Intimate Cartographies

For Jan
with love,
Lynne

Intimate Cartographies

L. A. Alexander

Duck Editions

First published in 2000 by
Duckworth Literary Entertainments Ltd.
61 Frith Street, London W1V 5TA
Tel: 020 7434 4242
Fax: 020 7434 4420
email: DuckEd@duckworth-publishers.co.uk

A CIP catalogue record for this title is available
from the British Library.

ISBN 0 7156 3011 3

Typeset by Derek Doyle & Associates, Liverpool
Printed in Great Britain by
Redwood Books Ltd, Trowbridge

Contents

'That's another thing we've learned from *your* Nation,' said Mein Herr, 'mapmaking. But we've carried it much further than you. What do you consider the *largest* map that would be really useful?'

'About six inches to the mile.'

'Only *six inches*!' exclaimed Mein Herr. 'We very soon got to six yards to the mile. Then we tried a hundred *yards* to the mile. And then came the grandest idea of all! We actually made a map of the country, on the scale of *a mile to the mile*!'

'Have you used it much?' I enquired.

'It has never been spread out, yet,' said Mein Herr; 'the farmers objected: they said it would cover the whole country, and shut out the sunlight! So we now use the country itself, as its own map, and I assure you it does nearly as well.'

From Lewis Carroll's *Sylvie and Bruno Concluded* (1893)

If trees cannot survive, humankind is not going to survive either.

Thich Nhat Hahn
Buddhist Monk and Peace Worker

Acknowledgements

There are so many people to thank: Marion Bennett, the Save the Beeches campaigner, whose work partly inspired this novel, and who so generously allowed me access to her files; Peter Jones for explaining the rules of Flatland, for hours spent fixing computer glitches, and generally sharing in the book's development; Kathleen Morison for her classes on Alexander Technique; Norma Alan for her reflexology session; Andy Fletcher for showing me how to climb a tree; Dr David Gorst for interpreting a breast x-ray; Dr Jim Morris for cases of bodies washed up along the Estuary; Jon Glover for providing the complete text of Flatland (even if it was inadvertently); Steve Padmore for information about mazes; Alice Meyers for her description of the electrically-charged ball; Chrissie Taylor for her useful feedback; and those I may have forgotten, with apologies.

I would also like to thank my agent, Clare Alexander, for her belief in me and her determination; and my editor Sarah Such, whose suggestions made this a better book; my Women's Writing Group for patiently listening; and to all my friends, whose love and encouragement has sustained me throughout the writing; and finally, Jacqui and Harvey of Silverdale, to whom I owe my life.

My special thanks to Julian Rothenstein for generously allowing me to reproduce several of the maps from *The Redstone Diary of True Places*; of the texts I consulted on maps and mapping, I am particularly indebted to Rudy Rucker's *The Fourth Dimension* (Penguin, 1985).

I would also like to thank the Arts Council for its generous support.

Lines from *Flat Stanley* © Jeff Brown (Mammoth, London, 1989) are reproduced by kind permission of the publisher. I would also like to thank Jeff Brown for his kind and helpful suggestions.

The publishers would like to thank the following for permission to reproduce copyright material. While every effort has been made to trace and acknowledge all copyright holders, we would like to apologise in advance should there have been any errors or omissions.

Map of the Rusland Valley: Reproduced from Ordnance Survey mapping on behalf of The Controller of Her Majesty's Stationery Office © Crown Copyright. MC 030497.

Mind Map: A *Mind Map* © Claudius Borer.

Three line drawings (pages 30-33): Reproduced from *The Fourth Dimension* by Rudy Rucker et al (1990), by kind permission of Penguin, London.

Map of the Rusland Valley, 1890: Reproduced from an Ordnance Survey 1st Edition. By kind permission of Cumbria Record Office, Kendal.

Map of Vishnu's Feet: Vishnu's footprints as constellations of his earthly symbols, Rajasthan, eighteenth century. Reproduced from *The Redstone Diary of True Places* ed. Julian Rothenstein & Adam Lowe (1997) by kind permission of the editors.

Map of the Underworld; or Ladies in Hades: The Ladies in Hades, back cover map for crime thriller (Dell Books, USA, 1950). Reproduced by kind permission, *The Redstone Diary of True Places*.

Map of the Hand: Palmist diagram, Rajasthan, eighteenth century. Reproduced by kind permission, *The Redstone Diary of True Places*.

Map of Grizedale Forest Sculpture Park: Reproduced by kind permission of The Grizedale Society, Ambleside, Cumbria.

Shadowland: Reproduced from *The Little Book of Hand Shadows* by Phila Webb & Jane Corby (1990, first published in 1927), by kind permission of Running Press, Philadelphia.

Map of the London Underground: By kind permission of London Transport Ltd. Registered user no. 99/E/1015.

Map of the Interior World: The Interior World, USA, 1930s. Reproduced by kind permission, *The Redstone Diary of True Places*.

Map of the Sexual Parts: The Male and Female Reproductive Systems. Reproduced from *The Anatomy Colouring Book* by Wynn Kapit &

Lawrence M.Elson (1993), by kind permission of HarperCollins, New York.

Map of the Face: Phrenological head mapping the sites of faculties and characteristics, England, nineteenth century. Reproduced by kind permission, *The Redstone Diary of True Places*.

Sand Map: *Earth and Sky*: Navaho universe in a pollen painting by Jeff King, recorded by Maud Oakes, USA, twentieth century. Reproduced by kind permission, *The Redstone Diary of True Places*.

Heartland: Poem map containing lovers' profiles and poem by Heinrich Heine, Germany, early twentieth century. Reproduced by kind permission, *The Redstone Diary of True Places*.

Map of the World, Upside Down: Reproduced from the Sunday Times/BNSC free CD-Rom: *Window on the World*, by kind permission of the British National Space Centre.

Map of Matrimony: Valentine card, England, late nineteenth century. By kind permission, *The Redstone Diary of True Places*.

Maze with Happiness at its Centre: England, 1941. By kind permission, *The Redstone Diary of True Places*.

1

Map of the Rusland Valley

To get to the Rusland Valley take the A590 west towards Ulverston and Barrow. Pass Newby Bridge and the Haverthwaite Railway Museum and take the next turning to Bouth and Rusland. Note the signpost to Grizedale Forest, one of the Lakes' honeypots, where you can play Spot the Sculptures hidden among the trees. We did, that day.

The Rusland Valley lies between Coniston Water and Lake Windermere, cradled by those two attenuated arms of water.

South of the Valley is the Cark Peninsula, in the shape of a duck's arse.

South of that, Morecambe Bay opens wide.

The Rusland Valley (OS Sheet 96: South Lakeland, 1:50,000 Landranger Series) is the greenest part of the Lake District, especially at the northern Grizedale Forest end. Surrounding it on all sides are brown contour lines, indicating the high Fells.

Normally Coniston Old Man and Dow Crag dominate the view at this point, but today the mist is down to the level of Torver Common, and with the fields flooded all you see is the Valley head opening out, flat and wet. Instead of grazing sheep, bobbing gulls. And here is where Rusland Pool begins, or rather ends: an innocent-looking stream or beck which extends for several miles along the Valley floor.

To your right is a yellow or 'minor' road (generally more than 4 metres wide according to the 'Roads and Paths' legend) which runs the length of the Rusland Valley. Pass a B&B on your left and, further along on your right, Abbots Reading Farm with its sign reading 'Rare Breed Pigs'. Keep on curving round to your left through the hamlet of Ealinghearth for another fifty yards. Ealinghearth Cottage is now on your right. Detached. Picturesque (i.e. needs new window frames and several coats of whitewash; drain clearance recommended due to rampant unpruned rose growth). Across the road is an even more picturesque (falling down) wooden garage. This is my property – but don't stop now. Keep on going to where the beech avenue begins. Park in the layby near the largest beech. Roll down your window so there's nothing between you and it. This sounds simple but it isn't – not for me.

Cumbria Ordnance Survey Office, Kendal

He hands me the photograph, a gesture somewhere between the toss of a frisbee and the pushing away of a meal he's had too much of. I take it at a tilt so that it catches the light, which slicks and skids in all directions. In place of an image, oily rainbowed slashes. Light waves hit the wet-look coating and tide across it. Beneath the blur is an aerial shot of a steep wooded hillside with a road running along the bottom: twisty in places but straightening out where the bulk of beeches line it.

'You know where it is, of course,' says the man who's my boss. How could I not know? Those trees, that place. Where I live.

I untilt the photograph. Mature beech trees telescope their way up from the forest floor; fresh limp leaves – it's a spring shot – wave to the sky to notice them, give us light. Overhead a buzzard pee-ews, hungry for some live thing down there. Forest floor humused with dead leaves; what more could live in such deep shade?

'The Authority wants a mapping of the trees,' he says. 'The Authority' stands for Lake District National Park Authority.

'What for?' A mapmaker doesn't normally ask this. Her job is simply to communicate using lines, colours, shadings and symbols – but I can ask anything I like. Exempt, object of pity, nothing to lose.

'They're thinking of felling,' he explains. 'A safety issue. I gather quite a few have had it.' His finger pogo-sticking from tree to tree. Had it? Wouldn't do to have branches crashing down on tourists' cars. No, it wouldn't. He shuffles some paper. 'There are, let's see, fifty-three, fifty-four beeches in total.' Shuffle shuffle. 'They want locations and levels for each of the trees.'

'Where are the specs?'

'There are none.'

I can't work without specifications and he knows it. Before I can begin a job I need a complete set of measurements. In any case, I can't work *there*: not among those trees.

I practise keeping my head balanced on my neck: an Alexander Technique exercise. To find your centre of gravity, place a finger either side of the skull just behind the jawbone at the base of the ears, where you'd test a child for mumps. From there imagine two straight lines pointing in and slightly down, converging about six inches up from the base of the neck. Point of Pivot, it's called.

'I can't do it.'

My skull wobbles on its fulcrum like one of those out-of-proportion troll dolls I once refused to buy for Molly. 'How could you want something so gross?' I said that; that's what I said. I tell him to let me know when the specs come in.

'Hang on,' he says, 'there won't be any. The team is tied up with other projects.'

I aim myself at him: body first, head follows; two distinct movements. My head has volume whereas my body does not. Today it has the quality of a razorblade, the old-fashioned kind with two slicing edges. Such a flatness could, if uncontrolled, go whipping around in a nasty cut-and-slash way.

'Sorry, but I can't do it. I'm a mapmaker, not a surveyor.'

'I know, I know.' His hand goes to his heart and bounces off. 'It's only a small job. A few acres of woodland, some trees to plot, won't take you long.' He reaches for the photograph but I'm not ready to give it back.

'It won't hurt you,' he says, just like that, without knowing a thing about it.

'Okay,' I tell him, 'I'll work from this.' It's not unusual to use aerial photography for mapping detail. 'It'll save me the field trip. Besides, I can't afford the time.'

'I'm afraid not,' he says, 'you'll need some ground control points.'

'What for? All they need to know are approximate locations.'

He takes the photograph and slides it into a folder marked RUSLAND

PROJECT. 'The Special Planning Board is getting involved, experts coming in on both sides. That means serial reproduction, multi-usage: we can't afford to cut corners. Some woman campaigner up your way making a stink apparently – you may know her, Bea Merriman.'

'We haven't met.'

'Anyway, you can go through the background material if it's of any interest.' His arm swings out with the file; this torques his shoulders, juts his chin forward and up. A few workshops in Alexander Technique and you begin to notice these things. In other words: go there, be among the trees. Huge, pallid, familiar.

The tree is a flowering plant with a woody stem called a trunk. The purpose of the trunk is to raise the leaves above those of competing plants. The tallest trees are able to dominate other vegetation including smaller trees. They are gentle giants, elephants of the plant world.

Thugs, they are, hoggers of light. Guzzling slurping absorbers.

Thomas Gray called the beech 'a very reverend vegetable'.

A very mad vegetable.

Trees are the oldest and largest life forms on earth. They offer sustenance, solace, beauty and shelter.

Might as well crouch between the legs of a cyclops.

Trees give pleasure to passing pilgrims. They give shade to cows, a home to bats, nuts to pigs. Giant green umbrellas, canopies for furry little Disneyworld critters.

Takers. Do-nothings. Limp-leaved dangling nut cases. Arrogant swaybacks.

Doolally bellies. Root-brained. Took everything.

The tree is a church, the tree is a temple/The tree is a snatcher and a thief ...

Were there any other witnesses?

Sorry, only the beeches.

The Peanuts cartoon blutacked to the door of my refrigerator shows Snoopy lying nose-to-sky on his doghouse roof thinking about visiting his brother out in Needles. Lucy's asking him if he can read a map. Naturally she assumes he can't; naturally he's indignant. Of course he can read a map, it's just that he doesn't happen to know what all those squares and dots and lines and colours and numbers and names mean.

Poor Snoopy. Poor carto-illiterate Snoopy. The difference between us is this: I *am* good at reading them, I *do* know what all those squares and dots and lines and colours and numbers and names mean. Matter of fact, I can do all sorts of fancy navigations and interpretations, not to mention making my very own maps complete with lines and colours and dots and numbers, etc.

The Peanuts cartoon isn't the only thing blutacked to the door of my refrigerator. There's also a so-called contour map of the Lake District, a cartographic joke in which Dollywagon Pike is bigger than Fairfield, Pillar bigger than Scafell, about everything bigger than High Street. It's out of scale to the point of idiocy but I forgive it, enjoy stroking the valleys, striding The Edge with two fingers.

Now why would a professional mapmaker have such a thing stuck to the goose-bumped chest of her refrigerator? Let's say it's for sentimental reasons; say it was given to her by someone who's no longer here; say it reminds her.

We drove through Needles. Molly was my daughter, Jay was my husband. We'd been camping and now stopped for breakfast at a truck stop: very hungry, all of us. Pancakes according to the menu were divided into Long and Short Stacks. 'What'll it be?' asked the waitress, aiming her pencil at Jay. (Women get to wait their turn in Needles.) 'Make it a Long Stack,' he said. The waitress chewed her gum while subjecting him to a full visual body search. 'That right?' was her half-time assessment. Chin, chest, crotch, feet. Down went her gaze and back it returned to his academic-size face and steamed-up glasses. Her final verdict was, 'I'd have a Short Stack if I were you.'

Some men might have puffed themselves up and insisted but Jay had the good grace to scale himself down in the pancake department.

Meanwhile Molly wanted to know what a Short Stack was. Wait and see, we told her. The waitress plonked down three orders of Short Stacks, each containing three pancakes the circumference of steak plates. We saw, she saw.

Later she found the cartoon in her Peanuts book. 'Hey, look, Needles! We were in Needles! That's where we had Short Stacks!'

Suspense sells – all those big fat thrillers – but what a stupid waste of space. Molly gave me the map and it was Molly who showed me the Peanuts cartoon and Molly it was who wanted to know all kinds of things. What's a map? What's Snoopy's brother's name? Who can eat a Long Stack? Why don't we have giant trees in England? Sometimes it was exhausting, sometimes we lost patience. How should I know? Give it a break, kid.

Explaining things after the fact is relatively easy. You can always come up with a story, or at least a set of possibilities. Prediction is something else. If, for instance, you found a tree lying in chunks you'd have no problem explaining how it got to be there in that condition; however, it's not something you'd normally have predicted.

By the same token, if you'd found a body, plus or minus certain body parts, washed up on various bits of North-western mudflat you might be able, although you wouldn't necessarily enjoy it, to explain its being there.

On the other hand, if you'd seen the owner of said body that morning (before the event that rendered her a body plus or minus certain parts), you would have had to be mad or telepathic to have predicted it.

The point is that often, both in life and in science, we can only give an explanation after the fact because we need the phenomenon to be explained itself in order to give us the evidence for its own explanation. There are limits, even with all the fancy technology, to what we can predict. Which doesn't make it any easier.

It happens even when I don't mean it to happen: innuendo, suggestion, filling up space with words. It happens because I'm not quite ready to explain. So I push it away and talk about other peripheral but not entirely unrelated things. It makes a kind of rhythmic sense. Time, preparation, avoidance. A natural response to an unnatural occurrence; a certain amount of faffing about before setting out. Suspense not as entertainment but as protection.

I run my finger along the Rusland Valley. The beech trees to be mapped are vaguely dotted along the south side of the road for a stretch of a mile. The whole area is a kiwi green with a swatch of brown at the top. Plasticky bumpiness to the touch. Originally there were a hundred and four beech trees. Fifty were cut down in 1951. That leaves fifty-four.

2

Mind Map

This is going back. The psychologist slid a piece of paper in front of her with the word TREE printed and encircled in an egg-shaped bubble. 'I'd like you to do a Mind Map of that word,' he told her. She was used to people using maps and mapping in loose, metaphorical, ways. 'Make free associations,' he explained. 'Or you could use the shape of the tree itself.'

While Magda was thinking, he went flipping through his Mind Map book. 'Ah yes!' He tipped her the illustration. 'Here, have a look at that.' Magda looked. It was in the shape of a tree showing how the application of basic principles, the 'roots', can lead to appropriate 'fruits'.

Roots fruits, thought Magda.

'I thought it would interest you.' The psychologist was mighty pleased with himself for finding a map that was also a tree.

Magda looked more closely at the Mind Map tree. Its 'roots' were divided between, on one side, the physical world of organic and inorganic chemistry, particle physics, electro-kinetics, etc., and on the other the living world of bacteria, amoebas, animals and flying insects such as the tsetse fly. Her German, unfortunately, wasn't up to translating most of the root-words; the so-called 'fruits' were such things as medicine, hydroelectric power, radioactivity, computer chips, etc. It was the sort of thing managers liked to use.

The psychologist was disappointed. If nothing else, she ought to be keen to discuss thought-processes and mapping. Seemed she wasn't. He tried again, showing her how to do her own Mind Map featuring a series of interconnected radiating bubbles. 'Images, thoughts, memories,' he instructed her: 'anything that pops into your head connected with the word "tree".'

Magda thought it wasn't really the mind the psychologist was talking about but the brain. The brain is an organ whose parts you can identify whereas the mind isn't. Soon, she thought, they must come up with a theory of the relationship between the two. In her map cabinet she had several 'maps' of the brain, showing it from different angles, whole and in cross-section. A map of the mind was impossible.

Still, she did as she was told. TREE, she printed and drew a ring around it. Unfortunately, the end of the loop failed to meet up with its own beginning. She added some more and with each one she got better at closing the opening. Pretty soon the page was filled with neat circles. She wouldn't have minded filling them with colour – pink yellow green – jelly beans rising off the page colliding with the psychologist's head. But in boring dimensionless truth they remained lying flat without colour or words, perfect stand-ins for Little Orphan Annie's eyes. The psychologist's mouth was another kind of oval shape: dry on the outside, moist within, rolled and scored. He opened it, transferring some of the wet to the dry via the tongue. Words came to him.

'They're blank,' he said.

'So they are,' she said.

The brain, you see, is a bit slow. It doesn't forget but sometimes it fails to remember. Take, for instance, the problem of phantom limb pain. An aid worker out in the former Yugoslavia was asked to massage a man's blown-away leg. Don't worry, he told her, it won't bite you. She imagined it there and so did he. Ah, he went, aah.

A limb no longer there? True in one dimension but in another – which we know relatively little about – the neural connections remain. How to alter the circuitry? Apparently it takes time to re-map itself, to find a new route for the new information. In some cases it may never succeed completely, and so the 'phantom' pain remains.

Soon, say the neuroscientists and evolutionary biologists, we will know everything. The human brain will be reconstructible, consciousness reproducible. We are making real progress, they say, towards realizing an architecture of the mind, a geography of the brain. God the Cartographer, with an inordinate fondness for maps.

3

The Map Cabinet

One of the best cures for tension is an Alexander workout: twenty minutes a day flat on your back and the discs in your spine re-fill with rejuvenating fluid. Think of a bellows, skin-thinned leather all plumped up. It's called The Semi-Supine. I began doing all sorts of 'therapies' after Molly disappeared. Some helped, some didn't; none harmed. Alexander Technique is the one I continue to do.

First, place three thinnish or two thickish books on the floor, preferably on a warm rug or carpet. Molly's rug has blue, green and yellow geometrical shapes against a dark red background. Primary colour jolliness, children's colours; woven in India by women organized by an aid worker and shipped to Oxfam in Kendal where it was bought for Molly for her room, for Christmas. *For Molly.* Let a yellow magic marker highlight that.

Getting into position involves curling sideways into the foetal position then uncurling onto my back while propping my head on the thinnish or fattish books (*Principles of Surveying, Trees in the Wild,* the latest MoD *Manual of Land Navigation*). With luck I may absorb something of them through the back of my skull. My elbows are splayed out and my fingers rest over my hipbones. I'm concentrating on the various contact points between me (elbows, heels, shoulders, back of skull) and the floor. My eyes are closed.

Imagine yourself flattening and spreading, spreading and flattening.

It doesn't come easy. I never was a spreading and flattening sort of person. It took time, a suspension of cynicism and a certain amount of self-brainwashing. Gradually I came to like the way it slowed time down, turned the positioning of a body on the floor into an event equal, say, to the spreading out of a map. Preparation for work.

My razor-self softens, edges wandering, arriving finally at some uncertain jellified stop. I should have told my boss I couldn't do the Rusland job; told him, if necessary, the whole gruelling gruesome Tragic Story so he'd let me off. Filled in the blanks with more blanks.

So what happened?

She disappeared.

Just like that?

Just like that.

No clues, no evidence?

No nothing.

And it was there, among the beeches?

There, yes.

'Oh dear, yes, no,' he would have said, all contrite and flustered, 'I quite see it's not the job for you, don't give it another thought.' The job would have gone to someone else, no problem. But I didn't; it didn't.

The idea of Semi-Supine is not to stay flattened like a pancake forever but to come out of it all puffed up. *That is the end of this exercise. You should now feel released and rejuvenated.*

In order to produce a topographical map of the Rusland Beeches – survey them in the field – I will have to pace them out, take measurements, plot distances, and so on. That's not part of my normal job; normally I do not do that. I am a simple mapmaker.

Dr Magda Beard, Cartographer.

Spreading and flattening, flattening and spreading.

Nice flat maps in nice flat drawers.

The map cabinet had once belonged to the curator of the Map Museum in Stirling. Now it belonged to her father. It was taller and wider than either of them, a serious hunk of solid Edwardian oak, seven feet tall by six feet wide with two ranks of flat, shallow but extremely deep drawers – twelve each side – with bellied brass pulls.

She called it her Map House. Compared to her friends' doll houses with their mock-period furniture the Map House was solidly of this world. Indeed it contained worlds, stacks of them made flat for easy storage and separated by onion-skinny sheets of specially treated tissue paper to protect the worlds from contaminating one another with grease spots. When she slid them open – those drawers she could reach – smells were released. Dust, fungus, spores, spices she couldn't name.

1955, Edinburgh. Magda's father took her hand as they crossed Princes Street. Her right hand. When they turned right from Princes Street onto Frederick Street he do-si-doed behind her so that he fetched up on the side nearest the kerb with her left hand in his. The man must always be on the outside, said the rule which was never spoken but must never be broken.

They turned in just past the Steinway Piano showroom. Up the stairs they went, to the George Street Auction Rooms. Magda held onto the banister, which felt different from holding her father's hand, and not just because of the switch from flesh to wood.

They chose seats about halfway along on the aisle. Her father handed her a black and white striped feather. "When I touch your elbow,' he whisper-instructed, 'you raise it up: high, higher, that's right.' He unrolled his catalogue to point out Lot 80 circled in red, the start and finish of the circle crisscrossed like shoelaces. Map Cabinet, 18th century, Origin English, Maker Unknown.

Lot 79 was a bundle of felt: *'Bundle o'felt, bundle o'felt what'llyagi'me for a bundle o' felt … ?'*

Her father's hand cupped her elbow, hup hup, and up went the feather, that's right. Things were right or things were wrong; her arm went up, her arm went down but this time she kept the arm up. She couldn't see anyone else raising anything but she did observe men winking or tipping their ears. Those are bids, her father would explain later. Then the winking and tipping stopped and the feather was all by itself, higher than her father's head. *'Going once, going twice, going a third time to the young lady with the feather.'*

Bang. She jumped and the feather flew.

Light car traffic, the occasional bicycle, a tractor, a milk wagon, a winding, gently undulating road. To my left, a patterning of fields; dips and rises and stone wall boundaries; a derelict barn. Just visible behind one of the walls, a pile of brightly coloured clothes someone must have dumped. The countryside as a convenient tip.

Fifty yards past the turning to Finsthwaite, the line of beeches begins. A rocky layby lined with hart's tongue ferns. This is where I park, this is where I wait to get started. The waiting is to the starting, I think, as the mind is to the brain. Or maybe not.

Time to get started.

How?

Just start.

I could try thinking about them differently: say, not as trees but as power poles strung along the Valley. A power pole is a power pole – nothing to it. Except that the mind doesn't allow itself to be tricked that easily. Everything to it: branches, root systems, factual solidity. On the other hand, glass is such a confusing, refractory thing. I see in it the reflection of my own hair, a pattern of mist and clouds – and then, through this screen, moving among the trees, in some dimension or other –

'Hey! Look, there!'

'Where? What?'

'The Maid! The Ghost!'

Children have such vivid imaginations. I remember saying I saw trees, that was all, there were no such things as ghosts. Three years later, I see no child because there's no child left to see.

I see a line of beeches. *Noble sentinels ... Queen of the broadleaves ... trunks like the smooth, soaring columns of a cathedral.* The tired phrases jump into my head and out again. The alternative, I think, is to conjure malign robots, greedy pachyderms, thugs with scars and skin-grafts; a world divided North South East West. There be angels, there be devils.

They're none of these things, of course: not queens or monsters, not holy shrines or hulking horrors. Trees, that's what they are: trees generically, beeches specifically; not endowed, so far as we know, with consciousness (as we know it); certainly not capable of intervention, divine or otherwise. As for harm, the so-called natural world never intends, lacking intentionality, damage.

If a tree goes down in a gale just as you're walking by, tough luck.

Still I stay sitting, sitting still, protected by glass and metal. Protected from two-hundred-year-old beeches spreading upwards by their higher branches as well as outwards along the ground, clawing the bank – no, merely gripping it as roots do when exposed at a road cutting. Nothing sinister except that one day a child came skipping along and they invited her in and decided to make her their permanent guest. Except that she was mine, not theirs.

Was she skipping?

I picture myself pacing, measuring, plotting. Official, competent; unthreatened, unremembering. Moving among the trees. Except that I can't move among the trees because they've gone flat. This happens to me from time to time. The trees turn into a painting of trees: grey stripes in an overlapping arrangement. On the ground beneath them are a group of people-shapes bent over a naked figure, like the mourners painted by Giotto. Wide-backed humps draped in capes the colours of sugar-dusted Turkish taffy. The women-shapes keen, the men-shapes purse their lips and tut. Up in the sky between the tree-stripes, a whole troupe of angels tumble about, holding their cheeks and temples, arching themselves backwards in an effort to avoid seeing the state of the body below. One has its arms spread wide, another its hands to its cheeks; yet another leans on its elbows as if reading a book in bed or tucked up in a cloud. The angels are garbed in Italian ice-cream colours, hooting up to God. On the ground, the body of a child, also grey like the trunks of the trees but more luminous.

Still I sit. Breath and leaves and beech bark: a famous grey that holds light even in darkness. Comparisons have been made with elephants, rocks, ghosts. It's getting dark. The sky not a backdrop but a very forward foreground, up against the windscreen, crazed with branches. When space is flat, elements and objects merge. It's simpler this way, like a line drawing, like porcelain. A scene made of porcelain, however, runs the risk of cracking.

The agony of a mother robbed of her child. I read that sentence some-where and it stuck. I don't like it sticking but that's the nature of stickiness. *Agony, robbed*: hyperbolic, vague, emotive words. Was the child actually stolen? Did the mother suffer true agony? At what point does mere pain skip over into agony? How can we measure (express) emotional pain without using words meant for physiological sensations? I also read somewhere that hysteria is when the womb goes a-wandering in search of its lost children.

The map I draw will be used by the Park Authority, the County Council, various consultants and other local groups involved in deciding the trees' fate. What's it to me? A job. Go home now, start fresh Monday morning.

4

Ghostland

An ancient group of trees in South Cumbria are steeped
in legend of the supernatural. And when the trees look black
and near-alive in the half-life of an autumn evening, it is not
too hard to see how such powerful myths originated ...

The Evening Mail, *December 22, 1995*

The myth referred to above, concerning the Maid or Ghost of Ealinghearth, probably originated in the late 18th century but was popularised a hundred years later in a poem by a Mary Gregson, daughter of the Rev. J. Gregson MA, vicar at Rusland Church. The poem tarts up the myth into Victorian melodrama, while the present-day journalist turns it into soap opera.

The story is simple. The girl, daughter of a cruel tyrant of a father, falls in love with a travelling salesman and leaves home. She may have been running away with her lover or, having been jilted, from them both in order to hide her shame. Either way, she ends up dead.

The girl is referred to in the article as young, beautiful and motherless. Yes, she was young: girls are. And then, did the writer know for a fact that she, the Maid, was motherless, or had that been thrown in to make her seem even more pathetic? If only, the reader thinks, she'd had a mother to protect her. But then, the more wised-up reader knows that the presence of a mother guarantees no such thing.

The girl was called Margaret Taylor. This information will have come, Magda presumed, from the Ealingarth and Finsthwaite Parish Registry. She'd lived ('resided') at Ealin Garth Cottage. Ealin Garth was one of several alternative spellings for Ealinghearth – the same cottage where

Magda, Molly and Jay had been spending the Easter holiday when Molly disappeared. Other spellings included: Ealin Harth, Ealinharth, Ealingarth.

The poem was one long moan about her lonely isolated existence with her brutal, sullen, tyrannical, etc. father. The girl's own voice was one long self-pitying wail. Why must she always live in that lonely valley? Why can't anyone tell her she's pretty? Why are the days so perversely sunny ('sunbeams daily')? Why is Ealingarth so dark and bare? Why is her Pa such a mean old so-and-so ('never a word of brightness')? Etc.? Etc.? Etc.?

Oh dear, it was all so drear, so grim, all that sucking on the gloom tree.

But then (dramatic pause), drawn by legendary tales of her beauty there came, yes, a suitor; and the world was instantly, as after an eclipse, made lighter and brighter by the information that her curls were dandier than her daffydowndillies.

But what of her rivals in town? This was a worry. And so, when a pedlar knocked at the cottage door, tempting her with his basket of trinkets and ribbons, she let herself be tempted. Pearl, silver, gold, copper, tin: the poem doesn't say what kind of necklace she bought. Not that it mattered. Her father's face, Magda read, was like the face of the dead.

Best leg it away.

But where could the poor Maid (or, as she subsequently became known, the Ghost) of Ealinghearth go? Where on earth could she flee ... ?

'Nestling,' crooned the auctioneer, 'in the picturesque Rusland Valley ... in a sort of Sleeping Beauty ambience.'

Molly in her glass bed: not alive yet not exactly dead.

Ealinghearth came up for sale at auction almost immediately afterwards. Perverse timing, Jay said. Magda waited for him to leave for work before phoning the estate agent. By 4 p.m. the For Sale sign was already strapped to their driveway gate.

'How can you,' he said.

'I have no choice,' she said.

He said, she said.

'I'm sorry,' he said, 'but I can't do it.'

He let his hands meet one another, matching finger to finger, lined up digits and thumbnails, base of palms. Now they were close but they could be even closer. It didn't take much. All he had to do was let the pads of the fingers slip sideways so those of the right hand filled the gap between those of the left. Holding his own hand.

'Let's be clear,' she said. They were arranged like people visiting in a prison. One kitchen table, painted blue, with a single banana between them, two green stripes on its inbent side. Jay used two fingers in a blessing, sliding them along the banana's back. So long as finger and fruit were connected everything would be all right. But then he reached the banana's black tip, and had to dive for it. The drop from tip to table potentially life-threatening.

'You want clarity? Okay. If you go for Ealinghearth,' he informed her, 'I'm leaving.'

'You've decided.'

'I have.'

Normal people discuss things normally. If this doesn't sound like a normal conversation it's because these were not exactly normal circumstances nor were the people in a normal condition, which may explain why their phrases came out sounding clipped and trimmed.

'Why?' she asked.

'It's too much.'

'Too much of what?'

'Morbid,' he said.

'I don't see it that way,' she said.

He said, she said: this is how it went.

'How do you see it?' he asked her.

'A chance to be close.'

'To what?'

'You know,' she said.

Which was true. He knew and she knew.

'What for?'

'Something.'

'That doesn't make sense to me. I'd rather get as far away from this terrible place as possible.'

'Then you go ahead and do that.'

'Okay then. I'm sorry. You asked for it.'

Three tidy phrases.

'What does sorriness have to do with it?'

They knew Ealinghearth well. They'd rented it three summers running, plus Easter vacations, sometimes Christmas. Magda, Molly, Jay, the beeches. Occasional manifestations, according to Molly (with the parents sometimes playing along), of the Ghost of Ealinghearth. Swallows nesting in the drains and those sexually active Amazons. 'Ealinghearth,' the auctioneer reminded his bidders, 'was occupied for a time by Arthur Ransome. It may still be, for all we know.'

Literary ghost cachet upped the starting bid by several thousand.

Going once, going twice. Sold to the lady in the alcove.

Abbot Hall Museum, Kendal

It was a rainy day. Magda, Jay and Molly were staying at Ealinghearth for their summer holidays. They'd decided to spend the morning at the shops and the library followed by lunch at the cafe by the river. Molly wanted to go to the museum first; wanted in particular to see Arthur Ransome's chess set.

Arthur Ransome had spent a summer at Ealinghearth Cottage, wow. 'Was it my room he wrote in? *Swallows and Amazons*, right here?' Nobody knew for sure, they told her, which room he wrote in or which books, and maybe he hadn't written at the cottage, maybe he was taking it easy, he was on vacation, after all. 'Maybe,' Jay finally proposed, 'old Ransome did nothing else but play chess.' Molly thought about this. 'I think he wrote a bit and then he played chess for relaxation.'

So now they were on the trail of the famous chess set.

The floor of the entrance hallway was made of marble in a design of congruent forms, gradations of pale grey to black. The rest of the building had wide dark oak floorboards, dampness overlaid by furniture polish. The trio-family walked around in their anoraks on the creaking floorboards, looking for a case with a chess set, but all they could see were paintings of mountains and stags in ridiculously ornate gold frames. Finally, they asked the woman at the front desk where the Ransome collection was and she pointed out the door to the next building: the Museum of Lakeland Life. Oh, they said, flipping their anorak hoods up for the trek back across the courtyard. Shook themselves at the entrance like dogs.

Here Be Not Art But Life.

The ticket seller was pleased. 'Not many ask to see it,' she said, 'except of course people from the Ransome Society, and visitors from the States; oh, and Japan, we get a surprising lot from Japan.' And then she handed them a map of the layout of the collection and pointed them up the stairs and left along the corridor.

They creaked past strings of bobbins and glittering rocks, rusty wheels and wooden mallets.

A large working loom from one of the nearby mills which once made cloth worn by Robin Hood and his Merry Men.

A large rocking horse, polished but not rocking.

An overfurnished Victorian doll's house with a lonely porcelain lady sitting amongst all her treasures.

A doll in a bonnet, looking extremely cross.

Another fat Queen Victoria doll carrying a parasol and a motheaten corgi.

Rows and rows of toy soldiers.

And then:

Swallows & Amazons forever!
THIS WAY TO THE ARTHUR RANSOME ROOM

Ransome's white handlebar might well have had a separate identity. As Molly said, 'It comes alive while he's asleep and goes crawling off his face.'

'To do what?'

'Have adventures.'

The face attached to the moustache: jowly droopy sad.

There were several maps on display including Wild Cat Island and Ransome's Lakeland. 'Hey, look!' cried Molly. 'Ealinghearth Cottage is on it!' And so it was.

His chess set was covered in plastic. It wasn't very interesting. So was his desk complete with Remington Home Portable typewriter and a selection of pipes. That was more interesting. *He was an inveterate smoker, and his studies were invariably nicotine stained.*

'What's "inveterate"?' asked Molly. 'A habit you can't break.' 'What's "invariably"?' 'Not varying. It means he always left yellow stains from the cigarette gunk on his fingers.'

The desk itself was quite small, as Molly observed. 'How could he write so many words at such a small desk?' She stood still and listened. Tick tick, went a very loud clock. 'We've disturbed him,' she said. 'Who?' 'Him, Arthur Ransome.' So her parents said what did she mean and she said, 'He's been here but he had to leave when he heard us come in.'

According to Jay, the author Wilkie Collins lived with a constant female presence at his back. *Lived with.* Now there's an interesting way of putting it. Magda pictured a couple trudging up Coniston Old Man, the man in front, the woman behind. His hoverer, he called her. She seemed quite real to him but whenever he turned to look at her, like Eurydice, she'd disappear.

'Poor Wilkie,' said Magda.

'Nah,' said Jay. 'I think he got off on it. A real woman would've scared him out of his wits.'

'Still, she kept him company,' Magda suggested. 'In a way.'

'Did his every bidding.'

'What does that mean?'

'Your guess is as good as mine. Obviously the protoplasm of a repressed Victorian sexuality.'

Magda checked behind her. She'd been living alone at Ealinghearth for six months when the Maid began following her. Get lost, buzz off. But the Maid kept mooching along in her ectoplasmic way. At one point she stopped short but the Maid kept going, straight through and out the other side, then stood there looking tragic. Optical hallucinations tend to have a limited range of facial expressions.

Magda went poke as to a breast but the finger met only disappointment. She accused the air of doing Molly in. '*Doing in?*' snorted the Maid, peeping out from behind Molly's beech, where she'd wrapped herself like a photographer's model trying to imitate a fawn. 'Why, what a quaint turn of phrase!' A smirky kind of simper.

Magda clunked her forehead three times against the trunk, I don't believe this, and headed for home. The Maid followed. Some hoverer, Magda thought. When they got to Ealinghearth she turned. 'You're not coming in, no way,' and slammed the door in that pasty faceless face. The wooden sign reading EALINGHEARTH COTTAGE did a double flip on its chain landing upside down.

Magda stopped going to the beeches and became a shut-in. Spent most of her time up in her study playing with map programs on her computer, but sometimes took a break and sat with her coffee downstairs at the open bow window, staring at the overgrown sycamores that blocked her view of the estuary. One day, the Maid came up the garden steps and bent herself swoonily backwards over the sundial like something out of a painting by Caspar David Friedrich. No normal semi-rigid backbone could do that.

'Sexy, hunh?' croaked the Maid, her windpipe suffering partial compression.

'Only if you're into necrophilia. I'm not. Go away.'

'I've got something to tell you.' She appeared to light a cigarette.

'That's disgusting,' Magda said and shut the window. Opened it. 'What?' Too late, the Maid had evaporated. This was terrible. The creature might have told her what happened, given her at least a clue. Too late.

Magda went through to the kitchen and switched on the radio – coincidentally, a programme about ghostly manifestations. Rational explanations, mostly to do with wind and optics, were offered. One typical scenario featured a window left ajar on a windy day. The wind blows over the sill setting up a low vibration as in an organ pipe. The low pressure sound waves can actually make your eyeballs vibrate, thus causing you to see a blur.

The vibrating eyeballs scenario wasn't all that convincing but just in case, Magda marched back and pulled the window to. Through the glass, the Maid gave one of those cute little independent-finger waves, hi y'all.

5

Map of the Rusland Beeches

Molly preferred books with an edge, characters who got into trouble or caused trouble. The Wild Things, the Moomins, Roald Dahl. Pooh was too tame. Her tastes changed over the years of course, and she'd have temporary weird crazes, but Flat Stanley remained her all-time favourite; and the way his family, the Lambchops, responded to his tragic condition was hilarious.

It happened during the night. On the wall above Stanley's bed hung an enormous bulletin board on which Stanley and his brother Arthur pinned messages and maps. The board had fallen slowly off the wall to rest at last upon Stanley, who woke the next morning only when Arthur shouted for Mr and Mrs Lambchop to come look. Lifting the big board off Stanley, they saw that he was now four feet tall, about a foot wide, and half an inch thick.

'Darndest thing I've ever seen,' says Mr Lambchop.

Now Stanley's mother speaks the best line of the book. 'Let's all have breakfast.' This is what she says and I will always love her for saying it.

Molly, when she was quite small, once lay down on the floor with her own bulletin board on top of her. She yelled out, we came running. The script went according to plan. Jay lifted the board and pronounced her flat as a pancake. She was holding her breath to within half an inch of her life. 'Darndest thing I've ever seen,' he said in his down-homest accent. I said, 'Let's all have something to eat.' 'Wrong!' yells Molly, sitting up, right-angled as one of those poor unfortunate morgue victims. 'Let's all have *breakfast*,' she corrects. Anyone with kids will be familiar with this. You have to get the lines exactly right or you're in trouble.

I load the boot with surveying equipment. The steering wheel fills my hands. Rain comes in rapid, shallow sloshings, the car an amphibious beast rolling with the waves. The fields are flooded again. The Coniston Fells, over in the next valley, are misted in but still you can feel their presence, three thousand feet of rock and scree giving way to land that barely makes a bump on Molly's contour map. Eventually you come to the estuary at sea level. Earth to map, map to earth. A mapmaker should move easily from three dimensions to two, and back again. The problem is getting stuck in two.

This is where the famous avenue of beeches begins: guardians, so they say, of the mile-long stretch of road. Rain slithers over the windscreen and pools along the ledges. It's time to shut off your windscreen wipers, and go.

Wax jacket, wellies, thick green socks. Monster canvas bag slung over my shoulder, containing OS map and compass, measuring chain and clinometer. Notebook and pen in pocket. I brought the theodolite just in case but probably won't be able to use it since there are no clear sight lines: the trees are blocking each other.

Beech no.1: inland and uphill from the other beeches in its immediate grouping. Big, wide-spreading, solitary. Under the canopy of branches its bark apppears neutral, non-committal; lower down it's streaked. Crocodile grey, not to be trusted. Beside it a stream runs diagonally downhill crossing the road under where I stand.

Check it out on OS map. (Always begin with a fixed point.)

Point compass at tree.

Take bearing.

Using chain measure follow track beside stream directly up from road.

Get out chain measure and secure it around tree. Take measurements for distance from road. Height is more of a problem. One of the bones in my neck makes a nasty popping sound. Drop head to chest: opposite movements ease tension. Up, down, up, down. It's okay to circle round if you do it slowly. Think of the head as a hollow earth. In the centre a sun shines permanently. At times its light escapes through the polar openings, causing an aurora borealis. Airy-fairy but nice. Try to keep an open mind. To get an exact height measurement I'd have to use the theodolite which I can't do because of sight-line obstruction, and besides I don't have an assistant.

Guess.

Okay. Height: 60-70' (est.)

Now go back to the car and pick up the Waywiser. Continue up the Valley, balancing on protruded roots that flex my arches right through the wellies. Most trees support their above-ground growth by reaching far down into the earth, but not the beech. The beech is top-heavy and therefore inherently unstable. Roots more like seaweedy hair by Beardsley. Shallow, just there under the surface. Obviously too close to the road, as the Authority has said. Obviously a danger to the public.

I put out my hand, feel furry velvety green stuff growing up its trunk. On top of that another kind of scaly, paler-green ruffly lichen. Externally the tree looks peaceful and solid. *Silent, noble, dignified* ... internally it's a starveling, a guzzling roto-rootering sapaholic.

It's not true that sap rises only in spring. The tree feeds all year round. It never stops. All those baby buds, you see, to feed.

Overhead a buzzard's pee-ew.

Reach up. Stretch for the lowest branch and pluck off one of the old fruit pods. Hairy, dried flower cupule, no nuts within. When new there are two seeds, a pair of offspring. We'd thought about having another, Jay and I, but it didn't take. On the side of the branch, borne on a short stalk, a furled-up-tight bud. Oval, tapering to a short point. What am I doing? I'm supposed to be mapping this tree, not doing nature study on it.

One down, fifty-three to go. Return to fixed point. Take a second reading using the corner of a stone wall beside the stream. Double check. The next six beeches are close to the road, lined up one after the other at roughly similar levels. Looking down the line, they should begin close then retreat into the distance, one roughly behind the other. They don't.

It's happening again: the space between them closes up. Rather than wait their turns politely, one behind the other, they all come crowding forward. No manners, these beeches. No depth, no space. A stripy design on the plane of my vision.

I close my eyes, will them to behave themselves, get back as they were. Tree no.7 obeys: 6, 5, 4 and 3 follow. Gradually they make room for one another and the scene rights itself according to the rules of single-point perspective. Viewer with normal 3-D field-of-vision sight views trees in their setting in a normal in-depth way. Carry on.

For trees 2–7 I use the Waywiser (basically a wheel attached to a walking stick with a counter attached). Check it against a fixed point, set the counter at zero, wheel it along the road to Beech no.2. Drop coin on ground, make note of distance, then carry on to Beeches 3–5. At each one note clinometer reading, girth, height and approximate levels. (There's no really accurate way to assess levels without a fixed bench marker but never mind, it's only a rough presentation.)

So far so good. I've got my two-dimensional plottings (distances on the flat plane) more or less accurate; for the levels above the road I'll have to continue with approximate calculations using the clinometer. Look through it, take reading for inclination, pace out between trees then using a trigonometric equation, plot height levels.

When I get to Molly's favourite beech I notice, about twelve feet up, one of those round pruning wounds. Rolled scar-tissue; puckered kiss-mouth. My neck goes back, click. Nose to sky, position of maximum strain to the cervical vertebrae. I roll it forward so my chin hits the zip tab of my wax jacket. Up again, this time to a more comfortable eye-level. Among the graffiti scorings of hearts, arrows, names and initials, and stencilled in bright yellow from a spraygun, is the number **31**. Tattooed, marked. The bark isn't scaly, as it looks from a distance, but soaking wet and cold – and squashy. You could squeeze it out like a washcloth. Moss thick and spongy with moisture from all the rain. Meanwhile, I'm absorbing water through the seams in my wellies. Knees, hands, wrists, neck and face running with it. No longer Stanley-flat, now paper-flat. Newsprint, front page story. *Lost Girl ... Local*

Tragedy ... Sucking up, swelling. Bits falling off, mixing with last year's leaves, turning to mulch.

It took me a week to map the beeches. By the end spring had snuck up: wood violets, primroses, early cowslips. (Molly: 'Do cows wear slips?') Beech leaves are said to break into leaf in April, but that isn't how it was: more an unfolding, a letting themselves be unfolded.

New beech leaves. From close up fringed with soft silvery hairs, almost see-through. From a distance pointillist dots against the sky. Or: not against but cut-out-of. Fresh green, fresh blue: that special vibration close-valued colours make. Flat but alive. Some of the other trees, still minus their leaves, looked wintry and a bit twitchy. That drawing – or etching – in one of my mother's art books, by Goya, of a madman with his hair and fingers like leafless branches or exposed nerve endings.

When the last beech had been plotted I climbed a rise above them and sat on an outcrop of rock. To go up high, as my father taught me – quoting Herman Melville – was not only a fine thing in itself (a 'noble point of observation'), but the best way of viewing the land about. Near my feet, primroses and violets; below me, the beeches. Out with my flask and sandwich. What would it be like to feed through your feet, become a living straw? All that distance from roots to topknot working against gravity. Hardwoods lift water at the rate of 50 metres an hour. Buds need to feed in order to flop open.

The bread fell apart, then the cheese, but not the lettuce. I picked at the makings, always in the same order: bread, cheese, lettuce, bread, cheese, lettuce, and so on, until the plastic box was empty.

I loaded up. The Valley had allowed me to come into it and was now letting me out again. Long narrow winding. The trees were no longer superimposed on one another nor was the space between them flat, negative or otherwise. They stood in the round, one behind the other, behind the other. Nice and proper.

I drove, moving through space, or rather, I inside the space of my car moved through another, deeper kind of space. Fortunately, no one was behind me. I put the car into neutral and let it roll. When it levelled out or climbed, I put it into first. At this speed I could drive with my eyes closed for a second or two. Like this, I saw tractors and woodsmen. Heard chainsaws, saw the trees go. They would go like Pick up Stix, the weakest first leaving gaps. Then some more, then all of them. I observed hulks then stumps, smiled into the rearview mirror.

6

Flatland

Magda's father gave her a book called *Flatland: A Parable of Spiritual Dimensions*, written back in the 1880s by a man called Edwin Abbott Abbott. Yes, two Abbotts, or as her father pointed out, Abbott Squared.

Flatland is a two-dimensional plane inhabited by two-dimensional creatures. 'How do they move?' Magda asked her father. 'Do they stand up at right angles and walk about or do they just lie flat and sleep?' He reached for a pair of scissors then extracted a piece of paper from one of the drawers of his double-sided knee-hole desk. He cut two shapes: one with a skirt and one with straight legs. This meant female and male. He let them flutter flat onto his desk blotter and pushed them around with one finger. Sometimes the edges of their arms or legs got tangled or sliced into one another. 'Of course the problem here,' he explained, 'is that these cut-outs, albeit thin, do have some thickness whereas Flatlanders – indeed, Flatland itself – strictly speaking has no solidity at all.' He slapped the palm of his hand down on the cut-out creatures. 'Think of a slick of soap film, or an ink spot on a sheet of paper.' Abbott Abbott himself, she later read, suggested thinking about the creatures as shallow bumps or mesas on the rubbery sheet of Flatland's space.

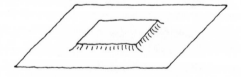

A Square as a bump in the plane

The main character was a square called A Square. A Square wasn't like other book characters such as Jane Eyre or Anne of Green Gables or Fred with his 'flat blue eyes'. A Square had one eye of no apparent colour. Its shape was a slice of pie with the tip eaten away but that couldn't be right because a slice of pie was thick with layers of pastry and apple and rhubarb in between. In fact, A Square's eye wasn't an eye at all but a triangle; and as for the eyeball, that was merely another smaller triangle inside the larger one.

She'd been puzzled about Fred's flat blue eyes. 'How can an eye be flat?' she asked her father. She'd felt her own eyeballs moving around under their loose lids. 'Go fetch one of your dolls, then,' he told her, so she did. The doll had eyes that were slow to react: shall I open or shut? Click click.

But now, off with her head. Magda's father reached up inside the doll's empty skull and plucked out an eye.

'Hold out your hand.'

The eye was spherical. The back part, which you didn't see because it was sunk into the doll's cheek, was made of some kind of pale wood while the eyeball part was pasted on. The lashes, stiff and straight, were stuck on with glue around their roots. Her father still wasn't satisfied.

'The human eye is actually ovoid.'

'What's ovoid?'

He produced a polished egg-shaped stone, greeny-grey with pink patches, smoother than a real egg or a doll's eye. 'No two will be identical in shape,' he told her. Cupped the top of her head. She thanked him but was now even more puzzled about why, if it wasn't true, her book said that Fred had 'flat blue eyes' . So she asked her mother. It wasn't to do with real eyes at all, said her mother, but with the feeling the eyes conveyed.

'The author is telling you something about the character through describing his eyes as flat. In other words, a flat expression. Flat-seeming, dull, not shiny and curious like yours.' She painted a swatch of colour on a piece of cardboard. Blue. Her arm and the brush moved together, skimmed the surface then took off again. There. Her brush hand hovered.

'You see, that kind of paint has no highlights or gloss to it. That's what your author means about the character's eyes.'

Fred had flat blue eyes.

Her father didn't want to know about *expressions*. 'Now there is a flat eye for you,' he said pointing to the illustration of A Square in his copy of *Flatland*. Magda considered the pie-eye located in A Square's upper right-hand corner. Below that was a curved cut-out banana of a mouth. No nose.

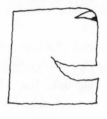

A square

Magda didn't like the look of him. She thought the grin and the pie-eye gave him a wicked expression but an expression couldn't be proved, wicked or otherwise. Then there was the problem of how he could breathe without a nose or see out of the single flat eye.

'Ah,'said her father. 'An interesting question.'

This time he reached into his pocket and pulled out a handful of coins which he placed on the edge of his desk. 'Now,' he instructed, 'if you lower your eye level with the desktop, what do you see?'

Magda bent one knee, unbalancing herself. She grabbed onto the desk edge but it was polished slippery and so were the ends of her fingers with perspiring. She felt wobbly. The fear of collapsing made it hard to concentrate on the coins. She shut one eye. What she saw were not whole coins but only their edges. Were the edges curved or straight? The lamp above them lit the edges so that shadows formed which allowed her to distinguish the big coins from the little ones; the round ones from the angled ones; thick from thin. But if the Flatlanders were truly flat – flatter than these coins – surely they would see each other only as lines. (But what if she was wrong? What if she was using stupid girl reasoning? On the other hand, if you don't try you'll never learn.) So she tried:

'Line segments?'

'Correct,' said her father, sounding surprised. 'Just so. Since Flatland is covered in a thin haze the glowing sides of the Flatlanders shade off rapidly into dimness. This means that they can tell each other apart only by their shadows.'

Flatlanders cast different shadows because they are different geometrical shapes.

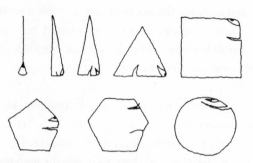

Eight Flatlanders: Woman, Soldier, Workman, Merchant, Professional Man, Gentleman, Nobleman, High Priest.

As you can see, he told her, the lower classes are triangles with only two equal sides. The upper classes are regular polygons, that is, figures with all sides equal. The more sides one has, the greater one's social standing. The highest caste of all consists of polygons with so many sides they are indistinguishable from perfect circles.

Magda's mother thought it was really a satire on staid and heartless Victorian society.

'Who's that?' Magda asked, pointing to the first shape in the diagram, of a thin line with a segment of pie-eye at the bottom. Her father sighed, 'I'm afraid that's a woman. The women of Flatland are not even the meagrest of triangles; they are but lines, infinitely less respected than the priestly circles.' He placed his hand on her forehead, lifting her fringe as if to protect her from the hurt of this truth.

'Oh.' Magda was disappointed, but when she compared her own body with her father's she had to admit it was less than a triangle in relation to his priestly circle. On the other hand, it might also prove her mother's point.

Here live people who have big swollen feet ...

Magda made the globe spin. It belonged to her father. It was originally made in 1492 by a man called Martin Behaim. It was the earliest surviving terrestrial globe in the world. *Erdapfel* it was called, which translates as Earthapple.

In 1492 Columbus sailed the ocean blue.

In 1492 Columbus sailed the ocean blue but it was several years before he returned to Queen Isabella of Spain to present his findings. In the meantime, Martin Behaim of Nuremberg made his map in which there was no America and no Australia either. There were a lot of islands, however.

Magda stuck out her finger to slow the spinning globe. When it stopped she opened her eyes and peered at the place her finger pointed: two tiny islands with the names Masculine, Feminea. Beneath them, in olde worlde script which she could just make out through the varnish, she read: *In the year 1285 after the birth of Christ one of these islands was inhabited by men only, the other by women only, who meet once a year.*

She imagined her mother living on Feminea and her father living on Masculine. She pictured their once-a-year meeting. Would it be on her island or his, or somewhere between the two on a boat? She pictured them rocking about trying to have one of their discussions.

'What about perspective? Depth?' cried her mother.

'What perspective? What depth?' shouted her father. 'The picture plane is flat. Art is an illusion. Any child can tell you that!'

After that the sound of the waves was so loud they had trouble hearing each other. *What? What was that you said? ... I said ... Look here ...*

By now her mother felt sick. Her father began to explain to her about the inner ear and balance. Her mother threw up all over him. The vomit was like fireworks mingled with the pretty gold-coin bubbles of the waves. Then it was time for them to go back to their separate islands for another year. Faced with parting they became curiously fond. (*Goodbye, dear ... Oh dear, goodbye, take care ...*)

Magda did one more spin (three spins allowed at any one time). She closed her eyes, sent her finger out into space and let it touch down. You had to be careful not to let your nail touch or you'd scratch the varnish. The globe had a bubbly texture as if grains of sand or dust had got caught in the varnish but her fingertip felt nothing. She had no idea where she'd landed.

Her finger divided two painted galleons, their sails swollen with wind. Beneath her finger – almost completely hidden by it – was an island called Angama. She moved her finger and read: *The people of this island have heads, eyes and teeth like dogs, and are much misshapen and savage, for they prefer human flesh to other flesh.*

Magda looked at her finger. She had never landed there before. She much preferred Java, for instance, which told you about spices such as her mother kept in jars in her spice cabinet (nutmegs, cinnamon and cloves ... forests of sandalwood). Best of all, however, was the island marked *Here Be Dragons*. If you landed on *Here Be Dragons* you would have a lucky day. Magda put her finger in her mouth and sucked. Human flesh was not so lucky.

'So,' said the psychologist, 'we'll continue where we left off last time, shall we?'

'Where?'

'With the flatness.' The psychologist reviewed his notes: FLATNESS, it said, followed by a whole row of question marks. 'Flatness' in clinical terms normally stands for depression, as in 'I feel low, without energy ... *flat*.' But this flatness was different: it was literal. The psychologist proposed a little game. 'You like games, don't you?' Eyebrows eyebrows. 'No Mind Maps today. All you have to do is finish my sentence. Ready?'

' ... '

'Right. Flat as a ...'

'Flatlander.' The therapist didn't know what a Flatlander was but he let it pass.

'Flat as a ...'

'Tree.'

More eyebrow. 'Flat as a ...'

'Child.'

'I see. Fine, good, excellent. Just one more, Magda. Flat as a ...'

' ... me.'

' ... '

Allowing space – time, that is – is crucial to the therapeutic process. It offers the client an opportunity to hear her own words and to register any contradictions which may in turn prompt her to question her own assumptions. It also gives the therapist a chance to observe the client. What he currently observed was a more-or-less normal woman in a normal body:

Who had her legs crossed.

Who was rotating the top foot 360 degrees by the ankle with such freedom of movement as can be exercised by any extremity in a three-dimensional world.

Whose legs outproportioned her torso, slotting into her pelvis at a point more than halfway up. A sort of Stonehengey shape: wide across the pelvis but rather flattish from the side. Unshapely in the conventional sense but not unattractive although still on the non-vivid side. Would not stand out in a crowd, he thought.

Hands and feet narrow and delicate; so too the bones in her face. One of those higher-at-the-nape-than-at-the-ears haircuts giving her a vulnerable schoolboy look, from the back anyway. The word 'subtle' sprang to mind. Forced you to look closer.

And so on, up and down the body.

Arriving at the conclusion that she did indeed exist in space just as he did, that she *took up* space. He must not however say so. If he were to say, 'A child is not flat! A tree is not flat! YOU are not flat!' it would give her the message that she was wrong.

The client is never wrong. What she had, in this case, was a different perspective, i.e. from inside-out. The psychologist, on the other hand, assumed an outside-in perspective. It assumed he could walk around her, 360 degrees-worth, appraising her from different angles as she sat, legs crossed, in the leather chair with the tubular steel frame; that he could touch her, poke her, run a tape measure around her bosom, waist, hips.

It assumed too much.

'So those things,' he dared to pursue, ' – child, tree, and so on – are flat?' Turn the statement into a question and hand it back to the client so she can see for herself what's wrong with it.

'Yes, if you perceive them in a certain way.'

'And what way is that, Magda?'

She smiled, possibly her first since her first appointment. 'Flatly,' she said. A sound escaped from the psychologist. Creak of leather, crack of bone. He could kick himself.

Monday nights between 7:15 and 9:15, you can forget everything – who you are, what you have been. The map of the beeches, the map of rising damp crawling up the back wall of your cottage, your rotting garage, the sycamores that need felling.

Monday nights between 7:15 and 9:15, you are a loosely-dressed skeleton balanced on your sit-bones on a straight-backed schoolroom chair. Monday nights you are a soft-boned child waiting for Sara, teacher, to tell you what to do. Monday nights you are a body, flesh around back-bone with added-on extremities, de-skilled, willing, waiting to be touched with the received wisdom of the Alexander-Technique-wand which will make you free: free to move, free to be, fully alive, fully *rounded*. I give you my body, my head is empty of all preconceived notions, do with me what you will. Now we'll just sit ... now we'll prac-tise standing up ... now walk around the room with your eyes closed ...

The class meets in the Alexander Centre on High Fellside in Kendal. Bare cork floor, generously-proportioned astragalled windows, diagrams of the human body. Giant beachballs, yoga mats, piano, washing machine, a human flotation tank.

'Well done for coming out on such a foul night,' says Sara. She calls it ark weather, apologizes for the lack of heating. She sits in her straight-backed chair with her feet in front of her, their outside edges lined up with the edges of two tiles. Her body describes half a swastika. The floor is cold. I'm wearing footsocks from Afghanistan (via Oxfam) and my gardening jumper, pilled and smelling of compost, down to my knees. Nearly summer, who would think it.

Tonight we're a roomful of spines. Sara instructs us to stand and begin walking: 'I'd like you to imagine your spine at the front of your bodies. Okay? Begin.'

I weave in and out of the others with my spine shoved forward, throat to groin. Like this, my shoulders and arms are forced back in order to balance the weight of so much frontal bone. A pregnant-type waddle.

Now she tells us to switch. 'Imagine your spine all the way to the back.'

This forces a hunch, shoulders shrugged forward, chest caved in, eyebrows up, chin down. One of Melville's tortoises, black as widow's weeds, heavy as chests of plate. I hump my shell.

Last part of the exercise. 'Now imagine the spine in the middle.'

This is obviously where it's meant to be, centred, the body in balance. When I try to walk like this I tend to wave about, my spine more like a reed or a sedge than a tower of bony matter. The others have no trouble, look happy, swing their arms.

When we're back in our ring of seats Sara asks for feedback. The others, expressing varieties of wonder and revelation, confess they have been walking badly all their lives. From here on in, they vow, they'll amend their ways. They have that light and buoyant look, like Flat Stanley after he's been blown up.

Sara also looks pleased: her experiment has worked. She dangles the plastic spine-model between her knees, passing it through her palms, twiddling its lopped-off pasta-tube nerve endings, raising it so close up to her face I think she's about to slurp at it, but no, she's merely admiring its intricacies. Great thick sausagey things.

Now she eyes the spine-model as if for the first time in her life. 'It's funny,' she says, 'just how much space it takes up inside your body. People forget just how three-dimensional they are.

A pool of poolwater which, judging by the burning in my eyes, contains unnecessarily high levels of chlorine. I used to take Molly to the Whitewater Hotel just up the road but now I prefer the caravan site down in Hawkshead.

I pay the entrance fee, find a cubicle and change into my swimsuit, black regulation. Push into the water, let it close behind me. Fall forward breaststroking my way towards the deep end which is not really very deep. Neck kinked hard back contrary to good Alexander practice. I enjoy swimming, so did she.

Ringing the walls of the pool building is a painted frieze of blue sharks' fins or waves, it's hard to tell which. Three compass-perfect terracotta suns, one for each wall – North South West – but no rising sun since the East wall is made of glass: Several palm trees which look more like over-grown cannabis plants. The white plastic tables and lounge chairs are not painted, nor is the lifeguard reading a book. Pop music pops. The real waves in the real pool are by Hockney; once they get churned into action they repeat themselves, lap lap, to match the frieze of sharks' fins or painted waves. I swim on my front going forwards and on my back returning; every other time, float. This is the pattern.

Did they have swimming pools in Flatland, and if so, who would have had the advantage, the big-shot males (circles, squares, polygons, etc.), middle ranking military and business professionals (triangles), working class males (extremist of the triangles), or the lowest of the low, the linear women?

On the fifteenth lap returning the walls of the pool building go flat – slit like a box down one of its corners and opening out into a scenic back-drop. It's necessary to hold on so as not to slide off the face of the scenery-world, along with the sharks and the palm trees and the three bully-boy suns.

I make my escape into the steam room. Timed puffs of steam suffused with eucalyptus to clear the nasal passages, a gathering of moisture and menthol. I sit with my legs gathered hard to my chest, the back of my head steamed to the wall. Study direction of drops as they circulate around the cubicle, do a flow-chart in my head.

Edmond Halley reduced the world to a set of maps and charts, tables and maps; tables of latitudes and longitudes; tables of stars and of comets and trade winds, geomagnetism and tides; specific gravities; maps and charts of coastal waters.

The steam room tilts. I slide on my bottom, listing from one corner to the other, my sense of direction in that featureless, shadowless, angleless room gone. After another four-minute interval, another hiss of steam: at least this was predictable. But then comes a more serious tilting during which I slide clear off the bench and onto the floor. Reach up for something to grab onto but meet only slippery slidey plastic. Edmond Halley milled the edges of coins, etched isolines, girdled the globe in graphic coils. Texture, definition: without it you slip and slide and don't know where you're off to next. Flat Stanley must have experienced something similar as he clutched his thin sandwich inside his envelope in which he would be posted off to California. His mother, Mrs Lambchop, calls to him inside the post-box. 'Can you hear me, dear? ... Are you all right?'

The steam room is constructed like a modern torture chamber. Walls floor benches all made of the same whey-coloured, moulded plastic.

'Wait a while before eating your sandwich,' she told him, 'and don't get overheated.'

Can you hear me, dear?

Everyone, I remind myself, is a mapper: the blind person feeling her way around a room, a bat flying around in the dark, a fell-walker navigating in thick mist, a child lost in a woodland. Only the female Flatlander would be too stupid presumably to figure a way out.

I grab the U-shaped handle and pull. Try pushing but it won't push. Write HELP in the steam with my finger but the door is made of some opaque material with the open-pored texture of a tangerine. Raise up my arms, flatten my steamed-up body against it and make three lewd wetfish slaps with my pelvis.

A female Flatlander might be stupid all right but she'd have other resources at her disposal. She had a temper, not to mention an invisible, deadly non-lustrous point. With that, needle nosed and hot, she'd take aim, back up and hurl herself straight through. Fine javelin shot skewers steam room door.

I pull back and knee the thing.

The lifeguard comes running over: 'Are you all right there?' he asks. I'm breathing hard but I'm fine, I tell him, just fine. Glad to be out.

Outside the real sun is low in the sky, with no clear outline. It isn't tangerine-coloured but the colour of light and heat. X billion degrees of hot disc suspended in a Spaceland sky.

7

Map of the Breast

'Slip off your bra and put your sweater back on.' Two other women are waiting, both mothering leather bags with gold clasps. I don't have one of those. They read magazines, I do not. My mind wanders. Where does the wandering mind wander to? The cartographer plays God, said my father on more than one occasion. I was innocent, at the time, of the patriarchal nature of such a perspective: not that my present wisdom necessarily protects me from repeating the error.

The mapmaker's space station is, as it were, an imaginary cloud or lily pad in the sky. From up there you get to decide which objects to include or exclude: tables, chairs, waiting women – all very well but what about the cubicles, the windows, the magazines (*Cumbrian Life*, *Company*, *Cosmo*, *House & Gardens*)? What about the wet coats and bras (over-the-head and hooked-round-the-back) left in the cubicles? The handbags and the things inside the handbags? The thoughts inside the women's heads?

The cartographer must be, among other things, part mathematician, part production expert, part student of graphic semiology and part geographer. As Arthur H. Robinson put it, 'His is the critical role equivalent to that of an author.' There weren't many female mapmakers around in Dr Robinson's time; there still aren't.

The cartographer, also like God, likes to think of himself as objective. What he sees from above is what anyone in his exalted position would see: what is there. Factual, undisputed, ascertainable. A nonsense of course. What you get on any map is what the mapmaker chooses to put there. This partition wall and not that, those three chairs but not those three women, a red dot and an arrow marker saying YOU ARE HERE.

Barefoot, gown gaping at the back, I pad back to the cubicle to get my notebook and pencil. In it I draw three circles arranged to form a right angle – one way of representing the three women, myself included, in this waiting area. The function of the map must also be considered, so given that I am here to have my breasts scanned, I must add two smaller circles at the top half of each of the three main ones.

Big circles = women

Small inner circles = breasts

One of the Circles wants to know if I'm an artist. 'Oh no,' I tell her, 'I'm just making some notes.' At first they seem disappointed, then suspicious. I could be making notes about them. Proper female Flatlanders, they contract into themselves. Lines waiting for a greater eminence to measure them.

Them/me/us. I am one of them. Remember what I said about playing God? Unforgivable. I should go to cartographer's confession; say, Father, I have sinned. Or rather, Mother. We are in this together.

'Dr Beard? This way, please.' The technician turns her back and I follow her into the screening room. 'Remove your top please.' My nipples are lost in the general expanse of goose-bumps. 'If you could just put your left arm up here and try to relax.' I embrace the machine, more cold moulded plastic. She leans on my shoulder, presses down. '*Re-laax.*' Takes the breast and scoops it onto the plate. The plate is too low so she has to let the breast loose, raise the plate, scoop the breast back in and screw it down again. The breast is at right angles to the rest of the body. Observe it, specimen-like.

Chin up. She tightens the upper plate which is see-through plastic and screws it down harder. A rounded peninsula with subdivisions, it reminds me of an illustration in my map cabinet, from a French children's book, *Plouf, The Little Wild Duck.*

She repeats the same procedure for the other one. 'That's fine, Dr Beard.' The technician unscrews the top plate, releasing the breast. I expect two mini pizza bases to jut out at right angles from my body but they are as they were, two bags full. Molly breastfed until she was nearly four, a great girl kicking her legs against mine as she sucked.

There were no breasts (or wombs for that matter) in Flatland. The women, mere lines, were simply too minimal. Such appendages would have spoiled their very linearity. In any case, the private parts of women, or men for that matter, were irrelevant accessories, like handbags.

I put my jumper and coat back on and go through to the front desk. The receptionist tells me I'll be sent a postcard with the results. She doesn't say when. 'Could I be sent a copy of my mammogram?' I ask. This causes alarm: irregular procedure, you may have to pay. 'That's all right,' I tell her, 'I can wait, I can pay.' I could be a map of fifteenth century Nuremberg, from the way she looks at me.

Outside, the rain has let up but the weak April sunshine does nothing for my bones. It carries with it wind, and wind has the capacity to cut through coat, sweater, underwear, skin, fat, right on into bone. Bone has mass and density. What does a flat bone look like? Molly once found a sheep's bone: we were high above Haweswater. 'Put that down, it's dirty,' I told her. Scolding mother words kicked up from under some ancient peat hag. She didn't, I didn't expect her to. It was bleached clean.

'What is it?'

'A bone.'

'Whose bone?'

'A sheep's.'

'What happened to it?'

'It got sick and died.'

And so on. She soon got bored with the bone and gave it to me. Surprisingly heavy and solid but pitted. Molly knew perfectly well that bones could be heavy and chalky but equally that, as in Flat Stanley's case, they could go flat as boxes.

Stanley, remember, had been squashed to within half an inch of flatness. This was quite worrying so after breakfast his mother, Mrs Lambchop, took him to see Doctor Dan. Doctor Dan asked him if it hurt very much being flat. Stanley said it had felt sort of tickly at first but that now he felt fine.

My breasts feel sort of tickly too. Added to that, my torso aches. The muscles that look like stringy bacon in the anatomy books, having shrunk in the rain, are now yanking at my ribs. A muscle in my groin has gone into spasm, gnarled root too near the surface. Most of my muscles have forgotten how to stretch and contract so that my body moves from side to side as it goes forward. Not a fat person's waddle but a thin line's affliction.

In Flatland, it was understood that any Female, either walking or hanging about in a public place, must keep up a constant wiggle of her sub-lustrous (hind) end to protect any poor unprotected Male from inadvertently being run into.

At that moment a Male in a pinstripe suit, bespectacled and benign, undoubtedly a consultant, comes towards me.

The last thing in the world I feel is dangerous – but that's the whole point. What with our stupidity and near-invisible Cap, we women of Flatland aren't aware of our own deadliness, for all it takes is a single jab.

As it says in the Flatland rulebook: any Female suffering from violent sneezing, or any other fit causing sharp and involuntary motions, shall be instantly destroyed.

I veer dangerously towards the consultant. So polished he is, it would be a terrible thing to run him through, decompose him, splatter him with blood. So sweet-faced, I think, only just going grey at the temples and with quite an amused type of nose. Resembling a little the writer Ian McEwan. And so I steer myself towards the kerb, yes, in order to protect him but also myself for, as with the wasp, while the women of Flatland can inflict instantaneous death by a single poke, yet unless they withdraw their stinger from the struggling body of their victim, their own insignificant bodies are liable to be crushed.

He puts out an arm to steady me. 'All right?' he asks. 'Just had a scan,' I say. 'Fine now. Thank you. You can let go.' Which he does. I walk on, knowing myself to be that impossible being, a Flatlander with breasts.

4 a.m. I pour milk into the milk pan and place it on the cooler of the two Aga plates. The pan tilts, which means it's not heavy enough, not properly balanced. I pour in more milk to steady it; warm back against Aga and wait for it to heat up.

The back wall of my kitchen is an art gallery. The paintings, mostly of the beeches, were painted from many different perspectives. In one they're abstracted to grey stripes; in another they seem to march forward like the legs of Indian elephants; in yet others they are fluffier, leafier, more like trees. Their leaves change with the seasons: lime, mint, old green, coined fire, leather, ash. Painted by Molly.

The pictures are stuck on with pieces of sellotape, now yellowed and stiffened, creating gaps between the paper and the wall behind. The milk has foamed over. Start again using minimum amount of milk without pan tipping over.

Molly picked up a brush; then, with her left hand, another. Two brush-horns. She had her red plasticated painting apron on. She dipped the left brush in green and the right in red, pointing them bullishly at the easel. At first the left side of each stripe came slower and wobbled more than the right, but as she worked, her left-hand execution became as confident as the right. Soon they were working in parallel motion or, if she so wished, purposefully at odds, pulling the paint here and there, swivelling and slapping and drawing it down so that the primary colours became more subtle. Forest colours. In between the poles of colour the paper stayed bare.

'I like your stripes,' I told her. 'They aren't stripes.' Annoyed, she raised both brushes so they jutted up out of her armpits. 'They're trees, can't you tell?'

The mapping job is finished, the beeches are still there. Molly painted them from all angles and in all seasons. She loved them and stroked them and drew them and climbed them and then what? If I were Japanese I would thank them for letting me measure them. If I were Native American I would listen to their counsel. If Molly were here she would hate them being felled. But she is not here, that is the point. They are a danger to the public, past and present.

Dawn. The bitterns who live in the reed beds in Rusland Pool are waking up. Molly imitated them by blowing through the top of a milk bottle.

Bwhoobwhoobwhoo.

Wipe up your spilt milk, Magda.

I'd like to say I arrived at crack of dawn, that the pair of Rusland Pool bitterns were already booming and the larks larking, but it wasn't so.

Dawn cracked without me. I shrank further inside my extra-large T-shirt with the map logo saying *You Are Here*. Eventually I opened one eye and what I saw was a wasp on my windowsill curled on its side with its wings behind and its legs tucked up before. Warm furry dead.

Children look so sweet asleep. Open the child's bedroom door and the heat and smell of them hits you. Go nearer the bed, put out your hand, tuck it under the hairline. The weight of hair is negligible but the fan of it leaves a wispy impression on the back of your hand. And then, under the hairline, a sweaty sour smell.

Open the child's bedroom door and she isn't there.

Here witness an act of will in which the human female breaks out of her night-nest and its messy memorabilia. That small but significant shift in orientation from the horizontal to the vertical. How is this done? According to the Alexander Technique (which assumes freedom of movement in three dimensions), by rolling over onto your left side with your knees to your chest and landing more-or-less upright onto the floor.

But if you happen to be flat? Then it depends on the nature of your flatness. Flat Stanley was quite flexible, bending at the waist and at the ankles. His father could roll him up into a parcel, tie a string around him and take him out for a walk. One day they met an old friend of Mr Lambchop's who mistook Stanley for a roll of wallpaper. 'Wallpaper?' said Mr Lambchop. 'Oh, no. This is my son Stanley.' He undid the string and Stanley unrolled: an untrue two-dimensional being in a three-dimensional world.

A Square, on the other hand, represents the ultimate in flatness: the oily smear on a cup of black coffee, the shadow on a wall, a barely disguised theoretical concept created by a serious Victorian clergyman-mathematician.

Which leaves Flat Stanley, I'm afraid, as an endearing cheat, no more than a character in a children's book: not to be taken too seriously. My father would not have approved. If you're flat, then for goodness' sake observe the rules of Flatland! But then my father is dead and many other things besides have gone awry, which makes the observation of certain rules seem silly if not superfluous.

Flat Stanley, Flat Me.

Look here. I know I'm not literally flat. Nor am I mad, silly or stupid or suffering from some bizarre form of astigmatism or monocular vision. I know my body is a tube full of organs and fluids and viscera, that food goes in at one end and waste products come out the other, that blood and air travel round it. William Harvey and all that. When I get dressed in the morning I do not cut my clothes out of paper and attach them via rectangular hinges to my shoulders and hips, thus leaving my back surface exposed. I am not the cut-out paper doll my father used to demonstrate how a 2-D Flatlander could move in a 3-D world. Even so, mornings are tough; they always have been for me.

Still, here I am, not only cracked but the chick stepped out, bathed and reasonably fluffed up. A sunny, still quite early, morning in the Rusland Valley. I am heading north.

Baaa maaa

Maaa baaa

Which is it? Molly and I would listen for baas and maas. We grew keen to their sheepy variations. Sometimes we voted for one, sometimes the other, or neither. A noise that slipped between consonants.

Mmmbbbaaama.

Sound comes at you differently when you're moving.

Cuh ckoo, cuh ckoo

Between the cuh and the ckoo falls a glottal stop. Anything you happen to be missing could fall into that space.

Keep going. Notice every tuck and fold on Dow Crag. Along the verges, tracts of allium, unfurling ferns like seahorses with snouts curled modestly to their chests, new shoots of holly and hawthorne.

When you're bouncing along tarmac, what you see also bounces. Huff and puff, the pluck of images and sounds. Which shall we put into our wildlife map this fine morning: that particular bird's song, that cuckoo's koo, that low-flying jet's razz, that patch of sky, that cloud? What about the nettles and docks and candy wrappers and used condoms? As for the bluebells ... O, the bluebells! O, the stitchwort! O, the leaves! Blue against white against green, pinged and ponged with sunshine. You notice the effect colours have on one another, how the white of the stitchwort lifts the purple of the bluebells while the bluebells tinge the stitchwort with their blueness. The green meanwhile neutralizes both the blue and the white. They are in balance, in harmony, vibrating one against the other; together more than the sum of their individual plant-parts.

Is that how we were? Did my purple earth Jay's white lightning? Did he brighten my blueness? Did Molly green us both? Did the three of us make a rainbow? Am I now less?

A crowd, a host, a rave of bluebells bopping and swaying in the … Breeze, definitely a breeze. Come, it says. The breeze strokes my forehead, eyelids, back of neck. Soon the beeches will come into view. The beeches. Sudden and still, backlit by the sun. New leaves of a yellow-green. Everything in motion (arms, hair, branches, leaves, cows' tails across in the field); everything, as I say, is gently moving with the exception of the trees' trunks. Today the beeches are dry and thus a paler-than-sometimes grey. Black dots – shadows of the leaves – playing up and down the trunks.

Stare at something long enough and it grows more complicated. The bark of the mature beech is a solid grey, but if you take one patch and isolate it, you begin to notice how it's stippled with browns and pinks in shapes suggesting whorls, butterflies, a map of Antarctica, the snout of the elephant seal. Damage scars, puckered and blistered, evidence of biological wear and tear. You notice how the colours change as the surface curves around, pinks to oranges to greens. Even those are not discrete areas of colour since the green patch also contains salmony pinks within it, and vice versa. The moss that was so sodden a week ago is now dry; warm and dry and velvety and crumbles off when touched.

I head uphill from Beeches 17 & 18, and sit on a mossy rock. How high am I, how far from the beeches? If I were a 'primitive' person I would know not by metres or yards but by holding that distance, that space, inside me. I would know every inch of ground. On the other hand, if someone put a piece of paper in front of me and said, 'Now map it,' I'd probably look quite blank.

A sailor would probably conceive of the distance in terms of wave patterns.

An Eskimo would measure the distance in time rather than linearity (say, fifteen seconds' trot downhill).

A child would–

It is very unstill. The breeze is soft as watercolour brushes, it lifts the hair from my forehead with great delicacy. Growing around me are wild sage, oak seedlings, grass, mosses (or are they liverworts?), twigs, last year's oak leaves, wood sorrel. A lime-green caterpiller crawls along the cuff of my T-shirt. The greens flash against each other. I could just sit here and merge. How long would it take to become a green woman, rot down, take root? A long time. I would get hungry long before then.

The flatness stops here. Full 3-D, every leaf and plant, in spite of the blurring effects of wind, picked out as if with the tip of a blade; every swaying thing veined bristled feathered; beech branches going up and down and the flashing sun behind.

Young beech leaves are said to be edible. I pluck one from the seedling just near my elbow. Chewy and tasteless, not unlike sunburnt skin. (Molly did that when we were in California, peeled the skin off my back and put it in her mouth. 'Mm,' she went. 'Yuk,' we said, 'yuk.') But then the delayed hit of the acid gooses me in the jaw. The wind adds another dimensional effect so that what I see or claim to see next is not to be trusted. I feel I must say that beforehand. So be warned, it's only fair.

A car stops and a woman gets out. She looks around to make sure she isn't being observed, doesn't see me since I'm well camouflaged. Now she scoops something from the back seat of her car and carries it over to the pair of beeches numbered 17 & 18. It is white and trailing, she almost trips on it. She lays her bundle down between the trees. Again she looks around – warily? guiltily? – certainly self-consciously. The bundle is child-size, the woman herself is not very big. She wears wellies with blue jeans tucked in.

The day, as I said, is benign. Not a day of foggy dew or dewy fog, when mist slaloms around the beeches and rises spookily off Rusland Pool; when the light is not light but heavy and half-dark, a time when ghosts and goblins and bogeys and other assorted undesirables feel more at home. The Ghost of Ealinghearth has been sighted in fog because that is the environment in which she and others of her ilk thrive. Weather report of the supernatural. No. This one is different. This one manifests in bright pretty weather. Clear enough to know that what you see is what you see.

What I see is this. The woman unwraps the bundle and spreads it out. Goes back to her car and returns with a jar and a hammer. Pours nails into the palm of her hand, chooses a few which she sticks into her mouth and pours the rest back into the jar. Pulls one end of the sheet up and hammers it to Beech 18. Bends down and up. Hammers the other end of the sheet to Beech 17, a distance of maybe four feet. Four nails in all.

Job done, she moves out to the middle of the road to see how it looks. Is it smooth, visible to drivers approaching from either end of the Valley? Not perfect, says her gesture, but it'll do. She goes back to her car, puts away the nails and hammer and comes back with a camera. Click. Another angle, another click. Gets back in her car. Tyres squeal and she's gone.

From time to time the Maid of Ealinghearth's story reappears in the local paper, especially when other news is thin or like now, when the Rusland Beeches have themselves become newsworthy. Tale, ghost story, myth, legend of the supernatural, yarn, tragic history – so many variations. Myths, I thought, were about gods and goddesses. And is a legend assumed to be false or does it merely become so when it's too incredible to be believed? Just how incredible does it have to be before it 'passes into' legend? As for plain 'story'; is that assumed to be fictional, as distinct from history?

How then is the Maid's story different from, say, Molly's? The Valley was hotching, after it happened, with tales about the Beard family and their so-called tragedy. Have we, or will we, one day pass into legend? But then, Molly's story was palpably true. How do I know? Because it happened. My proof? The front page story, *Westmorland Gazette*, 6th April, 1995. Not that you can always trust what you read in the papers, but they were right; she isn't here anymore.

How do you know she ever was?

Because I have her birth certificate. I have the pink hospital bracelet saying Baby Beard. I have the scar. Want to see?

No, that's quite all right.

Seeing can be a problem. Many experiments have been done to test how people see. In this one, for instance, a child who had just undergone an eye operation was asked, 'How big is your mother?' She looked at her mother, then at the doctor, and blinked her brand new eyes. He expected her to stretch out her arms to her mother's approximate height but instead she placed her two index fingers only two centimetres apart. How extraordinary, he thought. Without eyes she could *feel* her mother's size, and therefore know it perfectly, whereas now, fully sighted, she had no way of measuring her and was, in a sense, 'blinder' than before.

How big is your mother, dear? What if the good doctor had asked Molly that? By the age of five, her relative size perception was excellent. She could tell that I was bigger than her, yet smaller in relation to Jay. 'My mother is only a tiny bit shorter than my father,' she might have said, placing her index fingers roughly two centimetres apart.

A 2 cm measurement can mean different things. It can represent a whole person or the difference between one person and another. On the Landranger map which includes the Rusland Valley, 2 cm = 1 mile. One of those squares contains most of the fifty-four beech trees. It's along this stretch of road that I saw the real woman nail the real banner to the real beech trees. She must have chosen those particular trees (17 & 18) because they're a convenient distance apart and because they're highly visible from the road. It's still there, the banner, slung between them. It reads:

DO NOT CUT US DOWN
WE CANNOT BE REPLACED

But the question remains: What did I see or not see at the beeches?

Monday night.

'Imagine there's a tube, a sort of fireman's hose, attached to the base of your spine going down, down into the earth until it's about half a mile under. This is your grounding cord.

'Find yourself a space. Make sure there's plenty of room between you and the next person.

'Feel the tug of your grounding cord.'

The idea, Sara explains, is to send any 'negative' energy down the centre of the tube: any pain, anxiety, anger or disturbance.

'Send it down the tube.'

What ho, down you go.

'See the little clusters of unwanted energy floating easily down that hole to return to the earth.'

Tubes of pound coins wrapped in green paper go flooping down the chute at Jenner's Department Store. Down you go, pound coins and pain.

The Maid, the Ghost.

But it wasn't a ghost, it was a woman: the evidence is there between the trees. Ghosts don't drive cars, ghosts don't go hammering nails into trees. But what if you saw both: a woman *and* a ghostly thing? Superimposition, transparency, double exposure. The Maid slipped neatly between eyelid and eye, the spaces between the spaces of the new beech leaves.

'Feel the tug,' she says.

You saw a ghost.

I saw a woman putting up a banner.

You saw –

What I saw, or thought I saw, lodges somewhere in my brain and like an erasure, shines through. (You see the light and the light sees you.) A lost map on my computer. I can't get it on the screen but I know it's in there somewhere.

The Maid of Ealinghearth and the Real Woman are one.

They can't be; impossible. Floosh floosh, down the tube!

'If you don't feel sufficiently rooted into the earth, try hanging a weight on your grounding cord.'

Let. Go.

'You may now notice a change in your state as your body contacts the earth's energy more strongly. You may find yourself breathing more deeply as your body responds appreciatively to the positive mental directions you're giving it. Stop and enjoy the sensation.'

The sensation is not positive, the pull too great. My feet can't support the rest of me. My knees buckle followed by the sacrum followed by each of the vertebrae in turn: all fold down. I grab for the piano keyboard, make a noisy splash and come away, hitting the wall with one shoulder. Slide downwards, knees braced, in slow motion; prepare for grounding.

One end of the banner is already down, toga'd across his body. He reaches for the other end.

'Must you?' I ask.

Sheeted, nailed, mooned.

9:30 p.m., mid-June, the sun only recently gone down behind Dow Crag. Twilight, a few pinkish blobs but mostly burnished silver. A night that calls for a softish turn of phrase. He yanks the other nail but this one's well in. A tearing, and the freed sheet falls across his body, pinning him to the night.

I hadn't planned to come here after the Alexander class, especially after the abortive 'grounding' exercise. What made me keep going past my cottage at this hour: telepathy, intuition, coincidence? The psychologist Ruth Blakeman has debunked it all. Let's say I had a feeling. Feelings mean nothing, it's actions that count. It didn't take a genius to know someone would try and take the banner down.

And there he is! Baby Bear discovers Goldilocks asleep in her bed – except this Goldilocks is wide awake and no breaker-and-enterer. In fact, the Rusland Beeches, insofar as they belong to anyone, belong to him: Alan Amwath, Park Authority Project Manager. A man with long wavy golden hair and a golden sports car to match, all three romantically highlit in moonlight. Looked at from his perspective, what am *I* doing here?

I try to think of my spine in the middle of my body but somehow it's developed a defensive twist to it, a slight pull back with each step forward which makes progress slow. The two of us meet in the middle of the road. A tawny owl flies so low overhead we both duck. It lands in the next group of beeches and hoots, one of those long drawn-out cries that must, I think, surpass biological necessity: more like a throat-catching sob; the fowl equivalent of lost-in-the-wilderness.

Whowhowho?

He pushes the bundle of sheet towards me. Is this a test? If I take it, I'm guilty. Obviously, he assumes it was I who put the banner up. I clasp my hands behind my back, a semi-guilty child. 'It wasn't me.'

'Of course not,' he says, 'I had no intention of accusing you. It's quite obvious who put it up, or was behind it anyway.'

'Who?'

'The woman running the campaign: Bea Merriman. Save the Beeches. Lives just up the road, one of the Rusland Hall cottages. Her husband works for the Authority. I'm surprised you don't know about her – and the campaign – it's been all over the papers.' I remember now. 'My boss over at the OS mentioned her, but we've never met.' He smiles at his banner-bundle. 'I expect you will.' Then he's also remembered something: 'Did you map the beeches for the Authority? Dr Beard?'

'Magda. That's right. Look, I'm just curious about why you took it down.'

'It's National Park land.'

'So?'

'So, it could be offensive to tourists. Also it would seem to prejudice the case.'

'What case?'

'The Planning Board will be deciding how many trees to fell at their next meeting.'

'Presumably that's why it was put there?'

Smile. 'And you're here because ...?'

'Let's just say, having mapped the trees, I have an interest.'

He shifts the banner from under his right arm to under his left. I hold out my arms. 'Would you mind if I took that?' I don't know why I'm saying this but I am. 'Don't worry, I'm not going to put it up again; as a matter of fact, I've been concerned about the trees myself. I hope they do come down.'

He hands over the bundle and apologizes for seeming to accuse me. I tell him that's all right. Well, well, we go, and yes, well. I get into my car, throw the banner onto the back floor. He's standing there, so I roll down my window. 'The meeting I mentioned is at Murley Moss on July 10th. Our arboriculturalist will be making his recommendation on behalf of the

Park Authority.'

'What recommendation is that?' I ask.

'I'm afraid we can't divulge that yet,' he says. Smile, ghost of a.

It arrives in a Do Not Bend A4 brown envelope: one breast, the left. An NHS identification label tells me it belongs to me, Dr Magda Beard. A shapely bag with a parabolic curve to its upper slope. If you imagine it in three dimensions, distinctly breast-like. Hard to recognize. Both quite normal.

It was the left she favoured, I don't know why. Yes, I do. If you're right-handed, it's usual to favour holding the baby in the crook of your left arm since that leaves your right free for repositioning the nipple in the baby's mouth; or when she was peacefully sucking, for pressing squeezing patting; or when it wasn't peaceful but urgent and biting, for pulling the nipple slightly away to avoid tearing.

I take the negative over to the window and hold it up to the light. X-rays are black with identifying features in white. It's clearer like this but flatter, a land with an impossibly smooth, rounded coastline. A mass of radiating white lines. At first I think they're blood vessels but they're too fine for that. Should I phone the Screening Unit? No, figure it out for yourself, says my dead father. Do a simulation experiment.

The nearest squashable thing – I'm at the kitchen table – is a paper bag which once held a bunch of grapes. I scrunch that into a ball, then pull its edges out straight. Hold it up to the light. If you translate the dark lines into white lines, you have a not too bad approximation of the breast X-ray.

What happened was this. My breast was flattened. Tissue, glands, fat, etc. all bunched together. What the mammograph shows are the edges of compressed tissue of different densities. A breast, that is, such as a female Flatlander might have had, had Edwin Abbott Abbott thought to give her one.

8

Map of the Rusland Valley, 1890

Dear Dr Beard,

I thought you might be interested in seeing the arboriculturalist's report on the Rusland Beeches.

Since our nocturnal meeting, my colleague George Braund and I have been to have another look at the trees. They are obviously in a bad way. No. 5 (or 6?) from the Rusland end has bracket fungi growing out of the butt; others have rotten branch stubs or holes and (no. 31) rot has probably penetrated down the trunk (a woodpecker has evidently found this). And so on.

However, as George points out, there are a number of trees which are of excellent form and appear healthy. Furthermore, I do not accept the argument that because the trees have hitherto formed components of a single feature, we should therefore blot the lot. Even a single tree can be beautiful, as witness the huge solitary beech outside my front gate.

However (just to put you in the picture), not all of my Forestry colleagues agree with this conservative (conservationist) view but are more in favour of radical felling and replanting, and that includes the head of the Special Planning Board, Ron Dellums. Jon Milligan, another arboriculturalist, has referred to the beeches as 'etiolated telegraph poles with a cabbage on top'. A humorous man, Jon. I believe this 'tidying up' approach will be very persuasive to the Committee, too. However, I think we all agree our aim must be to reconcile the sentimental attachment of the present generation with our duty to do our best for the future.

I hope to see you at the July 10 Committee Meeting.
Yours sincerely,

Alan Amwath

P.S. I hope this has put to rest any shadow of doubt as to any accusa-
tion of vandalism on your part!

Attached to the letter is a spiral-bound report. Arboricultural Advisory
and Information Service: THE RUSLAND BEECHES, by G. Braund. Its
cover is see-through plastic: fold it back and it cracks, leaving a milky
score mark. At the end of the report is a set of Background Papers
including a Tree Preservation Order, Rusland Property File 561.00, and,
then, as promised, a copy of my own map.

My map yet not my map. Where before each tree was indicated by an
empty, uncoloured, triangle, now they appear in four different colours.

According to the Colour Code:

- Green (dark) = Felling unnecessary
- Orange = Major surgery required short term
- Purple = Felling recommended
- Green (light) = New planting

The easiest way to make changes to a given map symbol is to add
colour. Any computer can do it, you can change your mind endlessly.
Colours and type can be altered or modified, allowing old and new to
marry up. I married my tree symbols to the old OS map: G. Braund
coloured them in. *Let's see now, which colour shall I make the felled*
trees? No, not black, that's too morbid. How about hot pink? Oh no, too
jazzy. Purple, that's it! Twenty-six pretty purple trees …

Ex-trees. A culling of trees.

Superimpositions, recolourings, tataptap. Choose four colours overall;
say, orange purple greens. Those are the colours he chose to colour in his
triangles. The eye is drawn to colour. Pretty colours, pretty trees. Ex-
trees. Twenty-six ex-trees, to be exact, according to Braund's
recommendation.

Map symbols are important, they tell you what's what. All sheet maps and atlas maps have a symbolic code or legend based on certain cartographic conventions. Symbols on flat maps, which this is, use point symbols, line symbols and area symbols. Point symbols mark the locations of landmarks and villages; line symbols show the lengths and shapes of rivers and roads; and area symbols depict parks, woods, towns, cities, etc.

Triangles are point symbols since they highlight a particular feature of the landscape. I had to decide which symbol to use to represent the beeches: circle square triangle, doodle doodle doodle. In the end I fixed on the triangle: three sides equal (equilateral). Flat solid tutu-wearing tree, branches fused solid.

Δ = tree

The same symbol, however, can also mean:

Δ = mountainous terrain (pikes)

Δ = Ladies' loo

Or, more fundamentally, simply itself:

$\Delta = \Delta = \Delta = \Delta$

A triangle equals a triangle equals a triangle.

It's important to bear these things in mind.

'Once upon a time there were three bears ...' Molly was in bed, Magda was reading to her, Jay was having a chat with the farmer up the hill. A happy little threesome of a family, freshly tucked up at Ealinghearth Cottage for their summer vacation, having just got back from Jay's sabbatical year in California. Nice and cool and green after all that heat.

'What's three?' Molly asked, referring back to the story of The Three Bears. 'Three,' Magda explained, or tried to explain, 'as in three years old. Like you.' 'Like me, three? Three "me"s?' She didn't get it. The problem was the abstract word 'three' which, by itself, had no meaning – it needed illustrating. So Magda pointed to the bears in the picture book. 'One two three,' she counted, moving from one to the other. 'Daddy Bear, Mommy Bear, Baby Bear: one two three.'

For example no.2 she held up three fingers and popped their tops: 'One two three. Now you.' Molly repeated the action. 'One two three.'

Gerald McBoing Boing of the fingerworld.

'Hey, now I get it!'

She got it because the fingers and the bears were visible, quantifiable. She could see them and touch them and count them, whereas the word 'three' was merely a sound sounding like 'three': arbitrary, meaningful only if you were already familiar with it. Which she now was.

'Now I know three,' she said. And turned over and went to sleep.

Next day she divided her things – dolls, stones, sticks, bears – into klatches of three. That evening, the family sat down to dinner and the child looked from one parent to the other and then to herself. And said, 'We are three.'

'Yes,' agreed the parents. Nod nod nod.

And then, as they say, there were two.

'What is a map anyway?' That was Molly's question. Magda, her mother, was busy at her new computer with the special cartographic software. When she stopped typing or mouse-clicking she became aware of the fan, and then, somewhere beyond that, the same high-pitched noise that quarry trucks make when backing up, a sound that sometimes stays long after you've shut down: *heek heek heek*.

Molly was trying to distract her. She did this by hitting her shoulder repeatedly against the edge of her mother's drawing table. Magda went on clicking with her right hand but allowed the left one to slide between the child and the table edge. Some part of her brain must have registered that the repeated bump-bumpings could cause inadvertent bruising to the child's soft upper arm.

'What is a map anyway?' she repeated, bumping away against the cushion of her mother's hand.

'Stop fidgeting and I'll tell you.'

'Okay.'

In Magda's hand was a paper clip. With her thumb she forced the inner segment out. The paper clip is the question is the paper clip. When it's straightened out and lying flat on the white surface, I will know the answer. That was the thought.

'Come on, answer.' Molly's paper clips joined together to form a train, choo choo. Her train nosed the question mark clear off the edge of the table.

'Answer.'

'It's a Big Question.'

'C'mon.'

'I need time.' Magda was teaching herself virtual (3-D) mapping. While she thought, the computer went into rest mode and began dreaming of foreign places: Antarctica, Monument Valley, Giant Sequoias. The problem was, there was no metaphor for mapping, no way of explaining it using some other image as there was with most other things. You could draw a 'map' of the central nervous sytem, for example, or the London Underground, but you couldn't draw a map of a map. You had to use words which, being abstract, were both more complicated and less clear.

Molly was now sitting cross-legged and cross-armed on the floor. Being Patient. 'Still thinking?' she asked.

'Still thinking,' Magda replied.

'About what?'

Spatial simplification? Surrogate of real space? What's real? What, for that matter, is space?

'Just tell me that one thing and I'll go.'

'But a map isn't just one thing, it's many things.'

'Pick one.'

'Okay,' Magda tried. 'How about this: A map is a … *representation* … of something else.' Pause before and after the big word. Molly got up. 'Does that mean it *equals* something else?' No, Magda thought, no no no. A common mistake is to say 'equals' when you mean 'represents'. Because 'equals' implies *the same as*. Which it isn't: so it's important, she told herself, to distinguish, even if you're a child of six. So she said, 'Well, that's almost right. It sort of equals something else but not quite.' And then she got out her local OS map and pointed to a tiny square beside the road. 'See that? Know what that is?' The child didn't move. Didn't ruck up her mouth or cross her legs as if she had to wee or do any of the cutesy things kids do when they're pretending to think. She was thinking. Hard. You could feel the effort coming off her, heat due to an acceleration of brain waves.

She tried: 'Does it ... *represent* ... our house?'

What do you say to a child who grasps a concept many undergraduates do not? Do you fuss? Tell her she's a genius? Congratulate yourself for having her? Hug her till she bursts? No. You say, 'Correct. That's very good.' But you don't stop there, you don't let her feel pleased with herself – not yet – you push her just that bit further.

'And now can you understand why it doesn't really *equal* our house?' And then you wait. Worry. Have you pushed her too far?

'You mean because it's just a box that tells you where our house is but isn't *really* our house because our house is big and we're here inside of it?'

She's there, spot on: represention, mapping.

'Just so,' said her mother the mapmaker. 'To equal our house it would have to *be* our house. Which it isn't. As you see.'

She put her finger against her mother's. Their fingers jostled, the house-symbol got hidden. Molly's nail was pinker, smoother. Magda's had grid line ridges, Molly's had milk blobs. Their nails caught. They slid the flat parts against each other, grids to blobs. Magda hockeyed Molly's finger into the next square. The child saw.

County Hall, Kendal
Public Records Office, Archive Division (Basement)

'So, how may I help you today, Dr Beard?'

'Rusland Valley 1st edition, 1890, Paul.'

'You don't happen to know the sheet number, Dr Beard?'

'Lancashire Sheet VIII.9, *Paul*.'

'Most helpful, thank you, *Dr Beard*. Twenty-five inch, I presume?'

'Thanks.' What do I have to do to get the man to call me by my first name? Don't bother. Move back to the States if I want to be pals with the archivists. This is England, North-west division. Let him be what he is. Let yourself be what he needs you to be, *Dr Beard*.

How beautiful is the old map (surveyed in 1888, published in 1890). Large-scale (overall dimension 36" square), hand-drawn and coloured on thick vellum, its lines and boundaries delicate and varying. The difference between this and the new maps. No grid lines, no uniformity; in their stead, wandering spidery boundary lines: say, that of Skinner Pastures. The master cartographer so laid-back, so sure-handed and deftly accurate. Then there's the ruled boundary marking a walled enclosure the other side of Rusland Pool, the Pool itself a narrow freehand snaking shape.

This is the pool that swallowed the Maid that fed the cat that lived in the house that ...

Hand-painted, painted by hand. A hand stained, no doubt, with blue-green ink, especially on the clerk's bump of the index finger; a hand that will have picked up a brush and filled in the pinks, blues, browns, greens. Back then you could buy the map coloured or uncoloured (Price: Coloured 4/; Uncoloured 3/). Rusland Pool, wiggling from top to bottom of the map, was done in a faded baby blue, the Rusland Valley road a kind of fawn. Dusky pink for Rusland Hall and the surrounding farm buildings and cottages.

Where Bea Merriman (Save the Beeches) lives.

Ealinghearth Cottage is off the map.

The beeches. Individual trees drawn by hand, rounded triangles with curve-waisted trunks. Stylized generic tree, more like oak than beech, soft and curly, yet differentiated from the conifers, with their pinnate branches like pairs of stuck-out arms and smaller than the trees in Skinner Pastures and White Busk Woods. Which helps to distinguish the beeches from the surrounding woodland.

No question, then, that the beeches were a special feature of the land-scape, special enough to draw them in, one by one, hugging the road, some of them on the other side; some in rows, some in groups as they are now, except that then they were denser and continued all the way up to Rusland Hall. Over a hundred at least. Individual trees, yet if you slit your eyes they become joined up. A piece of unstitched needlework, its design stamped in pointillist blue, or a bit of lacy stuff to decorate the bare collar of the road.

Large-scale maps are, of course, special. (It wasn't until the second half of the eighteenth century that the necessary surveying techniques were sufficiently developed to allow really large-scale mapping for 'topo-graphic' maps.) The nice thing is the amount of detail it can get in (walls, paths, footpaths, old quarry, woods, etc), though even so, some details will have been suppressed. Where for instance are the reedbeds, the rocks, the contours? But if the same cartographer had been working at a scale of 1:25,000,000, he would have had to be even more selective.

The beeches would have had to go.

Things get 'lost' on maps all the time, sometimes through deliberate omission, but often through simple, or not so simple, blunder. In the early 1960s, for instance, the AAA (American Automobile Association) 'lost Seattle' (the twenty-third largest city in the US) on its road map. The AAA confessed, 'It just fell through the editing crack.'

That's an amusing kind of glitch. It's not so funny, however, when boundaries are unilaterally redrawn, economic zones misdrawn, islands wiped off the face of the earth or their size and positions distorted, mili-tary grids added, deepwater routes misplaced, and so on, and on.

This is a distraction.

Another problem with maps is that the features they purport to repre-sent (vegetation, boundaries, buildings, etc.) are constantly shifting and changing. Maps have trouble keeping up, or else they go too fast. On the most recent OS map the Rusland Beeches have been lost. The neck-edge of the road is bare of its previous decorative loops. But then, my map put them back. Now Braund's map will, partially at any rate, take them out again. So it goes.

'Have you finished, Dr Beard?' I look at my watch: four minutes to five. Time for the office to be shut up, the maps to be slid away: the archivist wants to go home. He's got his fingertip on the edge of the map and the map is moving. Too polite to pull. A considerate man, he wouldn't want to shock. So he's inching – centimetring – the map along the library table away from me. How you take a book away from a sleeping child.

'In Max's room a forest grew ...' The mother and the child singsonged together. The child was in bed and the mother was reading to her from *Where The Wild Things Are*. Really, it was more a double-act than a reading because the child knew the story so well. What she liked best of all was the directing. 'You be the Wild Things.' So Magda roared her terrible roar and gnashed her terrible teeth and rolled her terrible eyes and showed her terrible claws. And Molly, the child, cried 'BE STILL!' and then Magda opened her eyes as wide as she could and willed them yellow while Molly – having practised this – stared into them without blinking and this caused her mother to look away and call her daughter the wildest thing of all. '*Most* wild thing,' corrected her daughter. Who became not the king but the queen of all wild things. (As queen she could make emendations to the text whereas her mother could not.)

'And now,' cried the queen, 'let the wild rumpus start!' Which was their cue to bounce up and down on the bed and throw their arms up in the air and howl at the moon, whether or not it was out, and swing from the branches of the trees that grew on the walls of the world all around. Which was not the most soporific thing.

'Now stop!' ordered the queen, and Magda, who represented the Wild Things, stopped and asked, 'Now are you going to send us off to bed without our supper and go back where you came from?'

Which is of course what happens next in the book.

'No,' said Molly, 'you can have your supper.' And she shovelled some food into Magda's mouth. Turnips mostly, and prunes. Which meant the Wild Things would fall asleep with full bellies and wake up quite refreshed with still more terrible roars and terrible teeth and terrible eyes and terrible claws and then …

'But now you won't be able to get away from us and return to your own safe room.'

'That's okay, I don't want to go back,' she yawned, taking the book from Magda's hands and pulling it against her cheek on the pillow. 'I want to stay with the Wild Things.' And with that she conked out and Magda slid the book away in case it stuck to her cheek or the edges of the pages cut her skin.

You put out your hand and slice air. Carve a gap and step into it. The curtain of space dividing you from that other space closes up behind you,

while all around you is another kind of space, a changing room of noth-
ingness. No one can come into it; it belongs to your atmosphere alone.
The changing room changes to an elevator. Going up, up from the
archives to street level. Cool to warm, grey to green.

Many others are leaving County Hall. Air spirals between you. They
turn and twist towards each other, open their mouths: *Good night ... See
you in the morning ... Have a good ...* A school of fish, an unkindness of
ravens. What are these, a woe of workers? Once released they scatter:
down the building's stairs and out into the carpark, or onto Windermere
Road, to cars, to homes, to loved or not-so-loved ones. And as they drive
and greet and peck and twirl or slump and grump and ignore, they
manage to create in the space around them – these human propellers –
mini-whirlwinds of energy. They may not be happy but they are buoyant
and best of all, not-flat. The air, thus displaced by these balloon-like
beings with their curves and depth-of-being, becomes breezy yet at the
same time warm. Normal people.

9

Plato's Cave

July 10th, Murley Moss
Lake District National Park Authority Headquarters
Jugglers are probably the most balanced people in the world. Molly had three penguins weighted with sand; she was a slow and thoughtful juggler. In true Alexander mode I would move smoothly, mindfully and efficiently from my car to the building up ahead. New wood and glass, low-slung, very parksy. Except that I'm late and frazzled, and late and frazzled people tend to perform late and frazzled actions. I have already parked in a Private Barclay's Only space, had to run back to the car and go through the whole palaver again. Dropped keys, picked up keys, picked my way through a maze of parallel-parked shrubs, practising inadvertent key juggling.

At the entrance, a woman in a green Park Authority uniform hands me a stack of papers and ushers me into the boardroom. Holds the door for me, 'There you go. They're only just at the main agenda item.'

Item 5: the Rusland Beeches.

The Authority's Forestry Manager, Ron Dellums, takes the floor. Behind and above him is the National Park logo, a 12' diameter inlaid-wood cartoon of the fells with a lake in the foreground. A giant wooden puzzle.

The ceiling is high, tongued and grooved like a box with its sides sloping outwards. About fifty inset spotlights, adjusted so they illuminate the Board members but dazzle the audience.

The Board are seated around a vast launch pad.

Members of the public are seated in four rows at the back. I take the last seat, last row. Dellums begins by summarizing the latest

Arboricultural Advisory report – not by Braund but by somebody called Jon Milligan. Why have they brought in another 'specialist' at this stage? And how can they call Amwath 'independent' when he works for the Authority?

Dellums: 'If I can just summarize the main points of our latest Arboricultural Advisory report:

'The first, and in our minds most important, point made – in answer to the question, "Are the trees safe?" – is that "no large tree can be considered completely safe". Many of the trees under consideration are in a dangerous condition and need to be felled for safety reasons.

'Secondly, a number of the remaining trees would need extensive tree surgery work to make them safe and the AA suggests this would leave unsightly hulks.

'Thirdly, the AA therefore recommends that felling all of the trees now and replanting with a new row of beeches is more important than the immediate if regrettable loss of the existing trees, which after all – like the rest of us – have a limited life.'

The man is a philosopher.

'So that's where we stand as of now,' he concludes.

In other words – if I've heard this right – fell *all* the trees not just twenty-six.

'So, if any members of the public would like to present their views, please do so now.'

Which they do. One after the other they do. Stand up, sit down.

Woman at the back: 'Can you explain what happened to the first arboricultural report, done by George Braund, suggesting felling only twenty-six of the beeches; and why you've gone to another specialist who favours complete felling?'

Dellums: 'We wanted to do an exhaustive enquiry and therefore have sought outside advice. Alan's report has certainly been taken into consideration, and indeed I believe Jon and George have met up to discuss the matter. Next question, Bea Merriman.'

The woman stands. She looks familiar. A small woman with a lot of bone structure. Not skinny but as if wearing her skeleton outside instead of inside. Shiny red ringlety hair, flash of gold when she turns her head. An earring, a front tooth, it's hard to tell. Now I know why she looks familiar – she's Banner Woman.

Bea Merriman: 'Yes. In the last twelve months there have been considerable gales. If any "dangerous" branches were going to fall surely they would have fallen during this time. Is the Authority aware of any branchfalls?'

Dellums (hum-humming): 'So far as I know, no serious damage has taken place recently. However, the point about the current proposal is to prevent any future damage. Next, please. Man at the back.'

Man at the back: 'You have given the impression that a partial felling will be unsightly, expensive and in the long run leave us with hollow unhealthy hulks. It needn't be like that if the cutting back and the surgery work are done sensitively.'

Dellums: 'I'm sorry to give that impression, but an awful lot of work does need to be done. Next.'

English Nature (the bat lobby): 'Can you give us some assurance that no bats will be in residence when the trees are felled or reduced to hulks?'

Dellums: 'I have to say that at the end of the day public safety overrides bat protection, but we're prepared to take advice on protecting bat roosts, plugging of the roosts in felled trees and generally working our timetable in such a way as to ensure the protection of the bats. Indeed, the bats might gain in the end. Yes?'

Bea Merriman: 'Aren't you putting too much emphasis on safety? I mean, no large tree is safe, so why not fell every large tree in the Lake District?'

An outbreak of smiles, wags and titters from the gallery.

Dellums: 'I don't honestly think I need to waste valuable time answering sarcastic questions. One last point, a serious one I presume. Yes, David?'

Man sitting next to Bea Merriman:
'I'm uneasy about this proposal.' Pause. I recognize him too.
'For several reasons.' Pause. From where?
'It ignores the value of individual trees.' Pause. Pause.

'Replacement planting will not recreate them.' Pause. He's from the Alexander class.

'These are two-hundred-year-old trees we're talking about.' Pause. That's it.

'History has shaped them.' Pause. Tall, very tall. A man who takes his time.

'Replanting will not achieve the same effect.' Pause. Yes.

Dellums (shifting in the speaker's direction while keeping his eyes fixed): 'Let me um state categorically that the Authority is deeply concerned about the trees. However, the question of safety must always come first and foremost. Let me also remind everyone present today that as landowners it is our prerogative to deal with the situation in the manner we deem in the best interest of all concerned. Having said that, we believe we are doing everything in our power to consult with local groups and objectors; indeed, when the final proposal is approved we intend to submit it to the DoE – which again we are not required to do as landowners. But in the short term it is not for me to decide: the proposal will be put to the vote at the next Management Committee meeting.

'So, now, if any of the Committee would like to comment on the proposal before we move on?'

Which they do. One after the other they do.

Member 1: 'Seems to me everything has a limited life. It's like the horse's leg isn't it. If we try to doctor 'em with bracing, festoon 'em with multicoloured wire, we'll end up with an unsightly mess.'

Member 2: 'Better to have 'em all out now.'

Member 3: 'It's outrageous to try and prop up a bunch of dead and dying trees. We've all got to go sometime, eh?'

Member 4: 'At the end of the day – not ours but our children's and grandchildren's – those newly planted trees will be a pleasure.'

And so on, and on, until the room – floor, windows, galaxy of spot-lights and mountain logo plus the entire round table the circumference of a flying saucer – goes flat. The roof folds outwards. The table rears up as if on a pulley and all the coffee cups and expensively produced reports go sliding off, along with Members' spectacles, mugs, spoons, pens and paper clips. Light smears over the surface of the table. The people with their backs to the audience settle to the bottom but the others float around to the top and sides so that you see them as if from above, or as in a child's drawing. Molly had a model house kit made of cardboard. It came flat and I had to fold here and there along the roof line, wall line, and so on. Once she'd put it together she got bored and squashed it flat again. Which is what happens to the boardroom with all the people in it. Banner Woman whose name is Bea Merriman, and George Braund whose report has been gazumped, and Amwath and the man from the Alexander class whose name is David Somebody. All flat.

Item 5 on the Agenda is being wound up. The Committee will meet again in a fortnight to debate the issue further and take a vote.

'In the meantime,' Dellums says, 'I would be very happy to meet with any of you at the beeches or elsewhere if you have any doubts about the decision. Any objections from members of the public can be sent to me and will be taken into consideration.'

AOB. I head for the door along with several others. Someone holds it open for me. Behind me, the meeting is taking place on a screen, the shapes of backs and backs of heads on a plane with the faces from the far side of the table. Shadows and shapes as on a telly screen – or projected in Plato's Cave.

PLATO'S CAVE

Imagine a row of men sitting on the floor of an underground den. They're chained in such a way that all they can see is the cave's wall directly in front of them. Behind them is a high ramp, and behind that, a fire. On the ramp is a row of objects: a vase of flowers, a chicken, a wine jug. The fire casts shadows of these objects onto the cave's wall so that the men – these prisoners in chains – see these shadows projected. To them they're real: reality. They have no idea the chicken, flowers and jug have width and breadth, or that they themselves have three-dimensional bodies. Very sad it is. They talk to each other always facing forwards, assuming that they and their fellows are also shadows.

Alternatively, you can picture a sitting room with the people watching a television screen and identifying with the figures on the screen. In other words, believing they too are flat projections.

The psychologist observed how she folded in at the waist, out at the knees. A sharp fold not unlike paper. 'So how does it feel to be flat?' A question. While he waited for her to answer he wrote in his notes:

Flatness? Two-dimensional?

What's going on here?

> *Neurological?*
>
> *Pathological?*
>
> *Delusion?*
>
> *Shock?*

Part of her wanted to go on saying, 'Flat,' Flatflatflatflatflat. But that would only have wasted his time and her money. Besides, it wasn't such a stupid question, just complicated.

'Could you describe the flatness, how it feels in your body?'

'It varies from day to day.' She looked down at her lap and observed two leg-shapes neatly separated and encased in jeans, white iron-line down the centre of each thigh. After Molly, she'd been curved plastic, delicate as a contact lens (easy to lose). Sideways, her edges picked up light and flashed it around. Slices of metal twinkling in the sun; potential candidate for the wind farm up on Lowick Common. That had been quite nice. As an envelope she could be posted, slid under doors. I am flatter than a theoretically flat pancake, she'd think. I can lurk in shadows – *be* a shadow; a shadow inside another shadow. I can float on the surface of things. Be the coating on a photograph, scum on a stagnant pool (that was one of the bad times). The danger with being a leaf, fallen, say, from an overwintered beech, was that you could be stepped on; eventually, in any case, disintegrate. In the worst phase she'd become the smear of blood on the pathologist's slide. After that she'd threatened to disappear altogether – which was when she made her first appointment with the psychologist.

She tried explaining about Plato's Cave but he didn't get it. Getting such a thing is tricky, especially if you have an agenda. His agenda was diagnosis while hers was first principles. In the end (this refers to her patience, not the duration of the session), she got up and passed out through the office door.

Passed out?

The door dissolved, melted, twisted off its hinges, turned itself into a magic carpet and flew her off into the wild blue yonder. The door stood aside to let her pass. The door didn't exist; it was an open-plan office with an alcove leading out to a passageway. The door was one of those sliding things with a sensor which activates on approach (it saw her coming, it slid). More likely, since light curves around massive bodies she, being two-dimensional and therefore resembling light, curved with it.

Monday night. He arrives on my blanket and stands. In order to look up at him – make eye contact – I'm forced to raise my head to an angle that cuts off the circulation between the third and fourth vertebrae. I pat the blanket, 'You first.' He obeys, folds nose-down, legs extending way beyond the fringes. I kneel beside him at right angles, knees aligned on two of the green tweed squares, place my hand flat on his lower spine. Feel the gathers beneath the waistband of his trousers, the length of body beneath. Could be an extra couple of bones in there.

Both hands now cupping his right hip. The idea, Sara explains, is to push forward then let the body fall back of its own accord; then another push, and so on until the whole trunk is moving freely back and forth. Sacrum Rocking, it's called.

The sides of his hips are like hard-packed upholstery over a wood frame. Long, surprisingly heavy for such thinness.

Once a wave motion starts it tends to keep going. Even when the force pushing it stops completely, the body doesn't stop dead. Inertia, it takes time. Gradually the periodicity of the wave gets slower, the arcs wider. Hipbone to hipbone, rock rock: over he goes and back again.

Now for an experiment. I like experiments. We start off rocking our partners but then at some point we're told to stop while *continuing to imagine we're still doing it*. 'Don't let your partner know you've stopped, but at some stage you can test them on what they're feeling.'

This isn't experimentation, it's trickery. Visualizations, hocus pocus; nothing observable or demonstrable; replicable only by faith. The language is embarrassing: energy, aura, reptilian brain, spirit. My poor exact father, I'm thinking, who would not be turning in his grave because, as he told me: I will not be there for long, I will disappear, rot down.

Did she, Molly, disappear? Do I know what became of her? I do, partly anyway, but I'm not prepared to say. I'm sorry, that sounds like a tease and I don't like teasing any more than I like trickery, but I'm just not ready yet. It will come.

And so I put out my hands and place them back on his hip and set him to rocking; and then, when I think he's not expecting it, away with my hands but keep on with the imagining. See a pair of shadow hands rocking the stranger's hip. You don't have to believe to make-believe. Be a sport, fill your mind with rocking. Rockrock, you never stopped.

And now, with my hands behind my back, ask:

'Are my hands still there?'

'Yes,' says David Somebody, 'yes, I can feel the heat and movement.'

'Wrong,' I tell him, producing my hands.

'Amazing,' he says.

'A little bit of magic,' says Sara.

My father groans but I ignore him.

Now it's my turn to be rocked. Nose squashed into blanket, not easy to breathe. Something warm on my sacrum; hot. A wide mat of hand, a living thing. Heat radiating through leggings and underpants. Maybe he's one of those people who can make their palms into solar panels just by thinking sun-drenched thoughts.

Now I'm being rocked by the hand with the electrical element. Clipped into a sling harness, rockabye baby. A Newbury Bypass protester said it was like being up a flying buttress on a cathedral. Molly was good at climbing trees. She said if she sat still the deer wouldn't know she was there and she could watch them chewing the tops off baby trees.

The heel of his hand pushing one way, fingertips pulling the other. Wide flat sheetmetal ending in bumps at either edge. Back and forth you go over the sleeping policemen of your own skeleton.

He catches up with me as I'm getting into my car. 'Would you,' he says, the rest of the sentence on hold somewhere in his brain, not quite ready to get tripped, or whatever it is words are supposed to do off tongues. Is the looseness of the body somehow paid for with the stuckness of the tongue? I have fitted my two hands around this man's hips and he has fitted them around mine: we have rocked each other on our blankets but he cannot speak a complete sentence to me. Divided into our own space cubicles. Finally he manages it: 'Would you like to go for a drink?'

He names the Station Inn up on Oxenholme Road. I offer a bunch of small response words that add up to something like agreement. He ducks down and in. We go in mine: a large person inside a small car; a smallish car containing an outsized person. Alice after the Eat Me cookie packed with growth hormones.

'David, by the way. David Housego.'

'David I'm sorry?'

'House Go.'

'An unusual name.'

'Suffolk,' he says.

'I've never been.'

Now what? I could ask him about Suffolk, or the Murley Moss meeting, or the sacrum rocking exercise. I could share my discomfort. When you're with a shy person it seems to me you have three choices: either (l) you compensate for their silence by chattering; (2) you try to draw them out; or (3) you join them in their silence. Do not add to the world's word overpopulation.

The Station Inn is at the top of the hill just opposite Helm Crag. In summer you can watch the sun go down over the Langdales. Pleasant fell-side garden area with picnic tables, a playground for kids, a tethered area for goat and ducks. Worn wood counterpointed against bright plastic. Dogs begging chips. Molly once lost all hers to the goat and a portion of her jacket too which was divided into quadrants of colour: the goat ate the blue quadrant plus a chunk of red sleeve.

I order half a Guinness, Housego orders cider. A map of drinking habits with gender as the major variable would show a preference among women for sweet drinks: cider, Appletise, vermouth, lime and soda, etc. 'We're statistical exceptions,' I inform him, raising my glass: information as gift.

He smiles. This response could be interpreted in several ways: (1) he understands but isn't interested; (2) he doesn't understand but is too shy to say; (3) he already knows this statistically ropy titbit and isn't impressed. 'I mean,' I'm not giving up, 'it's usually women who drink the sweet stuff.'

He smiles at his glass of cider. Very fond of it, he is.

A gap, a space where some words should be.

Jay had so many. Jay was my husband, you remember (I remember). Words all strung together; thoughts and questions and suppositions that rippled and curled, twining around some central premise like so many ramblers over a dead stump. Proliferating flowery verbals and their promiscuous connections. Never a dull audio-visual moment.

My father, like Plato before him, warned against such things. Metaphor, circumlocution, poetry. Called himself a scientist but failed to see that his was a geography almost entirely of the imagination, fashioned and imposed by empire on distant lands and peoples. The Mercator projection – not demonstrable truth but a story, a fib; furthermore, a gross distortion. Rockier than an Alexander exercise. Rockabye Daddy.

Let me recall Housego's words at the Park Authority meeting:

These are two-hundred-year-old trees.

History has shaped them.

Replanting won't achieve the same effect .

Three apparently simple sentences. A man of few words. And what of all the words being spoken in the pub by all of the people? There they go, filling the empty smoke-filled space above our heads, a 3-D mind map of words and thoughts and so-called sentences connected together by thought-strings like so many party balloons. And then someone cuts the cord and all the thoughts go flying off with their word orders scrambled up and their grammar awry. And then some words, thus freed, turn nasty: turn on others, rearing up, slicing into each other's spines, apostrophes slashing the tops off 'T's, exclamation marks javelining the more vulnerable 'B's, and so on. And then, what about the words of the people from last night and the night before and the night before that? Does the space in the pub still contain those words, does it remember and remember to remember? Dreadful thought, because then you couldn't breathe for the glut of words, for the memories of the words clogging the space. And thank god for Housego's gaps, for the breathing space he gives you between his words. And then I think, any other man would be asking you what you're thinking.

You think, she thinks, I think.

Housego smiles.

By now the sun is being gored to its fourteen-million-degree core, stuck this side and that by spear-shaped clouds. Sinking, severely reduced until all that remains is a curved slice, the Cheshire Cat's gums painted with gentian violet. Hi there.

I twirl the coaster one way, the glass the other: circles within circles. He puts his glass down. This allows time. Time to observe the other person, to notice how the twitch of muscle affects the flesh around certain parts of the face, the guy ropes up in the jaw around the ears. You can adjust your own guy ropes in response to the other's, or let them go slack lest he get the idea your expression means more than you mean it to mean. However, after a while this gets embarrassing so you look away. Housego goes for the next round and I go off to the loo. When I come back outside, all I can see is a pink jacket floating in space, the rest of him merged into dusk.

'So what's your interest in the beeches?' This is me asking him. He strokes the side of his glass with his thumb. 'Treecreeper,' he says. The only treecreeper I know moves in a jerky shuffle pressed against the tree but showing its white underparts from the side.

'Sorry?'

'Tree man, arboriculturalist. My speciality is climbing. I've been hired by the protesters – you know Bea Merriman?'

'The woman who spoke at the meeting? Writes letters to the *Gazette*?' *Put up the banner?*

'That's Bea.'

'The one who suggested they cut down all the trees in the Lake District?'

'Mmm. Actually, it was a serious point but Dellums brushed it off.' Pause. This gives him away. I know where his sympathies lie but he doesn't know anything about mine.

'And you?' He means, presumably, why was I at the meeting, and what is my interest in the beeches. Which is harder. What constitutes 'interest', and do I have one? Interest, as in return on initial investment? Oh, yes, I've got one of those.

'I live just down the road.' Wave to the west.

'Bea's your neighbour then; she lives at Rusland Hall cottages.'

'Other direction, I'm at the south end: Ealinghearth Cottage.'

'You mapped the beeches for the Authority, I gather?'

'I did, but each of the consultants has changed it to suit his argument. I expect you will too.'

'I don't work that way,' he says.

'How do you work?'

'I climb trees, examine them quite closely.'

'Each tree? All fifty-four?' Nose to bark? Meetings With Remarkable Vegetables?

'I can do ten on a good day. So a week, maybe a bit more altogether.'

'Then what?'

'Then I write my report and send it to Bea.'

'Then what?'

'I won't know until I've done the inspection.'

'When will that be?'

'Bea thinks there's some urgency now that the other consultant has been brought in. The Committee are voting in two weeks and will probably go for complete felling.'

'So she's hired you because you're sympathetic to her cause?'

'I'm as independent a consultant as Braund or Milligan on their side.'

This is true, I think. The bell rings, time to go. The air temperature has dropped. I'm swaying slightly, not with drink or cold but in an effort to find my balance point. Housego has no problem with this. Housego is balanced. Trees are balanced (rooted) and Housego the treecreeper must be balanced in order to climb up them and not fall down.

He still hasn't asked where I stand. Assumes, as would any civilized, right-thinking person, that I'm for saving them. He assumes too much.

Housego's report came hand-delivered. From my upstairs bedroom I heard the swish through the letter-box, got to the window in time to wave goodbye to the roof of his Land-Rover.

Housego's report is different from Milligan's. Well, it would be. Milligan didn't treat his trees as individuals: didn't climb all fifty-four, split specimen branches, take samples to assess actual damage. Milligan assumes they're not worth saving; Milligan thinks they're dead and diseased; Milligan thinks they can be replaced. And why not.

Monday night, Housego and I go for a drink again, to a different pub. This time we have something to discuss which makes it easier (for me). I begin by asking him how it is that he and Milligan, both arboricultural-ists, can come to such wildly different conclusions.

'Not really,' he says.

'Not really what?'

'Any survey of tree health' – he could be reading from his own report – 'is a combination of objective and factual description and subjective judgement based on experience.' He could be wearing a surgical collar, one that goes right the way up the back of the head and locks into place. What if I got behind him, took his two ears between my hands, said, 'Okay, I've got you, you can let go now?' Instead I say, 'You mean you think Milligan is wrong?' 'No,' he says – slight loosening of the skull-vice – 'just a different interpretation of the facts.'

'Go on.'

'If you look at Milligan's report, his main objectives are not so different from mine. "To maintain and enhance the conservation value recognized by the SSSI classification." Quote unquote.'

'I don't follow.'

He unspirals off his bench and rises, reaches down for his glass. Head, neck, shoulders: slow tilt over and down. When he comes back up, his head oscillates a few degrees on his neck before coming to a stop which isn't really a stop. He could be thirsty or needing time out.

When he comes back with his refill, he says, 'Trees.' That one word. And again, 'Trees.' His thumb tracing a triangle on the side of his glass. With each repeat, the word changes shape.

'In order to become "a substantial visual feature", as Milligan's report says, trees need to be at least a hundred years old. Well, the Rusland Beeches are two-hundred-year-old trees – which more than fulfils their objective – so I see no point in felling them until they're judged to become a really serious danger.'

'Which you obviously don't think they are?'

'I think it's a nonsense. As I say in my report, I consider the whole thing overstated, the extent of the rot and the assumption that branches are likely to split and fall. Most have a high proportion of solid stems and healthy crowns. They've withstood several severe gales, followed by an exceptionally heavy snow fall last winter. They're not going anywhere in a hurry.'

'But is it worth the risk? Isn't it better to fell and replant?'

A slight but noticeable retraction of the neck muscles, commonly known as a flinch. 'Think about it,' he says. Hands in prayer position, thumbs north. 'If you begin poking around asking questions about safety, what do you get?'

'Answers relating to safety?'

The hands part from each other, there you are.

'You think they're asking the wrong question.'

'What do you think?'

'I don't.' My jaw locks, the whole skull screws itself together. If he took my head in his hands and shook it gently, would the words of the story come pouring out?

'Surely,' I say, 'they must have some reason for asking it.'

'Sure,' he says. 'A few years back a branch came down on "an innocent motorist". It was up around the Rothay Bridge area, not near here at all – and not a beech. But the Authority is still paying for it.'

'So it's afraid of litigation?'

'Let's say it has an agenda, and its decision supports that agenda. Now it has to find evidence to back it up. Milligan inspected the beeches in February. It's almost impossible to assess the general health of tree foliage that time of year or the real extent of dieback.'

'Whereas you inspected them in leaf?'

'Correct.'

'So.'

'So. The debate isn't just about safety, it's about different philosophies. Their attitude, which seems to be yours as well, is that trees have a set period of life at the end of which they should be cut down and replanted.'

'And yours is?'

'Mine is ... I regard old-growth trees as special. I think it's our duty to protect them for as long as possible, felling selectively only when absolutely essential and replanting to fill gaps. Frankly, I think the Authority has lost it. Let the safety thing blow up out of proportion, sold out on its own stated conservation policy.'

By now we're headed for the door. We say good night to the bar girl, not quite in synch. Halfway up Beastbanks, he asks if I'll be at the protest meeting. 'This weekend. At the beeches. Bea's organized it. She's invited the press and some TV reporter. Quite a few'll be there. She's also invited Milligan and Braund. Braund may come but Milligan, no surprise, has refused. The campaign's going well apparently. Bea's collected over 2500 signatures so far – still hoping to get another 500 or so before Sunday.'

I stop on the steepest part of the hill trying to think grounded thoughts. If I don't, it will happen and then I'll lose my balance and have to hang on. Feel the sacrum tucked down and in, the neck directed upwards. 'I haven't signed, you know.' Statement/confession/blurt. Housego says nothing. On Fellside we begin to divide, head for our separate vehicles. Still nothing. I turn back. 'Aren't you going to ask me why?'

'Why what?'

'Why I haven't signed the petition.'

It's not his business, he says. 'You'll tell me when you're ready.' Which tells me that he knows already but it doesn't figure in the equation. What may have happened to Molly and what may happen to the beeches are two entirely separate questions. Only in my mind are they all mixed up.

10

Map of Vishnu's Feet

The phone rang, it was Magda's mother. 'How are you, dear?' The daughter told the mother about a computer mapping course she was taking to catch up with new techniques. Splendid, said the mother, splendid, your father would have been so interested – thus letting her know that *she* was not.

'And how's the counselling, or is it therapy, going?'

'Fine, I'm thinking of stopping.'

The mother took this to mean her daughter was cured. Double splendid, well done. And then she rang off with, 'I'm so glad you've found your feet again.'

Magda stood there with the empty telephone staring down at her found feet. She hadn't been aware of losing them but she had, it's true, been having trouble with them. A sensation of weakness, an unwillingness to function as feet should, to *be* feet, behaving more like a continuous keel or a pair of joined rockers than independent appendages. Or like one of those sand-weighted dollies, head describing a revolution while its painted-on feet hold the centre.

The chiropodist's office was at the top of Beastbanks: steep and cobbled. A couple coming down it were holding each other so closely they looked more like one wide person with extra limbs. So long as they stayed jammed together at the hip neither could fall, yet their doubleness made them awkward, unbalanced.

Magda also tilted sideways, testing her edges. Nothing but air. When she got to the wall she held on, walked one palm beside the other. Soon she could imitate this crabwise motion with her feet, but when she tried to swivel ninety degrees in an attempt to walk normally, the angle between her and the ground decreased. At this rate, the earth's face and

Magda's would soon kiss. Then what? She'd clasp it round the neck, only it would be too far away. Down she'd slide across the earth's flat belly before finally dropping into empty space. When the couple were passed she took to her knees, crawling the rest of the way up the cobbled alleyway to Beastbanks. Beached beast lands on chiropodist's doorstep.

She lay back in his chair. Better. 'So what's the problem?' Her hands were dirty with clawing cobbles so she slid them under her. Tried to explain about how her feet didn't seem to be behaving properly. 'They just feel weak. I don't know. I probably shouldn't be here.' The foot doctor shook his head. 'People don't take care of their feet.' Oiling and powdering and massaging, cutting toenails with one of those curved sprung professional clippers. When he got to the dead claw on her left small toe he filed it down to a chip of rough calcified matter. 'Can you feel that?' 'No.' He picked up his knife and started slicing away at a bump on the topside of the toe. 'And that?' 'Still nothing.' The slices were elegantly thin. He went on bemoaning how people don't take care of their feet whereas they do look after their teeth. It didn't make sense. 'We depend on our feet for everything, without feet where would we be?' Filing and slicing. 'You can get false teeth readily enough but false feet ...'

The paper mat under Magda's feet was thick with skin and nail dust. What if he kept filing and slicing until she was reduced to needing false feet? Was she being taught a lesson? She agreed with him completely, oh yes, people needed to look after their feet better, and he looked happier, and then she asked him what caused nails to thicken and die and he said it was part of the ageing process and that hers would probably grow back again horny but she could file it off herself just as he'd done and she said thank you, and he said that would be eleven pounds please.

Magda drove home.

Drawer 20 contained the Map of Vishnu's Footprints. Magda got it out and laid it under the anglepoise lamp. It showed the soles of Vishnu's two feet, viewed as it were from below: wide as urns, flat as copper plates, each toe perfectly round as if drawn and cut out with a compass.

Maps have every intention of simulating three-dimensional space – that is their business. And any mapper can distinguish between the flatness of the folded paper map and the not-flatness of the landscape it purports to represent. It is in the nature of maps to do just that. But Vishnu's feet were so impossibly thick and fleshly you'd swear they were real, the lined-up circular sequence of toes so convincingly three-dimensional you wanted to take them one by one into your mouth and suck them like amber glass baubles or miniature balloons, to press along the instep with your thumb, to push with the heel of your hand against his leathery heels to feel their resistance – only you couldn't, of course. However suggestive of 'reality', it remained only a picture, a drawing, a constellation, a contrivance of flat symbols.

Beneath the overhang of toes was a sequence of deep red stripes not unlike a geological map of sedimentary rock. Along the fleshy ball were: a teapot, a pickaxe, an oil lamp, a fish, a pair of scales, a bow, and a bird which may or may not have been a dodo. Along the instep: an eye, a new moon, a star, a spear, a meditating figure, two dogs or possibly lions holding up an imperial chair. On the heels: a flag, a flute and finally, at the very outside edge of the right foot, a tree.

It wasn't a problem with feet at all, of course, but the space around them. There was too much of it and it was empty of other feet that had once moved beside hers, stepped on hers, shuffled and fell between hers, made six baby steps to her one. Or that other owner of outsized feet that moved more or less in synch with hers, that could brake her fall with its flank like a sideboard or run up her leg with its toes on a hot night. Support system; family, husband, daughter. They came with names but not guarantees: Jay, Molly.

Another woman might have gone for the photo album but Magda was, after all, a mapmaker. Studying maps was familiar. So she studied the map of Vishnu's feet and then she drafted a paper on 'Metaphors and Maps' which got published in the *Journal of Cartography*. That also helped.

'So how are we today?'
    'As usual.'

'Can you describe the flatness?'

'Sheet of see-through plastic.'

Therapist probes, client embroiders.

'Ah,' he said, 'ah.'

Having a transparent body had imaginative possibilities. Magda 'mapped' her internal organs for his benefit: lungs blue, heart red, flat and colourful, as though giving a lecture with her own body as projected transparency: a kind of computer graphic update of a female Flatlander. Did he see her as horizontal or vertical, she wondered. Brown liver, green brain, your turn. But while Magda and the therapist quite enjoyed themselves – the session zipped along – it zipped nowhere. It could have, she realized that as soon as she got out the door.

It could have gone something like this. Thoughtful pause followed by suck of professional breath: ' ... and the womb?' Well now, this makes you stop and think. 'Womb, womb? How would you map the empty area below the heart? What shapes? What colours?' You begin rather tentatively with the birth canal – make that baby blue – and work upwards. Next comes the thick surrounding protective wall of muscle – palest pink – out of which grow the two rosy-fingered Fallopian tubes: skinny blippy Olive Oyl arms gripping a pair of gold ovaries.

'And the colour of the womb itself?' he tries (gently gently).

'Black,' you say. 'Or white.' White for empty.

'Ah,' he says. He likes this one even more than the see-through plastic.

It could have gone on from there. He could have. *So what does the emptiness feel like? Is it painful or just blank?* And so on. But he didn't, he blew it. It was an obvious lead but he didn't follow it because he was too busy thinking how to crack the flatness. Flat, empty and white. Black for mourning. So obvious, tut tut, the sin of omission. Perhaps you should have given him another chance. But you didn't, she didn't. Magda cancelled her next appointment and the next and then the one after that. So perhaps her mother was right after all and she was cured.

Magda drove along Morecambe Prom, keeping her eyes focused on a spot below a bird dropping. From time to time, she looked out the side windows (peripheral vision naturally distorted) at scenes which might well have been painted by a Flatlander. Square professional men, strolling gentlemen pentagons arm-in-arm with lowly lines, not many high priestly circles. To her left was Frontierland, complete with giant cardboard cacti, fortune tellers and casinos; to her right, the Bay. The tide was on its way out. Any bodies washed up today? A convocation of Hell's Angels at the Central Pier. Winos on the Prom. Bubbles.

'Why can't we go to Bubbles?'

'Because it's in Morecambe.'

'What's wrong with Morecambe?'

'It's too far and too crowded – and tacky.'

'What's tacky?'

'Like Disneyland, only worse.'

'But I liked Disneyland!'

'No you didn't.'

'Did!'

'Oh, Molly!'

'But they have a water-slide, I want to go on the water-slide!'

'Okay, okay, we'll go.'

'When?'

'Soon.'

'Oh, goody, I'm going to Bubbles.'

'Don't count on it, I said "maybe".'

'You didn't. You said, "We'll go."'

You said.

Molly never got here. Her parents took her instead to tasteful middle-class Grizedale Forest Sculpture Park, which didn't exhaust her the way swimming and sliding and being stuffed full of E numbers would have. When they got home she said, 'May I go and play at the beeches?' and her mother said, 'For half an hour and no more – be careful, okay?' Molly liked climbing the beeches, her mother knew that. So – think of it this way – if they'd taken her to tacky Morecambe that day she might have been sitting beside her mother right now, frowning at the men in cowboy boots, asking, 'What's reflexology anyway?'

The reflexologist invited Magda to sit. 'I'll just ask you a few background questions first, if that's all right, and then we'll get you to lie down.

'Name?'

'Magda Beard.'

'Age?'

'Forty-five.'

'Miss/Mrs/Ms?'

'Doctor. Not medical, academic.'

'What kind of academic?'

'Cartographer. Mapmaker.'

'Really. How interesting.'

'Sometimes.'

'Yes, well, you'll be interested in this.' The reflexologist pointed to a diagram labelled 'Map of the Zones'. It showed the body divided into striped blue sections running from the toes up to the top of the head, other blue lines coming from the crux of the fingers. Another so-called map. After that, she asked Magda if she knew about electrical mapping. Apparently there was someone in Japan who did electrical mapping of the meridians in the fingers and toes to detect energy blockages. 'It's called *seiketsu*.'

'How interesting.' *Get on with it.*

'Married?' – 'Divorced.'

'Children?' – 'No.'

The reflexologist made notes on a card. Big loops. Magda studied a reproduction over her desk, taken from the Physician's Tomb at Saqqara, Egypt. It showed one physician holding a patient's foot, another holding a hand. Above them were various symbols not unlike those on the soles of Vishnu's feet. The reflexologist interpreted, 'The pyramid shapes symbolize energy, the owl represents wisdom and learning, and the three white birds depict peace, health and prosperity.'

'And the tree?'

'Ah, that represents birth, death and regeneration. In other words, Life itself. So, where were we? Oh yes: children?'

'You already asked me that.'

'I'm sorry. And you said?'

'I said No.' *Oh forgodsake get to the feet.*

'You know, Magda, I don't need to be touching your feet to pick up vibrations. Just talking to you, I'm picking up tension in the solar plexus.' Magda's hand went to the depression beneath her breastbone. Anyone would be feeling tense in the circumstances. 'Look,' she said, 'I've come because I'm having trouble with my feet, not my solar plexus.'

The reflexologist looked at her. Pityingly, head shakingly. 'I'd better explain how I work so you can decide if you want to go on with the session. How I work, Magda, is not just with feet. The feet are the starting points, the laboratories if you like, for investigating what's going on in the whole person. I call it tuning in – you'll be uncomfortable with that but still – I tune in, to your voice, your aura, your past, present and future lives. And – I feel I have to say it – what I'm picking up from you is some enormous block which you may not be ready to deal with. You may have to work with this in a less ... threatening way. Have you tried a chiropodist, Magda?'

'Yes. He shaved a corn and a dead toenail.'

'But didn't contact the real trouble?'

'No.'

'I thought not – and that is?'

'It's hard to describe.'

'Take your time.'

'I get the sensation they won't hold me up. A feeling of flatness.'

'Do you wish to go on with this?'

'I suppose so. Since I'm here. Yes.'

'Then if you'd just lie down on the treatment couch. Come forward so your heels are resting on the edge, that's it. Now let me take them. Let go, you're quite safe.'

Magda let the reflexologist take her feet. 'That's good, ye-e-es, let it come. People have all kinds of reactions to this. Some feel the need to cry, some to laugh. One woman had an orgasm. Just let it come.' Magda felt none of these things. 'When we're born,' came the reflexologist's voice, 'when we're born we're foetus-like, like tadpoles, our feet are ...'

'Wrinkled.' The word popped out of Magda's mouth, a popped word. It popped out even though she was supposed never to have had a child to observe the feet of. Not that that's so strange since plenty of people after all have seen newborn baby feet. In any case, the reflexologist didn't ask how she knew such a thing; she just continued to hold while Magda pictured the map of Molly's newborn feet, a constellation of wrinkles more intricate than any map of the zones. After some more time the reflexologist took Magda's right foot in her left hand and, using her right index finger, began pressing from the instep down to the heel area in a straight line. She did this two more times, then repeated the same to the left. It should have tickled but didn't; in fact, it was quite a pleasant sensation overall. Quite relaxing.

'That's good,' said the reflexologist. 'Relaxed, very relaxed. Later, say in early childhood, the feet often smooth out again. Of course it depends on the child, if he's thin or chubby.'

She.

And they remained wrinkled. Quite simian.

They'd been travelling up the coast of Oregon and decided to stop for a picnic. Magda, Molly, Jay. Walked Indian file down a steep coastal path onto a pebbled beach. Magda in her mother-role unpacked the food while Jay began sifting through the stones.

'Hey, you guys, agates.'

'What's agates?' Molly hooked her chin into his palm.

'Those.' He was isolating the special stones: dark amber to pale urine, cloudy to clear with white salt deposits – a bit like white calcium splashes on nails – and varying in size. Tiny as a baby's tooth to fat as the Queen's diamond. Molly took them from him. 'Are there more?'

'I expect so.'

'Could I find some?'

'If you look carefully, I don't see why not.'

'Have a sandwich first,' said the Mother.

'First I need to look. It's important. I'll eat after.'

Molly with her feet stretched straight out in front of her and her back to the waves, the Pacific Ocean ordinary as a bathtub. Magda her Mother dumps her sandwich with the imprint of her teeth and tiptoes over to get her camera. Crawls on her stomach using her elbows like a trainee marine to pull herself along into shooting position.

Molly's feet fill the viewfinder. Magda her Mother goes on snapping: vertical feet, horizontal feet, parallel feet, V-shaped feet. Close-up feet filling the frame of the picture.

She, Molly, could have stayed there for days, weeks, years. If they'd moved to the States she might still be trawling for agates. If she'd lived, she might have grown up to be a stone collector or a geologist. Or an anything.

'It's all right, keep breathing.' The reflexologist had her hand on Magda's lower abdomen. It was their best holiday. Magda had had the best of the 'Molly's Feet' photographs made into a poster which she'd brought home in a mailing tube. For a time it hung on Molly's bedroom wall; later it got filed away in the Map Cabinet (*Feet, Molly's*).

The sole of her right foot was plumped against the reflexologist's stomach; the stomach soft and yielding, more like sand than stones. The reflexologist supported the foot with her thumbs, worked with her index and third fingers in an arc across the front of the foot quite far up where the ankle comes in. Two times, three times. Then the same on the left foot. 'Keep breathing.' Why do therapists insist on using that expression? Breathing is an involuntary action, you can't not do it, assuming you're alive.

Gradually she stopped working on Magda's feet and went back to holding. A box of tissues appeared beside Magda's left hand; a warmed towel over her whole body, which felt quite nice. 'Take your time getting up.' Magda shifted to the right and the box of tissues fell off to the left. So did the warmed towel.

Beached on the treatment couch, feet dangling a long way down, flatter than ever. Greeting-card feet angled open but too far away to read the messages. How to get socks on them, shoes? At some point in the future she sat dressed in the chair beside the reflexologist's desk.

'So?'

'So.'

'How do you feel?'

'How do you mean?'

'Did it bring anything up for you?'

Like my lunch? 'It felt quite relaxing,' said Magda.

'And your feet: how do they feel?'

Magda hung onto the edge of the desk. The reflexologist stopped pussy-footing. 'There's nothing wrong with your feet. The reason you're having trouble standing is because you haven't dealt with your womb stuff. Loss is my guess. Am I right, Magda?' Magda said, 'I'm sorry, I have no idea what you're on about.' And she paid the woman and left.

Bottom drawer: *Feet, Molly's.* I lied of course. I lied and I resisted, twin therapeutic crimes, but that's what I did. I lied and I resisted, and the reflexologist knew I lied and resisted, and I knew she knew, and she knew it.

I was disappointed in myself. Was the reflexologist also disappointed in me? Probably. I never went back to find out. The point is, I thought I'd dealt with all that stuff: griefwork, losswork (regularly, boringly, yes, like housework, the more you swab and brush the more grease and grime spring up, so here we go again, sweep and brush).

She was right, I hadn't dealt with 'all that'. When she asked me if I'd seen anything, as she put it, I said no. I couldn't at that stage have told her about the photograph because she might have got quite excited. I think she would have. I couldn't have stood another 'ah'. The 'ah' might have led to other 'ahs', strung together like so many cartoon fishes, mouths opening and closing in that fishy way, little graduated bubbles percolating excitedly up from their fishy lips. And then, what if she'd held out her arms? *May I give you a hug, Magda, I think you could use a hug?* No, I saw nothing.

Molly disappeared, that's true. I'd given her permission to go. I said be careful because I was worried about her climbing trees. She would shimmy up the smooth beech trunks then scoot along onto a branch and sit looking down on the world. I was worried but let her go anyway because we'd decided it was important to trust her so she would develop trust in herself and in nature. A lot of trust, a lot of nature. So off she went on her bike, got approximately halfway along the avenue, leant her bike against one of the biggest beeches (no.31), and that's where the story stops.

Before me are two arboriculturalists' reports. One of them, by Jon Milligan, says this tree is suffering from declining vigour; also, he's identified an area of dead bark with fruit bodies of something called *Ustulina deusta*. In view of its defects and its proximity to a major layby, he recommends: **This tree should be felled.**

The other report is Housego's. Visually important tree, he writes. Weight leaning slightly north but unlikely to fall towards road and layby. **This tree should not be felled.**

Beech 31 was her favourite. She'd sit up in the fork and swing her legs, no shoes or socks. I take the photograph of the soles of her feet and blu-tack it to the wall of my study, just over the long white door which, laid flat over a couple of drawer-bases, doubles as a desk. A darkish corner. I trace the lines thinking they might lead somewhere but somehow they do not. Fork, merge, peter out, skin into one another. No grid or contour lines, no fixed code. *Ustulina deusta*. She disappeared, she never came home, we never got to sit down to dinner together. She disappeared, yes she did – but not entirely.

11

Triangulation

Prime porkers, Saddlebacks. Pigs are the star attraction of the protest meeting, rare breeds kept by Tony Parks down at Abbots Reading Farm. (The condolence card from his wife, attached to a slab of bacon, read, 'We were so sorry to hear about your terrible misfortune.')

'The reason we're here,' Parks is telling a reporter '– aside from the fact that the pigs like beech mast – is my family and I wanted to do our bit for the trees as they're a famous landmark and important to the community.' He reaches into the pen, scratches the biggest porker behind its ears. *Hongh squee-hongh*. One of the others screams for attention, all of them bumping the side of the pen.

'Worse than kiddies, they are.'

The best way to attend a party is from a distance. Up on a rise, tucked into a depression, well camouflaged with bracken. My very own nest of rock and roots and mosses and shoots. BEECH PARTY the headlines will say in Friday's *Westmorland Gazette*: a nice pun, to lend class.

I am not part of the party, any more than the mapper is part of her map. 'The mapper is above it all,' as my father would have said. Omniscient, aerial, remote, objective. He died in 1985. Scientific detachment? Oh dear, Daddy, no one takes those things seriously anymore.

Prime porkers plus people with a thing for trees. Hot mulled wine in a cauldron, someone ladling it into styrofoam cups. Clove steam. My neighbours, the good people of the Rusland Valley, drink and mix with protesters from Kendal, Ulverston, Lancaster. How would it be if I skidded down the rise, arriving decorated in last year's leaf mulch, beside the clove-studded cauldron? *Magda, my dear, it's been ages, we haven't seen you since ... Magda, you do look so much better ... Time does heal, life goes on, isn't it a miracle ...*

Is any mulled wine worth it?

When you sit under a tree, as somebody or other once said, you feel humble and secure. When you sit under a tree, on a bright green moss-covered cushion, after a while the cushion detumesces and leaves you with a wet bum.

It was her favourite tree. I will guard it with my life.

If she hadn't gone to play at this, her favourite tree, she might still be here today. Get rid of it.

Squee-hongh-squee.

More people arrive – families from Rusland, Finsthwaite, Grizedale; Friends of the Earth, photographers, more reporters, neighbours from Ealinghearth (farmer, doctor, retired teacher). Bea Merriman and David Housego arrive together. She's carrying two sacks and two large banners, one under each arm. Housego carries nothing but himself. From this distance I could pelt them with beechnuts.

Everything depends on your point of view. If you are a lemming, what you see is food and more food, great spears of grass for nibbling on. If you're a snowy owl, you also see food but from a different perspective. The artist's view is different again from the mapper's. 'It's called single point perspective,' as my mother explained, demonstrating with diagrams and dotted lines how the scene had to be painted from one person's point of view or else the different objects – painted from different sight lines – would be inconsistent, and then the picture would be a muddle. David Hockney disputes this, of course, as did Molly.

She saw a face – mine, say – and drew its features like furniture placed in no particular order around a room. 'It's you,' she said proudly. 'Don't you recognize you?' 'Of course I do.' Synthetic incapacity, Piaget calls it: the inability to represent realistically. Children, it would seem, can perceive objects in space long before they can draw or map them. This ability comes in stages:

(1) First they understand proximity: nearness, nearby-ness, separation, enclosure:

> *Those pigs are in that pen.*
> *That man from the TV is outside the pen.*

(2) Next they understand spatial succession (this-comes-before-that-before...):

There's a lady weeing behind a tree!

(3) Now they begin to perceive relative shape and size:

That big man looks small next to that gigantic tree!

The construction of space, says Piaget, begins with perception but continues with representation.

By ages eight or nine, they begin to develop a sense of 'realism' but usually succeed only partially. Single point perspective confounded Molly. Her picture of the black dog walking on the table, for instance, tries to establish what is behind what, yet the whole thing is a nonsense because the table is flat to the picture plane.

Beech trees, people, pigs in a pen, space around them. All flat. One sight line leads me to Bea Merriman being interviewed by a reporter standing beside a portion of Housego with his head cut off. It's the same with the trees, I can see their trunks but if I want their crowns on my map-picture I have to shift the angle of my sight line.

Bea Merriman pulls things from her bags: food from one, reports from the other. Places the reports – Housego's, Braund's, Milligan's – on the ground balanced on the tree roots so people can browse through them. It's important for people to get all sides of the story, she tells the interviewer. The banners she hands to Housego with a nod to the trees. He scoops them up along with her hands, plunged inside the bundle of banners. This plunging business doesn't last long. Bea Merriman grabs back her hands and off Housego goes to hang the banners from Beeches no.30 and no.31. They feature paintings of trees: one by an artist, one by a child. From this distance you cannot see details.

Radio Cumbria arrives. People eat, people drink, people go behind trees to pee, people sign petitions, people congregate in groups to discuss the 'tragedy' of the lost Ealinghearth child, people bend down to read the various arboricultural reports. Children hang over the pigpen. One bonks the pigs with beech cupules; others run around, chasing each other. One small one trips over some roots and bumps its nose and wails. David Housego bends to it, and sets it back on its feet.

The child looks up at him: up up up. He looks to Bea Merriman. I watch them both.

I watch them move around, take up different positions, sometimes quite close together though never touching, and sometimes quite far apart. The Radio Cumbria man comes at Bea Merriman with his microphone, cord trailing behind him. 'Watch out, don't trip on the wire,' someone yells. I can't hear much else but I can see the people gathered around Bea Merriman and the Radio Cumbria man, a pattern not unlike a giant flower seen from above.

'Mrs Merriman, what do you think the chances are of saving the beeches?' Mrs Merriman's mouth opens and shuts. I move further down the slope in order to hear her reply. 'It's anybody's guess now,' she says. 'I think we've done all we can, now it's up to the Committee members.' Head thrown back, eyes raised to the boardroom-in-heaven.

Save the beeches
Save the beeches
Save the beeches

Another meeting took place at Murley Moss on October 17th, to reconsider felling all fifty-four beeches. There'd been a lot of hoo-ha in the local press (**Hope fades for beeches! Beeches face the axe! They want to destroy the Rusland Beeches! Stop the felling!**), a lot of over-excited exclamation marks, a lot of impassioned letters to the editor (including two more from a professor and half a dozen from Bea), and then there was Bea's petition with its 3000+ signatures. A public outcry, cried the press.

Everyone would be there. I put off going until the last minute, then had to speed. I got there late again but at least I got there, just in time to see Bea Merriman rise from her seat. Ron Dellums was looking at her the way CIA infiltrators must have looked at Fidel Castro as he got up to give one of his all-day harangues. She began by saying she'd lived at Rusland all her life. She said she'd grown up with the beeches and seen them change with the seasons. She said they were a fantastic part of the landscape and they were there for us all, they were our heritage, etc. etc. She said that any tree on the side of a road is a potential hazard but the risk was slight and surely could be monitored, and anyway, the whole thing had been an overreaction and you know it, she said, aiming two fingers at Dellums' pupils.

He tried to say something but she shut him up, then addressed her next remarks to the Committee members, telling them that before they voted they should search their consciences (if they had such things), and consider how they would feel driving down the Valley lined with hideous stumps knowing it was they who had given the order to fell and how would they face future generations, their own children and grandchildren with a clear conscience, and so on and so forth.

The trees are our children, she says, we have a responsibility to protect them. You wouldn't fell a damaged child, would you? You'd care for it and nurture it, and the joy of children is watching them grow and change and so on and so forth, which sets the room, and the gigantic conference table twirling within it and the people sitting around it also, going like a jester's hat with bells attached, and then someone goes stomp on the jester's hat so that it's now flat flat, the jester's hat.

The Impassioned Speech over, the Impassioned Woman Protester flopped herself down. Dellums and the Members had turned beetroot, but the gallery was all a-clap and a-whistle and a-hear-hear around brave Mrs Merriman, not to mention Housego looking at her as if to say, 'Isn't she a pip?'

My hands failed to clap, my eyes to blink.

In spite of the Impassioned Woman's Impassioned Speech the vote was still fourteen to ten in favour of felling.

Flash guns pinged the logo behind Dellums' head, shot back off curved glass and came to rest in repeat halos in the air over Bea Merriman's shiny coppery head. From the side her face looked slippery. Housego's was dry and helpless. Outside, the microphones were waiting for them.

All fifty-four: *Dead, dying, dangerous.*

Felled is such an interesting word. If a tree is 'cut down', someone has to do the cutting. But if a tree is *felled*; well now, that's different: gentle, peaceful, go-to-sleepish. Of its own free will, it lays down and dies. No *tiiiiiim-brrrrr*, no crashing or smashing, just a nice if-you-ask-us-nicely-we'll-pick-up-our-skirts-and-go. So considerate.

It will happen in the night.

No one will hear except a few Rusland residents.

In the morning it will all be over.

Pick Up Sticks.

Bea Merriman called the decision a travesty and broke down in tears. Poor little Bea! David Housego had no comment and anyway he was too busy steering her away. Next day, she sent out a press release to pull the heartstrings of the hardest nut, featuring soon-to-be-homeless bats and birds and squirrels, not to mention the Maid of Ealinghearth. (*Where, if the beeches are felled, will the ghost of the Rusland Beeches go?*)

She's gone bananas and anyway she's wrong.

The trees are not safe.

The wood is not safe.

It will be a relief, definitely.

Turn on the radio. People are tying themselves to trees, climbing up trees, marching up and down before trees. A Buddhist monk says, 'I know that in our previous life we were trees.' How does he know? Whose life? He says if trees cannot survive, humankind won't survive either.

Why should it?

'Where trees are fallen there be grief,' comes an intoning sort of voice.

Good. Fell them. Let there be grief.

12

Map of Losses

Try this. Take a roll of newsprint or brown wrapping paper and cut yourself a strip, five or six feet long. You will also need a thick black felt-tip pen plus another colour, say red, for highlighting. If your losses have been particularly colourful however, you might want a whole bouquet of felt-tips. Or crayons will do. You probably want to work on the floor unless you have a long table to lean on.

Now begin. Take your felt-tip and draw a horizontal line from left to right the whole length of your strip, thus bisecting it horizontally. Add a series of vertical strokes crossing this line at intervals to resemble a single-track railway line. Now, begin at the beginning, start plotting your losses. Try to include not just the big events such as deaths or divorces but the small everyday partings and leavings and disappointments such as moving house, giving up a friend or pet, not getting a job, failing an exam, being rejected by a lover, and so on.

The above instructions were given by a bereavement counsellor to a group of the bereaved at a hospice in Ulverston. What with it being a hospice all except Magda had 'lost' relatives to cancer. Still, as they said, bereavement is bereavement, loss is loss. As if by mere repetition of the words either side of the 'is', the insight would become weightier, shine out. Profound expressions on their faces.

They moved the old-fashioned armchairs out of the way and spread their loss strips on the floor. Magda got the bay window to herself. It was warm and light; the floor was carpeted in sea green wool; it was like playgroup. She took her black felt-tip plus a random selection of colours: green orange purple. Drew her single-track line and went slash slash across it. Ties, power poles, trees.

Magda floated up: smaller, lighter, moving away from all the black lines and ties and knots and crosses and whatnots. A speck of dust, a filament of fluff, a single atom, molecule, quark. Giddy with shedding. Loss-free, light as light. Dot on top. Doing what she was trained to do.

From above, what she mostly saw down on that flattened landscape was a series of repeated circles, so many bowed heads, inside the larger circles of backs. Paper rectangles with their faint slashes and faraway losses appeared to grow out of the blob shapes. As for the dripdrop of tears falling from the ovals inside the discs onto the black tracks, making them run in interesting patterns and smudging the words of explanation underneath – those could not be seen but could be heard if you listened closely.

'Try to include not just the big events such as deaths and divorce but the minor disappointments of your life.'

'Hey, this piece of paper isn't long enough!'

Some of the people divided their loss maps into years. Some years were heavy with losses, then there'd be a long length of line with no crossbars, then they'd come thicker again, remorseless as conifers.

'Oh God, I'd forgotten that one.'

'Not that!'

'Oh yes.'

'Oh no.'

'Oh no.'

'Oh.'

On some maps the losses were labelled and dated, some were starred, some lines were longer or thicker and blacker so as to distinguish greater from lesser where labels were absent. The losses piled up in the room.

We moved away

I had to leave my best friend

My best friend moved away and left me

I didn't make the 11+

I didn't get into Oxford

I couldn't go to university because my father couldn't afford it

I couldn't go to university because I went and got pregnant

I got pregnant
I had a miscarriage
I had an abortion
I didn't have an abortion
My first boyfriend left me for my best friend
My husband left me for my best friend
My best friend left me for a husband
She died   he died   they died   it died
I didn't
She wouldn't
He couldn't
I watched while ...
I came home to find ...

The losses, feeling welcomed, made themselves comfortable. Not just human losses but furniture losses and musical instrument losses, including a harpsichord and a violin; a map of Corsica representing a trip never taken which now took off by itself. The dead dogs joined in and began to whine. Standard poodle, retrievers both golden and flatcoated. The poodle flipped over onto its back, wanting to be scratched on its belly: through the white curls you could see black belly skin with six pink nipples poking out. A golden retriever smiled at Molly and, when she made nice, bit her. At this point Magda had to come down off her cartographer's perch. Bit the dog back; spat fur.

This is stupid, she thought. What have their losses got in common with mine? Plus, at this rate we'll need a landing pad. It isn't safe. One woman led her very visible losses around the room like the Pied Piper of Ghostland. Another enfolded the space at chest level, as if holding a globe. A man rocked in the corner, baby chimp at a zoo.

'You should be finishing up,' said the facilitator. She wore a long sweater-vest with deep pockets into which she jammed her fists, her voice vibrating at a low register inside her throat. Here is a woman, thought Magda, who has heard every grief theme there ever was. Sing me a new one.

'Is anyone willing to read out from their loss sheets?' she asked.

There were volunteers. The non-specific losses were harder than the specific ones with dates. For instance, one man began with, 'I lost my teeth,' and finished with 'sex'. A woman began with, 'Lost my virginity,' and ended with 'youth'. Yet another began, 'We moved,' and ended with 'never moved again'. Each one described a certain symmetry but not the stuck kind like the 'loss is loss, bereavement is bereavement' variety. No, this was different, this was sad but also musical. Magda imagined a spiral returning to the same place but on a different plane. Spirals describe change, she thought, even if on the micro-level. She began to feel quite happy among these people.

The dead losses piled up in the corners of the room while the more transient losses floated about. One child on a tricycle ran over feet and fingers. Some people were laughing, some weeping, some just staring with Greek statue eyes. Small rejections, mini-deaths. Ghosts with magic wands like riding crops or whips with barbs stepped gingerly among the mappers with their blessings: *I'm sorry I don't love you … I'm sorry but you haven't been selected … I'm sorry*. As they came down on the bowed heads, the wands lit up, *ping*.

Gradually they calmed down. Animals and children soon curled up and went to sleep; others less easy to placate, as in the case of the never-taken trip to Corsica, eventually shrank and slid into drawers. Lost houses could also be flattened and put away. The rest arranged themselves in layers like a well-organized linen cupboard.

Somebody had the nerve to ask what the point of the exercise was. 'It's to help you get in touch with long-forgotten losses; to help you see a pattern, how one loss calls up another; how our lives are filled with losses, many losses, not just the one great one you may be facing just now.'

Somebody else said: 'Hey, isn't it bad enough with the one, why load on all the others?'

Magda had to agree. All the loss map did was make painfully graphic the whole forestful of loss. 'That, paradoxically,' said the counsellor, 'is precisely what this exercise is meant to do – make you more aware.'

It seemed cruel, an exercise in relentless losings. But the people in the room thought about it and read out their litanies to one another and after a time they stopped weeping and began to laugh at themselves, to talk about patterns emerging, continuums, about placing loss in context. Sharing the similarities and overlaps. You too? Me too. Oh my. They were not alone, you were not alone. You were rejected too? Me too, but we survived, oh yes we survived. You lost ... ? So did I! Well well. That dog, that cat, that parent, that goldfish. And in between each they'd gone on breathing, so maybe they'd outlive this one too.

13

Map of the Underworld;
or Ladies in Hades

My compost bin – at the top of the garden on a terraced slope near the greenhouse – is made of thick green plastic, a triangle with its top lopped off. Squat and unbeautiful but with a certain *gravitas*, it does its job. The one we had before was black.

Molly decided to keep track of what was put in and when. Good idea, I said. First came the soil base, as the bin had no bottom, followed by grass clippings, rose cuttings, kitchen slops, wood ash. Repeat the layers. After three months or so we got out the step ladder and Molly stood on it. I held her around the waist so she didn't fall in while she poked with the fork to get it turned and aerated. 'What's aerated?' 'It needs to breathe, like you.' And then I explained about how it rotted from the bottom up. If you didn't stir it, the stuff on top would still be fresh and uncomposted while the bottom stuff compressed down. So she forked and turned and it got semi-mixed up.

Afterwards she read about separating the layers with some biodegradable material. 'You didn't put any carpet or cardboard like it said in the book.' She was right. So we decided to take the compost heap apart and start again. I began spearing all the half-rotted food and weeds and grass clippings with the garden fork but that was hard work so I ditched the fork and began digging with my bare hands. Molly stood on the ladder and helped. There were a lot of worms.

'Are they the right kind?' she wanted to know.

We'd taken her to the Centre for Alternative Technology and one of the exhibitions had been specifically about worm composting. What you needed apparently were brandling worms ('No heap should be without its colony of worms to produce the best and fastest compost!', or better yet, *dendrobaena* worms which are Even Bigger Than Brandling Worms And Will Digest Up To 30% More Material And Are More Acid Tolerant.

Unfortunately we hadn't actually bought any. The worms in our compost bin were common garden worms: pink and striped with a darker red, with see-through bodies. They wriggled all over the composter and up my arms. They do so now. There's a desperation to their wriggling, as if needing to get out instead of in. Two insert themselves between my wrist and watchband. So long as they don't burrow through skin, I think, it will be all right.

Going down. Once you get past the first two layers it gets easier: nice, even. Dark, and with an earthy smell. Peel back the layers gradually. Imagine the oldest layers rotting and trickling through the next layer, and so on, until the cooked stuff mixes and merges with the raw.

Keep digging. No going back.

Down you go. Don't forget to hold your nose.

THIS WAY TO THE UNDERWORLD

Magda had never before entered one of her own maps. She knew such things were possible – Tomb Raiders and so on. Was this such a virtual environment and was she the Lara Croft of her Underworld Map; and if so, how had she entered it? There, on the outskirts of Hades, along the River Styx, she could just make out some of the more infamous inhabitants' dwellings: Cleopatra's house, Salome's villa, Lucrezia Borgia's castle (with bubbling pit behind), Anne Boleyn's Waffle Shoppe, Eve's home in leafy Figleaf Park, Helen of Troy's Bar and Grill.

Magda wasn't as knowledgeable as she should be about the latest hi-tech. She could well imagine Molly twenty years from now snacking on hyperdoughnuts, heading the field in gravity mapping, black hole mapping, curved space topography. Could just hear her, in her acquired CalTech accent, going, 'Oh, *Mom*, you're so old-fashioned!' Chill out, get real, get a life.

'Get in,' said Charon, ferrying Magda across the Styx, which looked remarkably like Rusland Pool on a steamy morning, except wider. He tipped her out at Ferry Landing which resembled nothing on earth she recognized. 'Which way?' She was heading for Charon's Office. Not manned so she followed the Landing directly to a raised walkway made of duckboards, which turned out to be a catwalk carpeted in red. As she mounted it, she felt herself wreathed in a heady incense rising from The Bottomless Pit, a jagged-edged blubbertubs crematorium. Best to avoid. Below, on each side, a welcoming committee of what you might or might not wish to call Ladies:

Helen in a toga

Cleopatra with golden snakes on her arms

Eve with regulation leaf

Salome plus veils

'Help! Lemme off!' Magda's instinct was to jump except that she was surrounded on one side by the stinking, bubbling Pit and on the other by a Vinegar Bath. No choice but to keep on going down the catwalk.

'Okay, let's see ya strut yer stuff,' belted out Cleo. What stuff? Magda was naked, except for the worms crawling all over her and a couple of half-composted grapefruit halves suctioning her breasts. Add a tattooing of herbal teabags with dangling strings. Skin browned with manure and soil. 'Here, take that.' Some kind-hearted soul handed her a vine leaf.

Magda started down the catwalk, arms crossed over her chest and legs in a double-snake wrap – a near-impossible method of ambulation. The women took her number through green slitty eyes ringed with lots of raccoon-style mascara. 'Hey, you!' Stuck their fingers in their mouths and blew.

'Say, who we got here, Little Miss Muffet?'

'Ha, bloody ha.'

She saw she had no choice.

Magda thrusts out her hip and struts. Stops. Thrusts out the other. Bump, strut, thrust. The Ladies whistle clap cheer grab. Magda goes for it: pouts her lips, shakes her head so a hank of stick-straight hair flops over one eye. Right shoulder to cheek and rub. Left shoulder to cheek, rub. Legs apart, crotch-ho.

'Whooooeeee!'

When she collapsed off the end of the catwalk they dumped her on a litter drawn by two dragons, who took her up to a caravan plonked out on Medea's Moor. 'She'll look after you,' they reassured her, slapping the dragons' flanks.

'Geeyup!'

It took time to settle in. A maid came daily to bathe her in a hot tub spiked with vinegar and eucalyptus oil; brushed her hair and dressed her in toga and sandals. Warm down there.

One day she received an invitation from The Ladies, who preferred to call each other Girls, to go drinking in town, and you don't refuse an invitation from The Girls if you know what's good for you.

So there they were at Helen's Bar and Grill.

'What'll ya have?'

'Something cold.' Magda was thinking of chilled white wine but a double shot of fluorescent green stuff appeared before her.

'Try that.'

She did: soon felt green all over.

'So.' Medea kicked off the interrogation.

'What about you, Kid?' They meant, why was she there? Magda felt like a parking ticket defaulter among serial axe murderers. She was about to say she'd offended the gods, or goddesses, but just then they were distracted from their questioning. 'Hey, look who's here.' All eyes, green and otherwise, looked out the murky pub window. A woman was in the act of dismounting from a camel, on top of which was perched a litter with a striped canopy. In this she had ridden. The animal was on its knees. The woman looked like Rita Haworth.

'Hey, Salome, in here,' waved the Company of Girls. Salome joined them as the interrogation continued.

'I lost a daughter,' confessed Magda.

'Say what?'

'I lost her.' Mumbling into her chartreuse glass.

'Nice one,' said Lucrezia.

'They're good at euphemism up there.' Helen, this was.

'How careless,' yawned Medea. Every helmeted, henna'd, tarblack head in her direction. A slapping of thighs. 'Hell,' said gravel-gullet Salome, 'look who's talking. This here Babe fed her kids to Jason.' Medea shrugged, 'Hey, what choice did I have?' 'Nobody talkin' 'bout choice down here,' grunted Cleopatra. 'With sauce,' poured on Lucrezia. Then there was a brief pause after which a small voice said, 'I had a daughter too.' It was the one called Anne. 'Aw, shut up,' jeered Helen. 'Maudlin bitch.' She smiled at Magda. 'Don't listen to her. And now, Magda, more about you.'

'I let her out.'

'Alone?'

'Alone. It was such a peaceful Valley, she was used to going out on her own. She was an independent kid. Anyway, what could happen to her?'

'Uh-huh.'

'Neglect, carelessness, a lost child.'

'Ooh-whee.'

Magda was starting to feel her crime was worse than all of theirs put together when Salome took pity on her. 'These tarts have hearts of marble – all out of the same Roman quarry.' And then she started up a rhythmic slapping of her knees which brought the others in: left right, slap slap. 'Hey, you telling us that all?' 'You kiddin'?' 'Hey, that ain't nothing, babe, wait till you hear this!'

Magda heard, and how.

On her seventh day in the Underworld, King Hades (aka The Big H) paid a visit to Medea's caravan where Magda was staying. Barged in without knocking. 'Where Medea at?' 'Out washing clothes.' 'Gooo-oooh,' dripped King H, pressing a button on the wall. Muzak came on. He grabbed Magda around the waist and bent her over backwards. She was wearing a hand-me-down cerise ruffled skirt and a tube top, not her usual style. To complete the ensemble, King H stuck a salmon-coloured rose between her teeth, which unfortunately clashed with the skirt and also made her gag. Spit spit, she went. Crash crash, counterpointed the cymbals. The Big H was by now tango-ing her around the caravan, bumping into things and singing, if you can call it that,

Lady of Hades, I adore you ... Lady of Hades, I deplore you ... Lady of Hades, I abhor you ... Oh, Lady of Hades, be mine!

He swings Magda around six times until the world is spinning faster than any globe and then he throws her down on the pallet bed and rapes her. 'All the girls get it,' he explains afterwards, wiping himself with the spat-out rose. 'It's part of the making-you-feel-at-home routine. Welcome, Kid,' he says, 'enjoy, d' goils'll show ya d' ropes.' For some reason he talks with a Brooklyn accent.

On the eighth day The Girls invited Magda to a group therapy session. They began by shrugging off their sins at which somebody called 'Denial!' Anne Boleyn was the first to break down. The others soon joined in, getting weepier by the minute, beating their breasts and pulling their hair and showing pictures of their children and generally saying 'if only' and how they wished they hadn't, and so on and so forth until the River Styx began rising dangerously with their tears.

Only Cleopatra and Medea's shoulders failed to shake. Cleopatra was doing her nails the colour of black figs. Medea was busy with her accounts; Eve with one of her snake-charming routines.

'Time for work,' they pronounced.

'What work?'

'Everyone here has a job, what can you do?'

'Draw maps.'

They snorted in unison. 'Don't need no maps 'round here, everyone be's lost, s'posed t'be. Lost Souls Tabernacle take care of that end of things.' The Girls consulted. 'Okay, we've decided. Report for work at 5 a.m. tomorrow morning.'

'Where?'

'Babe sure do ask a lot questions. Medea's Department Store.'

'What department?'

They looked at each other, winked. Eve produced an apple from you-know-where. 'That'll keep you going.'

'Children's Wear,' came the reply.

Going down.

Level l: Lingerie and nightwear

Level 2: Furnishings and garden supplies
Level 3: Children's wear

The racks contained Molly's clothes: jumpers, jeans, skirts, blouses, T-shirts from California, little polka-dotted shorts. Racks for her shoes, her backpacks, her hats. Her smell. She could hear The Girls guffawing.

Magda fainted.

It was *Start The Week*. Magda left off her early morning compost sorting and went in to have some breakfast. Deep in the bowels of the BBC, Melvyn Bragg kicked off with the subject of 'Galileo and Guilt'. His guest, a 'new' scientist whose name Magda didn't catch, explained that if we continue to push back the boundaries of three-dimensional space – as Galileo did – to include what we would now call infinite space, it follows that we also push back the boundaries of – create the right conditions for – infinite guilt.

'I find that quite fascinating,' said Melvyn. Then the telephone rang – it was Magda's mother. 'You may have gone through hell,' she told Magda, 'but you survived.' And then, as she never tired of repeating, 'Once you've hit bottom, there's no place to go but ...'

14

Map of the Hand

Rusland Church stands on a rise above the Valley. Built in 1745 and remodelled in 1868, tower at the front, elongated mid-section and added-on tail, it squats up there like some top-heavy beast on the look-out. For what?

To approach the church from the south-west you go through a farm gate and up a steep field. Frosted grass, rocky outcrops, cowpats with deceptively thin crusts. Twenty or thirty cars are parked on the low road while the people from inside the cars make their way up the hill. The effortful angle of ankle, foot, knee; eyes raised in their sockets to the tower or down at the parted grass. Tweeds and wax jackets; boots and wellies. Left right left: so many pullstrings attached by so many juicy bits to so many splendid spinal columns. By the time all of us have found our way there will be a squashed-down path of a darker wetter green.

I trudge along with the others, an Alexandroid who has practised her routine semi-religiously but hasn't really learned its lesson. The Semi-Supine with its horizontal spreading and flattening is the precondition to rising up ever more expanded and expansive. Sometimes it works but today I remain in Flat Stanley mode, an epidermis of parts that touch air, that are trained to meet and greet. An organ pipe is an enclosed column of air which has depth and therefore can be made to resonate, boom or beat. I am less.

We are here to hear about the latest Department of Environment pronouncement on the Rusland Beeches.

At the top of the field we go through a second gate and up the steps to the church. Don't forget to shut the gate so the sheep can't nibble at the grave bouquets. Arthur Ransome, Evgenia Ransome, Molly Beard. Distinguished company all round.

Inside the church, in an alcove of the back window, propped against the stonework, is a photograph of Arthur Ransome. 'This famous author,' it says underneath, 'spent the last years of his life in the Rusland Valley. His chess set and desk are now on view at Abbot Hall's Museum of Lakeland Life.' Where we went that day. Molly, Magda, Jay.

The south-west wall of the church is decorated with a display by children from Rusland and Finsthwaite Primary School. I take the sixth pew against the wall. The crayon drawing just above me shows a nun or angel figure with a halo over her head and a deep pink embarrassed face with one blue eye. **Anne Boleyn** is her name, pressed out in six-year-old lettering. Sugar and spice, what little girls like. Not all. Another little girl might have drawn her slaving over a hot waffle iron down in Hades, face puce with sweat.

Ron Dellums leans on the lectern eagle's back and welcomes us to the meeting. We know why we're here, he says, just managing to spit it out: the DoE has refused permission to fell all fifty-four beeches. Bea Merriman stands up and applauds. David Housego rises up beside her. It takes him several seconds longer. Other people stand and applaud; some cheer. Magda Beard, it's noted, remains sitting on her hands with her feet on an embroidered tree stool. Having a wall to lean against helps. Anne Boleyn offers what comfort she can. Ron Dellums waits, not very patiently, for the hoopla to die down.

The Department of the Environment, he explains, is suggesting taking a more gradual approach to the problem, including topping and heavy pruning rather than clear felling. 'If we follow its advice,' he says, 'that means twelve to twenty trees will require no work at all and thirty-two out of fifty-four will. So that is the position, if any of you would like to comment.'

'What about the bat roosts?' asks the woman from English Nature.

Public safety, he says, must override bat protection but they are quite happy to make sure the bats are not in residence when the trees are felled or reduced to hulks. Indeed, he says cheerily, the bats might gain in the end.

'Next question.'

Bea Merriman wants to know if the Park Authority is prepared to take the DoE's advice or can it still do what it likes?

There is muttering and there is clapping. Dellums' upper lip shows signs of twitching. As owner of the land, he says, it does not have to abide by the Secretary of State's decision. In other words, it's legally free to carry out any felling work it deems necessary without notifying the Department.

'Having said that' – glasses back on – 'we're prepared to go along with the decision.' A slash of light from his lens jumps the gap to Bea Merriman's and back again. Wait, he hasn't finished.

'However, if at any point we deem a tree to be dead, dying or dangerous, we still have the right – the responsibility – to act accordingly.'

Bea Merriman, good at translations, puts it this way, 'You mean fell.'

Dellums: 'That is what I mean.'

Bea Merriman: 'So this is just a window dressing exercise?'

Ann Boleyn's face, which is about to get chopped off along with her head, is flushed pinker than ever.

'I'm sorry,' says Dellums in a not very sorry voice, 'but I really don't feel obliged to respond to such antagonistic questioning. Suffice it to say, it's up to the Committee to determine which trees are to be felled. It's the Members' prerogative. At the end of the day, it's the National Park which is responsible.' He grips the sides of the lectern. But then, as if some sweet heavenly voice, perhaps Anne's, has sung out to him from the rafters – *hang in there, don't lose it now* – he flops forward and reaches out, O water lily of peace.

'Look, we needn't have consulted with you people at all but we have. We have agreed to take the DoE's advice even though we don't agree with it. We have compromised and done everything in our power to meet with you people more than halfway. And this is how you respond.'

You people.

'Last question. David?'

David Housego points out that dead and dying doesn't necessarily mean dangerous. It's sound ecological practice to leave a tree alone and keep an eye on it rather than fell it. 'In any case,' he says, 'of the fifty-four, I haven't seen any dead or dying trees.' Dellums' lamb-like lip rises over an eyetooth. A snarl escapes.

'Well, you will soon.'

The Farmer's Arms is a large rectangle with a series of poky low-beamed rooms leading off at different angles and levels: slate floors, inglenook fireplaces. Dutch-inspired still life with dead pheasant and fruit. Housego folds himself nearly double to get from the small side room into the main bar area; beyond that is the added-on dining room wing. 'Your party is in there,' the barlady's pointing.

Two nights ago there was a knock on my door. I could see Bea from my upstairs study window, from that angle not much more than a tangle-headed stick figure with a child-hump on its back. Just as she was turning to go, I opened up.

'Sorry, I was working. Come – come in.'

'Can't stay,' she says. 'Just stopped by to invite you, we're having a sort of celebration, at the Farmer's Arms. I don't really know where you stand on the beech issue but David – Housego – thought you might like to come – we saw you at the church meeting the other night.'

'What's a "sort of" celebration?'

'The DoE decision – not going ahead with the felling.'

'But they're still planning to fell ten at least, plus hulking another ten and bracing the rest. What kind of victory is that, I mean, from your point of view?'

'I know, but it could have been worse, it could have been all fifty-four. Anyway, come or don't come, it's up to you. I just thought I'd let you know.'

"Thanks," I said. Come or don't come.

And then, on Monday after our Alexander class, Housego said he could pick me up and I didn't say no. Why? It had nothing to do with me, after all, this half-hearted, better-than-nothing excuse for a celebration. But I'm here. Here I am.

Bea turns and waves. The man sitting beside her has his arms locked together at the elbows. Pull the chair and table out from under him and he'd probably stay poised momentarily in space before crashing to the ground. As Housego passes behind him one shoulder blade bulges out and back in a muscular twitch. Housego ducks to avoid a cross-beam.

Bea Merriman, Mick Merriman, David Housego, some other protesters and supporters and their partners, and me.

I sit at the end near the window with my back to the wall. Bea and Mick are two-thirds along on the opposite side. Housego is one away from me on the right; between us a tall blonde woman.

'Hi,' she says, 'I'm Janet.'

'Magda.'

'Oh, you're the one who mapped the beeches, right?'

'Right. And you're ...?'

'I'm not really involved – I'm just with David.'

'Oh.' I study my menu, a studious menu-studier. Just With David studies her menu too, asks me what I'm having.

'Brandy and coffee. I didn't realize it was dinner, I've already eaten.' I thought a meeting at a pub, at this hour, meant just drinks.

'Couldn't you manage a starter, something?'

'No, I really couldn't.'

The shape beside Bea Merriman is still cuddling his own elbows. I lean closer to Just With David. 'Is that her partner?'

'Husband. Know what he does?'

I said I didn't.

'Mick – for a living? Mick works for the Park Authority. He's their Head Forester.'

This is absurd, this is like a vegetarian being married to a butcher.

'You serious?'

'Completely. And he's convinced all the beeches should come down. We weren't sure he'd be here tonight – it feels, I don't know, like having the enemy in your camp.'

The enemy's wife waves me over. 'Come and meet Mick.'

'Excuse me.' I make my way round to their side of the table. Mick is saying, 'You people are way off. Most of them are rotten. We've done tests, gone into the heartwood. I'm telling you.'

'Mick, this is Magda.' She tugs on his shirt. He swings around, the locked arms pulled in against his chest. He could break himself in two.

'She lives at Ealinghearth Cottage. Magda, Mick.'

'Nice to meet you.'

'And you.' We shake and he swivels back into position. Bea looks up at me and winks. Yes, she does.

We are both dressed in black and white. Bea Merriman in a sort of schoolmarm outfit with high lace-up boots, while I am in black jeans and cream silk shirt. Whistler might have been keen to paint us.

The argument continues. Food is brought but none of it lands in front of me. First course: soups, pâtés, melons. Main course: blood sausages, Cajun chicken with chips, lasagna with chips, steak (thick/thin/medium) with chips, ham steaks with chips.

Forks rise, knives rise; one impales while the other cuts. Elbows move up and down. Ten out of the eleven eat with their right hands and one with his left. Most are able to talk while they eat and quite a few gesticulate at the same time. I try to separate fish smells from fowl from meat – the combination isn't good.

'Mind if I open the window?'

'Sure. Go ahead.' Just With David tells me she's a mature student at the Uni, with five children and just about to go off to Africa to study women in nomadic tribes. 'How interesting,' I say. This is not original. Nor is it clear if it refers to the five children or the African research. I ask who'll look after the kids. Just With David forks to her right. 'He will.'

Desserts: mousses, meringues, sticky toffee puddings, ice creams, Death by Chocolates or is it Deaths by Chocolate?

'You have children?' she asks.

'Who me? No.'

Coffees, teas; cream mints. A last drink and a toast, 'To the campaign … To the beeches … To Bea …'

'To Bea!'

Drawer 13 contains a Map of the Hand, 18th century Rajasthan. Each finger is divided into three sections, the tips decorated with spiral-shapes, the lower phalanges with parallel pucker marks.

The palm is divided by its famous lines. The heart area contains a peacock and something that looks like a cannon; in the 'head' area, a tiger, an elephant, a prancing ox plus the sun and a moon; the 'life' area contains a ship, a horse, a bow and arrow, a fish, a flag and a pagoda; and finally, on the Mound of Venus, a temple, a match, a flower, an egg and a sperm.

Drawer 13 contains another set of prints, of a child's hands. Channels, rivulets, hair threads; close whorls and open whorls, curved lines and jagged ones; galaxies of stars; knots and crosses, the letter 'M', waves, trees, mountains. Each one a whole complicated landscape, its coastline dotted with indecipherable doodles. I'd forgotten they were there, those hands, slipped inside a see-through envelope to stop them curling. Flat, encapsulated, not attached at the wrists.

'Roll up your sleeves and hold out your hands.'

Drawer 13: *Hands, Molly's.*

Afterwards – after I'd 'taken' her hands – still hot with the friction of the roller, she'd walk around flapping them like blue flannels.

Slip the prints out of the plastic, place them side by side (left, right), my own hands lapped. Why did I do it? Because I knew how. Because my mother 'took' mine. Because certain practices, having been experienced, get repeated. Other parents kept growth charts.

'We'll keep a record of the changes in your hands, shall we?' Experimental, methodical. Molly stuck out her palms to be inked with the roller.

'Ee ee. Hey, that tickles!'

We began on her third birthday.

Having inked her right palm I took hold of the wrist and turned it over onto the paper, then placed my hand over hers to ensure a good overall contact and closed my eyes. Concentration, it was called.

That pressing warmth, that mother-ironing.

I peeled the print off her palm; repeated the procedure for the left hand.

There are three sets of prints: green, red, blue. Three years wasn't enough time for any significant – measurable – change to take place.

Her hands were 'water' in texture but 'earth' in shape. The thumb on the right hand angled off by itself.

'What does that mean?'

'A need for independence.'

'What's independence?'

'How you like going places by yourself.'

But then the thumb had a curve to it which signifies a certain malleability.

So? So nothing. I have a cartography colleague who can tell you everything about maps but practically nothing about the terrain they refer to.

There was also a marked difference between the hands. On the left, the fingers are gathered closer together as if the world were not an entirely safe place to sprawl out in or grab onto, or stroke.

Molly was left-handed.

'Are those my hands?' I was studying her prints. 'No,' I replied, 'Those are *prints*. These' – I held her wrists and flapped – 'are your *hands*.' Important to distinguish.

'What do they mean?'

Discrepancies, contradictions, a riddling of branchings; every-which-way lines. Not like a map, which clarifies and simplifies. How do you interpret such a thing? The Heart Line for instance ends messily in cross hatchings and prunefaced puckers: railroad ties, in mapping symbology. Then comes the Life Line, prematurely truncated; that is, cut off at a fraction, a mere inch, less than a fifth of the normal Line of Life (i.e. ten years of life or less). And finally that naughty, haughty Fate Line what done the damage: swung round and sword-like gone chop: *Off with your Life!*

'What does that short line mean?' What could I tell her, tell myself? Something unexpected? A surprise awaits you? You will soon embark on a great adventure? Is it possible to read the marks on a person's palms as map hieroglyphs, portents of change, routes to potential disaster or some major revelation? (Should I have known? Should I have taken this hand-

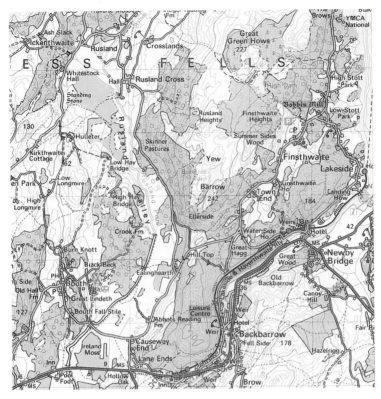

1. Map of the Rusland Valley, p. 1

2. Mind Map, p. 8

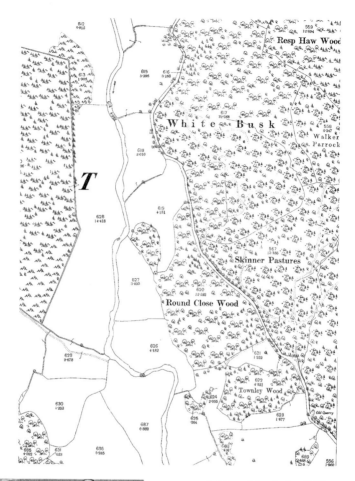

3. Map of the Rusland Valley,
1890, p. 56

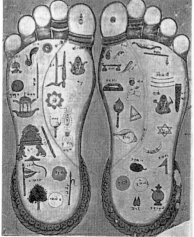

4. Map of Vishnu's Feet, p. 82

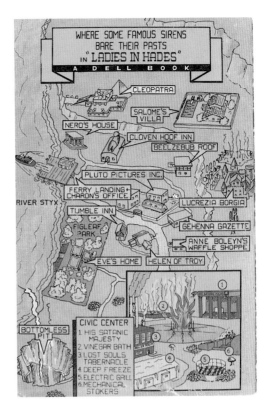

5. Map of the Underworld;
   or Ladies in Hades, p. 104

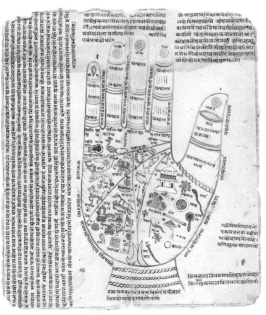

6. Map of the Hand, p. 111

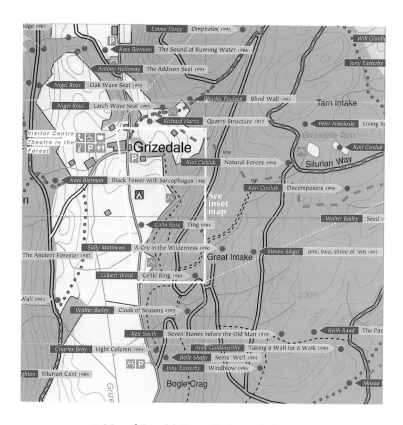

7. Map of Grizedale Forest Sculpture Park, p. 122

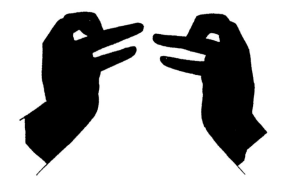

8. Shadowland, p. 127

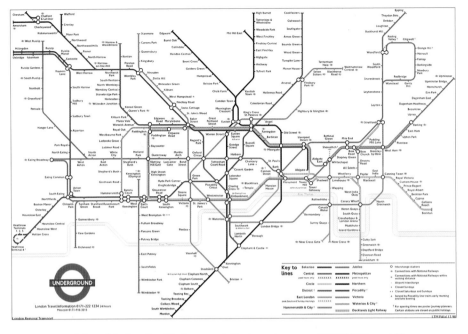

9. Map of the London Underground (Registered user no. 99/E/1015), p. 152

10. Map of the Interior World, p. 173

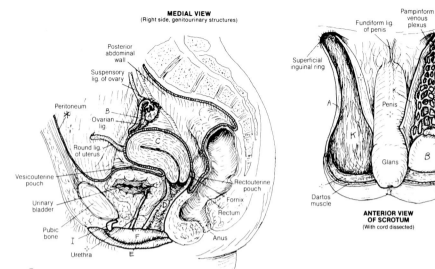

MEDIAL VIEW
(Right side, genitourinary structures)

Posterior abdominal wall

Suspensory lig. of ovary

Peritoneum

Ovarian lig.

Round lig. of uterus

Vesicouterine pouch

Urinary bladder

Pubic bone

Urethra

Rectouterine pouch

Fornix

Rectum

Anus

Pampiniform venous plexus

Fundiform lig. of penis

Superficial inguinal ring

Penis

Glans

Dartos muscle

ANTERIOR VIEW OF SCROTUM
(With cord dissected)

A Ovary
B Uterine (Fallopian) tube
C Uterus
D Vagina
E Labium Majus
F Labium Minus
G Frenulum
H Prepuce
I Clitoris
I¹ Glans
J Body
K Crus
L Bulb of the Vestibule
M Vestibular Gland/Duct
N Vestibule:
O Urethral Orifice
D¹ Vaginal Orifice /P Hymen

Mons pubis

Posterior labial commissure

Perineal body

SURFACE

A Scrotum
B Testis
C Epididymis
D Ductus Deferens
E Seminal Vesicle
F Ejaculatory Duct
G Urethra
H Bulbourethral Gland
I Prostate Gland
J Penis
K Coverings
+ Constituents:
D Ductus Deferens
L Testicular Artery
M Testicular Vein

11. Map of the Sexual Parts, p. 175

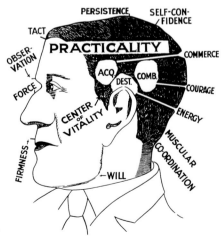

PERSISTENCE

SELF-CONFIDENCE

TACT

OBSERVATION

PRACTICALITY

COMMERCE

FORCE

ACQ. DEST. COMB.

COURAGE

CENTER OF VITALITY

ENERGY

FIRMNESS

MUSCULAR CO-ORDINATION

WILL

12. Map of the Face, p. 181

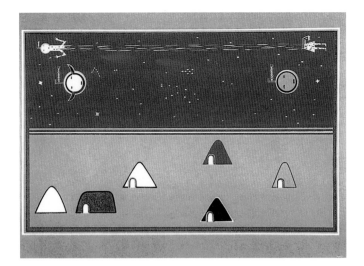

13. Sand Map, p. 187

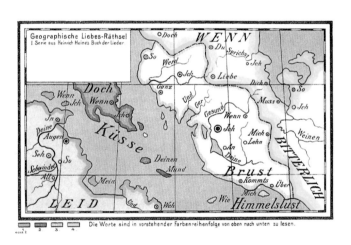

14. Heartland, p. 192

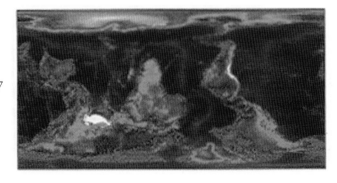

15. Map of the World,
    Upside Down, p. 237

16. Map of Matrimony, p. 251

17. Maze with Happiness at its Centre, p. 260

mapping game more seriously?) I hardly think so, but it's foolish to reject such things entirely.

Neither science nor art.

To create the effect, in paint, of a dog sneaking across a table top she bunched together the fingers of her left hand – a cartoon Italian about to throw a kiss, *mwaah* – and dipped them in a mixture of blue-grey paint. Dab, he went, all over the red tablecloth, black dog makes tracks. If you look closely you can see those Molly marks, the trajectory of those farewell kisses.

How did I answer her? I didn't. I had no answer. Instead I employed my hands, fingers, nails, dancing them here there and everywhere up and down and round the back of her body.

'Hey, that tickles!'

What else could I do?

And now, to still my own flapping flannels, I put one over the other. Try it. Place the left hand over the right. The left one feels a knuckly articulated fleshy mass. The right is aware of itself being touched, and between them at the point of contact a certain warmth is generated . But what does the left, or for that matter the right, feel of itself? Nothing. What do you know about these strange things growing out of your wrists? You slide a ring on your finger, rub hand lotion into your palms, bite your cuticles, have the occasional manicure and polish – but do you know them? Could you pick out your own hands from a series of hand prints?

There's a basic principle operating here. You cannot see your own eyes, hear your own ears or taste your own taste buds. Your mouth cannot swallow itself nor can you smell your own nasal tissue. Your hands cannot touch themselves. All they can do is hang on to one another.

'Bend over,' he says. He's in my kitchen.

'What?'

'Bend over.'

Simple words describing a simple motion or possibly two motions, a bending and an over, the body forming an incomplete arch or, more angularly, an 'L'. Now why would he want me to assume such a shape?

Normally the heart is one of the most internalized of the internal organs: not until it's exercised do you know it's there. It's being exercised, I know it's there. I consider the possibility that I have invited a 6' 5" sex maniac into my house. When he's finished he'll stuff my body into the larder behind the stocks of malt whisky which I have inherited. Gentle Treecreeper Attacks Rusland Divorcée. Ill-Fated Family Struck Again. If only my mother had studied the art of prophecy. See that forked line there and there, that petering out, those trauma lines?

Patsy for punishment. Perfect victim. Bentover duck.

What *is* he doing here?

Perhaps he's come to talk about the 'sort of' celebration at the Farmer's Arms? Maybe he and Bea have decided Further Action Is Necessary and they want my support? He can't make tomorrow night's Alexander class and he wants me to pass the message on to Sara? He wants me to look after his kids while Just With David goes off to do her fieldwork so he can Be With Bea?

Housego's right hand supports the small of my back while the left grips my right shoulder. Left forearm up against my throat. Like this he draws me to him, dragging puppet feet. Left hip rests T-wise across his front, chin hooked over the arm sack-wise. He holds me there for another thirty seconds then shifts his weight so I'm forced to balance by myself. This takes some adjustment. Now my back is parallel to the floor providing a reasonably flat surface for the smoothing of his hand. Neck to waist – pause – neck to waist.

'You looked so tense,' he says, as if that explained everything. I, on the other hand, am in no position to question him further. Beast with horizontal spine studies the slates on her kitchen floor: grubby, unshiny. Housego has five children?

'I wonder why my slates are so dull compared with those at the Farmer's Arms.' My own voice comes back at me courtesy of my bentover body creating a sort of echo chamber.

'They wash their's with milk,' he says.

'Really? How do you know that?'

'Shhh,' he says. 'Let me.'

Milk, I will have to try it. I may even do it tonight, after he leaves.

In the Alexander Quickie Massage your back should be flat and as near horizontal to the floor as possible. Usually there's a hump but he continues to press all along the complicated bony ridge so your body forms an 'L'. Imperfect, but never mind. His left hand supports your chest decorously above the breasts while he massages the sacrum. Your breath makes clouds on the slate floor. Up your spine he goes, sticking his thumb into each of the spaces between your vertebrae: left side, right side. Then drumming strokes with the side of the hand and then slapping and then he brings you into an upright position and now, still supporting you across the shoulders, rub-a-dub goes he in circles all around and when he's done that he just rests with his palm low down, your shoulder against his ribs. He reeks of tree bark.

The surface of beech trees, their cambium layer, is particularly sensitive to both light and injury. You picture your own skin tattooed with the print of his hand; unfortunately you can't see back there to read it. You can feel it though, and flesh remembers. The kettle is screaming its head off.

15

Map of Grizedale Forest

'Is that a sculpture or a natural bridge?'

'I think it's a sculpture.'

'Natural bridge.'

'What's the difference?'

They'd taken Molly to Grizedale Forest, where they cycled up the dry dusty forestry track playing Spot the Sculpture. Low gears, rucked-up shoulders, one steep hairpin bend after the other. Molly wobbled but managed to stay on, Jay stood up in his saddle. When it got to a twenty per cent incline Magda got off and walked. 'Look!' cried Molly. 'Another sculpture.'

An organ perched on a rocky outcrop, carved out of green wood. Jay took the bench and played Lon Chaney playing *Phantom of the Opera*, feet fugueing away on the pedal-board. Poor Bach.

Afterwards Magda tried to work out who did what in what order. Jay played, Molly fell off her bike, Magda laughed. Or Molly played, Magda fell off her bike, they all laughed (to see such sport?).

You can't forget so you try to remember, not just the events and who said what to whom but the movement, sequence, pattern and feel of it in various parts of your body. If you're not careful you forget the drift and flow, and are left with a sequence of carefully arranged tableaux.

'Are those real people or sculptures?' Wooden giants, tall as the trees; the woman, with her arms over her head, directing the stream's flow over her mate. Baptism by sluice.

'I think they're real, don't you?'

'No, they're too big!'

Magda's bike slid sideways in a dry rut. She managed to stay balanced on one leg with the bike half on top of her. Hopalong Magda. Molly and Jay came to the rescue. 'Hey, look!' cried Molly the look-crier. The parents looked where she pointed. Down a deep dell: a three-piece suite. Coffee table, TV, window (framed, no glass) complete with drapes. Each piece carved out of wood, chunky and solid, shady cool. Sitting there, waiting to be sat upon, curled up in.

The three people looked at each other, parked their bikes, trotted down the bank and took up position in the empty expectant living-room. Molly got the chunky armchair, Jay and Magda the settee. Molly zapped the remote. Magda gazed out the glassless window.

'What should we watch?'

'How about a nature programme?'

'About a forest?'

'About a forest with sculptures in it.'

'Good idea.'

So Molly and Jay watched the wood-faced telly while Magda stared out at a sylvan scene through a wooden window with quite a solid frame, drapes hanging in heavy folds from a heavy pole, hands on top of thighs or possibly slotted between. Or did two of the hands touch? Molly's rested high on the armchair's arms. They sat. It was very restful. They heard various scuffling foresty noises but no one came to surprise or disturb them so finally they roused themselves. Shall we go now? Had enough? Two more minutes. I'll just go for a pee, be right back.

He said, she said, they said.

Higher still and higher. At the very top they stopped again at a Gaudí-type structure made out of willow branches, labelled 'Cathedral'. Jay said if all churches were like that he would become an attender. Magda and Molly stood while the light played in and out of the spired twigs.

'Hey, look!' cried Molly.

Molly cried, Magda looked. Jay was still worshipping. A moon hung high up in the branches of a tree, appearing to float. What kind of tree was it? Pine larch beech oak birch? And the moon? Was it polished steel, beaten silver, aluminum?

Molly wanted to know what was holding the moon up. Jay hunkered down, held her by the waist and moved her three inches to the left. 'Look, there, can you see?' A branching of semi-invisible wires attached the moon to the tree.

'That's cheating!' said Molly, who having asked to know, preferred that it stay up by magic.

Was it full or was it a sliver or a gibbous thing lolling on its back among the branches? Magda couldn't remember. She did however remember Molly saying it seemed funny having the moon out in the middle of the day. 'It often does that,' said Magda. Jay looked thoughtful. 'What is it?' Magda asked. 'Don't you like it?'

'There's something wrong.'

'What?'

'I don't know.' He continued to look thoughtful. 'Yes, I do. It's the only sculpture so far not made of wood.'

'What's wrong with that?' asked Molly.

'Nothing, just that it doesn't fit so well.'

'I like how it shines.'

'Me too,' said her mother, 'I think it's wonderful.'

She enthused, he regretted. Downhill all the way. This was the off-trail part which was so rough and steep and full of tree roots Magda and Molly had to carry their bikes. Jay rode his bucking bronco. At the bottom he climbed back up and helped Molly. 'I can do it myself,' she insisted, even though she couldn't really.

'Do you remember that part?' Magda asked him later.

'Of course.'

Then: 'How do you remember?' A semi-theoretical question.

'What do you mean?'

'I mean,' she said – he was the philosopher after all – '*how* do you remember?' She was asking him: in flashes or snatches; in fixed pictures or moving ones, in time or out of time? 'And what about the bits in between? How do you decide which ones to remember, which to forget?'

He said, 'It's a complicated subject.' Which she already knew.

'How?' Try again.

'In flashes.' In flashes, he said, more or less. To simplify. Which seemed necessary or it couldn't be spoken about at all. But still worth pursuing.

'Do you put yourself in your memory pictures?'

'No, I don't think I do.'

'Hm,' she said, wondering if it was a gender thing; and then, how in mapping it was quite different. In mapping you were outside the picture, above looking down. Though in map *reading* of course it was different again. *You are here. We were there.*

At some point they went round in a loop and met another sculpture – or it met them. Under a group of extremely tall Scots pines white stuff covered the ground – only it wasn't snowing. The three people observed the puzzling phenomenon mouthing the word 'snow?' *snow?*, not daring to go closer. The three people might themselves have constituted a 'living sculpture' as they stood in their huddle, near but not too near, the patch of snow whispering possibilities.

Jay guessed, 'White glass.' Magda said, 'Stones: white pebbles.' And so it was: a thick strewing of clean white pebbles beneath the pines, contained within a frame of wooden battens, like a three-dimensional painting. But then, in the places where the trees cast their shadows, those places were bare of stones. Long bold earth-dark shadows. It was very clever. Shadows forever. And if you looked carefully you saw the other, real, shadows, which were not cut-outs but a pale play of light on the paler-still pebbles, depending for their appearance on the real sun, which at that stage was low in the west. Sculpture shadows and real shadows, how interesting!

Molly asked, were you allowed to walk on the pebbles? She whispered because while people can be very loud around snow – say, when sledging or skiing – at other times they might want to be quiet. This, even though it wasn't real snow, was such a time. Or maybe the wonderful fakery made it all the more advisable to be hushed.

Molly snuck up close to the frame-line and the parents dared to follow. Jay said, observing some footprints, 'It looks as if people have walked on the stones.' And Magda said, 'It doesn't say not to.' But none of them made a move to enter the white rectangle under the trees. When they came upon a scatter of white pebbles outside the frame Molly squatted down and, one by one, placed them back inside.

The three people cycled home along the Valley. A quiet route, perfect for cycling. Mostly downhill so they were going quite fast, the man and the little girl ahead of the woman but not by much. An altogether quite fit family, quite close together. The man began doing tricks, sticking his legs out in a 'V' and crossing his arms across his chest. 'Showoff,' yelled the woman at the man who was too far ahead to hear. The little girl copied him, which made the mother worry, as mothers do, about oncoming traffic and wobbling under wheels and so on. The last bit was uphill again so that slowed them all down.

They were now passing the famous Rusland Beeches. The last memory picture is arriving home dead tired. Alive tired. Tired and alive. The woman went upstairs to run a bath while the man made tea – a small but occasionally necessary role reversal. The little girl asked, may she go out and play at the beeches. Father at his kettle, mother in her bath. Both said okay, but just for a little while. Fifteen-twenty minutes, half-hour at the very most then back for tea. Got it? Got it, said the little girl. Then no more pictures, only shadows.

16

Shadowland

The therapist said they would begin where they'd left off. 'Which was where?' asked Magda. He re-checked his notes.

'You were saying you felt like a shadow.'

'That's correct.'

'And whose shadow would that be?'

'Perhaps you can tell me,' she said.

The therapist began to doodle: one upright figure and one lying-down figure, flattish and attached at the feet. The lying-down figure he darkened in with horizontal strokes to indicate shading.

'Your own?' he tried. The shaded figure in his doodle was obviously meant to be the shadow of the 'real' or original (non-shaded) figure. In other words, she was feeling like her own shadow. He looked quite pleased with himself. Magda wondered why she was paying this man. 'What I said,' she said, 'was I am no one's shadow. I AM the shadow.' The therapist scratched his head. 'But surely you can't have a shadow without a body to cast it?'

'That,' she said, 'is the conventional understanding of a shadow.'

'I presume,' he sighed – oh dear, you really shouldn't argue or try to reason with a client – 'that means you have a different understanding. Perhaps you'd care to share it?'

Or perhaps not. How to explain her 'other', autonomous, shadow? More essential than the cast shadow; a purer version, so to speak, of Flat Stanley or even a female Flatlander? More than a line and entirely separate – separated – from her bodily self?

'It's a thing in its own right,' was how she finally put it.

'So you are an independent shadow-being entirely split off from yourself?' He scribbled 'schizophrenic split?' on his notepad before she could reply. Magda shook her head. He'd failed to appreciate the elegance of her proposition. She'd be better off going to a palm reader or a teller-of-fortunes by tea leaves or coffee grounds or, better still, a reader of shadows like the eighteenth century Johann Caspar Lavater. 'Physiognomy,' as he wrote, 'has no greater truth than that imparted by shade'.

What the person conceals the shadow reveals ...

'Once upon a time,' the woman began. The child listened. They were sitting on cushions, one yellow, one blue. The room was dark except for a single spotlight on a chrome base.

'Once upon a time a poor boy called Peter Schlemihl was out looking for work when he happened upon a society of millionaires.'

'What's a society?'

'A group of people.'

'What's "happened upon"?'

'Met. The poor boy met a bunch of rich men. Okay? May I go on?'

'Yes.'

'So there was this bunch of millionaires being entertained by a man in grey who was pulling all sorts of unusual objects from his pocket.'

'What objects?'

'Well, let's see: a plaster, a telescope, a carpet, a tent with poles, three saddled horses ... how's that?'

'They must have been very small horses,' said the child.

'I think they were normal-sized horses because the man was a kind of magician and the things he pulled from his pocket were meant to thrill his audience. What they liked best, you see, was to be REALLY SURPRISED.'

'Is that because they were so rich?' asked the child.

'Yes,' said the woman. 'I suppose it was. Since they could buy almost anything in the world, they wanted to see things they couldn't buy. Anyway, seeing the boy in rags gave the guy in grey an idea. "Pardon me," he bowed to Schlemihl.' The woman imitated the bowing rich man and her shadow bowed too. ' "The noble shadow at your feet there ... might you be disposed to make this beautiful beautiful shadow over to me?"'

The child clapped, the woman sat back down on her cushion and went on with her tale.

'The man proposed to Schlemihl that in exchange for his shadow he would give him a magic purse which would always be full of gold. "For this inestimable shadow" ' – once again she imitated his pompous manner of speaking by lengthening her jaw like a camel's – ' "I hold the very highest price too small." So Schlemihl agreed. And with that the man in grey was able to loosen Schlemihl's shadow from top to toe, roll it up and put it in his pocket.'

'Flat Stanley got rolled up too,' observed the child.

'That's true,' said the woman. 'Anyway, now the man could produce it with a great flourish, the most unusual thing that had ever been seen. As for Peter Schlemihl, he was wealthy beyond his dreams – but lacking one thing.'

'His shadow.'

'Correct,' said the woman. 'Shadowless, imagine what that would be like.' The child imagined and so did the woman. The child said it would feel like something was missing only you wouldn't quite know what because although you weren't always thinking 'that's my shadow', you somehow knew it was there with you.

The woman smiled. She was thinking that by most definitions the shadow was irremovable – undetachable – from the body it duplicates. To trade it is to prove its separate existence. She continued, 'When people saw Peter Schlemihl was shadowless they became very suspicious. "What, no shadow? Must be something wrong with him." "Must be bad." '

The child said, 'Serves him right.'

'Mmm. People shunned him. He was all alone. Children threw stones and dogs bit him. He became very unhappy – as you can imagine.'

She said she could. 'So what happened to him?'

'Well, eventually he begged the rich man to take back the magic purse and give him back his shadow.'

'And did he?'

The woman couldn't actually remember so she tacked on a quick made-up ending. 'Oh yes,' she said. 'Because our shadows are very important, d'you see?'

The child saw.

According to Pliny – this was a long time ago, in Corinth – it all began with a young girl who was in love with a young man. Unfortunately, he was about to leave the village and go abroad.

The girl wanted to keep him; what to do?

'I know!' she thought and drew in outline, using charcoal, the shadow of his face on the wall behind him. Later, after he went away, she went over it in paint. In that way he was preserved. His real shadow would, of course, accompany the young man on his travels but the painted shadow would belong to the girl; indeed, unless defaced, would probably last longer than the young man himself.

Thus, the girl 'captured', so to speak, the image of her beloved.

His shadow made up for his absence. It kept him alive. It was him.

It was evening, wintertime at Ealinghearth. In the corner of her study there stood a stilt-legged Dickensian clerk's chair made of oak wood. Molly had often climbed onto it – it had lived at their other house too – while Magda worked at her cartography. From up there she could observe many unusual things: spiders' webs, her mother's parting, the top edges of pictures and photographs like slices of light.

Now Magda's desk lamp was in the opposite corner from the tall chair. She switched it on. What she saw was not the chair but its shadow against the white wall. The shadow chair was more interesting than the full frontal chair: its tall legs and crossbars translated into a sequence of flat white rectangles divided by black bands of various widths, the seat a simple parallelogram. A painting by Mondrian.

On the wall to the right of the clerk's chair hung a photograph. It showed three people walking along the shore at a place called Silverdale with the sun behind them. The people themselves were quite far away but their shadows were quite near. The child's, especially, was shaped like the stilt legs of the clerk's chair. 'Look,' said Molly, 'my shadow is taller than the clerk's chair!'

And so it was.

Magda switched off her desk lamp, which made the chair's shadow disappear. This made her angry. She sat in the dark having anti-shadow thoughts. Fraud, bluffer, bully, she addressed the wall. Blow out the light and you disappear. She switched it back on – the chair's double came back again.

Still, something was missing. Magda went to her supplies drawer in the map cabinet and pulled out a sheet of blank cardboard; from her box of instruments, an X-acto knife. With this she cut out the shape of a sitting-down child which she placed on the clerk's chair.

There.

Now the shadow showed a clerk's chair with a child sitting on it. Which proved – just as the Mondrianish shadow's existence proved the chair – that the child must also exist.

A ghost, being an emanation or phantom, will not cast a shadow. If a shadow is cast – as the therapist had tried pointing out to Magda – it proves that something or someone has thrown it. Which must mean that Molly – see how her shadow perches on the high clerk's chair's shadow – that Molly couldn't be a ghost; and if she isn't a ghost, then she isn't dead.

Crackers, but that was Magda's reasoning.

On Molly's seventh birthday (this was after her disappearance) Magda threw a party. She baked a chocolate cake, iced it with pink icing and carried it up to Molly's room where she plonked it down on the carpeted floor. Popped seven candles around the perimeter of the cake and one in the centre.

Now for the guests. She invited Molly's toy companions: dolls, teddies, a Victorian American dollhouse, a stuffed dog, her origami Loon Woman, and two of her puppets.

All pleased to accept.

Capturing the Shadow was once a popular party game. All those who

took part did so, apparently, with a mixture of apprehension and anticipation: apprehension because they were worried they would reveal some
terrible flaw in their character, anticipation because they hoped they
would reveal, for all to see, some valuable hidden qualities.

Magda placed a candle on the floor just behind the assembled party.
Lit it. On the wall, Molly was bigger than her toy guests, so Magda
moved her closer to the wall. 'How's that.' (Now she, Molly, was her
normal size.) Magda then moved the toy guests still farther away which
made their shadows on the white wall quite enormous. The puppets
loomed up onto the ceiling dancing and slapping their knees. They
were joined by a huge growling lion and the Loon Woman, who
covered the entire ceiling with her spideriness until Magda felt herself
cringeing.

'Okay, calm down, you lot,' Molly told them and they all swooped
down and took their places around the party's centrepiece again.

'How about some cake?'

'Cake! Cake!' came the echo. Some voices were louder than others.
Molly slid down off her high chair and picked up the knife that lay on
the platter beside the cake.

'Wait! First you must light the candles.'

'And then you must make a wish.'

'Make a wish!'

Molly's shadow reached out for the matchbox. She scratched a match
and spread its flame to the candles on the cake. With each succeeding
candle, the guests grew greyer, less distinct. By the time the eighth candle
was lit (for luck) the whole party, including Molly and Magda, had
become near-invisible. (This was because the candles on the cake were
brighter than the single candle behind them.)

'Wish,' Magda whispered. 'Quickly.'

'What shall I wish?' came the child's voice out of the gloom.

'Anything you like but you mustn't tell or it won't come true. Now
blow: hurry, before the wax melts all over the cake.'

'Wa-hoooooooo,' went Molly, which blew out not only the candles on
the cake (not to mention toppling some of her lighter guests) but also the

single candle on the floor which had illuminated them all in the first place. To the sound of clapping and cries of 'Cut the cake!' the shadow party was therefore snuffed entirely.

Magda reached out in the darkness and clasped the same old piece of cardboard.

The next night Molly's Shades were restless (which was understandable since it was Hallowe'en). 'No more shadows! No more cake!' they cried. 'Then what?' 'We want a dog!' they racketed. 'A dog – what kind of a dog?' 'Any kind! Dogs dogs!' they whooped and moaned. So Magda said, 'Oh all right if you must,' and took them off to Cark Station in her car which she parked and they all trooped over the lacy iron overpass bridge (painted white but rusting and flaking) and onto the train heading south.

'How many?' asked the ticket collector.

'One,' said Magda.

They rode across the estuary in the dark. On either side of them, slick-shined tidal mud in '30s-style hair-wave patterns merged with the reflections of her shady crew mooning at the windows, sniffing up cold round the edges. Molly and the Maid of Ealinghearth holding hands. The Loon Woman off by herself, making strange loony noises.

They got off at Lancaster. 'Follow me,' said Magda. Gloom & Doom, Inc. glooped along behind. Left turn down Meeting House Lane, another fifty yards, stop. 'Now look,' she ordered her jolly troupe. And sure enough, there, behind a locked gate, installed on steps which once led to a grand house but now led nowhere, were the dogs, arranged in a pyramid: at the bottom, half-hidden in foliage, was one sniffing dog; in the middle, two bayers-at-the-moon; and at the top – inside a pergola – was the dancing dog on its hind legs. All four were white. Tin dogs. 2-D façades sprayed white so they glowed at night.

It had been raining so they gleamed. Drops of scummy water slid off their 2-D muzzles and dropped onto the stairway that led, plop, down to the street.

'Hey!' cried Molly. 'Look!'

At the stroke of nine on the Priory clock – *bong bong bong bong bong*

bong bong bong bong – one white paw moved, shook itself; no longer straight and tinny but round and soft like a puffball or a marshmallow. Molly stuffed the Maid's apron into her mouth. The other dogs tested their paws. Magda and her non-apparent family vamped aside to let them pass.

The dogs came down in waves, poured over one another like milk until they got all churned up into a head of pale cappuccino froth. Landed on the street with their seal-shaped snouts tucked into one another's necks, tails all entwined. Eventually they unscrambled themselves and stood. Shook themselves dry. Looked around. Barked at the shadow-people and were off.

Magda's lot followed at a trot.

By the time they got to the cemetery the moon – made of the same material as the dogs – was well up in the sky. 'Oh,' said Molly. This time the ghost-dogs were leaping and dancing in the moonlight – dancing and leaping and pirouetting among the bones. So the shiny white dogs and the dull white bones waltzed and tangoed and said, 'May I have this dance?' and the dogs bowed and the bones bowed too (if painfully), and Magda and hers joined in and their different whitenesses flickered in the moonlight like a grainy old movie or an underwater ballet except without the water.

By 10:30, they were pooped. The dogs leapt back up onto their perches, top dog to its pergola, still (always) dancing. 'Goodbye! Goodbye!' waved Magda, Molly and their gang, now spiralling up Meeting House Lane to catch the 10:58 to Barrow (known affectionately as the ghost train due to the pallor of its late-night riders under the non-designer overhead lighting).

The car awaited them at the station. Magda drove back to Rusland, peering hard at the road to make sure it was still there. When they got back to Ealinghearth, out tumbled her troupe as from a clown's two-dimensional Mini. 'Upstairs and straight to bed, all of you!' she commanded, inserting herself amongst them.

A heapful of pale sleepy puppies: warm fur, naked bellies, tongues and paws. Molly in the spoon of Magda's stomach.

'night, sleep tight.

Zzzzzz.

'The past is a shadow,' said Magda's mother over the telephone. She was ringing from Edinburgh. How banal, thought Magda. 'You don't know anything about shadows.'

'What's that got to do with anything?'

'You said the past was a shadow.'

'I meant it figuratively: gone, over, done with. Time to face the future, reality, a new dawn. Speaking of which, have you planted the climber I sent you?'

'Not yet; and not true. The shadow isn't nothing, you know, and it doesn't just represent the past.'

'Magda, do calm down, dear.'

' ... It represents life as well as death. It's where darkness and light intersect ... the place where opposites meet, it's ...'

'Magda, I wasn't actually talking about shadows, I was talking about the past: an unfortunate choice of imagery, perhaps but ...'

'What about the future shadow – when the sun is behind you – and the side shadow?'

'Oh, dear, you do have such a literal mind,' complained her mother. 'I must say, sometimes you're worse than your father.'

'Has it occurred to you that the shadow can both defy gravity and prove it at the same time?' Her own shadow lay at her feet. 'The point is, why think of the shadow as past – done with, over, dismissible – when it's demonstrably true that a shadow can precede us? Why not, in that case, allow it to represent the future?'

Magda's mother tucked the phone between ear and shoulder and began sketching a figure with a shadow leading it. 'That *is* interesting, darling. By the way, have you decided to go back to work yet?' The shadow looked jaunty, future-oriented. She decided this train of thought was quite positive.

'Magda, do get the New Dawn planted soon. Lots of muck, it's a thirsty brute. Darling?'

Her daughter had put the phone down. Her mother tutted but didn't ring back. Instead she finished the sketch and put it in an envelope with two stiffeners and a sticker saying DO NOT BEND. Later she posted it.

Molly never drew shadows presumably because, like medieval paintings, the objects in them were full frontal. The crayon drawing on the larder door, for instance, featured a line of trees with blue and green leaves suggested by rapid diagonal crayon strokes. This made them look windswept. Gold stars and a gold crescent moon sprinkled the sky-part of the picture. A sequence of hoop shapes below the trees was meant to represent the stone wall running along the road. Peeping out from behind one of the trees was a black dog. The dog cast no shadow.

Medieval painters also ignored the shadow. Why was this? Because the painters didn't wish their figures to represent physical reality – they were more interested, according to Magda's mother, in stylized shapes, icons, colour and pattern. It was only later, post-Giotto, she supposed – after the discovery of perspective – that the shadow came into its own. If the shadow exists, then a body must exist to cast it: not a flat thing, not a cut-out shape but a real, voluminous body. With that came the portrayal of 'real' emotion.

Expression, it was called.

Magda's shadow met other shadows. The world became even more crowded than it was – Kendal's Highgate worse than Hong Kong on a Friday lunchtime. Really you couldn't go anywhere without being stepped on. When it got really bad, Magda retaliated. Stomp, she went with both feet until the owner of the shadow dragged it away by its feet. Come along, you!

It was hardly less crowded along the Rusland Valley road, although the shadows she stepped on tended to originate in the sky: a low flying jet, a pair of buzzards, several crows plus some black-headed gulls and a heron headed for Rusland Pool.

Magda walked along the road in her wellies. When she got to the layby at Beech no.31 she cut in and stood beside the tree. As its shadow approached, she fell to the ground and lay on her back – a version of the

Semi-Supine among the crunchy carpet of old beechnuts – covered in shadow like one of those Rab sleeping bags which weigh nothing but are surprisingly warm.

By the age of five a child understands that a shadow 'belongs' to an object. When Molly was five her mother held her hand up to the wall. They were on their way upstairs, one lamp was lit below; the mother's hand cast a shadow. She flapped it and made it fly; made semi-convincing rabbit ears. Molly laughed anyway. When she was pyjama'd and tooth-brushed and tucked into bed, the mother asked her if she knew why the shadow was there. 'Of course,' said the child. 'Because your hand was there.' And she touched the mother's hand as if to make sure. It was!

When she'd fallen asleep the mother dug through some of her old books and there she found the *Little Book of Hand Shadows*. This Book Belongs to Moira Webb. That was the mother's mother's mother.

Molly's mother spent many hours practising. Snail, Pig, Panther, Dog, Tortoise, Moose, Crab, Frog, Kangaroo, Two Flying Birds, Two Baby Birds, Snake, Hippo, Sly Weasel, Clown. She didn't have a job at this time so she had time to practise. Sometimes she had strange shadow-puppet dreams which she could never remember.

Two Baby Birds – that was the child's favourite. It also happens to be one of the most difficult of the shadow puppet positions:

Form the 3rd and 4th fingers into open-scissor shapes – these form the beaks – then curl the 1st and 2nd fingers over them with an opening for the eyes. To make the baby birds open and shut their mouths, waggle the bottom two fingers (if you can). Let your hands sway as if the birds were being rocked in their nest.

> These baby birds go rockaby,
> In their tree-top nest when the breezes sigh.
> Rockaby baby, in the tree-top,
> When the wind doesn't blow,
> the cradle will stop.

That was the rhyme in the book.

The child tried but couldn't get the hang of it. At that age, finger independence is limited. 'Never mind,' said the mother. 'You'll get it eventually, it just takes practice. Try one of the easier ones.'

'What one?'

'How 'bout Snake?'

'Okay.' So she did Snake, which required only one hand. 'Good, very good,' said the mother, and then she showed the child how to improve the Snake by cutting two narrow strips of paper for fangs and holding them between her first and second fingers. Hiss, went the child. Oooh, said the mother.

When the child was a year older the mother asked the child if she knew why the shadow was black.

The child considered. 'Because ... because your hand has bones?' Which was the absolutely correct answer.

According to the psychologist Piaget, this is the Shadow Stage of Development. Unfortunately the child progressed no further.

17

Map of the Moon (1)

Monday night. Housego stretches himself out beneath a huge mirror. I kneel at his head-end and lift his skull into my lap. Striped soft hair tumbles up my wrists, fingers an interlocking hammock in which the skull lolls. I begin with a gentle bounce. The head, being a trusting sort of head, lets itself go heavier still, which is risky. I manage not to drop him but my knuckles do graze the wool of the blanket.

The point of the exercise is to demonstrate the weight of an average head – approximately two gallons – and its effect on a normal spine. Housego's must weigh three.

I hold the head in my two hands like a snifter. 'Don't worry,' I tell it, 'I've got you.' I tilt the head so its chin is higher than its crown. The poor grotesque thing rolls its eyes up (down) at me and smiles. Upside down features, ugh! Now I turn it this way and that, thinking there's a brain inside sloshing about in its cranial fluid. At which point I picture a coconut and then a melon, say, honeydew, and that spoils it because a melon, like a child's head, is so easy to squash.

Crash goes the head.

'Sorry.'

'Time to switch partners,' says Sara.

Housego slips his hands under my neck and rolls my head around as I rolled his. 'Don't be afraid to give the full weight to your partner,' Sara reminds. 'It's a question of trust.' How does she know he won't get distracted, as I did, and drop it? 'I've got you,' he says, index fingers of both hands plugged in where neck meets skull, pressing up and in. I'm being milked.

*

The head leads. Neck and shoulders follow while the spine trails along for the ride. Curved trajectory through space, plotted in time; map of motion. This movement isn't sudden, however, which is a relief. Objects and people often come at you so fast you have no time to memorize them. Cut them out, paste them facing this way and that. Important for when they're no longer there.

When you feel the bones, the teeth, the hollows of a person's face with your thumbs, you know they're getting close. The porch enclosure where you're bunched together is not a roomy place for even one ordinary-sized person, and Housego is not ordinary. There is a moon. Your key is in the lock but the door remains closed. You have driven him home but he has not gone home – he is at your home. Ealinghearth Cottage. The wooden sign clunked him in the forehead as he passed under it.

He's making for your lips, you'd better get ready.

Lip skin tends to want to stick, pink budlet to pink budlet. Then come the teeth which, having displaced yours, are followed by the tongue with its too-blue veins sloping far down into the throat. How are you supposed to respond? Does your own mouth and its attendant parts understand the word 'anticipation'? Is it willing?

These are perfectly good questions but there isn't time to answer them, so you become dimensionally, so to speak, minimal: dark and flat; stretched, pulled wide. It's possible to do many things in this form, including curving up and around the other form. As Mr Lambchop discovered, his son Stanley could be rolled up without being hurt at all. It avoids being jostled or knocked down by unflat forces; also, when you're rolled up you hardly get wet – just around the edges – whereas if you're unrolled, and therefore exposed to the elements, you get properly soaked.

Deep space can be dangerous. It can also of course be interpreted pornographically, assuming as it does that the single point which we call perspective will vanish into the distance taking us with it, seduced, cone-wise, towards infinity. So you don't touch yet. Imagine the hairs on an arm introducing themselves to the hairs on another arm.

*

It's obvious that a Flatlander, being flat, has no bulk and therefore can contain no organs of generation. However, the question of how they would do it if they could – well, it could be fun to speculate.

Take one Flatlander – A Square, for instance. A Square could in theory send out a kind of snorkel device. This device would itself have no thickness, of course. We are free to imagine any shape we like from a straight to a wiggly line, or for that matter, a triangle, lozenge or even bow-shape. As for its tip, that could be curved, hooked, barbed, squiggled, arrowed or even question-marked.

Now – remembering she's a mere line – for the female Flatlander. We'll call her Ms Line. What part of her slim anatomy does he aim for? Is there one spot in particular or several erogenous zones and how on earth does A Square find it/them? Does he go nosing blindly along with his snorkel until he hits The Spot or does the snorkel contain some radar device that leads him directly to it? How, in other words, do they do it? Is the connection by subtle collision or a clear banging together of their edges? Is there a moment of penetration, of envelopment? Of swallowing and spitting out? Do we see the line in a temporary state of engorgement rather like the snake that swallowed the pig?

Stop. Think more radically, more two-dimensionally. Why, for instance, assume a penis-substitute on A Square's behalf? A hole in Ms Line? Why, for that matter, limit Flatlanders to sexual parts at all? Why not suppose that they are such evolved creatures that they have no need for such complicated, messy, smelly, embarrassing sexual parts?

Imagine two oil slicks sliding towards one another. Imagine, if you like, the female wriggling like a worm, the male more like a blob. Eventually their edges touch. The female jumps back as if shocked, then forward again, then back. The next time she goes forward she touches the blob with her pink tip and begins a sucking action. The blob's substance is sucked in until nothing is left of it.

Alternatively, imagine two shadows. These are more subtle still. Their edges are sometimes soft and unfocused, other times deep black and definite as whips. They approach one another, naturally, sideways-on. We have no way of knowing what their expressions are since shadows, by definition, have no features.

Now imagine A Square-as-shadow moving slowly, dramatically if you like, over Ms Line-as-shadow until she is completely covered. Alternatively, imagine Ms Line turning ninety degrees (on the same plane) until she is at right angles to her wide-boy partner. She moves straight through him, no rim or ridge to stop her progress. As before, when A Square slid on top of Ms Line, nothing of her can be seen given that he is the wider of the two. They are merged all the same. And yet this way round – Line sliding over (or through) Square as opposed to Square sliding over Line – is subtly different. Think about it. Do the experiment for yourself working with shapes and a light source, or two. Let them proliferate; grow and shrink. Imagine Flatlander shapes with human shapes superimposed, or vice versa. Imagine, if you like, extrapolating from this, Housego and Magda having sex.

According to the rule of non-penetrative sex your bodies may do everything but. Tease, tickle, tongue, brush, rub, caress, stroke, etc. Desire is stimulated. The conjugation of surface bodies is exciting yet kind and respectful. Parry, deflect, slide and glide but remain within your own skin: in other words, no invading. No breaking and entering, no enveloper or enveloped, no yin-yang of body parts. You can touch and be touched but you may not dissolve into one – that is against the rules. Still you are two: you are you and he is he.

But if the rule is broken, then what? A headless body comes towards you, an outsized cookie-cutter shape of a man. Who goes there? Where does Housego go? Does he dare to overstep your precisely drawn boundaries? And do you let him, invite him in, allow the map of your body to be disturbed?

As Stanley might have said, it's so much easier being flat!

This is where the messages start flying. Spinal nerve fibres penetrating inward from the body's surface, innervating sense organs and anatomical structures previously hidden, beyond our gaze and touch, beyond the reach of our experience. Outside joined to inside. Sharp localized sensations deep in the body's depths – which could, of course, be perceived as threatening: an invasion, an occupation, the colonizing of a space that was once exclusively yours but is no longer. But then you remind yourself it's only a temporary absorption: the act of taking in and pushing away. When you're sated he'll go away, and although your recessive tissue layers will retain the memory of him you will be left with you, and therefore, well, why not enjoy the experiment while it lasts?

It happens gradually of course. You have been prepared like a canvas: wrapped round, stretched, primed. The first brushstrokes depress your surface but you bounce back, youthfully elastic for your age. But this surface conjugation only lasts while you're a shadow, a film. So long as you're flat, that is, this thing can go no further.

Don't misunderstand me. Flatland has its advantages. You can do many things in this form, which cause your partner to wonder if you are there at all. A wave motion, he suspects. And then, although he is normally so much heavier than you, when you enter Flatland you both become weightless – dimensionally, let's say, liberated. Which means all positions can be reversed with some pleasure.

Still, it has its limits. Eventually there's a shift. Forget canvas, glue, staples, size. Your picture-surface is wiped, your paint dissolved. You are now leaving Flatland behind. Your surface body stands aside while the internal body comes forth – its first appearance in, oh, a long time, its awayness becoming less away by the minute.

As for the intruder – your muscles do quite a lot on your behalf to make him, whom you no longer perceive as quite so intrusive, feel at home. You can afford to do this because by now you're plugged into your own deep reproductive circuitry and therefore feeling certain inexpressible feelings accompanied by certain untranslatable images: flappings of leaves, the generation of heat expanding outward in a pattern of concentric circles, an outside and an inside system featuring bark, rings of fruitwood, heartwood; intertwining boughs, branches, stems.

Limp-leaved, newborn. And all against the rules.

'Have a look.' The moon is full and Housego has brought his telescope. Other favourable experimental conditions obtain: (1) We are in a highly relaxed, expanded state; (2) We have been drinking wine; (3) The night is cold but clear.

Free of gravity, lunch and dinner, we move in astronautical ways, doomed to wasting muscle disease but bearing our fates bravely. Our new address: The Sky.

I carry the stand; Housego carries the telescope childwise in his arms, a cylindrical papoose. Three feet in length, ten inches in diameter. The electrical cord trails behind him. Do be careful, it wouldn't do to drop it. Up three steps from the road and around to the paved area abutting the house. He places the stand beside the sundial, loads the telescope onto the stand. There are no city lights for miles around.

When you look at the moon without a telescope – the eye naked as a sink – it appears to be flat.

'Here,' says Housego, 'have a look.'

The moon looks kindly on lovers, it can't help itself. By the same token, lovers are supposed to look kindly on the moon. Me, I'm a lunar cannibal. I have swallowed the moon and it has floated up into my head filling my eye sockets with bolts of luminous cheap voile. Instant glaucoma, eye cells popping off like stars. You can't take such a thing for long.

'Here, you have a go.'

He bends to the viewing lens. After ten minutes the moon has moved out of focus. He makes the necessary adjustment and then it's my turn again. The telescope is covered in dew. By now I'm sober which means I can see what there is to see. Are those dark shadowy shapes craters or seas? Craters, he says: some rounder than others, deeper than others, some with rims higher. Around each of the craters a kind of bracelet effect, like so many tambourines. These are cliffs.

Montes Pyrenaeus.

The moon is demonstrably global. Orbiting. This can be proved by following the movement of a crater – best to choose one quite near the underside – as it curves round and disappears. You want to put up your hands and say Catch! Gather it to you for warmth except that, as everyone knows, it's very very cold.

Hecataeus ... Humboldt ... Gassendi ...

'Extraordinary.'

'Yes.'

'Moving.'

'Yes. Literally.'

What can you say?

What is there to say?

After looking at the moon through Housego's telescope I had a dream about a beaver – not a very British mammal but this was a dream beaver, a mother beaver. She had planned to go for a morning's fishing in Rusland Pool but before doing that had crossed the road and stuffed something into a hole in Beech 31 for safe keeping. A special beech for a special thing, now what could it be? Her young one, correct. Having done that she beavered back to the Pool where in due course – in dream-time probably three or four seconds – she caught an enormous pike.

Now it was time to return to her young. But just as she was approaching the tree, with the pike in her mouth, she saw something fingering its way towards the rim of the hole. The hand was creeping further into the hole of the bole and, yes, it was about to remove the pup, or whatever it is you call a young beaver.

Caught in the act! Stop! Thief!

The mother beaver drops her pike, and how. Her mouth opens, her gums clear her teeth. They look more like axe blades. Her cheeks stretch and her whole body arcs. She clears the distance between her and the pup thief easy. Her mouth closes around his leg somewhere just above the thigh. The axe-teeth break through trousers, skin, flesh and bone. The man breaks apart like a rickety chair and the beaver's young is saved. A close shave.

When I woke up Housego was gone and I was left with the dream. What to do with it? I got up and trailed into my study, feeling like The

Groke in Molly's Moomin books. Wherever she goes, The Groke freezes the ground she walks upon.

I stood forlornly at the window. Rusland Pool was just visible beyond the trees in my wood. The map cabinet held all sorts of maps but not dreams. If you tried to map a dream that would spoil it, or it would escape. Still, I could try. So I switched on my computer and mapped the basic configuration. Added numbers corresponding to the stations, as it were, of the beaver, to be explained in the key at the bottom.

The mother beaver begins at (1) along the river bank. Crosses the road and enters the beechwood (2) where she drops her pike and chomps the leg off a poacher who was obviously on the verge of plucking her young from its nest with the intention of who knows what dastardly deed.

The dream ended there but the map journey, I saw, could continue with the beaver and her young returning to the site of the dropped pike (2) and from there proceeding further upstream carrying the big fish between them to a safe place (3) for a picnic.

'Where is it?' Molly asked.

'Where is what?' asked her mother.

'Dreamland.'

'Oh, it's all different places – depends on your dream.'

'Is there a map?'

'Well, each dream could have its own map, in theory.'

'No, I mean the place called Dreamland.'

Magda explained that in this country grown-up people didn't believe there was such a place and therefore they'd be disinclined to map it since that conferred a kind of reality. 'However,' she added, 'I believe they do in other parts of the world; Australia, for example. They have a concept of dreaming they call Dreamtime. I believe the Aborigine peoples have something they called Churinga, or dream mapping.'

'Could you get such a map?'

Magda hadn't added anything to her map collection for quite a long time.

'I could try,' she said.

18

Map of the Moon (2)

'I'm hungry,' said Magda's partner Jay. At first she thought, how could you? but then she realized she was hungry too. Starving. They hadn't eaten for several days – it was just after it.

So what should we do, they asked each other. 'I don't feel like cooking,' said Jay. 'There's nothing in the fridge,' said Magda. 'I know,' said Jay, 'let's go out.' 'Where?' asked Magda. 'How about The Moon?' said Jay. 'Okay,' said Magda.

He said, she said. Even monsters have to eat.

Jay didn't believe they were monsters, merely human. Some such phrase. You mustn't blame yourself. He didn't blame himself so why should she?

Not your fault.

Did what you could

Did what you thought best.

Good, well done. Now where to eat?

'We could go to The Moon,' said Jay, which was a repeat of what he'd said earlier but no matter, Magda had clean forgotten. Brain, stomach, kitchen cupboards all spick 'n' span. Fine, The Moon, let's go. And then Jay said, 'Let's go,' and together they said, 'Let's go' and so saying, they sat on the edge of the bed gradually losing substance which meant they slid more easily so by now they were almost on the floor and it was nearly too late to go, at which point something in the lining of Magda's gut twitched and she leapt up and grabbed Jay by the paw.

They were wearing clothes, don't ask me what kind. Skirt, trousers, shirt, blouse – generic clothes. Belt to keep trousers up, shoes and socks of different colours but never mind. Hair combed. Earrings plugged into holes, feel the jab, the popping of nearly grown-over skin. Magda hadn't worn earrings in a long time so now there was blood. Gory grume! Add lipstick, an attractive undead blue-black colour.

And now we take a little jump avoiding the drive and the parking and so on, and present them in the doorway of the restaurant known as The Moon, with its lickable high-gloss burgundy and green painted wainscoting and a tasteful sprinkling of moon motifs. Indeed, each portion of homemade ice-cream came with a sliver of chocolate moon. Food for a Flatlander. They also sold T-shirts in adult and children's sizes saying, I'VE BEEN TO THE MOON. Molly had one.

'Where would you like to sit?' the waitress asked, leading them to a table next to a radiator – this couple needed warming. As for deciding what to eat she began recommending things. 'The tomato and orange soup is very nice.' 'Yes, yes, we'll have that,' they agreed. They were very agreeable. 'For the main course I'd have the fish, everything else is quite heavy.' Oh yes, fish. Nice light fish.

Jay ate, Magda ate. Once they started they couldn't stop, Magda in particular. The more she put into herself, the hungrier she felt.

An emptiness inside that needed filling?

You could put it that way.

And then the others walked in. A family: two adults and two children. The children were facing her, so Magda had a good view of them; in fact, you couldn't not view them. They were blond and foreign, Dutch or Swedish perhaps. Beautiful, of course, all shiny and blue-eyed.

'Pudding?' asked Jay and Magda said, 'Oh yes, pudding.' She'd had some kind of starter and a main fish course but was still ferociously hungry.

Or maybe just ferocious?

Ferocious, yes. And just to prove it, when she looked down into her pudding bowl, there they were. The children, reduced to the size of a Weetabix, all snuggled together in the bottom of her bowl.

Imagine that!

Magda placed a restraining finger on each of their sweet narrow chests. The girl – call her Gretchen – had gone floppy, but the boy – Hans, say – was quite rigid. A nuisance, Magda thought, because his muscles will become tough and chewy. Gretchen was whimpering or praying. She would slip down too easily. Hans was shaking his little fist and shouting in his Swedish accent, '*You cannot do this to me!*' to which she replied, 'Oh can't I?'

She began removing any indigestible items: hair clips, shoes, buttons, etc. Later, she thought, I will put them in a plastic bag with a label on for identification purposes.

The beginning of a career in eating children?

Let's just say she was feeling very organized.

But here comes the best part – undressing them.

Magda began unbuckling their little sandals. Gretchen was too floppy to stand up so she had to be wriggled out of her dress while still on her back. A pretty sprigged pinafore dress. Magda crooned a Victoria de los Angeles song to soothe their nerves, while stroking Hans with a finger which she'd first dipped into some chocolate sauce from a separate bowl.

She encouraged them to do some yoga breathing. She wasn't heartless, you see, but Hans began whimpering and his little penis was red and sticky. It began waving about like a raspberry but his sister kicked him and told him to stop being such a baby and then ...

Yes, go on, it's all right.

It wasn't all right, it was disgusting. As she said to Jay, 'This is disgusting,' she said. And he said, 'Do you want to send it back?' – and that's when she began to laugh and couldn't stop and they had to leave the restaurant pronto.

You mean he thought she meant her dessert was disgusting?

'Thank you,' said Magda to the bereavement counsellor, for getting her meaning. The counsellor looked thoughtful: 'It's hard being a monster, isn't it?' And Magda said, 'Yes, it is.'

Wait a minute. Can this Magda-character really have been as cool as all that? Did she never let go, break down? *Cry?*

You mean: Did she weep and did she moan? Did her nose grow increasingly red at the tip, her cheeks and forehead blotchy, her shoulders shake 'n' quake?

See Magda turn Rusland into a Vale of Tears (and go floating away on her back like Alice in her salty sea)?

See Magda beat her breast?

See Magda run round and round some old beech tree like a demented squirrel?

See Magda pull out her hair?

Tears? You want to know about tears? Did they come in individual droplets or compound globules? Or were they joined up like writing in a linear flow down the bumpy landfall of her face? Were they proper tear-shaped, pear-shaped, tears? Of normal salinity, unusually salty, or salt-free?

Did they ever get heavy enough to fork into separate tributaries, end up going drip-drop off the tip of her nose, the ledge of her chin? Did they wet her bib? Sound effects? You want an accompaniment of snorts? Bubbles from the nostrils? Great gulpings for air? Strangled cries of 'Woe! Woe is me!'?

What more? Dramatic body language, expressive gestures? The rolling of eyes to heaven? The shaking of shoulders in time with the pumping of fluids?

How about some serious griefwork, some really hot cathartic stuff? Pillow punching, the flinging of mugs against the kitchen wall, wolf howlings up on the ridge behind the beeches?

How'm I doing?

Then there's the interesting question of flux: patterns of change, increase and decrease, frequency correlated with time of day, and so on. We could map the flow. Commence at the minute orifices, *puncta lacrimalia*, proceed inwards to terminate in the lachrymal sac. Note how the superior canal at first ascends then bends at an acute angle, how the inferior canal descends, abruptly changes course, passing almost horizontally inwards.

No? Not what you had in mind (enough of this cold, calculating stuff)? You want the *human* angle, the true True Confessions?

All right, here we go.

I cried. I cried a lot. Buckets? Easily. Bathtubsful? Quite possibly, although it takes an awful lot of water to fill the average tub. It went on, a daily thing, though not an equal part of every hour. Mornings, middles-of-the-night tended to be worst (a common pattern). There were triggers, of course, sure springers such as music and drink. The last thing I needed.

It went on for six months or so and then it stopped – they stopped – the most shocking thing of all. Oh, not one hundred per cent – they'd come sprouting out in the middle of a funny film, escape in dribbles during dreams – but the apparently unstoppable gush of them stopped. Other things took their place. Dry eyes, dry grief, call it what you will. I didn't pull out my hair, though some fell out of its own accord. As for sound effects, there was probably a whole gamelan of gongs and snorts, as well as a word I tended to repeat to myself, that went like this: *MollyMollyMoll* ...

Satisfied?

19

Map of the London Underground

Bea Merriman and I sit side by side, she in the window seat. From Cark the train crosses the estuary from north to south as the current moves east to west; and with this criss-crossing of moving bodies, water and train, we feel briefly stilled, as if they'd somehow cancelled each other out.

Leaving the Valley can be tricky. We are like moles, like badgers. Main roads, traffic flow, trains, towns, cities, the shock of it. The wider world is too wide and unfeatured: not ours. We are Rusland supremacists, beech bores. Leaving requires an act of will which exhausts us. Bea rubs her eyes and prepares for sleep. I keep watch over her. The outside world tips: canals like metalled bookmarks, rivers windings of experimental jewellery.

Let me explain. That flat world I enter from time to time, or that enters me, isn't always brought about by memory or sadness. Not a simple Molly equals flatness equation. A certain cast of light can bring it on, tiredness (an eye condition?), sheer laziness. In this case, if I had to map what I saw – make sense of that complex blur, that flying-by land-scape – I'd be exhausted in no time. This way it's easier: a pleasant but not overtaxing film, a screen to watch but not engage with.

Bea yawns. Soon after Lancaster the glass becomes her pillow, and what could be less comforting to a head? Even with that ticking of curls it rattles, skull dance against glass. I'm tempted to offer my shoulder – more motherly than glass – but I don't know how. Still, she sleeps.

Bea was nominated for the Andrew Lees Memorial Trust Award for her 'painstaking research and investigation as an environmental campaigner.' The presentation ceremony is in London. I'm going with her because she asked me. Why not Mick or Housego or her mother, or anyone? Because they were all tied up with work, she said. 'Somebody has to look after the kids. Anyway, I'm asking you. Come or don't come.'

Come or don't come. So I came. I will be of use.

'Did you remember to bring the A-Z?' she asks.

'Of course. How many other nominees are there?'

'Dunno.'

'Who're the judges?

'Dunno, journalists from the national press.'

'Who nominated you?'

'Housego, I suspect, or you.'

'Not me.'

She had no idea where we were going. While she slept I worked it out: Underground to Victoria, South Eastern Railway to Blackheath.

'Where are we?'

'Euston, nearly there.'

'You should have woken me sooner.' She could sleep forever. 'It's the break from the kids – and Mick,' she says.

Euston, this is Euston. All passenger journeys terminate here. Please make sure you have all your luggage with you. Mind the gap.

We stand in the aisle, waiting for the doors to open. Bea's hair attracts other reds: the furry chevrons repeated on every seat, the painted-on chevrons around the door, like some postmodern dog-toothed archway; that man's shiny red jacket. The doors open. Follow me, says her bouncing ball hair (it also attracts people). Red likes red. See there, up on the ceiling of the station, along the beams and struts, a dried-blood red with regularly occurring bolts to hold it together; and there, on the wall, that poster advertising a poppy-splattered painting; and almost everywhere you look.

Bea stops short so I almost run into her. 'Where are we?' Sweeping a finger from West Kensington round to Clapham Common, a blind diviner. But then, the Underground map isn't all that easy with its different lines represented by red brown black pink grey green and yellow, the stops by single or double bubbles. It may be eye-catching as a design but it's wildly out-of-scale. Scale is relatively large for the inner city areas where routes converge and connect: some stops in the central areas are only four or five blocks apart. Towards the outer areas station-blobs are probably a mile or more apart. The scale here can be smaller because the mapped features are less dense.

It's not about accuracy but about linkages, adjacency, relative position. By sacrificing geometric correctness to a schematic abstraction it addresses the Underground rider's basic question: where am I on the system? Where is my destination? Do I need to change trains? If so, where and to what line? In which direction, roughly, do I need to go? What is the name of the station at the end of the line? How many stops do I ride before I get off? Function, as it were, dictates form. A more accurate map would obfuscate, be confusing.

'Magda, where the hell are we?'

'Don't worry, just follow me.'

I lead her through the system; on, off, change here. Bea hanging by an overhead strap, long as a rabbit. 'Where do we get off?' Her shadow goes before her, pulling her along; even so she has to trot to keep up. 'Where is this place?' As if I should know. I've only been to London twice in my life: once with my mother to look at paintings and once with Molly. At the Science Museum she stood before an electrically-charged metal ball mounted on a pole. 'Put your hand on it,' I told her. 'What for?' 'You'll find out.' She closed her hand over the dome and her fringe stuck straight up in the air. She pulled her hand away and rolled her eyes up to see what the hair was doing. It was taking its time subsiding because she was wearing well-insulated shoes. She patted it down with her hand. 'My arm is still tingling,' she said.

A young man greets us at the front door of the gallery: 'Hi, there, and you're ... ?' Bea points to her name on his list, taps with her fingernail: 'That's me.'

Bea Merriman, tick.

'And this is ...?'

'Magda Beard, she's with me.'

The gallery is a white rectangular box with high ceilings and a polished beechwood floor, track lighting overhead. On the walls, paintings of trees, leaf patterns, rivers, rocks, mountains: mostly abstract yet identifiably Nature, fixatived against corrosion by cigarette smoke and human breath. Environmental Art. Fashionably appropriate as a backdrop to the prize-giving.

Waitpersons churn through with trays of wine and canapes, tiny pastries stuffed with cheese or fruit purée. 'It's more like some arty opening,' says Bea, grabbing with both hands. 'Nice space,' says a voice. Space, the stuff between the people and the paintings, between the canapes and their eaters, between Bea and She's With Me.

'Hey, Magda,' Bea's plucking at my sleeve: 'it's starting. In there.' So we troop through into a red brick courtyard, looked down on by fire escapes and spotlights. Designer plants in clay pots big enough to cook whole humans. Tables but no chairs.

'Who d'you think'll win?'

'Bea Merriman.'

'Oh?'

'Trees are big this year, everyone's into trees. You know, the healing energy of trees. Besides, she's a woman, isn't she, and cute.'

'Yeah.'

A representative for the Trust goes up and fiddles with a microphone. '*Bwhoo bwhoo*, can you hear me?' Thank yous and gratefuls for the support of followed by brief descriptions of each nominee's work and now the event we've all been waiting for: the winner of the Andrew Lees Memorial Trust Award.

Pause here. You can't just announce the name because people need to be surprised, and surprises need to be prepared for. The name of the winner has to be put inside an envelope and then the envelope has to be passed from one besuited chap to another; then it has to be opened with a view towards recycling the envelope; then the piece of paper with the name inside is taken out and unfolded; and then, in order to see the name, the Master of Ceremonies has to reach into his jacket pocket and put on his bifocals and peer at the piece of paper. Aha.

'The winner of the Andrew Lees Memorial Trust Award for her Save the Beeches campaign – Mrs Bea Merriman.' He peers over his specs, we all look around.

'Bea Merriman, is Bea here?'

'You. Congratulations. Go.'

'What'll I say?'

'Haven't you got something?'

'Didn't think I'd win.'

'Doesn't matter, say anything, talk about the beeches. You'll be fine.'

The Master of Ceremonies bends to give Bea her award. Two young women near me are deeply concerned with what she puts on her hair to make it so red and shiny. 'Henna wax.' 'Yeah, she must wax each ringlet.' 'Think it's a perm?' 'Nuh-uh, it's too all-over-the-place.' 'Yeah, could be natural.' Bea's gold tooth flashes, she might bite the poor gift-giver.

'It's stupid,' she says.

'One moment, please.' The Trust man inserts himself between Bea and the mike, lowers it.

'That better?' We can't have heard that right. Start again.

'I mean, there are lots of other people who feel as strongly as I do about the Rusland Beeches. I feel like an imposter, I don't deserve this.' She pumps iron with the trophy. What now? Will she launch it into the audience, bonk the Trust man over his head? People moue, assume modesty. She lowers her arm.

'I grew up with the beeches, and I'd like to die knowing they're still there, so I had to do my bit to protect them. In any case, we haven't won. So far we've managed to save most of them but ten are still under threat and eighteen more could be reduced to hulks. Do you know what a hulked beech looks like? An amputee. Once that's done, they're better off felled completely. So it isn't a complete victory, I wish it were. But a lot of people besides me have worked hard and will continue to fight. And besides,' she adds, 'I'm not even doing it for the right reasons.'

This is not seemly, not part of the script. Everybody is looking at everybody else except for those suddenly fascinated by plants. 'The right reason,' she ploughs on, 'is environmental. Supposed to be anyway. But mine is selfish. I grew up with the beeches. I love to look at them and I make most of my living photographing them. That's all.'

'Well, ah, that's quite enough for us. And now, I believe Bea has to catch her train back up north so, once again, thank you and congratulations, Bea Merriman.'

'Maybe it's enough,' she tells the mike.

'Ungrateful little git,' says the girl who'd admired her curls.

'And congratulations to the other nominees for their splendid campaigning, and to all of you for coming. Once again, thank you.'

Bea marches this-way that-way through the maze of tables. I grab her by the arm, through the gallery and out, then we jog all the way to the main road. Use her trophy for hailing a cab.

'Euston Station, please. Fast, we have a train to catch: last one tonight.'

'Where you ladies going?'

'Cumbria, the Lake District.'

'Nice place, took my kiddy fell walking once. Windermere way, or was it Coniston? Coniston, that was it. The Old Man of Coniston: you know it?'

'We know it.'

20

Map of the Zambu Tree

Monday night. Housego raises his arm to the angle of a Hitler salute only limper. I fit my palm over his knuckles and close my eyes. The object of the exercise is for the 'blind'-handed person to 'stick' to the 'seeing'-handed person wherever he or she goes.

Housego steps back, forward, sideways, around. Our hands, his and mine, slew against one another in ball-and-socket fashion while our arms scissor together and apart. Sight-free, just follow the hand that leads you.

Sticky Fingers, it's called.

Housego's arm describes various shapes in space: parabolas, spirals, the motions of Jupiter's moons, aerial balletics and tumblings. After a sudden loss of altitude my hand becomes detached from his – poor paw, lost in mid-air. That stomach-drop you get when an engine cuts out. Where am I? Are we going to crash? Of course you won't, you're just being teased, freed to flirt with gravity. It won't last, the hand-dive. Just before touchdown he'll swoop down and under. Hand-lifted to safety.

When it's my turn to lead I describe trade winds, lightning slashes, graphic coils, a chart of marital breakdown. His hand rides mine. The object of the exercise is to trust your own body; to let it go, as they say, with the flow. My object is detachment: to lose him as he lost me. Only it doesn't seem to work. However many suicidal moves I make, Housego's hand stays stuck to mine.

He's easily led, she said.

Bea Merriman, on the way home from London, said that.

This is only an exercise, of course. Once we leave the centre we're quite separate again. As we walk, our shadows appear and fail to appear. As with the moon, it has to do with the blockage of light. Leonardo believed the contours of shadows were impossible to define so he drew them fuzzily. Dürer, on the other hand, believed their edges could be clearly defined and therefore drew them clearly. On the pavement they merge, go their own way, join up again; stretch like snakes, ripple like runner carpets or the bore on the estuary, go flick like a tongue. They reach the Brewery bar before we do.

The shadow is an affirmation of the body. It proves volume, flesh. So long as you cast a shadow you can't be one of them. Shadows and ghosts, vampires and Flatlanders, as everyone knows, do not cast shadows.

At the Brewery pub we sit in one of the round booths. We are close but not-close. What we are in relation to one another – bed partners, Alexander partners, drinking partners – doesn't require further definition. Housego is married, he has five children. He has been and may continue to be in a long-term relationship with Bea Merriman. I am what I am.

I'm good at this. I may be kidding myself of course but I'm having a nice time too, so why should I worry? It suits me, it suits him. We're both easy. Mapping requires precision plotting, but this is in relief to that. Many women want 'commitment' but I do not. They want someone they can be emotionally 'open' with and with whom they expect to be 'open' in return. I do not. On the contrary, I worry that he will at some point want to talk about 'things' – and I'd much rather he didn't. I'd much rather a regular back-and-forth exchange of information. So I say isn't it great about Bea's award and he says it's only deserved; and then I say the DoE, did I hear, are sending another site inspector and he nods into his Guinness, adding that the DoE have been forced to think yet again; and I'm saying I thought they'd made their decision? – surely this whole thing can't be going round and round again? and he's saying oh, but it can.

'Bea wrote again to the Secretary of State, and so did a load of others. Things are really hotting up. By the way,' he asks, 'did you see that professor's letter in the *Gazette*?'

'I did. Father's ashes scattered under one of the beeches?'

'Mm. Apparently he makes a yearly pilgrimage – lives up in Edinburgh, I think. He appealed to the DoE as the trees' "ultimate custodians". That got to them.'

'Why?' I ask. 'Why should a national body be forced to backtrack?'

'Sensitive issue, the beeches – they have to watch their step. Plus I think they're genuinely committed to saving trees down south whereas up here we seem to be mad-keen on chopping them down. It's crazy.'

Maybe, I think.

'Media coverage helps too. Did Bea tell you? They're doing one of those Countryfile features on 'The Threatened Rusland Beeches'. Granada, I think, Wednesday night.' A finger on the wrist-bone of my left hand.

'You'll watch?'

'I'll try.'

My hand moves but the finger stays where it was. How does he manage this? How did he manage, in the sticky finger exercise, to stay so loose yet connected? It must be a movement and balance thing – climbers, like dancers, are good at this. Then again it might have more to do with that other thing. He's easily led, she said.

How does her garden grow? Not with silver bells or cockle shells but feverfew and hydrangea and still-dormant African daisies and hoop-shaped slates rolling encouragingly along the path. Framing the pretty cottage door, a rosette of stones; beside it, a stone bench. The pretty cottage door opens. Come in.

The Merriman cottage is part of the Rusland Hall estate, about a mile-and-a-half up the road from Ealinghearth. Mick, her husband, is out at the pub in Satterthwaite playing darts. Their kids are called Joe, Stewart, Simon. 'Ssh, they've only just gone off.'

We drink Sweet Peppermint tea. Bea is curled up in a beanbag, knitting, with a spotlight behind her. Elbows going up and down, she could be a fly.

'I'm just learning. This is only the foundation row.' She holds the knitting up to show me, an abacus of green wool loops. Her needles are made of bamboo with wooden blobs at the ends, like old-fashioned clothespin heads, to stop the stitches falling off. She holds them like crossed swords, secures them with her thumbs, raises her elbows. 'First stitch is knit, that goes into the back of the stitch. Second stitch purl, that goes into the front.' She holds the remote control at right angles to the TV screen and hits the 'On' button with her thumb. 'Once you've established the first row you do the opposite: where there's a knit you purl and where there's a purl you knit.' She says she likes the resistance each stitch puts up.

A picture of trees comes on, trees blowing in a wind. A gale, more like, which blows for two rows. Not that I have any interest in the gale or what will happen in the gale but I pretend to watch what Bea watches. I am to the telly as Bea is to the telly. Two women and a television set.

'Storm havoc,' says the voiceover, 'winds 100 mph ... trail of destruction.'

'Hey, wait a minute.' She stops knitting. 'That isn't Rusland.' The programme they were supposed to be showing was 'The Threatened Rusland Beeches'. The little bumps look like sphagnum moss over rocky ground. From an aerial perspective real moss looks like so many mini-trees.

Their eyes were fixed on the screen.

Imagine two lines originating at the back of each of our retinas travelling towards the light of the telly screen. The lines get closer and closer eventually meeting at their point of intersection. **Dangerous Trees**, says the dramatically delayed title on the screen. Each pair of eyes, according to the principle of triangulation, 'sees' the title. Bea Merriman leans forward, half in, half out of her beanbag, a semi-illuminated comma. The dwellers in Plato's Cave, remember them? Those cartoon oafs watching Cave TV with their arms dangling between their legs, mouths hanging open. Couldn't believe what they were seeing either. Me? I can believe anything.

A fifty-foot elm lays itself over a car – two-year-old Jaguar written off. The music that accompanies the images storms and crashes and bangs. Bea Merriman falls forward onto her knees and shuffles towards the telly.

'Over one hundred sightings of dangerous trees ...'

I sit on my hands to stop them clapping, it wouldn't be right to clap, she wouldn't understand, Miss Save the Beeches, it would make her mad, it would make her sad. Still holding onto her knitting, forehead going bump bump against the screen's safety glass like some stupid tup, stitches bungee-jumping off their needles.

By now, two children are hopping down steps in their pyjamas to see what's going on. Joe, Stewart, but not Simon because he's too small. 'It's nothing,' she tells them, sitting back on her heels, 'just something on the telly, go back to bed, shoo.' Pushing them in the smalls of their small backs. Baby Simon in his cradle doesn't wake. She waits for them to go before letting go.

'It's the wrong programme!' Cursing and shaking. 'Damn Park Authority, they must've leant on Granada. Damn Dellums, Dellums damn!' It sounds like a song. Little fists hitting little thighs, tomorrow she'll have bruises.

'Trees may provide shelter and aesthetic pleasure but they have also caused millions of pounds of damage ...'

'SHUT UP!' she yells. And then: 'Can you believe it?' Hoiking up her hair like the Bride of Frankenstein. Yes, I can believe it of the big green greedy plant, that very so-called reverend vegetable. Smash crash, there goes another house, another car, another child. Bea kicks the telly with her socked foot then goes hopping about. Mustn't laugh. By now I'm standing in the sitting-room doorway. Time to go. Bea pushes past me into the hallway and grabs the phone. The last tree falls in slow motion; someone is about to be crushed.

Knock knock, who's there? It's the professor, stepped from our conversation onto my Welcome mat.

'I hope I'm not disturbing you.'

Hope and disturbance, two interesting concepts. When he knocked, I was trying to plot the distribution of clusters for a local childhood leukemia research project. I've already done individual cases, basic control census data, morbidity rates, aggregation of enumeration districts; highlighted special features such as buffer zones and power lines, hospital sites with incinerators and the infamous slaughterhouse. The clustering is getting messy for the scale they want, what with all those overlapping circles. And then, how do you map a non-visual co-variable such as wind direction?

'That's all right. Come in.'

'I won't keep you long,' he says, 'I can see you're busy.'

'Do sit down.'

He sits, I sit. Compared with Housego he takes up little space. Ealinghearth's bow window is one of those '30s extrusions you curse from the outside but bless from inside. Sun streaming in.

'So, what can I do for you?'

'As you probably read in the papers, I'm here on my annual pilgrimage.'

'Your father ...?'

'That's right. I've just been to see Bea Merriman, to thank her for her campaigning work. Marvellous, isn't it, about the award, by the way. She happened to mention in passing that you also suffered a personal tragedy ... in connection with the beeches.'

'An interesting way of putting it.'

'Ye-es.' His stretched yes allows time. Time allows a gap; into the gap, quesions jump.

'I suppose she was leaving it to you to fill in the details – but only if you choose to, of course. If you feel intruded upon, you must say. But it would be a help to me, you see – how shall I put it? – Bea cares passionately about the beeches of course – she's marvellous – but I'm not sure how she would see this other ... dimension' – he taps his chest – 'I mean, in her eyes it must appear rather, oh, self-involved – not caring about the beeches *per se* but conflating their intrinsic value with this other thing we impose upon them – in my case, as the preserver, as it were, of my own family tree. I don't know if that makes any sense to you.' Fingers of his right hand hooked cliff-wise into the heart pocket of his shirt.

Answer the man, Magda.

'Actually the someone Bea referred to was my daughter, but she wasn't buried among the beeches.' (How do you say in a conversational way, I merely lost her there?) He doesn't ask for clarification, nor do I give it. He says 'I see,' and 'of course.' A soft man, a kind man. A man who needs to talk about his father.

'He loved the beeches, you see. He was an old-fashioned naturalist. He thought them one of the finest avenues in Britain. He would have been horrified, as indeed we all are, at the prospect of their being felled, even ten.'

I want to say, 'he smiled', but the expression that took up residence on the plane of the professor's face was too wobbly, too temporary ('a fleeting smile'?).

'It was funny really,' he's saying. 'I couldn't decide whether to go along sprinkling bits of him at the foot of each tree, or simply dump the whole lot in one go. Endless dithering, you see, walking up and down, running the ash through my fingers saying "father". You'll think me absurd.'

I don't think anything. 'Which did you decide?'

'I didn't for quite some time. If I scatter him, or so I argued with myself, that could be quite liberating, a kind of freeing of the spirit – the corporeal body is dissolved in any case – that sort of thing. But in the end I wanted to be able to return to one particular place. Terribly earthbound and conventional, I'm afraid.'

Not scattering his father's ashes, in other words, but dumping them all in one go.

Now that the professor has told his tale, the nervous little self-disparaging laugh can be dropped. He seems relieved. 'Thank you,' he says simply. 'Thank you.' Perhaps that's what he's come for. Thank you simply. And then I ask him which one and he says which one what and I say which tree meaning under which tree did he dump his father and he says, 'Oh, sorry: the great one, at the bend in the road – it now bears a yellow number 31 – you know it?'

His smile is encouraging and therefore I'm encouraged to say I know it, indeed I do, and so did Molly, followed by the words *daughter, child, disappeared*. And the words, once begun, aren't inclined to stop: explaining words and some distress words and quite a few unanswered questions come dashing out until there are no more laugh lines or broken lines left, you are at the margin, the place where your story-map ends and there you sit with no compass bearing and no footpath marker and no grid reference to follow but it so happens the thing you dreaded most of all doesn't happen. Your words, in other words, don't cause undue upset or pity or shock or wanting to put arms around for comfort, or for that matter undue anything except attendance, rather as if he were trying to follow one of those old series OS maps which has yellowed and torn along the folds and is stuck together with scotch tape and is blowing in the wind but somehow manages to keep hold, smooth it down, always fold along the horizontal, then side to side, according to my father's instructions.

At the end I say I'm sorry. It's the kind of thing you're taught to say. I was, he was. 'Not at all.' Generous to a fault. The earth under his feet opens up and he comes away brushing dust off his trousers.

I am a bit wobbly yet not entirely flat.

The professor's face is aglow. This is the problem with giving information: gift, responsibility, burden. I've been trying to tell him what I failed to do: *hold the body together.* Her body was lost, discarded, disassembled, not preserved respectfully in one place.

He doesn't get it. Why should he?

The professor asks had I thought of burying her under Beech 31 too – assuming it's not too crowded, what with his father already in residence and goodness knows who else; and I reply that no, we hadn't thought of it, but that she was in quite good company up at Rusland Church.

There's often, in conversation, a moment when you feel a shift. Delicate, yes. If the professor had been a little more curious, a little less polite, a little less in a hurry, I might have told him – more. Possibly. But such a moment doesn't last very long. Professor Ross – please call him Stephen – looks at his watch, he must get back, until next time and we shake hands but it's the kind of shake where you enclose the other's hands in both of yours like a pair of nuts, rattle rattle, and then the two halves of the shell are divided and he's gone.

Four fingers under the brass bellied handle and pull.

Wood against wood.

Smells of blue cheese, camphor, dry whips of vanilla pod.

First, yes, wash your hands: necessity, ritual.

Drawer 16: Map of the Zambu Tree (Burma c1830-40, polychrome).

The world of the Zambu tree is in fact an egg. The top half of this egg-world is divided into layers of pale green with several amorphous land masses in soft yellows, salmon and turquoise. In the centre is a constellation of tiny boxes representing houses, plus four tiny trees.

The lower half of the egg-world is unfortunately broken, so that teardrop-shaped blobs of yellow and salmon coloured stuff float over the bottom half of the map. A dotted line indicates where the bottom of the egg-world would have been if it hadn't cracked up and oozed its solidity.

All things flow downwards from the Zambu tree. Its roots are wound into a tight spiral tipped up to the picture plane. It could have been painted by Gustav Klimt in silvers and golds; it might have been an eye with a composite pupil but is obviously meant to be a nest.

The nest contains half a dozen smaller eggs. From the bottom of the spiral-nest – still working downwards – grows a larger egg or apple from which a further sequence of roots radiates into 'continents' or land masses. Below that are the broken bits which appear to bob around in space on their wide bottoms and pointy heads.

I haven't looked at the Zambu tree map since after Molly. I recall thinking at the time, 'How dare they? How dare they make a tree the divine centre of the world?'

The new inspector is a woman. Her name is Dr Chadwick. Ruth. She's an arboriculturalist and a Deputy Director of Planning at the DoE. Before this she was in charge of the Manchester Airport protest. Not what they'd expected.

Bea and Housego are here on behalf of the campaign and Mick Merriman, yes, is here on behalf of the Park Authority. Alan Amwath arrives late in his yellow sports car with the top down, blond hair streaked and streaming in the wind; golden retriever in the passenger seat also streaked and streaming.

I'm here representing no one. Bea stopped at my house and said, 'Come on,' so I came. She's With Me.

Amwath parks in the layby beside Beech 31. For some reason Bea thinks this is hilarious. He slips the dog's lead over the steering wheel and leapfrogs over the door. This strikes me as more hilarious.

'Hello, there, sorry I'm late, I was delayed.' The inspector shakes hands all round but doesn't get too close. Introductions over, she begins with Beech no.1 and works her way up the avenue, stops at each tree slated for felling or hulking. Beech no.2 comes first. The Park Authority's report recommends shortening by four metres all major branches hanging over the road. She's picturing it lopped. 'It will be okay with the foliage still on,' she says, 'but dire in winter. Have you taken that into account?' Mick mumbles something about safety over aesthetic considerations, and we move on.

At Beech no.24 she asks, 'What's the justification here?' Lays on hands. Is she conducting a healing session? Amwath reads from his notes, 'Crown growth becoming very weak; pocket of decay on north of trunk at one metre.' She bends back to examine the crown, then fits her hand to the 'pocket of decay'. Says it's too small a pocket to justify felling the whole tree. 'Besides,' she says, 'it's growing far enough away from the road so there's no threat to passing traffic. I suggest thinning some branches and stopping there.'

Amwath looks at Mick, Housego looks at Bea, Mick looks at Amwath, Bea looks at the tree. I look across the road at a waving hedge.

'Next,' says Inspector Ruth.

Bea tee-hees.

Beech no.31. Amwath looks down at his notes then up at the tree. The crown is weak and ragged. Indication of declining vigour. The main fork is holding water. On the north-east he's found an area of dead bark with the bodies of some insect. 'Anyway,' he says, 'it's too close to the layby. Our view is, it should be felled.'

The inspector strolls out to the middle of the road and examines it from there, then from the layby. 'Visually important,' she calls out. 'This corner will be devastated without it.' She wants Housego's view: 'Is it likely to fall?' Housego says since its weight is leaning slightly to the north, he reckons it's unlikely to fall towards the road or layby.

'Thank you.' Another stroll around the tree, stroking it as she goes. Could be a cat or a lover. 'A muscular beauty,' she says. Somehow she makes it sound original. 'But rotten to the core,' says Mick Merriman, not sounding quite so original. Bea Merriman reaches forth as if to protect the tree from the news of its rottenness.

'Give me some more evidence.'

'Arborsonic test. Advanced rot in the lower third with decay at the centre.' Mick Merriman squeezing like it's his granny. Then in with his thumbnail.

Bea Merriman moves in closer with her palm.

David Housego holds on round the other side and higher up.

The inspector is leaning into the tree with her whole body. 'Pity,' she says.

Pat pat, poor tree. Housego, Ruth and Bea go round and round the poor tree. I do not go round because I don't pity the poor tree. I stay perfectly still, just outside the circle of circling pitying people. Their arms form spokes.

The inspector examines the tree using no arborsonic device and no needles. Prior to the invention of the stethoscope, a doctor would bend his head to the patient's chest. Nothing between her and the tree – only the palpating of bark.

Amwath, on the other hand, is tapping with a device resembling a metal detector. Stethoscopes were invented to save the doctor the embarrassment of having to touch the patient directly.

Bea Merriman uses all of her fingers, scale of D on the piano.

Housego reaches further up.

Amwath doesn't touch, Mick doesn't touch, I don't touch. Not the touchy-feely brigade, we three. Housego rises and falls on the balls of his feet. 'I think the rot is actually regressing, not progressing,' he says. 'My feeling is it could last another fifty years or more. Keep an eye on it and let it die naturally. A bit of decay is neither here nor there, it's part of the natural life-cycle of the tree, its dying down.' The bouncing lends a rhythm to his pronouncements. Quite persuasive, if you hadn't already made up your mind.

'You don't kill a person because they show signs of weakness, do you?' chips in Bea.

The inspector is not saying.

'Besides, if you go around labelling trees dangerous or potentially dangerous, that gives you *carte blanche* to fell anything.' Bea again.

'Nonsense,' Amwath's saying. 'This tree is in imminent danger of falling.'

The inspector takes a good look at the tree (in imminent danger of falling).

Then she takes another good look at Amwath's car parked under the tree in imminent danger of falling.

And then she regards his dog going woofwoof in a car parked just under the tree in imminent danger of falling.

Allows a nice three beats or so before informing Amwath, deadpan, 'Frankly, I'd be more convinced if you hadn't parked your convertible underneath it with your dog inside.'

Ho ho, woofwoof.

And then she's serious again.

'I think we might just be silent for a moment and listen to the tree before making a decision.' That's what she says. A tree listener. Healing energy. Secrets waiting to be discovered. No embarrassment whatsoever.

Bea goes into meditation mode, Housego drops his head to his chest. They don't seem to mind this at all. Sounds of breathing, rustling, fidgeting, a zipper being pulled up and down. Mick turns his back, could be about to pee on Beech 32, Amwath flips his fringe. His dog makes strange whiney noises so he goes and lets him out. Housego hunkers down and goes pet pet. Mick is starting to lose it. 'You people are nuts. If you leave these trees standing you'll be left with a mess: hulks, ropes, bracings. It's crazy.'

'You people' now includes Inspector Ruth.

'You seem, gentlemen,' she says, 'to regard these beeches as things that stand in your way – our way, our cars' way. But let me remind you they were here before we were. Other cultures wiser than our own believe in the sacredness of the tree. They need our protection not our censure.'

A fine speech.

Amwath's got to go. Mick Merriman, about to go pop, says he can't believe what's going on. 'How can you let yourself be bamboozled by these people?' nodding at his wife and Housego. 'They don't know what they're talking about.'

The inspector begs to differ. 'We have here one of our finest arbori-culturalists.' Housego, she means.

'Balls,' says Mick Merriman and with that, as they say, he reaches into his back pocket.

Now what can Mick Merriman be wanting from his back pocket? The longest screwdriver you've ever seen, and before anyone can stop him he's got it buried to the hilt into Beech 31. Jiggles it around, causing dry dead wood to come tumbling out.

'You pig,' says his wife.

'See that?' Rotted through and through. Crumbling, dead. 'That satisfy you?'

This is what's known as a tricky moment. A large tree with a small hole in its side, losing bits of itself by the second. Stick out your thumb, staunch the flow.

Now eat your words.

Not a happy moment for Inspector Ruth.

'Oh, shit,' she says. 'Sorry, looks like you're right after all.' Kicks the ground. 'This tree, with regret, will have to go.'

And then someone else says, 'No.'

Now, this 'No' doesn't appear to be addressed to any particular person or action nor has it been properly prepared, with an intake of breath or an opening up of the chest. It just decides to come, but not easily. Not the open-throated release of an opera singer but the rusty gush of an old fumarole. Nuh ... nuh ... nuh ... guttering and stuttering. But when it comes, which it does, you sense it's a 'No' that's been hiding in there for years, and a 'No' that's been kept low like that, once let out, tends to go high and wide: an extra- 'No'; a last-of-the-fireworks- show 'No'; an off-the-Richter-scale of a 'No'; a 'No' that, once released, rises up into the roots of your teeth and splits you down the middle like a dead tree; a syllable both so low and so high it may be inaudible, except to Amwath's dog wherever it is by now.

And all of the people gathered round the tree stopped what they were doing while, down the Valley, horses whinnied and Tony's pigs up the Valley chased each other's tails, and the Wild Things plus the Maid of Ealinghearth swooped down, picked up the 'No' and gift-wrapped Molly's tree with it. Round and round the precious boughs: rag curls, mummy strips, raw silk bandages shot with pain-threads, illuminated cobwebs after rain.

Diva's trill, possession by coyote? Why the 'No'? As the sawdust came spewing out of the beech, so the 'No' came yodelling out of me. Instant Conversion? Transcendental Experience? Do I now quit mapmaking and go off to the Himalayas, join the Chipko Movement, the Green Belt Women; become a hugger-planter of trees, a rescuer from the axe and the chainsaw?

Or is it (was it) something much less specific, not to do with trees at all?

Molly's Beech.

Let's just recap for a moment. When all this began the beeches were a source of distress. It's true I could not bring myself to go past them down the Valley. To get to Hawkshead I'd detour for miles around the Lakes. Seeing them wasn't the only problem, though. All I had to do was think about them and the discomfort level would rise to severe. I didn't choose to think about them, they chose me.

On the other hand, I chose to be their nearest neighbour.

A curious contradiction, no?

No. A nay-saying, a bray of denial – it could have meant anything. No, don't fell any of the beeches? No, don't fell *Molly's* Beech? No, don't let it have happened? No, get me out of here? No, go away and leave me alone? Was it, in other words, a meaningful 'No' or just some generalized cry in the wilderness? My period was due?

The options are confusing.

The beeches are safe. They could go on for fifty more years with tending.

The beeches are not safe. Might as well start a fresh planting now.

No one knows the right answer, although some people think they know. Take a risk, care for what's there. Or: Play safe, think tidy, plant new.

This year I was asked to map the beeches. I went and sat among them, in the protection of my car. Forced myself to do the job. Measured and paced and stomped around the place in my great big semi-waterproof boots, a real pro. Kicked the beeches as if they were dumb car tyres until they began to lose their kickback.

Is this turnaround time, where I see the light? The beech not as enemy and destroyer but as keeper of life, guardian of memory. The Rusland Beeches? Oh yes, very precious, to be protected at all costs. That blissful identification with Nature, with rebirth. The tree is she. The culmination of a long and painful but ultimately healing process. It will come, predicted the bereavement counsellor, it will come.

On the other hand, I know perfectly well that the tree is not my dead daughter incarnate but a large leaf-bearing, bark-bearing, nut-bearing vegetable. Nor is it the divine centre of the universe.

I still feel queasy passing that strung-out bay of snatchers. Long for them, at times, to be disappeared out of this Vale of Swallowy Amazony Tears.

Beech 31. That night, after the 'No', I dreamt of stripping its bark off – and you know what happens to a tree without its bark. I used a wall-paper brush, first wetting the trunk thoroughly then stripping it off with my fingernails. Systematically, strip by strip, rib by rib. Tall enough and loony enough and taloned enough. The stripped beech ended up looking like an exposed supermodel.

So much for instant conversion, right?

21

Map of the Interior World

Drawer 11: Map of the Interior World.

Here is the Earth as we know it, with its skin of continents and oceans and so forth on the rim, but deep inside – buried beneath fifteen hundred miles of the Earth's crust – is the secret Interior World containing the lands of Bilbimtesirol or Plutusia, Atvatabar, Mylosis, Hilar ... ; and at the very core of that already deep dark world is their sun, radiating rays of warmth. *Swang*, it's called.

Magda was heavily pregnant at the time. She lay on the floor practising her panting, huff huff, belly stuck up in all its proud rotundity. Jay knelt by her side. 'How do you know you're pregnant?' he asked. She peered at him over her raised horizon. Did he think she'd swallowed the globe?

'What are you on about?'

What he was on about was that mostly we are barely aware of what goes on inside of us. Jay was interested in such matters: material bodily matters, matters of mind and matters of body and how the two link up – or fail to do so. He loved drawing Necker Cubes showing those parts of the body we're unconscious of; the autonomic nervous system, certain internal hormonal shifts, and so on.

Magda thought about what was inside of her – the thoughtfully skinned-over and enfolded-away bits, the vital but messy physiological functions. Organ-works, pump of pumps, dark interior; or, as her father might have put it if he'd thought about such things (he hadn't): *Terra Incognita*.

I could name it Swang, she thought.

'What I mean is,' Jay said, 'in depth disappearance, the internal body recedes. There's all this, this viscerality inside of us which we're barely aware of.' And then he added, 'Even in pregnancy.' So great was the urgency of his philosophical delivery he began panting with her. 'Even in pregnancy (huff huff) the mother experiences gestational processes only indirectly through their global effects on her body: nausea, craving for chillis and ice-cream, and so on, but she cannot really experience the inside of her body because it's hidden away – she only responds to signals that affect her bodily well-being on the surface, as it were.'

As it were? A fillip of acid shot upwards, unfathoming itself somewhere near her heart. 'Dead wrong,' she said. 'I *am* aware of the inside of my body.' She added the words deeply and keenly. Jay smiled in a fatherly sort of way, placing his palm over her keenly deeply-felt belly. He informed her she was in a highly-strung state. 'Of course, in the latter stages of pregnancy – such as this – there is greater awareness, what we call an interoceptive experience of the foetus's movements.'

Magda felt it.

This was an atypical experience.

He felt for the head pressing against the abdominal wall – there. 'Yet,' he continued, 'as with all visceral processes, such perception is highly limited.' He sat back, righted himself, gazed somewhere into deep space. 'Traces of a vast invisible realm,' he intoned. A lovely, impressive bubble formed around him. He became highly plastic himself so that all his inside stuff showed, and his surrounding fluid plus membrane were also see-through. It was quite distracting watching him float around in his heavy liquid environment, doing somersaults and backflips (in slow motion). Bubbles were coming out of his mouth, which were turning his life-liquid iridescent. He was speaking – not that she could understand a word of it through all that goop – but it was so impressive she didn't like to ruin it. But she did. Prick went the bubble.

'Listen to me,' she told him. 'I have an inside, a very definite inside; I have never felt so, how can I put it, inside myself. Nor does it feel limited; it feels absolutely unlimited: in fact, I'd say over ninety per cent of my awareness is located in there. Not the shell but the mollusc. So far inside myself you could almost say the foetus is enfolding me.' She nearly added 'Swang' but managed not to.

There was a pause during which her husband took quite a lot of air into his lungs. 'Ecstasis,' he went, expelling it again.

22

Map of the Sexual Parts

Drawer 13.

Yes, I've washed my hands.

First comes the Male, an Anterior View of the penis with the scrotum opened up. Next comes the more complicated Female including a Surface View plus an Internal (Medial) View. The Map of the Sexual Parts is no different from that of Rusland Forest or Grizedale Sculpture Park; no different, that is, in What Really Matters: Where you are and where you want to go. Each part is labelled and lettered. To match letter to part go to the Key, as you would on any map.

If you have lost your way a map can be helpful. However, if you don't know where you are to begin with the map will be useless or only serve to confuse you further. How can you know where you're going if you don't know where you are in relation to where you want to be or have been? It's important to have a starting or reference point.

If you are for instance a penis (J) you may begin your journey by gently parting (E) and (F) and entering at (D), pressing upwards at (I) along the way. Initial progress may be slow but exquisitely observed. As you approach the neck of (C) you are tempted to pick up speed but another possibly higher impulse from higher up your body tells you to slow down again, boy, slow down.

Tucked right up. Pulsing like a stretched star.

However, if you are a sperm your heterosexual journey begins now, here at the female's (C). Shot from (B), you go wriggling against gravity up through (E, F, D) into (C) where you will attempt to batter your way through the membrane of a bonny bloated ovum. Who may or may not have you. Who will probably coddle you in a substance so acidic you will go into instant decomposition.

Or, if she is in a receptive mood, you may be able to implant yourself. This event may be described variously as: (1) an invasion (the foetus's beginnings thus rooted in violence); (2) a mutually agreeable entrance (thus rooted in mutuality); or (3) the egg (x times bigger than a measly wriggling sperm) plays thumbs-up thumbs-down (the roots of female power).

Now change places. Suppose you are that ovum, that egg. Your journey is a shorter one, naturally. At the beginning of the month, having received a chemical message from the moon (circumstances auspicious for going on journey), you begin travelling that well-worn but justly famous path from (A) to (C). It will take you roughly two weeks to complete, at which point you will bury yourself in the lining of the womb which is now nicely plumped up for your comfort. There you will wait for a mate (see sperm's journey, above).

(C) marks the spot.

All of this assumes of course that you have not interfered with Nature.

The doctor's waiting room is a converted storefront, long and narrow with chairs lining both sides so it feels as if you're in a space capsule. Either you study the people opposite, and they you, or you try not to. Or you read one of the yellowing curling leaflets in the window.

For You in Your Loss
Healthy Bones For All the Family
Reducing the Risks of Cot Death
Cancer Care
Summer Studies

Or you watch the children playing or try not to watch the children playing. Or you read a magazine article on 'The Benefits of Sex'. Sex makes your skin and hair look clear and radiant. It has aerobic benefit (about equal to climbing two flights of stairs). It helps regulate your periods and makes you more fertile. It builds better bones. It relieves stress and stored emotional pain. (One orgasm can give you six pain-free hours. This can apply whether the pain is emotional or physical: arthritis, whiplash, depression following a major life trauma.)

But it has to be *REGULAR*. Being celibate is not so bad; the real problem is **getting a lot and then nothing**. Feast-or-famine; sex-fest followed by fallow-fest. This is the worst sex-life pattern because it confuses the endocrine system and you end up walking around with a post-menopausal level of oestrogen. *Masturbation may benefit vaginal tissue but it doesn't bolster oestrogen levels*. For that, you need a partner. Regular week-by-week and day-by-day and night-by-night sex is the message.

Question: How do you get it if you're not in a **REGULAR** relationship?

At this point the doctor stuck his head round the door and called 'Next!' It was Magda's turn so she left the magazine on the chair and went into the doctor's office.

'So, Mrs Beard' – she didn't bother to correct him – 'what can I do for you?'

What she was really bursting to ask him was why on earth the NHS didn't invest in an army of sex workers instead of health workers, since sex was obviously the universal cure-all. Instead she said, 'I'd like a new diaphragm.'

'You've had one before?'

'Yes. But it's been a while.'

'They don't wear out normally.'

'No, but I'd still like a new one.'

'Of course. You've had children, I see.'

'Child, one.'

'Not planning any more then, no, wise at your age, just pop your things off and pop up onto the examining table and I'll be right with you.'

What a lot of popping, thought Magda.

When the doctor had gone Magda pulled her knees to her chest and rolled herself up. The doctor pulled the curtain aside.

'Now if you can just slide down to the edge for me and spread nice and wide.'

Magda slid down to the edge as instructed spreading nice and wide. By this time she was completely flat however which made it difficult for the doctor to do his internal examination.

'You'll have to relax, Mrs Beard.'

'I am,' she told him.

'Try harder.'

The walls of her womb did an Edgar Allan Poe, her pelvic floor was floored and her womb hung in a 'Y' shape by its armstruts, like one of Goya's Disasters of War. She took a deep breath, held it in, then let go with a great whoosh. The woken-up womb stretched her Fallopians, just like Olive Oyl pumping iron!

By now she was well blown up. All those invisible, unfeelable, unknowable internal organs were now imaginable, feelable, knowable. I could map the whole area in swirling pulsing colour on my computer screen, she thought. She felt her heart contracting and releasing and shuddering, intricate rhythms just inside the girdle of skin, fat and muscle. She even became aware of her digestive tract which was joined in turn by other organs in its dance, a peristaltic wave, a gastrointestinal flutter. The sphincter loosens its grip, the bellows collapses in on itself ...

'That's mu-uch better, Mrs Beard. Lovely. You can pop your things back on now.' And he peeled off his rubber gloves and dropped them in the bin and went tap-tap on his computer, and then he handed her a prescription and Magda thanked him and popped out of his office.

Monday night. Sara is telling us about how the tree is the great symbol of being alive. We are trees, therefore we are alive. 'The umbilical cord of each newborn child,' she says, 'according to Native American legend, is said to be attached to a tree. A tree and a child both grow from a tiny seed.' A tree and a child, a child and a tree.

We work in pairs again, taking turns being different sorts of trees. One kind is light with shallow roots, like a birch or very young beech, while the other is well rooted, say a mature oak. As we're imagining ourselves like this, our partner tries to push us over. 'But be gentle,' Sara reminds us, 'a gentle pressure will do. We don't want any accidents.'

In Flatland being 'rooted' like a tree isn't possible since there is no ground, no up or down; you're simply there, floating in space. Gravity in the Flatland dictionary would probably be defined as *Sci-fi*: A purely theoretical concept by which the mythical creatures of Spaceland are held fast to the ground by what they call their *feet*.

Why not emulate a stream or waterfall or the sky or the very air itself?

'Who's first?' we ask.

Housego points at me.

'Am I the pusher or the pushed?'

'Which do you want?'

'Don't mind.' I shrug. 'Okay, I'll be the tree.'

I close my eyes and plant my birch feet as best I can, what with their inadequate root system. Housego asks am I ready and I say, 'Ready,' and he pushes me over, easy. Next I'm an oak with a vast gnarled root system disappearing right through the floor and into the ground. 'Ready?' 'Ready.' This time he pushes harder and I rock slightly backwards but stay standing. 'This isn't an experiment,' I grumble, 'it's a self-fulfilling prophecy.' Housego doesn't disagree.

'My turn,' he says.

As a birch Housego is also an easy pushover. As a mature specimen he's heavy, you can see how heavy he's growing, lowering his centre of gravity, pushing down his roots, his whole body quite trunk-like and grey and those big feet so well planted they may never come up again. Imagine giving an oak the heave-ho! Not possible, you think, but a beech, say, one of those grabby thug-like beeches, everybody knows beeches aren't safe and this one's stuffed with dead heartwood showing signs of advanced rot, a column of sawdust, a hollow sham, no sap sapping and anyway roots shallow and dry and more like claws, clawing the earth except the earth is dry too so it won't hold for much longer, except a few of the cleverer root-shoots find their way into rock and between boulders, which makes him/it bedrocked but still precarious. One big wind and ... Oh you like a good challenge so you breathe right down into your belly then take two fingers and jab fast as hard as you can at the stupid dangerous beech roughly level with where its branches branch out, which is obviously just the right place because it's now leaning over at a strange angle. The bigger they are the harder they fall, you're thinking, as a whole group of bystanders goes running to examine the damage. Poor tree.

David Housego follows me home in his Land-Rover. Are you all right? Yes, fine, but are *you* all right? What have I done? How can I say I'm sorry? Forget it, he wasn't really hurt and besides, it livened up the class. But still I'm having to check him all over for bruises, healing hands and healing lips, and since after all these things are better done with clothes off, up we go to my bedroom to indulge in some modestly aerobic healing following major life trauma. Coupling For Health and Well Being. Add a dollop of Alexander expansiveness and where does it get you? Attached not to the ground by your soles but to another person by your primary sex organs; more than the sum of your tangled parts.

And all the Flatlanders gathered round to watch through their wedge-shaped eyes and were sore amazed at what they saw. Two beings fused together at the hips yet wriggling about in three dimensions. Impossible! Treasonable! Oough! They shut their eyes and refused to watch. Everyone knew there were only two dimensions except A Square who, sceptic and scholar that he was, chose to believe the evidence of his own eye. What he saw baffled him. It also excited him. All he'd ever known was flat-pack sex. This was something else! It reminded him of a dream he'd once had, of Spaceland dragonflies doing their lilting bounding mating dance.

Housego took up space. When Magda was with him she was no more a line than he was. From time to time she was reminded of something she had lost but – like A Square himself – as a visitor in Spaceland, the experience of all that wraparound space was so very distracting she soon forgot. At one point she thought, Housego does not offer himself completely, bits of him belong to others. But then bits of her belonged to others too, so that was probably all right.

Gradually she returned to normal. At one stage in the detumescing process – imagine air escaping a lilo – she still appeared rather tuberous (a rooty sort of Line); but that passed too, and by morning she was returned to the packaging that was herself. When Housego had gone, Ms Line began – like all good Flatlanders – to deny that such a thing had ever taken place.

23

Map of the Face

Magda knifed a triangularish chunk of butter off the main slab, onto the side of her plate. Jay followed with a straight cut which corrected the lopped-off angle and also left the butter in better shape for wrapping up and putting back in the fridge. His butter pats, being flatter, tended to melt faster. Molly, meanwhile, was pointing to the mugshots in the line-up of muffin-tragedies catalogued in the recipe book.

'What's that one?'

'Read what it says underneath.'

Molly read.

It was the Sunday morning after Easter. Magda, Jay and Molly were sitting around the kitchen table at Ealinghearth Cottage where they some-times went for holidays. They were eating bran muffins made according to a recipe given to Magda by her American mother-in-law. Molly pulled open a muffin, only to reveal a mess of tunnels, as if worms or slugs had crept through; plus it was sunken in on top as if weary of life.

'How come it's like that?' Molly asked. Magda handed her the battered old cookbook, find out for yourself. 'What ... Can ... Go ... Wrong ... With ... Muffins', she read, pointing to the illustrations which showed four muffins in a row, three inadequate and one perfect. The problem muffins were: (1) lopsided; (2) sunken; (3) holey. The perfect one looked as if it was wearing a top hat, fine even texture.

Molly divided a butter pat, applied them to the halves of her muffin, observed them sink into the holes before delivering her judgment, 'I think this is a combination Wormy-Weary Muffin.' 'Could be,' said Magda who was fed up with muffin-typologies. I'm an okay mother, she thought, but sometimes I'd rather have an adult conversation.

'So what are you working on?' she asked Jay.

'I've begun collaborating.'

'With?'

'Somebody in the English department – you wouldn't know her.' He took a mouthful of muffin, shed crumbs.

'So what's it about?'

'Oh, Theory of the Body in Literature.'

'What does that mean when it's at home?'

'It means I do my body consciousness stuff and she looks at it in terms of, oh say, flat and round characters. Forster, for instance ...'

Unfortunately, what Forster thought would have to wait because at this point Molly poured herself off her chair and started lurching around the kitchen dragging one leg, 'What am I? What am I? I'm a Wobbly Muffin!' – so convincingly played that she fell over clunking her head on the Aga rail, 'Owowow'. 'C'mere,' said Jay, mouth full of depressed muffin. Rubbing Molly's head with one hand, taking up where he left off with the other.

'Forster is the spokesperson for realism. Round characters are best; flat ones are comic stereotypes. "Look at Mr Pickwick sideways and he's like a gramophone record." Quote unquote. But when you get to postmodernism it gets turned on its head.'

'I can do a headstand, wanna see?'

'No, not now, you just hurt your head – give it a rest.'

'How?' asked Magda.

'It flaunts its flatness. What was bad news before is now what it's all about. Flat characters, in a different sense, are in.'

'You mean like Flat Stanley?' This was Molly. The ends of her fingers were shiny with butter. The parting in her hair wandered like a road, creating a sort of tonsure out of which the hair was pulled up and tied with a pink wiggly elastic. She didn't blink although she turned from one parent to the other to observe the effect of her question on them. The elastic made it hard to rub the bruise on her head.

'Exactly,' said Jay, working his thumb under the elastic. They exchanged looks over her ponytail which said, more or less, can this kid be for real? Later that day, Magda noticed the buttons on her jacket were perfect hemispheres, shiny black, in which you could see a distorted version of your own face. They told her how clever she was.

But now they'd better get a move-on if they wanted to get up to Grizedale before noon. So, 'Let's go,' they said, and after putting the dishes in the sink and throwing jackets and apples into their rucksacks and panniers, took off on their bikes up the Rusland Valley towards Grizedale Forest. When they got there Molly had a go on the giant chicken slide. Magda and Jay watched as she crawled into its craw, mounted a flight of stairs behind six other children and, when it was her turn, slid down. Halfway down she flipped into one of the side troughs and from there over the side. The parents rushed over but she wasn't really hurt. They bought her a hot chocolate at the cafe, then at last took off for the sculpture trail.

I sit here, thinking about Molly making a scene in order to get a look-in while her parents are having some stupid academic conversation. Round and flat, real and not-real. And then I try to picture her in the round – the disc as a little globe – and I can't. Try again. Pinch out a neck which causes a smaller globe to bobble up on top; raise arms, divide legs, put down feet: Play-Doh of the imagination. How can it hurt, Magda? You are merely doing what people like E.M. Forster did: building a character.

Something is wrong. If only I were a sculptor, say, with a knowledge of anatomy, I could build her bone by bone, organ by organ – but I'm not. In any case, I could never reproduce the *progression* of her growing-up. It wouldn't be practical. A six-year-old, for instance, would take six years to build: the advancing of the skeleton, the mixing and bombarding of the hormones, the stretching and thickening of the skin, the formation and reformation of the features, and so on.

She had a flattish nose ... she had a small scar running diagonally from her left temple near her left eye ... In the end it comes down to a few static elements in a facial landscape. Provide a detail or two and leave the rest to the imagination or to some crude logic. Given a low forehead and flattish nose, the probability is her lower lip will be fuller than the average child's; given a deep roseate cheek chances are her hair and eye colouring will also be dark.

Go to your map cabinet, Magda. Put your hand on the knob of Drawer 9. Run your thumb around and over the roundness of the brass. The map cabinet was there then and is still here now. It reconnects you to a past which is older than any rogue memory too recent to count as history. Open Drawer 9, pull one out at random: *Phrenological Map* (English, 19th century). Notice how it's carved up and labelled:

Tact is located at the hairline.

Observation at the overhang of the browline.

Force lies with a doorknocker of a nose.

Firmness at the abnormally long top lip.

Will lies in the jutting jaw (mark of ambition).

This is how it was. Hokum and bunkum. Pseudo-taxonomies leading to pseudo-predictions, even more dangerous assumptions. Heads were routinely mapped and measured. Cesare Lombroso, the nineteenth century criminologist, headed the field, got off on measuring crania and assigning arbitrary so-called characteristics.

Thank heaven for progress? Not at all. Jay was addicted to the Science section of *The New York Times*. While I read about when Africa was last attached to Brazil and how old and far away everything is, Jay read about the brain, specifically the human brain, more specifically where things happen in the brain. He was into something called 'neural imaging'. 'So, how does it work?' I asked. He waved the paper around as if to conjure up a neuroscientific genie beside my cereal bowl or, read it for yourself, he probably meant, I can't be bothered to explain. But I carried on. 'I don't see where it gets us to know that the word for "bran flakes" excites a certain part of the brain whereas "toast" doesn't.' As Jay bit into his piece of toast, he became a model Lombrosian skinhead: over his right ear a tiny toast-shaped tattoo, lit up and flashing. 'Look,' I pointed, 'right there.' Molly joined in, clapping, 'Toast on the brain, toast on the brain!' Jay ignored us both. 'I should have thought,' he muttered, 'you'd be more excited about the brain being organized on geographical principles.' Except I wasn't (and I'm still not) so I said, 'The brain isn't a lump of land.'

Now he and Molly are both gone. Jay gone, Molly gone: do these phrases go ping in different parts of my brain and if so, what does it tell me? Is the organizing principle the word 'gone' or 'family'? Why should I care? I don't – not about Jay's current academic preoccupations. What worries me is this recent so-called subtle and sophisticated technological development. Map the brain? Do a Lombroso update? Why? The Victorians also thought they were being subtle, sophisticated, etc. and out of all that mess modern forensic 'science' grew; and here we are now in this mess.

Mugshots, identikits, photofits: the relics of his kinky phrenological taxonomy are alive and, if not well, thriving in the study of crime. The Museum of Turin has on display the preserved severed head of Lombroso himself, its cranial bumps betraying a distinct criminal tendency. According to his theory most of us suffer from 'apish stigmata': low brow, 'weak' chin, short snub nose. Molly certainly did. Her photograph reveals sure signs of incipient degeneracy. Delinquent and criminal-to-be. Count your blessings she didn't get the chance.

What did Molly look like? they asked. I provided a photograph. 'It's not a good likeness, I'm afraid; she was hard to capture on still film.'

What did she look like? They peered closely at the photograph, blew it up many times its original size, projected it on a screen. Big Molly. They outlined the area around her eyes in black, concentrating hard, taking notes. They were doing their job earnestly, I was not doing mine. I said, 'Look, this is a waste of time. If she turns up, she turns up. You'll know it's her.' They said, details help. They said the eyes reveal something called 'the micro-expression'. I said: 'There wasn't any one expression. She had a mobile face.' Finally they let me go, thanked me for my time, apologized for causing me 'undo distress'. I said, 'That's all right.' What else did they have to work with? A few scraps of material snagged on a tree. Possibly some footprints. Not much to go on.

The face is only a surface. Unless you're a geographer or an archaeologist, you map the surface features of the land. You read its expression from the visible. What you see is what you get.

Apparently we have forty-four facial muscles, more than any animal on earth. Imagine a face, say, a child's face. You say to her, 'Yes, you can go and play at the beeches, but only for half an hour, no more.' At first she's cross at being given a time limit. According to a bizarre nineteenth century Italian text called *The Mimicry of Ancient People Interpreted Through the Gestures of the Neapolitans*, there are ten possible expressions of anger from flaring the nostrils to the facial equivalent of 'pretending to bite one's elbow'. The child's expression is none of these. It's true some brow-knitting muscles are doing their thing but further down her face the pout-muscles are negotiating with the smile-muscles, which causes an asymmetry as well as a mini-tremble in the lip. The bottom, yes. And then there's nothing more to be seen because the child has run off with her mobile little face and her remaining twenty-minutes' worth of precious time.

Flesh out your character, pump air into her lungs, make her 'live'. Go on, cause her to breathe: in out, in out. I dare you, Magda.

No.

Why not?

Because it's the last thing in the world I want to do. Why would I want to conjure Molly? She's dead, gone, disappeared, vamoosed. She keeps trying to slip into the story – I can't help that – but in the end she has to be made to slip out and never show her sweet live face again. Where's Molly? Gone to the beeches. Gone.

Flat as Stanley. Slide her neatly away.

24

Sand Map

Monday night. 'Imagine you're lying on sand,' says Sara. 'Feel how your body sinks down into it, how the sand gives way to your body. Now, think of the map your body makes in it.'

She doesn't mean 'map', of course, she means imprint or mould in which the shape or outline left in the sand corresponds actually to the body that has pressed itself into it. A map is different. A map converts, scales down, represents space and the things in that space in a symbolic way. How do I get from here to there? What are the landmarks along the way?

'If you're having trouble focusing your attention in your body, try closing your eyes.'

I close them, but not too quickly. Prepare the dark, gather space around me like a duvet – but only summer weight, I wouldn't want to smother. My back is soft but heavy. Certain parts stay straight but others – backbones, bum, elbows, calves – sink below sea level. Strange earth forms seen from below.

Imagine grains of sand dropped one by one onto a flat surface. In time a pile forms; builds and builds until – this is the critical point – one more grain and you get an avalanche. The particular grain that triggers the avalanche may have caused it but doesn't explain it. To find an explanation, you have to move from the motion of the particular grain to the overall structure of the pile. This gets well into complex systems. The sand I am lying on is simple. Sand painted with a single swipe of an ochre paintbrush.

I continue to lie on the simple sand, a woman-shape spread out in the sun, drying. Wavy oatmeal-coloured seaweed. A man bends over the woman-shape, covering her in his shadow. He holds out a hand which she grabs onto, allowing herself to be raised up. At this point the scene begins to come to life, begins to change. She changes from weightless seaweed to waterlogged driftwood but the man, whom she recognizes, perseveres in lifting her up. He is her husband, partner: together they were once called parents. Now they have been given a new title, Bereaved Parents.

Hand in hand, the Bereaved Parents walked. Looked around them. Noticed a landscape bordering an estuary, an interesting area of limestone cliffs and scooping shifting tides. Familiar. Where they went just after it. Nosing out over the limestone cliff above them was a colony of environmentally-friendly green caravans. 'Pity,' said the Man. 'Pity,' repeated the Woman. They were now strolling along on the sea-washed turf with its cookie cutter cut-out shapes.

Their feet walked while their fingers foraged. They picked up shells and stones and driftwood twisted into dragon-shapes. The habit to do this was still there but then they'd forget why and drop them again. Still, their feet kept walking. A pair in their condition, predating, it seemed to them, the classification 'Bereaved Parents'.

'The thing about coasts,' the Woman began, 'is that they don't just end where sea begins. Land – stop – water: no, that is not how it works. What you have is a submerged, gradually descending, shelf. Any decent geological map will make this quite clear.' Such a clever woman, thought the Man.

They carried on walking, making footprints. Not a map of the foot but its imprint. Along with their own were those of: wading birds, horses, dogs, Nikes, walking boots, tractor tyres, worm tracks, arrows in a figure of eight made by oystercatchers, random pogo-stick holes (made by some mystery creature) and ordinary tide tracks: a whole shoreline of criss-crossings and scribblings.

They held hands, the turf was bouncy under their feet. Every few yards they had to stop because of a channel. Normally they would have jumped but jumping requires spring requires energy. Besides, the channels had deepened and widened into mini Grand Canyons. At first they stared into them, feeling helpless, then walked a bit further inland, paddling across isthmuses like children or very old people.

Where the sea-washed turf and sand ended, the mud flats began. Great clumps had broken off and stood stacked on edge in size-place formation, one slotted in behind the other, facing the sea, as in a school or large family portrait. The Woman thought of A Square and his Flatlander family, a collection of trapezoids, triangles, circles and lines, standing on edge, posing for a Victorian photographer. Cheese! Pop! But soon the effort of standing on end would be too much for them – boomph! They'd fall flat again and the sea would claim them back.

'Why does it happen?' This was spoken by the Man. It was something to say. A conversation. The exchange of information back and forth, back and forth. 'It happens because the sea hurls itself at the land. The estuary is tidal. Waves work by hydraulic action.'

'Hydraulic action,' repeated the man. It sounded nice and clean. The way he saw it was the sea shat or vomited up a lot of garbage onto the shore, here take this, which they were now wading through.

They stood with their toes hanging off the ragged trousered edge. They could do a song-and-dance routine, entertain the waves. They jumped down off the turf onto the tumbled clumps. Holding hands probably made it harder but they daren't let go.

'The waves come up and smack into the land,' continued the Woman. 'You can see how thick and matted the turf is – but that wave action is stronger. As it smashes against it, the wave crams air into the crevices between the layers, all that jumble of roots and stuff – anyway, it does it with such explosive force that when the wave retreats, the air left inside the clay expands and causes cracks that have already started to open up, and eventually it breaks off as chunks. As you see.'

He saw, she saw. Layers and levels. They continued over the muddy clumps: balanced, wobbled, slid. From time to time one of their feet would get stuck between two mud blobs. A long way down.

Down down, going down.

The Woman could see it wasn't that simple, that the fibrous turf was incredibly strong and would hang on, not breaking off from its roots even when the clay beneath let go. Hanging on by threads for, what, dear life? Connectedness?

She imagined, as the bore smacked, a ripping and wrenching louder than burlap, followed by a tremendous plop as the turf fragment fell into the sea. But then she doubted that it happened like that. Too sudden. Nature took its time, worked by a process of slow erosion. Months it would take, years.

She imagined the untwining of the fibres, a patient unkinking of wind-tangled child's hair – Ow ow ow you're hurting! – until that particular undermined chunk just let go, gave itself up to the splitting off and fell into the sea, leaving some fibres hanging on.

They kept going, out beyond where the dry mud and turf pies ended and the mud flats and river channel began. The tide was ripping in. That was called the bore.

In comes the tide over shiny green rocks
Out goes the tide washing everyone's socks

The Man and Woman were sunk up to the ankles in squidge. The mud rose or their knees lowered. Finally the Man shouted (over the roar of the bore), 'Tom Mix stuck in mud!' The Woman didn't get the allusion, which was American in origin, but she haha'd anyway. Played a piano piece on his palm: *Für Elise*. The bore karate-chopped them behind their knees, roared and bored while the undertow tugged. The wave left debris behind: a child's trainer, a driftwood dragon, plastic soda bottles.

'The oceanic equivalent of pooping,' the Woman commented.

'That's funny,' observed the Man.

And still the once-parents stood, or rather wobbled about, letting themselves be slapped and punched and generally knocked about by the boring, roaring bore. Stick figures back on the shore shouted at them but the mud was there, nearly to their knees, give or take, allowing for size difference. Out there the horizon was flat, you couldn't tell where water ended and land began. Piel Island, Barrow, even Humphrey Head, were misted in. They would become part of it.

The Woman thought about how a couple of Flatlanders would go about killing themselves. Why, they'd send themselves skimming onto water like frisbees – except they wouldn't drown, they'd float! Floating frisbee Flatlanders, hey! She started to laugh and then she doubled over

and couldn't stop. Flatlander Frisbees, circles, squares, triangles, ha ha
ha! She laughed till she toppled. The plop of her toppling snapped the
Man out of whatever numb-dumb state he was in so that he grabbed the
backs of the Woman's knees and pulled her legs free, one at a time, then
had to push her back up towards the shore with quite a lot of force before
the mud sucked her down again. This caused him to sink further. 'Wait
there,' she said, which was still more hilarious and set her off again. Even
so, she managed to find the driftwood dragon which he grabbed onto
while she pulled. Plop, they both went as they landed on their backs in
the higher, drier sand.

'And now open your eyes. Prepare to get up from your place in the
sand. Take your time, don't rush. Come out of it in the usual way. Over
onto your side in the foetal position, then roll up.'

I take my seat in the Alexander circle. A lot of dazed-looking people,
some still half-buried in sand. 'So, what did you leave behind?' She means
what worm-like tensions have we managed to cast off. Headaches, neck-
aches, backaches; fears, pressures, body constrictions. One person claims
to have shed her coldness, another her dislike of her own body.

'And you, Magda?' The class turns to me. I try to think of something
but nothing comes, so I pass. Perhaps I have lain too lightly on the sand.
There is comfort in this. I have caused the least disturbance, left nothing
behind. Such is the nature of flatness.

25

Heartland

'Now which of you,' asked Molly's teacher, 'thinks the earth is flat? Hands up. Okay, who thinks the earth is round? And who isn't sure? Molly Beard, you haven't raised your hand.'

'That's because it isn't round or flat – it's pear-shaped.'

'I see. Who told you that, Molly?'

'My mother, and she's a cartographer so she should know.'

(Her mother doesn't believe it's pear-shaped either but that's the closest fruit-approximation she could give her daughter, and also it depends on what kind of projection you are using, and so on; but anyway, it's in flux so it's quite wrong to suggest to small children the idea of a fixed forever geometrical shape.)

'Well, now,' says the teacher, 'that's very interesting, Molly, but for our purposes I think we can say it's more-or-less round.'

Magda's father stood beside his globe of the world. 'It isn't really round, you realize.' He poked and the world twirled: full turn, half turn, quarter turn. 'Get me a grapefruit if we have one,' he ordered. 'If not, an orange – oh, and a knife.'

'What kind of knife?' Magda, having learned the niceties of knife differences from her mother, was for once more precise than her father. 'Filleting or parer?'

'Sharp,' said her father. Her mother's knives were all sharp for cooking.

How do you hand over a knife? Handle first and you risk cutting your own hand; blade first and you look as if you're trying to stab him. The only solution was to put the knife down on the table beside the globe. As she did this, Magda wondered if he'd seen her problem, and if so why he hadn't tried to help her. He picked up the knife. In his other hand, the grapefruit.

So, how would she map the earth? She was not prepared. She should have been but she wasn't. What did mapping the earth have to do with knives and grapefruits?

He could see she was lost but the problem must be pursued. 'How do you go from the round planet which we call Earth' – tipping the globe with the point of the knife – 'to a flat representation?' In other words, how do you take the skin of the earth and open it all out, North Pole to South Pole, Eastern to Western Hemisphere; lay it flat and wide so people can take it all in in a glance?

The clue she knew was in the question. Skin of the earth. She pictured him slitting the skin off the world and laying it flat but in doing so the land shapes would be distorted.

Still, she didn't know. (A knife for cutting out your tongue?)

He explained, patiently, about tangents and secants; conical projections and triangulation points. He put the knife to the grapefruit, the tip went in through the skin to where the fruit began. Stopped there. You couldn't tell if the knife-hand or the grapefruit-hand did the impaling; or if each played a willing part.

He undressed the grapefruit, slitting its skin into patterns for Ali Baba's pantaloons. Squashed them flat with the heel of his hand. 'There you are,' he said. 'There lies the solution.'

It lay on the beeswax polished table.

The party is held at one of the campaigners' houses in Kendal. We travel together – Housego, Bea and me. I drive, Bea sits in the back to give Housego more leg room. Her hair is sprinkled with glitz & gleam, distinctly in a shiny mood. Mine hugs my scalp like a shadow. Bea says I have the right-shaped head for such an extreme haircut. 'I'd look like a monk or a concentration camp victim. On you, it's elegant.' Say thank you, Magda.

'Thanks.'

Snow, also shiny but sluggish, is happening around us. We stop to pick up Housego who lives, as befitting a woodsman, in a cottage deep in

Satterthwaite Wood. He's wearing a new fleece. Crystals adhere to it, causing it to sparkle, the fibres to bloom into mini flower heads.

'You're so pink,' Bea tells him. Pink, a single neat but very plucky type of word. He looks down at himself as if he's forgotten to get dressed. Then Bea says, 'Only four, isn't it fantastic?' Housego says he supposes it's better than ten but even one unnecessary felling leaves something to be desired.

'Still, a victory,' she pronounces. The real thing this time, not that sad excuse ('it could have been worse') we had at the Farmer's Arms.

She'd had a letter from Ruth Chadwick, the DoE's inspector. They were refusing to lift the Tree Preservation Order, thus going against the Park Authority's latest plan to fell ten and operate on eighteen more. In the end, they recommended felling only four. 'Which four?' I ask, and she says she's not sure, she can look up the numbers, but definitely 31. Housego's hand briefly covers mine on the gear lever, a gesture which could be interpreted in several ways.

The party is in one of those grand Victorian villas on Kendal Green, up fifty slippery steps. The door is open. At one end of the room is a refectory table with a forest of bottles plus bowls of nibbles and things to dip. We add our offerings. On the wall behind hangs a banner saying WE WON! with a stencil of spray-painted marching tree-shapes. The consensus seems to be that four is a small price to pay for keeping an avenue of fifty. Housego still begs, quietly, to differ. About twenty to thirty people have already gathered. In the background, music.

Bea curls herself onto an enormous black cushion on the floor. Silver-rimmed spectacles, silver fingernails, earrings and bracelets, transparent bubble shoes with silver flecks. Look at the moon's reflection beamed across water, where is it aimed? At you, of course. That is how the eye sees: selfishly, stupidly. You are never the only one drawn.

Mick Merriman? He's at home babysitting.

Janet Housego? She's at a research meeting. A babysitter's looking after the kids.

Housego fetches Bea a paper plateful of food and a glass of wine, then stands guard while she picks and drinks. When she's finished, he takes her empties and returns with a slice of chocolate cake on a clean paper plate with a clean green napkin folded on top.

Darwin described religious devotion as consisting of love, complete submission to an exalted and mysterious superior plus a strong sense of dependence, fear, reverence and gratitude. Only when the revered one is completely sated will the worshipper consider feeding.

I fill my own plate and join a woman called Jo who's doing research into gender and self-esteem in four- and five-year-olds. Well, how interesting! And how do you assess such a thing? Using a questionnaire, of course. Questions about dressing themselves, what they think they look like, how well they can read, write, draw, play a musical instrument; are they good at helping mother/father/granny/grandad/ brother/sister? etc.

'What about measuring self-sufficiency?'

'Oh yes,' she says, 'we have a question, "Do you often play on your own?" We also have, "How far do you go from home to play?"'

'And this presumably measures adventurousness?'

'Yes, and confidence. We have a scale of confidence.'

'What if their parents have forbidden them to go beyond their own property? What if they live in a bad neighbourhood? Your findings could be skewed.'

'Sure, we've allowed for that by asking, for instance, "Do your parents tell you not to go very far/play with strangers, etc.?" Then we weight that against their answers. Some are less inclined to obey than others.'

'How do you know they're telling the truth?'

She smiles. 'You should be a social scientist. We try to take bravado into account.'

'How?'

'Through observation. You get good at spotting when a child is starting to embroider or exaggerate. Voice, body language, that sort of thing. Not always, of course: some children are natural-born actors.'

'So the data isn't a hundred per cent reliable?'

'Of course not, but nothing is.'

'And your findings so far?'

'So far,' she says, 'it's as you would expect. Little girls are more timid physically. They also worry about how they look and about pleasing their parents or other adults.'

'If it's so predictable, why do the research?'

'Ouch,' she says. Better get some chocolate cake before it all disappears.

It's one of those long two-knocked-into-one rooms. At the window end people are dancing; at the back people are eating and drinking; in the middle they're discussing the DoE decision and the forthcoming Management Plan. They seem to think the four trees will be felled quite soon.

'When is quite soon?'

'April – before the bulk of the tourists arrive. Isn't that right, Bea?'

I'm sitting on the floor near Bea. She says she supposes so, but Mick will know for sure. Housego sits down beside me and as he does so, manages to slosh some of his wine on the grey wool carpet. Our host runs for the sea salt.

While the rug absorbs salt, we dance. Housego removes his pink fleece. Underneath he's all in black (black rollneck, black trousers); around his neck a cerise pink silk scarf. That World War II photograph where everything is black and grey but for the poppies and blood.

By candlelight, our shadows accompany us. Soon the room is crowded with double, triple selves, black to smoke grey depending on their proximity to the light. I'm wearing black silk: loose floppy trousers and top. On the wall I'm a swish of shadow. Mountain retreating into the distance. A giant hand. Above that, an obelisk of a candle with no flame. 'Why doesn't the flame cast a shadow?' asked Molly. Because it's brighter than its own light source. Look closely, in fact, and there is a shadow only it's very faint. On the ceiling the silhouette of a flying putto, reaching out to touch me.

Now it's Bea's turn to dance with Housego. This is something to watch, you can't not watch. Picture a miniature Ming vase beside a Knossos burial urn. Such a pairing ought to be freakish but it isn't. As if they've been dancing together for years.

The music stops. About ten of us remain sitting around on cushions, our shadows lying low. (Even when you're perfectly upright your shadow can lay itself down to rest.) Housego curls his fingers into a peanut bowl. We raise our glasses. 'What shall we drink to?'

'To saving the beeches.'

'To saving some of the beeches.'

'To all but four.'

Housego (consulting his peanuts): 'To the four not saved.'

Thus revising and correcting, we finally succeed in coming to some kind of toasting terms. Not so much a clink as a plink, plastic being what it is.

'To the beeches.'

'To Bea and all her fine work.'

Bea: 'To all of you – '

I hold the bowl of my wineglass with two hands, tip the liquid one way, then the other. This causes aeration. Bring it up to the level of my mouth and sip. Certain areas of the tongue are good for tasting particular tastes. Housego and Bea are now drinking from the same wineglass: the dipping of dippers, one up one down, one in one out. Every so often they meet in the middle.

My glass is made of pink plastic. The stem edge picks up light from the candle and runs a neon line around the flat disc of the base, and from there up the other side and around the rim. Soon the whole goblet is outlined in pink, sizzling like a neon current. The liquid inside has boiled down to a black syrup inside the pink glass. No more, Magda, you're driving.

'Excuse me, where's the loo?'

'Beyond the kitchen – apologies for the mess, it's about to be renovated.'

The downstairs bathroom is an old lean-to that had once been painted a vicious pink but which is now faded and peeling. Lumps of plaster have fallen off. Around the clawfoot bath, some sweet pink tiles with a rose in the corner of each. I sit on the toilet lid. The sweet pink of the tiles looks more vicious than the vicious pink of the walls. I close one eye, form a triangle with my fingers which I move around, freeze framing map shapes of no country in particular.

When I get back, people are eating strawberry ice-cream. Why is everything pink? How funny. Think pink. Our host hands out spoons. Housego takes one and so does Bea. Candlelight bounces along the edge of Housego's spoon and up into his left pupil. Bea digs in: strawberry, pale pink with darker fruity bits. Housego's spoon lolls in his hand. He says it's too cold for him; it hurts his teeth. He snuggles back into his pink fleece. Thin as an After Eight, he chills easily. A spoon's shadow goes up and down on the wall opposite the flame.

I put out my hand. It gets to within an inch of Housego's sleeve which causes a few fleecy fibres to respond, particles of energy prepared to jump the gap. The other day I held a newborn lamb, the fingers of both hands buried to the knuckles in its baby-pile. Housego's pink fleece, by way of comparison, takes my fingers only to the first joint.

The pile of salt has turned to pink slush. Housego offers to vacuum it up but our host tells him not to worry, she'll do it in the morning.

We drive home. I drop them in reverse order: Housego, Bea. That leaves me.

That Valentine's Day (1997, her last), Molly came home in tears. 'A boy said my painting of a heart looked more like a catfish!' 'Let's have a look,' said Magda. It did rather but she did her best not to laugh. The heart, complete with its many-tentacled blood vessels.

Three years before that the child laid her head on the mother's chest. 'Listen, can you hear?' The child listened. 'Of course I can hear.' 'And do you know what that ticking sound is?'

'It's your heart! How could I not know **that**?'

How did she know? Magda couldn't remember ever telling her. A simple pump? Well, quite complicated, actually. So she took her by the hand up to her study and showed her a map of the heart.

Heart. Remove the 'h' from the beginning and scoot it around to the end and you get: **earth.**

The map cabinet is in my study. Studies are for studying. The red anglepoise lamp creates a pool of light, not round and deep like Red Tarn or flowing and serpentine like Rusland Pool but rather flat, a pool for Flatlanders to swim in. On the far wall is the banner with the red lettering DO NOT CUT US DOWN/WE CANNOT BE REPLACED. Sagging but still there.

Drawer 15 contains two reproduction sixteenth-century 'cordiform' projections of the earth. What was the point of this heart-shaped peeling of the earth's skin? The world thus laid out could be seen from a great height – the famous bird's-eye view– each hemisphere relatively undistorted, thus allowing the viewer to see how far the world extended. It suggested, too, according to contemporary sources, the earth's rotundity, its 'living' character.

Drawer 15 also contains a German cartographic poem-map, or Valentine's card.

I am trained to see topographies. I see before me, therefore, two main land masses divided by a sea with a dotting of islands. Normally I can identify even a fragment of international terrain, but what on earth is this? At the south-west corner is a land-triangle with a rather bodice-like coastline, while across the sea of *Küsse* is a highly indented coastline, jutting out, at one point, to a promontory resembling a manicured goatee.

They aren't bodies of land of course but the outlined torsos of lovers gazing at each other from across the impossibly wide blue sea of *Küsse*. Female, male. Her bodice heaves, his goatee quivers; two tears depend from his port-eye and drop into the sea, forming tiny offshore islands. What is to become of the lovers, thus separated by a sea sadistic, ironical and cynical enough to call itself *Küsse*? The answer is that unless a sudden freak event in plate tectonics closes the gap between them, their poor parted lips, foaming with salty frustration, are fated to stay that way forever. Yearning yearning.

The words, from a poem by Heinrich Heine, are sprinkled here and there (Love, Breast, Bitterness, etc.) as if the poem had been cut up into so many single-word strips, then gathered into a sack and dumped. Left to flutter down in their own good time, land where they would.

My neighbour, who lives fifty yards down the road in the hamlet of Ealinghearth, is a retired medic. He tells me it's possible to 'map' the surface of the heart using echocardiography. He supposes, as a mapmaker, I will be interested, and so I am. But the point of mapping an area of terrain, say, is generally as an aid to finding your way around in or on it; whereas the heart's surface, I would have thought, is not particularly interesting in itself? 'Ah,' he says, 'but it can tell you about what's going on *inside* the heart; for instance, a flat sound tells you there's a deep cardiac dullness.' A geological mapping, as it were, of the heart. Layer of dull, dense rock. In which case, how would he map the heart of a female Flatlander? A trick question, of course, since she's a mere line with no external organs. Heartless (lucky) line!

This neighbour walks his dog, a 'flatcoat' retriever, past my house each morning and evening. Its muzzle points up the Valley, its tail towards the estuary, aligned positively as a compass arrow. Sometimes its owner and I make do with the clicks and nods of greeting; sometimes it's weather code (fine, lovely, foul, etc.). On occasion – such as now – we stop and chat, mostly about the ongoing saga of the beeches. He thinks it's all rather tedious. He thinks, along with Mick Merriman & Co., they should all come down and be done with it, plant new. He doesn't know what I think. I lay my hand on the dog's skull. The bony shape just fills it with two fingers between the eyes.

26

Horrorland

Once bitten, soon bedded – as they say. Strange bedfellows, stranger bed: lined with beech leaves and blood. Add the company of freaks – vampires, bogeys, ghosts – sick company but company nevertheless.

Misery loves it; Magda loved it.

She waited for dark then slipped, via the side door, into The Duke's in Lancaster, that underground den with its prisoners all in rows, many holding hands for comfort. All they could see however were the shapes on their cave's wall. Known as a film theatre.

Magda sat in the first row. The screen was studded like a painting by Vermeer, pointillist points of light lighting up the Weimar child-killer's eyeballs, pearling his bottom lip. The projection beam pinged over her head, hissed in her ear. Comet tail, bridal veil. Having the screen so close, at such a worshipful angle, forced her neck back on itself: an extreme angle, not recommended by Sara.

Just you wait, it won't be long
The bogeyman in black will come.
And with his little chopper
He will chop you into bits.

Hear the sweet children singing their not-so-sweet rhyme. See the letter 'M' stark naked on a black background.

Eine Stadt sucht einen Morder

'M' for murder.

Magda stuffed her mouth with salted peanuts to stop herself giggling like a maniac. It felt, as Flat Stanley might have said, sort of fluttery. Above her, Peter Lorre, complete with famous mobile forehead and inno-cent moon face. Peter Lorre as Beckert, the 'curiously sympathetic

Weimar child murderer', as it said in the programme notes. Peter Lorre as Flat Stanley before he got flat.

Peter Lorre rolls around the streets of Weimar. Where to go, what to do? Poor ninny. He sees the child playing with her ball, something grabs him like a gripe, says 'do it, do it', the tell-tale whistle rises in his gullet. Loom goes the shadow over the still-life with child, while the child continues to pup the ball on the ground and then pap it against the poster advertising a reward for the child-murderer. Pup pap loom. The shadow's connection with the verb 'to loom' derives from the fact that it can draw itself up from its horizontal position, swelling as it goes, until it blots everything in its non-substance.

Nothing to be afraid of, thought Magda, since the film itself is a nothing (an 'electric shadow', as the Chinese called it). But then she revised her thinking to think, it can't be nothing because it derives from something. It precedes, foretells, if you're paying attention, danger. Lays itself out before you, up and over, lovingly as a soft pet. Pleased with herself for arguing her way back to fear. Welcome home, Magda.

The child-murderer looks down at himself: two hands of stumpy bananas. These hands do not belong to me! They do such nasty things, these cannot be my hands! I must get rid of them! But the pudgy hand which is not a hand, not his hand, holds the orange out to another little girl. Holds it and rolls it and juggles it back and forth tee hee, while the child goes up and down with her skipping rope, while the still-life grey orange blobs back and forth and Peter Lorre's eyeballs slip and slide in their sockets. Oh, that unexplained urge!

Little girl, would you like an orange?

Oh yes, please, kind sir, yes …

And then everything stops, the jumping the juggling the giggling, the eyeballs ready to pop out of his head, the music, the eating of peanuts in the audience, the slooshing of beer. Everything stops when the hand flips open the penknife.

Flip slip flip, goes the knife.

Peter Lorre with black blood on his hands. Yuch, get it off! So he wipes it on his tummy, his funny stuffed-with-old-socks-tummy in its button-down waistcoat that strains across that infernal front, that rollercoaster of tumps and trenches.

As for the children – thanks to director Fritz Lang – you do not see them after he has done what he has done to them. According to the programme notes, Lang believed in a subtle, non-prurient approach to film-making, less voyeuristic and violent than that of some contemporary directors who positively revel in blood and gore and dismemberment. Lang chooses instead to indicate a child's death through symbolism: a rolling ball, an abandoned balloon. Knife. Orange. The oblique angle.

How long does a rolling ball take to stop its rolling? That depends on the angle of slope.

The no-more-child's ball goes rolling along, into a derelict plot of waste ground with a derelict-looking oak seedling and some scrubby-looking scrub; goes on rolling, though without the hand to pup or pap it can't go on moving and so it begins to wobble, starts to stop, seeks for a place to come to rest. In a shallow dip it arrives at a shivery shimmery not-quite standstill before finding its balance point, its equilibrium.

The film ends but Magda stays sitting. If she stood up she'd fall right over. So she sits and thinks: how strange, while people squeeze past her legs. How strange that the children went with him. *Elsie, what a pretty name! ... Little girl, would you like an orange, a balloon? Oh yes, please, yes* ... How they held out their undernourished little arms in a gesture hovering somewhere between welcome and surrender. Embraced, so to speak, their fate.

Peter Lorre, the curiously sympathetic monster, rushed away into the night: skin without body, necktie without neck to fasten round. Beanbag of wickedness. Magda for her part – sated, sickened – also fled, up Moor Lane and into the night. Shadow trailing shadows.

When she couldn't take any more child-killer movies or true-life child-killer books she turned to Self Help (Finding Your Way, Wisdom of the East, Support Systems for the Bereaved, etc.). She learned about the six stages of grief: (1) Denial; (2) Anger; (3) Bargaining; (4) Depression; (5) Acceptance; (6) Hope. Where was she on the star-spangled ladder towards Number Six? Third rung, second rung? *First?*

The words she read were so inspirational they made her salivate. *If not for death how could we ever appreciate life? ... Were we to shield canyons from the windstorms, we would lose the beauty of their carvings ... What is death but the transition from this life to another?* ... She supposed such stuff was helpful if you were feeling like being helped. Probably she wasn't ready. They made her either hungry or want to throw up.

When she couldn't read any more of anything she took to riding around in her car with no fixed destination in mind. Her cassette collection at this time included some jolly little numbers such as Schubert's 'The Erl King', sung by Ian Partridge, whose voice she found quite light and airy; Strauss's 'Four Last Songs' sung by Christina Schäfer: a dryish version but preferable to an over-sentimentalized one. Her most contemporary work was James MacMillan's 'Seven Last Words'. Deliciously harrowing, this.

Then there was the Portuguese fado: mournful, wailing, ululating, squeezed from the twin jelly bags of the singer's heart. Bearable only within the close confines of a car.

Magda got out her Bartholomew's – 1½ miles to the inch – and drove north along the M6 from Kendal. At Carlisle she took the A698 over the Scottish border to Canon and from there turned off onto a 'B' road. Kept going along Liddel Water River until she got to the high back road and turned off at Kielder onto a track overlooking the Reservoir.

Fado means fate, by the way. To sing fado, according to the notes on the tape sleeve, you had to be a woman. Women were not only experienced sufferers, they were experienced fatalists. When tragedy struck, they would shrug their shoulders, go away and weep quietly to themselves. Get out the black dress, black stockings. A very circumscribed, over-determined and culturally-specific view of women – but there it was.

She parked under some forestry trees. It was starting to snow. The snow piled up on the branches, causing them to lower in stages according to load-bearing principles: every so often another groan, a further lowering. Depending on the flexibility (moisture content) and strength of the branches, by morning some would be broken.

She depressed the button. *Play*, it said. The snow melted away. She saw herself sitting on a low stool in hot sunglare, wearing a pair of thick black lisle stockings, thighs apart. Fly-swatter in one hand, wineglass in the other: vicious little swats to the swoopings of the fado. She shrugs, rolls her tragedy-lidded eyes. Asks the question with no answer, 'What can you do?' By the time the tape was finished Magda reckoned she'd become an honorary fadista.

In the meantime, real snow had piled up on her real windscreen in a panoply of monster-shapes. Pure projection, unfair to snow, but there:

Giants' eyeballs

Fiendish fingers

Gruesome ghouls

Screaming bats

Sinister skulls

On the top shelf in Molly's room was a box containing Creepy Cookie Cutters sent to her, Molly, by her American grandmother. Jay's mother, a child psychologist, believed Molly was suffering from a fear of bogeys and other such creatures of the dark, and that to make light of them – i.e. to shape them, bake them, eat them, etc. – would cure her. Nothing to be afraid of, chomp chomp. The set included four scary cookie cutters plus creepy cookie coffins (self-assembly) for use as gift boxes. Gift tags.

Wrong. She respected the so-called creepy things too much – accepted their 'reality' if you like – to consider toying with them. 'Take them away,' she said, handing over the cookie cutters, 'they're silly.' Closed her eyes, arranging her teeth on the curve of her bottom lip like stumpy white nails that glowed in the dark.

Molly wasn't frightened of ghosts and shadows; if anything, the opposite. She was drawn – fascinated, obsessed – these words are too easy. She liked the Wild Place and being close to the Wild Things. How could anyone in their right mind be afraid of them with their peg teeth and over-easy eyes? Her favourite was the girl Wild Thing with her parted-in-the-middle hair and sawblade teeth.

Cute as pie.

'If they invited me to go with them, I'd go.'

'You would?'

What I mean is, she was no more afraid of the so-called 'dark' crea-tures of the forest than she was of the creepy cookie cutters. It was she who gravitated to them; she who climbed into the boughs of the beech in order to wait for what, I do not know.

Don't get me wrong. I'm not saying she held out her arms to pain or death. (Kidnapping, molestation, strangulation: I'm not saying she wasn't lured or that she invited these things – most chillingly, in other words, willing – how could I?) Not at all. What I mean is, the trees were her life, where she lived. That they also happened to be where she died is unfor-tunate.

Magda sat in her car until it grew light, until the light grew. Snow makes light grow and light, as she observed, snuffed shadows. No it didn't, not really. All it did was to provide an atmospheric camouflage. The shadows, in a sense, still existed; they just weren't visible.

Frost glittered. People had been found frozen inside their cars, like lumps of coagulated peas. Frozen peas are good for aches and pains. But Magda wasn't injured, and the cold wasn't painful – it was just cold. Nice and numbing. And not to worry, she thought, I know where I am, I have my maps. And she played the tape again and ran her car engine: *fado fado*.

It could have been worse, a lot worse; a lot realer as they say. She could have shot up; she could have drunk her way through the five cases of malt whisky left in her larder; she could have hung herself from a tree branch, preferably Beech no.31 for best strangefruit effect. It would have been understandable, seemly even. Many parents of dead children commit suicide in one form or another. They blame themselves, of course they do.

Jay fell in love. Falling in love is a common response to death, explained the bereavement counsellor. Magda tried imparting this infor-mation to Jay but it bounced like unbuttered popcorn off a garage door. 'Contingency,' he said. 'What does that mean?' she asked. 'It means I want her.' Magda supposed a man who spends his life studying philos-ophy was entitled. 'Her skin reeks of sunshine,' he said. 'So does a fig's,' she countered. He insisted his wasn't stereotypical midlife behaviour and in so saying became stereotypical. He said he couldn't help himself; he said, in the end, such unoriginal things Magda wondered why she'd married him in the first place. Within six months of Molly's disappearance Jay had moved back to the States with the fig-person and Magda had moved into Ealinghearth Cottage which she'd bought at auction.

She pruned the 'New Dawn' down to a porcupine's spine. Having done that, she curled herself into an armchair, with a crocheted blanket around her legs, and read or watched garbage. Horror by mail order, vampire voyeurism, mainlining via black squiggles on the page, light projected onto the retina, sound waves delivered direct to the auditory canal for quick passage to the brain. A glut of Gloom & Doom, Menace & Blood, Inc. When the writing got so bad she couldn't read another word she went back to films. Fritz Haarmann as the Nosferatu-like child-killer ('*Tenderness of the Wolves* lacks the moral conscience of *M* but makes up for it with buckets of blood ...'). Buckets of blood, that was good, but it had to get worse before it got better.

A little girl runs and runs through a forest. Her head is detached. It turns on its axis North-East-South-West. The head opens its mouth but no scream comes. Would she, Magda, have heard her, Molly, scream? The radio had probably been on. Five o'clock. *Jazz Record Requests*. 'Hello there ...'

More, more, I need more, she thought (detail, description, closeups). The need to taste and smell; hear voices raised, lowered; a hand clapped over a mouth, a pair of eyes growing wider over the clapped-on hand; the flash of a knife, a snatch of dialogue: 'You're scared? That's good ... tha's *va-rry goooo*.'

Magda's neck hurt with craning her neck back at the screen plus she'd developed a tic in her left eye with too much reading of small disgusting print. Also, by this time she'd gone through months of mind-body stuff: reflexology, Reiki, shiatsu. I've tried the lot, she thought. Dunked a toe in the glow of their so-called positive energies – and felt nothing. Stepping into water when it's too close to your own body temperature: senseless, sensationless, dimensionless.

Magda staggered to the foot of the stairs where her shadow took her by the hand – she'd left a light on – and led her up to the bathroom. Half an hour later, having emerged from the bath, she bent over to dry her feet and couldn't get up again.

After a while, people noticed she wasn't around. A neighbour knocked on the door – fortunately she'd left it open. 'Your back is in spasm,' the neighbour informed her and called the doctor. The doctor came. He said, 'Your back is in spasm.' He wrote out a prescription which she couldn't get filled due to the fact that her back was in spasm.

She lay flat on the floor. Her mother came to help her out. Brought her cups of tea, managing to put them just out of reach. 'Thank you.' Her fingers stretched forth but the synapse couldn't be jumped. The tea cooled, Magda's arm got tired of stretching into cup-free space. Pain. Gen-u-ine 100% guaranteed pain. Good, this was good.

Her mother said, 'If you don't eat something you'll turn into a shadow.' 'I already have,' said Magda, maniacal giggle only half-muffled by the rug she was lying on, face-down. 'Oh dear.' Magda's mother didn't like this kind of talk. Since Magda's father's death she was into Being Positive. 'I say, have you tried the Alexander Technique?' she chirruped. 'I've heard it's very good for these back-things.' Magda sensed a plate of cucumber sandwiches placed squarely on her backbone. 'I'll look into it,' she said to the rug.

27

Map of Rusland Pool

If you look at a map of the Rusland Valley, you will see that Rusland Pool is not a pool at all in the sense of land-locked water, but a flowing body. Narrow and undulating, it originates at Grizedale Tarn, divides into two minor becks (Grizedale and Dale Park), rejoins at Satterthwaite, gathers speed at Force Mills and Forges before flowing into the Valley as 'Rusland Pool'.

From Rusland Hall, where Bea lives, it snakes along past Skinner Pastures, flows under Low Hay Bridge and High Hay Bridge, turns westerly where it narrows at Ealinghearth (running along the bottom of my wood), keeps going in a southerly direction, passing under the A590 at Pool Foot, where it joins up with the River Leven before emptying out into the Bay at Greenodd. Mostly it's quite shallow but there are a few notoriously treacherous rocky pools where the Maid, among others, is believed to have drowned.

(What does it matter about the ins and outs of a meandering pool? *She's gone and lost the plot.* An interesting expression, that. Stories, maps, land – indeed 'plots' themselves as in kidnapping or terrorism or espionage – all involve plotting. Have I lost mine, gone a-wander along Rusland Pool like some poor crazed Ophelia? No. I haven't forgotten my compass and I haven't lost the plot. Soon. I'm almost ready to tell you, and myself, what happened to Molly.)

We are headed for one of the pools: Bea Merriman, Simon Merriman and I. She has invited me for a swim and I have accepted. The job for the Regional Health Authority is finished plus it's the Easter holidays and the weather is hot – one of those early freak spells. It will probably snow next week.

In wet weather, the path along Rusland Pool is unwalkable bog but today it's dry. Bea knows an enclosed bit of pool which is safe and good for swimming. Bea's two older boys are with Mick, doing treework on the Rusland Hall estate.

We walk in single file. Bea holds Simon over her head to stop him getting snagged. Small Bea, large package – the thought of him inside her is absurd. Her arms must be aching. A machete would be useful. At a steep bank we hang onto bare tree roots, slide, catch each other. Simon thinks it's fun. The pool, when we get to it, is lower than usual because of the drought. Protected on all sides, sun conveniently overhead, a patch of sand for getting in and out. It will be warmer and stiller than usual. Rising up from the pool, a high vertical slab topped by trees and scrub. Aside from the sand beach, a heap of rocks and boulders.

Bea plops herself down with Simon on her lap. It's the kind of weather that makes you think of words such as 'plop'. Way back in geological time the rocks did their own version of plopping.

We agree to take turns: me first. Splash splash, I make it up to my knees and stick. Jay had a story about a dog, a crossbreed half terrified and half in love with water who'd stand up to its knees, tail wagging one end and howling the other. Molly in a pool would imitate that dog. Bea tosses a pebble – 'Get in! Do it!' Shame loosens me, winds me down.

At first I let the water take me. (Is that how it was for her?) Then I break into my usual routine – forward breast stroke, returning back-crawl – it could be any tiled, chlorinated swimming pool. The routine helps. Upstream gives you something to work against (Was she exhausted? Already dead?), a bit of resistance. Up down and around. The water closest to the vertical rock is deeper and colder, fishier smelling.

'Brrrrr. Your turn.'

Now I'm holding Simon and Bea's stripping off and I can hear a rustling noise, human feet – someone's coming! Bea says so what, and finishes undressing. 'Come on in,' she waves to Housego (yup, that's who it is), 'it's wuuunderful.' She swims over to the waterfall at the bottom then flops onto a flat slab which slides her into the next pool, wha-heeeee!

Housego says hello and I say hello. I scoop Simon under his bum, pulling him closer against me like an overfilled hot-water bottle. When will he register it's not his mother's stomach or breasts pressed against his back? Housego picks up a stone and flips it back and forth, says he's sorry about the other night. Nothing to be sorry about. Simon my skinful of rubbery hot baby.

'I guess I haven't been very clear,' Housego says. 'The truth is, I don't really know what's going on myself.' Still no waving kicking flipping or pat-a-caking. Inert baby. Something wrong with you, hmm? Sun-addled, Simon? 'Things are still quite messy at home as well.' Household mess, hard to avoid with one child around – but five! Imagine! All those toys!

'Want to go in the water, Simon?' No answer. 'Give it a try then, shall we?' Yes, why not. Over hot rocks – grey granite mottled with pink – to the edge of the pool. Heavy Simon. When I carried Molly on my back I'd have to lean forward slightly or she'd pull me backwards. Musn't drop Inert Baby into water.

Simon's skin slips over the stuff of him. As I lower him down his legs retract. Hey, he's alive! Not a hot-water bottle after all! Limp baby fat turns to a solid ball of contracted baby muscle. Non-Inert Simon knows what he wants and it isn't meltwater off the fells, and who should blame him. Nice and cooling for hot baby but hot baby doesn't agree. Nice and cooling however for hot Mummy and hot Housego.

I step backwards making sure to keep my balance on the hot stones (baby skulls are so tender!). Wobble on one leg. Watch the man and the woman in the pool splashing and laughing: Simon's Mum and Simon's Mum's friend Housego. The person holding the baby is me: Simon's Mum's female friend Magda. We are all friends, one two three.

Three is a closed system in geometrical terms but in human, living, terms our angles are not fixed: we are free to pull apart and reformulate. Equidistant is best but it can't always be like that. Patience is required of the far angle. Once, out on the fells, I lost my coat in a gale. It was the middle of winter, near freezing. The wind whipped it straight off a cliff. Look! a flying jacket! At first I ran about flapping like the Loon Woman, like a flying cagoule, like a woman who'd lost her jacket in winter; but after a while I calmed down, took sensible steps. A question of survival, of coming to terms.

There are no terms to this particular situation but that's part of the challenge. As for the lost winter coat, that's hardly relevant here since it's a heat wave.

Simon's Mum's friend Housego gets out of the water. Simon's Mum splashes his back. 'Coward!' His private parts, which are no longer private, are affected by the cold. He comes closer; his shadow looms and drips. The droplets appear televised, but when they land they are real and cold – sort of tickly, as Flat Stanley would say.

'Shall I take him?'

Now it's my turn again to swim with Bea and after that she gets out and holds Simon and it's Housego's turn to swim with me.

Musical Baby, we're playing.

In the seventeenth century what foxed Newton was the 'three-body' problem. His system could handle attractions between, say, Saturn and the Sun, but when he had to take into account the gravitational interactions between Jupiter, Saturn and the Sun his exact-solution broke down. The best he could offer were approximations.

28

Map of Molly's Passage

The history of mapping is a flowline from guesswork to virtual certainty, from blank spaces to terrain fleshed out. Centuries of artfully drawn question-marks and phantasmic beasts, a blueness that goes on forever. *Grand espace de pays dont on n'a point de connaissance particulière.* Not Much Known.

Then follows an interim period when coastal regions were mapped while the interiors remained uncharted. The explorers and soldiers moved in and the sailors sailed out. Progress, it was called.

Now we leap a couple of centuries. The 1920s turned to engraving in glass; the '40s to plastic sheets and transparent overlays. In the '50s photography replaced lithography in reproduction. From there we skip to iso-mapping where places of equal value are linked by lines. Flowlines, computer mapping, digitization. Mapping becomes a game and an adventure. Colours, type, shapes – you can change your mind endlessly; no problem getting the old and the new to marry up. Rescale at the touch of a button.

The vocabulary: *Virtual. Pan. Zoom. Refresh.*

The hardware: satellites, computers, digitizers, plotters, printers, lasers, cathode ray tubes. Computer driven image analysis systems. Satellite captured (electronic, photographic) images.

So many images!

Now you can take a 'surrogate walk' (stroll down any street) in different parts of Britain: take a hike in the Lake District; explore the beautiful tree-lined Rusland Valley; have a swim in the notoriously dangerous Rusland Pool which is only dangerous when it's in spate. This you can control in your virtual experience.

Mapping is no longer a sheet with marks on it but a video display that transforms itself by the second.

Cartography is in a state of near-revolution.

It's hard keeping up, but boy! – as Flat Stanley might say – is it exciting!

Other women go to their refrigerator; I go to my map cabinet. Old-fashioned paper maps may be museum pieces but that doesn't mean they aren't worth a visit. Free admission, nothing to lose (and you may be surprised!).

Twenty-four drawers, which one will it be? Close your eyes, go bumpety-bump down the brass pulls. Where she stops nobody ...

'This isn't going to be pleasant,' said the pathologist. Pathologists do not have pleasant jobs. Magda made a gesture similar to the one which secured her Ealinghearth Cottage at auction. The pathologist went on to explain how after heavy rains, which there had been, a body could be washed out to sea. 'Is this hypothetical or actual?' Magda asked. In theory, he said, a body beginning in Rusland could be found washed up as far south as Blackpool.

'Blackpool? Really?'

'Yes, really,' said the pathologist, and he produced a folder of maps.

'May I have a copy of those?'

'They may not mean much to you.'

Jay butted in. 'My wife happens to be a cartographer.'

The pathologist stopped what he was doing and looked at her as if she were a real person. He was quite flustered. He wished he could start all over again by shaking her hand more firmly, professional to professional.

'Well now,' he said, and adjusted his vocabulary accordingly.

The body – in plain language – was not found floating, nor did the frogmen find it at the bottom of the deep pool. But a week after her disappearance her right foot, still in its K shoe, was found at Sandside; three days later the rest of her was washed up on the Morecambe mudflats. Yes, it happens; it happened.

It/her/the body/she. Free of foot and free of fancy and generally free of that burden we call Life.

Jay waited outside while Magda went into the mortuary with the pathologist to do the identifying. Surely only a formality, they must have identifying fingerprints. Wrong. There were no fingerprints because they'd disappeared along with the skin on her fingers.

There were troughs on either side of the wooden slab-things where bodily fluids drained away. The pathologist was wearing green paper hatties over his shoes.

'That's her,' Magda said.

'You're quite sure?' asked the pathologist.

Magda was quite sure it was Molly even though the body was bloated and smelled like rotten eggs (hydrogen sulphide due to bacterial growth in the tissues); even though the face was bruised, one eye was missing and the body skinned; even though her hair had lost its pony grip and the nails had gone altogether; even though she'd had a chunk of thigh bitten away (naughty fish!).

'Quite.' Magda assured the pathologist: that was her daughter and that was her daughter's right foot. Same shoe, bought at K's in Kendal.

The pathologist held the door for her. Outside she nodded to Jay. The nod signified Positive Identification. After that, a policeman drove them back to the inspector's office up Moor Lane on the other side of town where they unrolled more maps of the area, including special ones of the estuary showing 'tidal drag' and the play of currents. The police diagrams were crackly and full of arrows, black marker lines and red Xs. It was quite gruesome.

For weeks she did nothing because she didn't know what to do. Then all of a sudden she did. Or maybe it wasn't sudden, maybe she'd been thinking about it without knowing she'd been thinking about it. After all, water flows and paper does not.

Magda got into her oldest blue track suit with its mud shadows around the inside leg cuffs. When Jay stopped her at the door to ask what she was up to, she replied, 'Imaginative reconstruction.'

(1) Begin at the beginning (Beech 31: X marks the spot).

(2) Cross the road, through a gate, across a field to the bank of Rusland Pool.

(3) Turn left for fifty yards to High Hay Bridge and the pool. Stop there. Point A (entry): X marks the spot.

(4) Pause here to consider how she came to enter said Point A. Entertain each of the following:

    (a) she jumped in;

    (b) she fell in;

    (c) she was thrown in alive but drowned;

    (d) she was thrown in already dead.

Remember, Magda told herself, you aren't a detective, you're a mapper. Don't try to come up with an answer, just follow the question. Begin walking, stopping at the places marked with a red X where traces of her (bits of clothing, hair, etc) were found. This sandbank, that rock shelf, that overhanging bough. Take your time, do not be afraid to touch. Note several Xs in a row then nothing for miles where she presumably took off, with the help of a river in spate. White-water rafter without a raft.

Magda began to run. The dipper went faster: great bobs over the water, rock to rock. When she heard the voice, her voice, she began to run faster, harder. Began to understand something she'd only suspected from before Molly was even born, that once let out she'd just keep going.

Magda decided to keep her company, a lonely business drowning. So she ran with her past Ealinghearth, along Ireland Moss to Pool Foot. Together they crossed – the tide was still low enough – through Roudsea Wood to Ashes Point where Greenodd Sands begin. The Bay was dry except for a sequence of shiny ribbons of channel water. This was August. August is the month for cross-channel walks, when tides are lowest.

Off with running shoes and socks, park them on a rock. Continue walking in a south-southwesterly direction towards Canal Foot. Pass under the Leven Viaduct just as a train is approaching. Oystercatchers and gulls and shelducks scattered. Magda kept on accompanying. (Ulverston Channel would probably have taken her, they'd explained, past Ulverston Sands and on, out into Lancaster Sound; from there she'd have been swept in a great south-easterly rush across the Bay. This will have been where part of her (right foot + shoe) parted – travelling north to Sandside – from the rest of her which kept going until it eventually fetched up in Morecambe.)

Magda could feel the rumble of the train over the bridge transferred to the water to the sand to the soles of her feet. She curled her toes and allowed the mud to suck at them. Think how clean they will be, she thought, a bit wrinkled but never mind.

Once across the channel it got better. Long swathes of ripply sand. Corrugated sand, corrugated feet – what a good foot massage she was getting!

Beyond Canal Foot now, midway between one coast and another; but for the gathering birdlife and the map of Molly's passage, Magda was completely alone. Silvered hazy light, solid edges smudged as by a thumb drawn across the horizon. All the known landmarks – Heysham Power Station, Blackpool Tower, Humphrey Head, Walney – wiped.

And now. Between Magda and the next bit of shore came a widening channel. Waves doing what waves do: waiting their turns or jumping over the backs of others, thus disturbing a neat mathematical progression but introducing a more playful one. The channel under the viaduct refused to let her back. Sea smell in the air, breeze blowing up.

A word about the bore. The trouble with the bore is it's boring. Relentless remorseless pitiless merciless etc., the way it just bangs on. Once it starts it can't seem to stop, shoving against the backs of your knees. But Magda was strong because she had a purpose; or rather, she'd *had* a purpose (to follow Molly). But now her purpose, as purposes are wont to do, had changed. Her purpose now was to get from one sand-bank to another and from there across to land. (Problem: How long does it take for a woman to get from A to B with the water travelling at x mph and the woman at ... ?)

Important to keep going. Once on the other side, she told herself, you'll be safe: that's what she thought. In any case, she couldn't go back so she had to go on – no choice here – so she pushed across, with the boring bore bashing away at the backs of her thighs, somehow managing to exert a greater-than-equal force against it.

Safe. Lovely hard sand under her feet, the tidal flow safely to her left, flowing along between her and the shore, but that wasn't a problem because soon she would get to the shallow part where she would simply sloosh across the channel, thinned at this point to ankle depth, kicking water and watching drops fly up and singing like a child.

Except it didn't happen like that because somehow, in spite of all her careful navigating, she'd managed to cross two channels not one and the tide was coming in fast now and there was no shallow place at all between her and the shore.

What she'd thought was the shore wasn't. It was an island.

Chapel Island, a nesting place for birds.

Go back.

She couldn't, of course, since the river channel behind her was now uncrossably deep and treacherous. She'd come across it earlier but that was then and things were different now. Water closing up. Empty spaces filling up. Water seeks its own level. The gulls thought it a hoot.

Try not to panic, try not to cry, try to keep moving. Magda was good at thinking calming thoughts. *This is how it was for her.* And then she thought how it would all be over soon. She hadn't planned the reconstruction to parallel events quite this closely but now there was no choice but to Go, as the saying went, With the Flow.

So there she was, jogging along, with the bore boringly lapping away at her heels. Plop went her feet in the water: you wouldn't believe how fast that bore can follow! Ballroom bore, Strauss waltzer. Mirrors and champagne; last of the curlew bubblers before moving inland to lay their eggs. By now, water was flowing off her like a bridal veil. She was also forced to discard her jacket and all other excess weight: wallet, identifying objects. Finally she was light, ballgowned in water, coiffured and necklaced in tidal suds. Salt, she tasted.

I'm coming, Molly-o.

By now, the water was well over her head, pulling her out. Eye-level with water, so much of it! So strong! Magda tried to swim but the current had other ideas. Tricky current! Let go, come with me, it crooned, but another, higher-pitched voice was yelling, swim! Magda swallowed water, coughed and spluttered and began to fight the bore for real. On the other hand, it was at this point she realized the edge of shore she'd been aiming for was not the mainland at all but an island.

Chapel Island belongs to the birds.

Soon it will be under water. The birds will fly off, heartless things.

But the next time Magda looked she saw people-shapes on the island. A mirage, she thought but no, there they were, a man and a woman, passing the time of day there on the island's edge.

It *must* be a vision. Humans are rare on Chapel Island.

'Are you all right?' yelled the woman-vision. She had quite a convincing real person's voice.

'No, gulp, no, help!'

Now it was the man-vision's turn to yell, 'What the hell are you doing on the wrong side of the channel; don't you know this bay is dangerous?!'

Ha! What a time for a lesson on estuary safety! Magda felt quite cross but semi-drowning as she was, didn't have strength or breath or time to argue.

'Help! quick! please!'

Drowning, not waving.

The man was quick, and as it happened, he was togged out in a swim-suit which meant he needn't lose precious time undressing. Time was being lost all the time and Magda calculated at this rate thirty seconds more and she'd be the bore's seaweed bride forever. Well, she was dressed for it. Molly as bridesmaid.

He was in now, throwing out a raft-like arm, only Magda couldn't reach. A floating version of the Creation of Adam, except the divide between their fingertips was getting wider, not closer. But the man, a strong swimmer, was able to heave himself up and with one powerful lunge – gotcha! By this time Magda had little strength left. She crawled along, feeling for the island of his chest leading to an isthmus of neck. Wrapped her noodly arms around it. Both now in danger of going down. Together, *tous les deux*, down and along, washed up and out at Morecambe.

O la! The thought of being washed up at Morecambe mudflats,

however, appealed to neither of them. Magda's rescuer was now kicking hard backwards with Magda flopped on top of the hairy fleshy raft known as his body. She was cold and wet but saved. Her vision was no vision. Her vision's name, as she soon discovered, was Harvey.

Harvey and Jacqui's cottage was right down at the edge of Bardsea beach. They held Magda's wet body between them, arms around each others' waists.

'I'm Jacqui, he's Harvey.'

'Magda.'

'Pleased to meet you.'

One of Magda's hands held a fistful of fabric, the other a handle of flesh. It made walking difficult. The three of them staggered like jolly drunks, babbled like the saved. Hold tight, don't let go whatever you do.

They walked along the beach, barefoot muddy wet. Every few yards, Magda squeezed their hands and they squeezed back ('It's okay, we're here'). The sand felt wonderful, unsolid in places as it was. Jacqui asked Magda what size she was. What size? The question brought tears to her eyes; next she'll be asking who her favourite film star was. (Who was her favourite film star? She couldn't think.) 'I'd say you're about a ten, same size as me.' Jacqui's concern was getting Magda something dry to wear, Magda's was being alive. Very simple, very basic.

When they got to Harvey and Jacqui's cottage they wrapped her in a blue and black striped beachtowel, the kind that's not too thick because it's been used a lot. Jacqui brought her tea with sugar for shock; Harvey rang Jay. When he arrived Harvey instructed him not to let Magda ever do that again, didn't they know those sands were dangerous? Jay nodded obediently; Magda shivered, grinning like a maniac.

'I'll take her home now – throw her in a hot bath.' He put his arm around her and led her away, with her bare flapping feet and her wet flapping towel. Magda offered to wash and return it. Jacqui said, 'Yer all right.' Harvey said, 'Keep it as a souvenir.'

She said, he said.

As they were leaving Magda remembered something else. 'Thanks for letting Harvey jump in after me.' Jacqui laughed, what you on about? Lots of women, she meant, might have held onto his arm, not let him go. (Would she, Magda, have? Hard to say. She might have jumped in herself.)

Jacqui said, 'Get away. Don't be daft.'

'So what did you discover?' This was Jay. They were driving along Priory Road. Discover? Who did he think she was, Vasco da Gama? She suppposed he meant, what did she think she'd accomplished nearly drowning herself and another person and causing a lot of unnecessary bother all round.

What *have* I discovered, she thought, and why did I do it in the first place? Answer: because when someone goes missing, when they slip away, when you reach out your hand and they're gone, you have a need to go after them, put yourself in their position. But after all that, was she really any wiser about how Molly got into Rusland Pool in the first place or about what happened to her among the beeches?

(1) Q: Would she have jumped into a cold body of water in spate in April?

A: No way.

(2) Q: Did she fall in accidentally?

A: Possibly.

(3) Q: Was she thrown in already dead?

A: Possibly.

(4) Q: That means someone – or something – may've nicked her. A heron?

A: She was too big.

(5) Q: Then who?

A: Who knows.

So the upshot was that, according to Jay, they were no further along: she'd found out precisely nothing.

'Wrong, I found *her*.' This is what she said. Quite definite, quite categorical.

'What?' The car swerved, then righted itself. A BP truck came towards them. She repeated, 'I found her.' Surprise surprise: invisible geography. And then she began to sing:

Heigh ho! my angel's name is Harvey
He has no wings and his chest is hairy
Heigh ho! how good it is to be alive
And have a great big hairy fairy!

Jay looked alarmed, which was understandable. 'You're suffering from shock,' he said. Which was true.

The existence of a map (data) is the existence of something. Something is better than nothing. Something you can pin up on a board and point to with a long-handled pointer (tap tap); a transparency you can run through a projector (whirr whirr): 'See that? And that? Now with regard to ...' Something to put into another thing until you've amassed a bulging file of speculation and guesswork.

Good work, men.

That journey of Molly's; the police maps didn't do it justice.

Mapping the gaps, filling the pictorial blanks. It's not true that all mappers are fact freaks, landlocked, gridlocked Gradgrinds. In fact, scroll back far enough and what you find are a whole brood of medieval cartographers mapping the maybes, the who-knows, the greatly-wished-for-but-even-more-feareds. One-armed, one-eyed men, hairy-bodied women, fire-breathing gila monsters, lions with stretched tongues, flying salamanders, and so on. Impalpable and impossible but, well, you never know.

They mapped what they saw but also what they couldn't ever see. The distinction wasn't all that clear, after all. Pierre d'Ailly and his *Tractatus de Imagine Mundi*; Giovanni dei Marignolli and his *Purgatory in the Antipodes*; Simon of Taibutheh – they were all hooked on the unmappable, the bits in between and beyond. Knowledge, as Simon argued, must not be limited to the senses but go beyond. Beyond where? What? Beyond compass, ship-power, human endurance, ability to withstand extremes of heat or cold or whatever. Beyond the blue horizon. Beyond the bore.

What did the police know? What could they say about the actual journey: bobbing like a cork, being picked at by herons, nibbled by fish?

But then she was already dead, so what matter a few bits removed? These things did not figure on their map.

Magda began with rough sketches on newsprint. (No, she thought, I will not use the computer.) When she had some idea of what she was doing, or trying to do, she went on to experiment with some old techniques, using a roll of her father's vellum which she found in the supplies drawer of her map cabinet. The map she eventually produced – not being an artist or calligrapher – is probably a Curiositie, a mishmash.

The Map of Molly's Passage overlaps two 1:50 000 OS maps. It includes the Rusland Valley plus the Cartmel Peninsula, the Kent Estuary and all of Morecambe Bay; in other words, the whole area traversed by Molly on her journey from Beech 31 ending up, in parts, at Sandside and Morecambe.

Magda's equipment: water colours, sepias, a book of palest gold leaf, a set of Chinese brushes and three rapidograph pens, one with a #0000 nib, producing so fine a line you hardly know it's there.

Drawing in the contours was the easy part; she enjoyed that to the extent that she almost forgot the map's sadmad purpose.

Think fluid yet precise.

Next came the channels and sands. How to represent the tides: in or out? Modern maps show great expanses of sand with fingers of pale baby blue. Quite still. Magda's waves were cream-stuffed brandy-curls. The bore ended up a cross between a high speed waterborne tumbleweed and the East Wind, with blown-out cheeks and ferocious pop-eyes, crouched at the helm of a hovercraft.

Then came the hard part. How to incorporate Molly's journey? How do you express such a thing in cartographic terms? Magda doodled, trialled and errored for a week, drank too much coffee, took up smoking again. In the end she could brush-paint, with something of a flourish, the herons and the fish-with-many-teeth nibbling at the one-legged, one-footed, one-eyed child.

There Be Dragons, oh aye.

Then came the lettering – you couldn't call it calligraphy – more like writing in mud, the letters closing up around themselves as soon as they were formed.

In place of Lancaster Sound: Molly's Passage
In place of Sandside Bay: Bay of the Right Foot (with K shoe)
In place of Morecambe Bay: Here Endeth Her Journey

When it was finished she added the warp and woof of grid lines, best open weave. And the thing they call grief? That was written in invisible ink (sniff like a dog and you'll find it's still there); in washes of Cézanne blue and Turner's gold, colours that dripped and bled but let Molly's skin shine through. Varnish to cover and seal in.

It finished up, no doubt, a stramash: a bordered, starred, embroidered, fleur-de-lis'd illuminated Thing. A thing that lasts in the wake of leaving something more important behind. A thing that dissolves past and present, low tide from high tide, lost from found. A little mad but also beautiful, a little.

The drawing of a topological map depends on certain conventions; it also requires spatial intelligence. Some psychologists claim men are better endowed with the gift than women, but I wouldn't agree with that, would I. My father, after all, was determined I should not be silly about maps and I wouldn't want, even now that he's dead, to let him down. Or myself.

Nervous hands produce sweat and sweat produces sweat marks. Sweat marks on maps are not a good thing. *Always wash your hands before going to the map cabinet.*

Twiddle the left-hand tap and out comes the water, cold at first but getting hotter – the miracle of modern plumbing! Plug in, hands in. Let the warm water sag me with its pleasure.

Mirrors and sinks are great devices for looking into the past – films do it all the time. In *The Last Emperor*, for instance, the ex-Emperor locks himself in a People's Republic loo, cuts his wrists and plunges them into a sink full of hot water. His hands and the water, now red with blood, swim before his, and our, eyes – and, easy as killing yourself, we're back to the year 1908. A fat cherub is being handed over by its mother. She's doing it for the baby's own good, only the baby doesn't know that so it's very distraught.

Separate fingers, pull on each one in turn. I could be a pianist getting ready for a concert. The third knuckle of the left hand cracks but that's nothing to worry about; as Sara says, cracking of the joints is a sign the body is getting limbered up. The soap slips up and down and in between. Put down soap, pick up nailbrush: nails, knuckles, skin and bone. Rinse. Shake off excess water. Dry on a clean towel.

Drawer 24: *Map of Molly's Passage*

It's quite usual, when doing the Semi-Supine, to feel chilly. The temperature of a body at rest tends to drop, so it's a good idea to have a blanket handy. I don't have a blanket so I'll have to improvise.

Warm and light, the map serves my purpose well. Soft as a good cotton sheet that's been washed for years, an excellent insulator. As it makes better contact with my body, it settles closer into the rises and falls and folds. North to South from the head of the Rusland Valley to Morecambe, West to East from Ulverston to Sandside.

The map and I are now one: Molly and her journey traced onto my skin – a tickly itchy business as she goes sliding out from under an armpit like at Water World, up and over my chest – Sorry, can't stop now! – slooping over my belly where the heron grabs her in its beak – Hey, let go! – before it drops her, plop! onto Morecambe mudflats (not far from Water World) minus one foot in its K shoe, as well as one eye. Goodbye. As I lay Molly's Map carefully back in Drawer 24, I pray it won't imprison her there, fix her forever: varnished, sealed and labelled; over and done with.

I have strayed a long way from the conventions of mapping. But a curious coincidence. I have been asked to map the routes taken by cross-Bay walkers over the past ten years. Doing that changes everything. Now the Bay becomes not just a place where a body is torn apart but a place where friends and families + dogs go for a ritual day out on the sands, a jolly swish-swish through the river channel and the mud on their way from Kents Bank to Arnside and vice versa. All those people mapping that normally no-go place.

This is where the computer comes into its own. The finished map of the Cross-Bay Walks will show a sequence of lines all ending up in the same place but arriving via different routes. It will tell about the changes in the channels over time and the types of journeys taken.

I sit and stare at this map-in-the-making for a while, and then I go back to Drawer 24 and get out Molly's Passage and stare at that for another while. Lay them side by side. Look at one, look at the other. Then get out a plastic transparency from the supplies drawer and trace the shape of the Bay from the first map. Then ink in the trajectory (approximate) of Molly's passage. Do this in red. Place this over the Cross-Bay Walks map. Notice it resembles a palm print.

Now there are two maps, one on top of the other. The problem of true (truer) representation remains, so I return to my computer. Begin setting up a new kind of programme for mapping the Bay. This one wants to go back centuries, include everything. (But what do I know beyond some shadowy impression of a much-crossed, much-used yet empty-seeming place?) Never mind. I know it's a place of memories, layer upon layer – throw in the lot. That's the beauty of the computer, after all: simultaneous images; temporary crossings; ever-changing routes. The Cross-Bay Walks map wants to show it all: layers of sedimentary rock, stepped, compressed, smoothed by ice; stippled and gouged, veined with ores and ribbed with the skeletons of seabeasts; wants to reveal all the routes taken over the past X years; to show a place not just where a body was torn apart but where many another was fished out; where folks have gone slithering and crossing and crossing-over; the trajectories of horses and wagons, and also worms; the crabbers and fishermen and swimmers and a lost motorcyclist and …

The problem of course is too much information, layers and layers overlaid and overlapping. The computer can handle it but the human brain can't. Like playing tunes on top of one another, after a certain number the ear becomes confused – even Bach couldn't manage more than six. In any case, as I once explained to Molly, the map is not the real thing but a representation, a recollection. Its fundamental inarticulateness, its experiential blankness, remains shocking. What you want to come back, cannot.

29

How to Climb a Tree

Things start to happen quickly now, start to finish. The Park Authority has taken two years negotiating and re-negotiating about the beeches, two years' worth of appeals and meetings and protests and petitions and refusals by the DoE and another round of all that followed by a final agreement and more committee meetings followed by another turn-around thanks to Ruth Chadwick, followed by a final final DoE decision and a final final submission of a Management Plan and then, now, soon, it's about to happen. Today is Friday; Monday is a Bank Holiday. Tuesday morning, is when.

We have been given two weeks' notice. Two weeks to find other ways to get to work and school and play. An enforced holiday for those further up the Valley, whose exit and access routes to the main road will be blocked. Two weeks, fair enough; besides, it wouldn't do to give people too much time to get nervous.

Four beeches will come down. Mick Merriman will run the show, as he calls it. He personally, according to Bea, would have preferred to carry out the felling hit-and-run style, but the Authority is a Responsible Body which has to be seen to be doing The Right Public Relations Thing. All above board, nothing hidden. *We apologise for any inconvenience. However we hope to carry out the felling in such a way as to cause least possible disruption to residents and other visitors to the Lake District. The felling of four beech trees is being carried out with your safety uppermost in mind.*

You Have Been Warned.

Early Tuesday morning the JCBs, chainsaws and work force will arrive. The road will be closed off to traffic, with warning notices at the A590 junction suggesting alternative tourist routes. Three days have been allocated, allowing for unforeseen difficulties.

It will happen. The thing's been dragging on for too long. It has cost millions in people's time. It has been, what with residents, protesters, committee members and the DoE all with conflicting interests, an administrative and bureaucratic nightmare. The biggest headache we ever got ourselves into, according to Mick. Bea, who is here in my front room, getting ready to leave, says, 'I don't see what more can we do.' We have been drinking coffee, talking things over: the beeches, Housego, this and that. Simon's been vandalising *Cartography Today*.

Time to go, so she humps herself into the baby sling. Simon's crying, probably because his trousers have got hoiked up in the leg holes. The stiff sling fabric chafes. She asks me if I wouldn't mind reaching in and tugging down his trousers. No I wouldn't, and while I'm doing it I'm rubbing Simon's back and thinking about a paper Jay once wrote about babies, or rather not about babies but babies in novels. They're never real, he said, they arrive as if they've been posted, flat as a letter. Somebody goes and picks up a baby, say, and remarks to the reader, 'Isn't he/she cute?', and then it gets forgotten about until it can talk or is needed again as a literary device.

I told Jay I found this very strange indeed; I mean, a baby is a very real thing, I said. 'You don't understand,' he said. Which was true; or rather, I did understand but I didn't particularly like what I understood.

Hup hup hup. It takes three hups for Bea to get Simon into a comfy position on her front. His suit is padded and edged with scallopy red blobs, too hot for indoors. She doesn't understand, she says, fitting her underlip to the outcrop of his head, what I mean about doing something more. 'We've won, it's over, what more … ?' According to her I'm now out of kilter with events: time to get on with our lives. Simon's nose and mouth snuffling in the gap between her breasts. Sliding her hand inside the sling to massage his back.

'If we keep going at this stage there'll be a massive backlash.' Clap to baby's back and a puff of smoke from the recesses of his bundled-up neckline. 'Poof, there goes our local support.' Smell of baby powder.

'They'll be saying, "Don't those people know when to give up, when enough is enough?" and I wouldn't blame them. Four trees just aren't worth it.' And now she better be getting back, Simon's getting over-heated.

Four trees: dead dying diseased. A thinning-out exercise; a trim, a snipping-out, a positive type of pruning; more room for the others to grow. Bring light in, let the dead wood rot down. Think of the wildlife soon to be housed in the great felled trunks; the mice and moles and insects and larvae and voles soon to take up residency in the huge rotting stumps and trunks.

Besides, only direct action would make sense at this late stage and who in Save the Beeches would be up for that? Not Bea Merriman, nor David Housego, nor the Kendal or Ulverston people. Which leaves one other person, and can you seriously picture the professor laying himself down in front of a JCB or chaining himself to a tree?

Monday night, August Bank Holiday. The class is predictably thin, only three of us. No, I don't know where Housego is.

'Shall we go ahead anyway?' Sara suggests.

'Why not.'

'Might as well.'

'Sure.'

So we begin: (1) Sit on a straight-backed chair on your sit bones; (2) Be in the present; (3) Place right hand on right thigh; (4) Place two fingers of left hand on right bicep; (5) Raise your right arm.

As my right arm moves the muscle contracts, narrows and bulges up like a small mammal rising out of sleep.

'Muscle tension,' Sara explains. For almost all of the actions we perform we tend to overuse our larger muscles, and tense them more than we need to.

'Now go through the same procedure,' she says, 'doing exactly what you did before, **only this time imagine a string attached to the knuckles of your right hand helping to raise it up.** How does the muscle feel now?'

What muscle? I hardly know it's there. It doesn't bulge but remains fast asleep in my upper arm. The arm rises without fuss or bother, apparently more efficiently.

'You have allowed your arm to make the same motion as before but without the tension.'

Well done. My arm is soft. I have learned an Alexander lesson in softness. I am pleased. I almost didn't come to tonight's class because of having to prepare for tomorrow, but something made me come and that something was obviously right because this is the lesson I needed to learn, the best preparation I could have done. Forget spike-walking, just stay soft and imagine a sequence of strings raising me up. Think about Flat Stanley being flown as a kite, how he went soaring high over the trees: freely, effortlessly, without tension. Stanley Lambchop demonstrates the Alexander Technique!

Change doesn't happen overnight, except when it does; when you find yourself at that overnight stage, that deep-breath, about-to-act-out-of-character phase. Then it can seem so sudden, so unbearably sudden, that on the threshold of the morning in question you ask yourself what you are doing and why, and shouldn't you just go home and get a good night's sleep; be like Bea (shiny cheerful adaptable); when you wake up it will all be over.

No. Or rather the answer isn't yes or no but both and neither; a thing so complicated there are no words and no conclusions. Sometimes I think one thing and then the other. I will not be fixed in my position vis-à-vis the beeches. Or rather sometimes I am fixed but the fixing is temporary. It happens, it still happens that I look at the beeches (no.31 in particular) and what I see isn't a splendid two-hundred-year-old specimen but a Peter Lorre-type creep or one of those ferocious Indian gods with far too many arms. And then it changes; and changes again.

Uncertainty is the only really tenable position whether in science or in life. However, this is about action, a different story altogether.

So here I am, making for the beeches with a weight of backpack on my back, pretending not to recognize myself, except that I do. Hindsight helps. It tells me I have been preparing for this – a part of me has – for quite some time. I have been doing my change homework, my building-myself-up-to-whatever-it-is until the time is right for me to do whatever-it-is I plan to do.

And now is the right time.

I am making my way in the still-dark phase between night and morning, the back beneath my pack a skinful of bones and blemishes; a landscape of trepidation, of oh-god-what-am-I-doing.

I have come prepared; taken instruction mental, physical and spiritual. I have observed David Housego climbing the sycamores in my wood (now felled) togged out in full body harness, straps clipped together at the chest. 'What's that for?' I asked. 'To stop the shoulder straps slipping off when I'm hanging upside down.' 'Oh,' I said. Asked about more dangling clanking clip-things. Carabiners, he called them, demonstrating the difference between a screwgate and a clip fastener. The former is used at the waist because it's more reliable. 'That's your lifeline,' he said. Further tree-climbing equipment included helmet with mesh face mask, leg irons with spurs, one rope and one strop.

I do not expect to hang upside down, or to need ropes or strops or clanking things, although I have brought a chain, just in case, and some sexy sticky climbing slippers. But equipment and technique are not what it's about. Purpose, focus, concentration, what to call it? I have practised my morning Alexander lesson in muscle softness, as well as plotting my plan of action. 'If you think an action first the doing of it will be easier' (Alexander Technique); or as my father would have put it, rather more poetically: *And what I must doe then, thinke now before* (John Donne).

But now there's no time to waste on poetry or anything else.

4 a.m. A darkish dawn, chilly but clear.

Dry bark! Thank heavens!

Slip off my pack and get into climbing slippers. Feel instantly balletic. Do some Nijinsky noodling about. Trip on outspreading tree roots. Floored! Flatlander Absorbed Into Ground. Try again. Get moving in another plane.

Back on with pack but minus down jacket.

Already sweating, how to begin?

The first move is always the hardest. Who said that? Housego.

Fine, but other trees have ridges, plates, corrugated. This is like climbing a giant plastic flask. (A beech is not a sycamore! Would that it were!)

Deep breath. Think rising up thoughts. (If Molly could do it, so can you!)

Left leg up, wrap arms around tree.

Great. What now?

Right leg still on ground, needs to follow.

Oh.

Go.

Hoop.

Well done. Small rest here. Let bottom dangle while mind visualizes going up, propulsion by imaginative direction. Uh-pup-pup. Arms holding but relaxed, leg muscles gripping but soft.

Also shaky.

Fine, go with the shake. Bounce. Establish a rhythm. Wood gives, the body gives. Resting but not still. Body pulls down, mental energy springs up. Keep knees loose and springy. Think of a rubberband.

Ve-ry good.

Breathe in, get ready. On the out-breath – go!

OH!

Whoa now, easy. Creep and dangle but not too much bum-dangling or your own weight will bring you down. Creep and dangle but keep on thinking Up. Take the treecreeper's advice. Think Alexander (rising) thoughts. Trust those velcro'd soles!

Take advice from the tree: those scars are ladders.

Pimples and blemishes, eye-shaped shallow hollows, island-shaped tears, scar-tissue – all these make hand and toe-holds.

Notches, grooves, graffiti.

Don't look down.

Forehead to bark. Turn head ninety degrees. (Dancing cheek to cheek ...)

Don't worry about ripped nails. (At least you don't have to hang upside down.)

Don't look down.
Can't move. Help! I'm stuck!
Lean out.
Can't.
Can.
Come.
Who said that?
Come.
Oh.
Up I go.

The time is 5 a.m. Good timing. I have timed it this way to allow myself time before the forestry team arrives. An hour of unscheduled time to prepare for whatever it is I need to prepare for. Sitting and doing nothing time. Adapting to the shape of my perch which is rather grand and throne-like now I'm in it. It has taken some wriggling and shifting about, right leg slung over one branch, left leg slung over another branch: a wider split than is comfortable, but I wouldn't expect a tree to be posturepedically designed. Having said that, I can see why she came up here, lined as it is with moist leaves, this year's and last's, softened at the edges with bark rolled like a bunch of fine if musty-smelling blankets. Her nest and now mine. Back support lined with delicate dry fungal platelets, finely edged in three shades of brown with wavy edges. For extra cushioning I have gathered my sleeping bag around me, around us both. The tree's low-hanging, dark-leaved branches, heavy with nuts. Leaves at the end rather than the beginning of their greening – thick-skinned and stringy – you wouldn't want to eat one. Quiet time, rest time. Head back, eyes to the sky. The smell of my own nervous sweat. Everything in motion around me: branches, leaves, clouds, circulating air.

Haven't you forgotten something, Magda?

Oh that.

The chain attaches. Like this, I am nice and snug and chained up, more aware of the root-like vibrations threading and spreading. The beech in September, full-skirted and generous, gathers around me.

The tree holds me: back upright, legs splayed. Minor discomfort in left hip which is twisted more than the right. But I'm pointed in the right direction, the direction the Head Forester and his team will come from, for it is time, the sky is lightening and it's true I can feel a different vibration, a rumble that doesn't originate inside the tree or the ground beneath but from the road. People are arriving. Surely I must prepare in some way but now it's imminent I don't know how. Grip the tree with one hand, the other flies to my chest. Test chains. Oh, my, I feel awfully strange, which is not surprising under the circumstances. Hang in there, as they say. Close your eyes, think calming and resolute but non-violent thoughts. We-shall-not-be-moved type of thoughts. Don't forget to breathe, Magda, you're doing fine.

No I'm not, I've gone weak, weak and flat. Flat is how I have been in the past and how I am again now. Welcome back to Flatland, Ms Line. The problem is, having a sub-lustrous, and therefore deadly, Invisible Cap is not particularly useful when what is most needed is solidity, weight, staying power. Nor is a Flat Stanley-type flatness. This is not about getting rolled up or blown away but …

Yes, Magda?

I could try breathing deeply into my chest to make it expand and see what happens.

Well?

Nothing.

Listen.

'I'm tired of being flat.'

Who said that?

Magda did.

And now she remembers that Flat Stanley also grew tired of being flat. He was sick of it, he said.

It was making her feel sick too; she'd had quite enough of it.

Stanley's brother Arthur had an idea. He went rummaging through their toy box until he found an old bicycle pump, put the end of the hose in Stanley's mouth and pumped him up.

'There stood Stanley Lambchop as he used to be, as if he had never been flat at all!'

Brilliant idea! And so it was for Magda, too.

But who was at the end of Magda's pump?

Guess.

Which means she is now strong and rounded out and ready for anything?

Yes. Yes she is.

Look down and what do I see? Housego waving a bunch of ropes. The professor peering up rather soulfully then closing his eyes in – it could well be – prayer. Bea Merriman looking like a rainbow on legs, in a pink and purple striped woolly hat, violet and blue jacket, bright purple leggings with lime-green stripes, neon pink gaiters and walking boots with purple laces. On her back, Simon in a turquoise carrier (this one has an aluminum frame). Simon himself is in his lumpy red suit and hood with matching gloves pinned to his cuffs. Waving waving.

Get ready. Here come Mick Merriman and the tree cutters.

Once upon a time – this was before we moved to Ealinghearth – there lived a child-crier.

I'm not talking about Molly here.

Like a town-crier, this neighbour-child cried; cried and cried as if not knowing how to stop, how to do anything but cry. You would go into the garden to weed or read or mow or water and there would be the sound of the child's bike wheels on gravel and you would know that within thirty seconds she'd tumble over and it would start again. *A-ha a-ha*. I can find no satisfactory combination of letters to represent that sound, how it began, swelled, dipped and curved through space and then, quite quickly, got narrowed down. Imagine the shape of a diminuendo in space, a nosecone drawn to a point at infinity.

Her mother hid her away.

The child was snatched off its feet and rushed into the house, *for shame*. The sound retreated. Quiet invaded our garden but further inside that house, I knew, the sound continued. The breaking of the face, the open drawer of mouth, the unstoppable hic-hic. It did, of course, stop.

Eventually. But the pattern was being laid down: the predictability of the child's reaction set for life.

You can't have that: *wawa*!

You're so wonderful/ beautiful/ talented, etc: *waaaaahhh*!

I wish you wouldn't do that: *wa*?

I love you: *wah*!

That at the slightest tumble or toss or criticism or even (or perhaps especially) a compliment or expression of love, she will automatically burst into sobs or need to stuff something inside to fill up the panic.

Crunch go the plastic wheels lodged in gravel.

Over goes the bike: crash! crunch! *bwa wah*!

Her mother came running out. Every time, guaranteed. Thirty seconds of bwaa-ing and out the mother flew to take the sound inside: oh dear, the neighbours will think I'm murdering her. Scoop you up, in you go. Trail of the wail through space, tapering down: big small smaller. Slam goes the door on the wail.

Did I think her mother was killing her? No, I only thought she was protecting her to death.

Molly never cried, or hardly ever. Sometimes she would stare, her eyes ratcheted open, held at their extreme position. Blink not or you'll break. The owl lives in the tree. Bwhoo bwhoo.

It was good to move away from the wailing child. The trouble is, I can still hear her. Now is such a time. Mostly the chainsaws drown her out, but not entirely.

30

Map of the World, Upside Down

'You looked so cool,' says the professor. We sit, so, at my kitchen table, our wineglasses and the cheese plate between us. The table is coated in a glossy marine blue; when its leaves are folded down you can see the original plain pine, sown with two neat rows of crumbs. Time for a clean-out. The cheese is a ripe Gorgonzola brought by the professor from Edinburgh's Valvolla & Crolla.

Cool, did he say?

The professor sips his wine. 'I suppose one's perspective from below is inevitably distorted.'

I sip mine. 'Not any more so than from above. Distortion occurs whatever the viewpoint.'

For a while we make do with the rituals of eating and drinking. A veiny chunk of cheese placed on the end of the tongue followed by another tipple and another. Very pleasant. We discuss Edinburgh and how it has changed over the years. We discuss aged cheeses. One more creamy dreamy lump popped on the tongue to melt and then:

'It was quite moving, you know.' The professor has a way of slipping from one subject to another.

'Sorry, what was?'

'Oh dear.' The professor looks to an overhead beam, seeking aid perhaps from the humble woodworm. Then to the floor, now quite shiny with being milk-polished according to Housego's recipe. No help from above or below, unfortunately. What he means, he says, is that he felt moved by the events of the day: by my 'action' as well as the felling itself.

Whereas I was distracted by other things: chain-cutters, for instance.

The professor collects his briefcase from the front room, scrabbles around in it and produces a photocopied print. 'Have a look at that.' He slides it down near my plate, dangerously close to the Gorgonzola, and peers over my shoulder. 'It's from a book by a seventeenth century Florentine artist, Jacopo Ligozzi.'

A large beech tree with a door-shaped hole at its base.

Virgin and Child in the central fork of its boughs.

Uh, oh, here we go.

The professor is half-embarrassed, half-surprised, half-amused. That's three halves. I wish he wouldn't hang over me. He's probably used to lecturing at a podium. The beech, as he points out, is cruciform in shape ('In much early iconography tree and cross were conflated'). The Virgin and Child equals nativity. So far so good.

'So what's the hollow cavity at its base?'

'Tomb of the Resurrection.'

'Ah.' Map symbols, I'm thinking, are so much more sensible.

'It's all so ... close, don't you see.'

Do I? I trace the veins of the Gorgonzola with my knife. Think maps, rivers, the varieties of blue. The professor's eyes: cheesy orbs! Don't giggle. Too much wine, yes. Do away with the footnotes, the Key to the Symbols. Eat up all your cereal and it will be there at the bottom of your bowl. Promise? Promise.

'Listen,' I tell him. 'It's different when you're actually sitting up a tree. You don't think about anything much except sticking it out as long as you can without getting hurt.'

'Yes, quite ... of course.' The professor turns his head one notch which aims him at the back wall, a wall of paintings (the beeches the beeches the beeches).

'Molly's.'

'*Uh*-huh,' he says, accent on the first 'uh'. And then he's off again on cycles of rebirth. Stirring stuff but at this moment, oh just too out-of-this-world for me.

'I can just about cope with the symbolism,' I tell him, 'but not the religion, I'm afraid.' He doesn't disagree. 'No, no, of course not ... people invariably misconstrue ...'

Filling things out, making historical and poetical connections.

Pop ... pop ... pop!

'Look I'm 3-D', as Molly would say.

'Transformation, metamorphosis, evergreen resurrection ...' He stirs the air not unlike Jonathan Miller going on about opera. Again, '... it's all there ... don't you see?'

What I see are Molly's painted trees, and what I know is that fifty of the real trees are still left standing further up the road, plus or minus a few limbs. I wave a bag of newly-ground coffee at the professor, smell that, but oh, good heavens, no! – one whiff and he may never sleep again. Try waving a bottle of malt whisky: yes yes, here the prof is game.

'Water?'

No, he's a neat-man.

And now it's time to go through, as they say in Edinburgh, so I stick the bottle on a tray with two glasses and lead him to the sitting-room, the room for sitting in. But first, the professor seeks a toilet. 'Upstairs to your right.' While he's up there I attend to the fire, chuck on half a firelighter to help things along. Close my eyes; open them; make the whisky go round and round in its glass bowl.

The professor returns with a moving apology. I mean, he's moving down the stairs and apologizing at the same time. Seek and ye shall ...

'Find the loo all right?'

'Yes, look, sorry, I've been going on ... habit ... the truth is, was, I felt so damned useless ... standing there while you were ... risking your life.'

Risking my life? Whoa, now, let's not get carried away!

'Listen,' I tell him, 'I planned to come down before things got nasty. Which I did, and here I am. Nothing dramatic about it.' A screw of paper still in my hands which I twist, hard.

'Yes, but what can it have been like for you up there all alone while we stood gawping?'

'I was glad to be alone. And it was great to have support below.'

'I almost didn't come.'

'I'm glad you did, all of you.'

By now we're curled up either end of the sofa and I'm looking at him through a rolled-up *Cartography Today* which makes him appear even further away than he is. There are more things he wants to say to me but can't because I'm too far away or because he thinks I won't understand, which is probably just as well. As I observe through my spyglass, his eyes are closed and his lips are moving.

Don't mock, Magda, this is for real.

'So ... were you really praying for me when I was up the tree?'

The prof tee-hees, he really does.

And now I'll have to put it in my own words because if I quote the professor you'll think him mad and I don't suppose he is. A bit dotty, perhaps, but not mad.

Not me but the tree.

There was this tenth century Anglo-Saxon visionary who had a vision of a tree with consciousness. When this tree got felled, he saw it as a surrogate for the torments of Christ. And then he heard the tree speak. Yes, he did.

'"They pierced ME with nails ...

'"They marked us together ... I was all bedewed with blood."'

He sips up the last of his whisky: perhaps he'd like a straw? But come, I'm being silly and insulting and failing to take the man seriously. On the other hand, I did what I did for my own reasons and he's not overly interested in that. So there I am and there he is and the truth is there's a lot of space between us; in fact my sofa has grown wide enough for the whole lineup of people down in Plato's Cave.

'It was, symbolically speaking, such a close re-enactment ... the analogy ... quite irresistible. Can you understand? "From whose four boughs the great rivers of life flow..."' he quotes.

I twirl my glass. 'Not that it accomplished much in the end.' An attempt to ground him, as Sara would say, bring him back down to earth.

'On the contrary, taking a stand ... seat, rather ... oh help ...' Fluster fluster, the professor is off again. Oh, do stop faffing about!

'I mean making a visible protest ... yes, to be admired ... not to mention – as I've been droning on all evening ...'

Where oh where will it end?

'... the magic of it.'

The magic?

So this is where it ends, with something the professor calls magic. Let the word simmer. A sauce needs to simmer down to its essential sauciness, why not a word? Magic. The professor is full of it. He is so full-of-it he barely sees me-as-me. I wonder if he even sees the trees. Magic and symbols, the professor's way of mapping the world.

Naturally, one doesn't like to disturb such a sweet mental construct, but in the end ... one must. One is so inclined. Truth time for academics and cartographers and whisky drinkers. Time for a comeback, for a statement in the shape of an arrow. On the in-breath, take aim. And on the out, 'It was not ...' Here a pause, taking a leaf from the professor's verbal style book. Not 'it wasn't' but 'it was not'. And now:

'It was not magical in the path lab.'

Which puts an end to speech and speechifying, and ushers in a tsunami of unsound. The child-crier in reverse, a tendency towards perfect notnoise.

Good work, Magda!

The professor nods, the hit head heavier than Housego's at half its volume: oh the weight of guilt! But then there's the lightness of an 'aha!', and gradually these two combine to produce a condition which might be described by the phrase, 'For a moment there he was struck dumb'. And so it was.

Eventually, of course, it comes back. Speech: poor, pathetic, inadequate, the need to use words as pathmarkers. The professor is sorry; he is professorial in his sorriness; he even slaps his forehead in sorriness, *mea culpa*. How could I have forgotten? What a duffer! As if all the public school education, which embarrassed him and plunged him into a loneliness he will never recover from, were all too much; as if to say, I am like you, I am less than you. I know not, is his motto, and yet here I am, a professor, which must mean I have things to profess, and yet I feel as ignorant and helpless as ever I have – and this proves it.

'Can you ever forgive me?'

'Don't be silly.' Now that I've said the hard clear thing, it's over, eased and onto the next phase. 'Of course. Forget it.'

His eyes, if eyes can do such a thing, are perspiring. His apologies are wearing and endearing in equal measure. His shirt puffs out of his trousers, regulation elbow-holes in his jumper. The arms themselves are full of dirty dishes. We stand hip to hip at the sink. As the dishes are dried and put away I tell him about my map collection. He is interested, of course, but rather tired so for now may he be excused? Of course. I take his hand, very gently so as not to frighten him, and up the stairs we go. Molly held onto two fingers. The stairs were pyramids, Alps, Himalayas. Do the treads remember? Molly's bed is now the spare bed.

I park the professor on the spare bed with its clean sheets and a clean towel folded on its pillow. Tell him if there's anything else he needs to let me know and sleep well.

''Night, then.'

'And you.'

The next day, the professor left for Edinburgh. He'd thought about strolling along to view the devastation – he should, really he should – but in the end he didn't. 'You're more robust than I am,' he said. I didn't think robustness had anything to do with it. I was glad to have it to myself.

Beech 31 – its severed central trunk – lies in a semi-supine position. The remaining stump is around four feet in diameter, criss-crossed with saw marks; some straight slashes, some curved. Dampness makes the stump slippery but it also brings out its colours, warm golden syrup to blackstrap.

This is where I sit. Sit and sit and stare. Map shapes with black liquid outlines that tend, if you stare at them as I do, to flow into one another.

My sixth form geography teacher pulled down the Map of the World. He was called Mr Dorling, and we supposed, because he dressed nattily and moved in a more fluid way than our other male teachers, that he must be gay. Homosexual, a fruit. That being so, every morning there appeared on his desk an apple, pear, banana, like that. No morning did he fail to show delight, no morning did he cotton on to our idiot heehawing. And then, one morning, he pulls down the Mercator as usual – that lovely flat oh-so-inaccurate cartographic projection – and it's upside down; only he doesn't notice because his eyes are too misted over with gratitude, what with that morning's bunch of grapes. He points to South Africa when he means Northern Siberia.

My first Mercator projection showed Europe twice the size of South America, the Soviet Union larger than Africa, Scandinavia as big as India, and Greenland bigger than China.

The Peters Projection is ideologically sounder and cartographically more accurate. **FAIRNESS TO ALL PEOPLES**, announces the Peters Projection: *In this complex and interdependent world, the peoples of the world deserve the most accurate possible portrayal of their world.* The Peters Projection is the **MAP FOR OUR DAY.**

This is where I sit. Sit and sit and stare at the configurations produced by sap and moisture and age:

The oldest known map (China, 2100 BC) painted on the outside of an ancient cooking vessel;

The map of a graveyard uncovered from a tomb around 300 BC;

A Biblical map including Paradise, the Garden of Eden and the route of Exodus;

The painter Vermeer's map of nowhere in particular: fuzzy, blurred, beautiful;

A medieval *mappa mundi*: florid, artistic, complete with dragon;

Maps and more maps, I see; maps of poverty, maps of rural gardens, maps of Queens and of crime; maps of contaminated water, of cholera, of madness; maps of fatalities (showing coffins); maps of sewers (showing putrid matter, public privies, etc.); maps of family trees, maps of nuclear installations; maps of the ear and brain; maps of the meridians and chakras; maps of the stars and the planets; maps of animal and bird populations; Buddhist 'roadmaps' to higher states of consciousness;

A sixteenth-century cordiform projection: twining vines, a heart with roots –

There is no end to this.

The heart of Beech 31, as Mick Merriman and others predicted, was spongy and hollow and rotten. I go in with my nail. So they were right after all. Housego still insists it could have gone on another fifty years. Other trees, he says, are rotten inside only we don't know it. What we don't know, he says, doesn't hurt.

It's getting dark but still I go on sitting. Sitting with the body of the tree which lies horizontally against the earth. A great grey body. Think of it as a wake. I scrub the soles of my shoes into the sawdust around the base of the stump. The professor's father down there; funny thought. Fathers/Sons/Men/Women/Trees/Children. Write these simple words with one of the many beech twigs lying around, then scratch them out.

English Nature has launched a national register of ancient trees. The Fortingall Yew in Scotland (five thousand years old), will be the first on the list. The measuring is to be carried out by children.

Beech 31 is now in pieces. With luck, it will be allowed to remain where it is, to be colonized by all kinds of creatures and plant life. That's good. Its main boughs have been logged, its smaller branches taken away for compost. What, then, is left? I peel off bits of bark, scrabble some more in the sawdust. Looking for, what, some kind of memory-leech in amongst its remains: all that broken-down vegetable and mineral matter combining into a rich mulch. Griefs ancient and modern, oh yes. They say a tree carries a memory of its storms, that its rings record their history. They say that even after it's been felled those memories somehow continue. Does that mean it remembers those who have climbed it, perched in it?

A child sits in the fork of a tree; the way she sits, her posture, her gestures, her stillness. All this creates – what to call it? – vibrations. These go on spreading. How far do they spread? This cannot be known. In theory to infinity: planets, stars, universes. Who knows. Not the physicists, not yet. As for this place, this stump, what of her memory does it contain? A thrill, a breeze, a shiver, a something. Not to mention the Maid and the professor's father.

Rest well, all of you.

Each of us, so they say, has an inbuilt 'map of the self'; us in relation to others. In bereavement, they also say, this map gets destroyed; at some point, add the thing called hope, and it gets reconstructed.

31

Map of Three Worlds

We sit in the bay window staring out at the now-clear view of the Bay, much improved without the sycamores. 'So much lighter,' says Bea. I agree. Simon crawls, we sit. We don't drink coffee, don't do much of anything. Simon reaches up for a magazine and pulls it off the coffee table. We observe this but do nothing about it. The lost art, doing nothing, falsely named because we have no name for what it is we are doing or not doing.

Think about how, at the end of a film, you find yourself sitting while the credits scroll away and the curtains swish closed, and still you sit. Eventually, but still reluctantly, you gather your things and shuffle out. Just so we sit. Eventually we say, 'So.' Roll our lips, chew our cheeks, sort-of-smile, tilt the line of our shoulders, cock our heads and point our eyes – if that's possible – in the direction of the beeches. Gestures play their part in this dance of head and shoulder. Unfortunately, our repertoire of movements is limited so we continue to grope towards language.

'So it's over?'

'I s'pose.'

'Seen it?'

'Hm.'

'Hm.'

Each waiting for the other to pronounce. Assuming the worst until one of us says something like, 'Oh, it's not so bad.' Which happens; Bea says it.

'It's not so bad. Really. You have to admit.'

'Do I?'

'C'mon, Magda.'

'All right. It's better than having forty-four down, or all of them or even ten of them. But it's a mess. They look like amputees.'

'The cuts are still raw. Mick says they'll weather. By the summer with the new growth, you won't even notice.'

Won't I. Mick says. Mick and his chain-cutters, Mick and his saw. Bea says she's sorry it was Mick who had the job of cutting me down.

'It's all right, I don't hold it against you.'

'He was quite gentle, yeah?'

'Yes, he was.'

'He could have been rougher.'

'Yes.' No, Bea, you're not married to a monster.

'And the big one ...' she says. 'Beech 31. Mick was right about that – have you seen the stump? Squashy as an Aero bar.'

'Mm.'

'Stop that!' Simon is eating *Cartography Today*: good teething matter. Bea wrenches it away from him and picks him up. Not roughly. He wails. 'I'll have to get on. I just wanted to tell you about the new proposal, it's been jointly agreed.

'What proposal?'

'The sculptures.'

'What sculptures?'

'Magda, forgodsake where've you been?'

Where have I been? 'Working (face in a computer screen). I haven't seen the *Gazette* and I haven't spoken to Housego.'

'Okay. Four sculptures have been commissioned.'

Four sculptors to make four sculptures to replace the four felled trees.

'Who's commissioned?'

'The Park Authority, local sponsors and Northern Arts. So what do you think?'

'You're joking.'

'No. They asked me to ask you, informally, if you'd do the map for the brochure.'

'Who's they?'

'The committee.'

'No.'

'Don't be stupid.'

'I'm busy with other jobs.'

'Make time for this one. The thing is, I'm collaborating with one of the sculptors.' The difference between her and the professor is when he feels guilty he hangs his head – she cocks it.

The sculptor's plan, it seems, is to embed four of Bea's photographs (of the four felled trees) inside a trunk-like structure, so that when you look inside you see the images of the trees that once were but are no more.

'It's called "Memorial". Have a look.'

She hands me a sketch. Simon tries to grab it, succeeds in getting a corner. 'Oi!' Bea smacks his hand, then rubs it. How confusing!

'Listen, Magda,' she says, 'at first I didn't like the idea either but I changed my mind after I met the sculptors. They're really sweet. I mean, they don't see it as replacing the trees. They know that's not possible. They're not going to do anything crude or obvious or sentimental. Not like a theme park or anything, if that's what you're worried about.'

'It'll encourage more tourists, more traffic.'

'It's only four sculptures, Magda. Pretty low profile as these things go. More like the Eden Valley sculpture trail – seen that?'

'No.'

'You have to walk, in some cases quite a distance, to find the sculptures. They blend in with the landscape. With any luck, ours will too.'

'It doesn't work as a sop, you know.'

'Why d'you have to see it like that?'

'Because I do.'

'I'll drop off details and some more photographs. You can think about it.'

'When will they be installed?'

'The opening is pencilled in for next spring, assuming the sculptors can get the work delivered by then.'

'They'll never make it.'

'They want them installed for the millennium.'

'Good luck.'

Simon's grizzling, she's got to go.

'Hey, how'd it go with the professor?'

'How'd what go?'

'You know.'

'Nothing. He's nice. Writing a book on tree symbolism. He'll want to know about the sculpture plan.'

'I'll send him a copy of the proposal. You'll see him again?'

'We might meet up at Christmas. I'm going up to see my mother.'

'And Housego?'

'I haven't been to Alexander classes in a while.'

'He thinks you're avoiding him.'

'How d'you know?'

'He told me.'

'What about you?'

'Wife Mother Photographer: that's me. It's not like that with us anymore.'

Not like that. I tell her I don't really know how we are. 'Not serious, anyway.'

'You're so cool, Magda.' This is what she says.

'You're the second person who's accused me of that recently.'

'Well, you may be missing some important signals. Anyway, look, I've got to go. And about the map for the brochure – think about it, okay?'

The professor's postcard is up on the refrigerator door, round the side from Molly's contour map. Along with the card came a legend about a woodman from Thessaly who cuts down a sacred oak tree. His punishment, meted out by the Earth goddess, is eternal hunger. The poor guy snaps air, his stomach gripes, he calls for food, but the more that appears, the hungrier and emptier he gets. In the end he devours himself. Poor Mick Merriman. Seems the professor has a sense of humour after all.

On the other side: a woodland pond with fish, the reflections of three trees. 'Three Worlds' by M.C. Escher.

Look closer, Magda.

The leaves, beech and oak, mostly, float on the surface of the water. They get smaller as they go from bottom to top of the picture plane, thus demonstrating the receding surface of the water.

The fish (one of those giant goldfish with pop-eyes) is in the foreground just under the surface, peering up at the viewer. Not a pretty beast.

The three trees, in the background, are shown in reflection, presumably the only proof that they exist. Of course, the floating leaves could well belong to some other trees on the other side of the pond ...

So there are three separate elements: (1) that which is on the surface; (2) that which is underneath but clearly visible; and (3) that which is merely reflected.

At first I imagine the professor chose it simply for the tree imagery, but the professor is never simple. There must be another message besides the one he scrawled on the back thanking me for putting up with him, and inviting me to visit him if I'm up that way for Christmas.

On the surface, under the surface, in reflection.

I go on studying the picture until my own brain is swimming with surfaces that contain, reflect, float. It's all there, of course, but not in any solid or usable way. I'm tired. The week has been exhausting one way and another. I keep returning to the one relatively clear space on the surface of the pond where the fish's eyes stare up and its whiskers jut out, and frankly I can't help thinking it looks rather like the professor.

Chapter 32. Map of Matrimony

Signals, she said. I slide the Map of Matrimony onto the drawing table. Centre it, frame it; adjust the table's tilt to a more horizontal position. Lean over it in a more or less relaxed – released – way. All that small print, those barely decipherable but possibly important details. Adjust the anglepoise lamp so my own shadow doesn't blot the thing out.

Map of Matrimony (19th century, English). Who else but the Victorians could have conceived of such a thing? The central land mass, shaped rather like a legless flying elephant wearing a hat, is divided into seven main states:

Country of Compliments
Land of Kindnesses
Province of Jewellers and Milliners
Feeland
State of Agitation
Wedding Cake Land
State of Solemnization.

Before gaining access to these blessed regions, however, you have to show your mettle. Between Feeland and Wedding Cake Land, for instance, lie the Mountains of Delay. The perimeter is sprinkled with come-ons: Cape Billet-doux, Bay of Mirth, Point Hope, Valentines Bay – if only you could get there; for the coastline of Matrimonyland isn't represented by one easy-to-skip-over line but several overdrawn ones. Skin within a skin of impenetrable cliffs.

Coast of Spoons, Port of Hymen, Point Joy.

Ships founder on coastlines, hit rocks in fog, come adrift. Between Flirtation Point and Settlement Bay comes the Sea of Doubt (what scale is this map anyway?). And there, miles out to sea, is the Island of Spinsters. Not exactly partytown, not your great little Greek island, not hotly pursued in the tourist stakes. More like the back alleys of Nowheresville where the widows in black wail their laments.

Languish Town, Widow's Bay, Old Maid's Coast.

The Country of Single Men is also an island but rather closer to the mainland and separated from Spinster Island by the Sea of Propriety. As a Single Man, Our Hero may set up shop in Dismal Town, City of Uneasiness, Town of Discontent or Make-up-Your-Mind City. When he tires of all that, however, he will be free to jump into his stripy T-shirt and sail around the Ocean of Admiration. His trajectory (marked by dotted lines) takes him from Lonely Isle into the Sea of Doubt and from there ...

But meanwhile, back in the Land of Spinsters, Our Heroine is setting off, in her ropy rowboat, from Point Want Husband towards the Island of Fear. From there she zooms south making an unscheduled stop at Jealousy Isles. (Where she, what, jumps up and down gnashing her teeth? Roars her heart out to the stone-blasted sea? 'Liar! liar! you played with us both! I demand an immediate explanation!') This, however, is exhausting (but quite cathartic) and at dusk she rows peacefully home to knit, tend her goats, mumble ifs and buts and on-the-one-hand-on-the-other to herself. Grows her nose long.

Meanwhile, only recently recovered from cruel rejection by his married lover, Our Hero continues trawling the coast of Matrimonyland until he washes up on Parson's Bay. Strolls along the heathery cliffs to Cape Billet-doux, shields his eyes from the western sun and sights, a pogostick's hop across the Ocean of Felicity, the Land of Spinsters. 'Oh yes, tomorrow!' he exclaims. 'Tomorrow I will set sail.' Which he does, there delivering (this being Victoriana-land) his proposal down on his knees.

What else would you expect?

Housego's eyes aren't sea-blue and in any case I'm not looking into them. We're sitting on my garden bench staring out towards the estuary, a reasonably clear view now that he's cleared the syacamores. So there we are, two more-or-less-right-angled bodies, lined up one beside the other on a stone slab: one arboriculturist, one cartographer. Expanded labels for contracted people. We are too pooped to stand. We could be posing for 'American Gothic', seated version. All that's missing here are the pitchforks.

No smiling, now.

Housego isn't good at this but the offer seems to be there.

'Well?'

'Well what?'

'It's not impossible,' he says, and I say, 'Nothing is,' which he agrees with in principle, but then I say it doesn't make much sense either; and then he asks why does everything have to make sense, to which I don't really have an answer.

Housego: 'You're making this difficult.'

Me: 'Is it meant to be easy?' I'm thinking about certain not-so-easy subjects such as wife and children but Housego seems to have taken care of all that. He uses the word 'together'. 'We could be together,' he says, and I observe that we are at this very moment together sitting on a stone bench getting cold bums, watching the sun set over the estuary. Fine sight.

Housego: 'You're so cool, Magda.'

Me: 'If one more person says that.'

Housego: 'What?'

Me: 'Nothing.'

I'll spare you some dialogue here. What?/Why not?/It could/This isn't working is it?/etc. Suffice it to say, it went on until some kind of communication took place. Housego explained that, although still legally married, he was well into the process of unmarrying (by mutual consent), though five children complicated matters somewhat.

'Somewhat.' The word had an understated quality to it.

'Oddly enough,' he says, 'she doesn't want custody. I'm assuming women normally do, but perhaps I shouldn't make that assumption.' Generous and self-questioning.

'None of them?' I ask.

'She wants a clean break: marriage and motherhood were never for her,' he explains. 'She's one of those committed academics. You know?'

'I know.' Like Jay, like the professor.

'Anyway,' he says, 'she's off to Africa again, more demographic research. Promises continued financial support at least but a settlement will have to be worked out.'

'So what will happen to your kids?'

'I'll get custody, as I said.'

He had so many children, he didn't know what to do.

'How can you be so sure?'

'It's just what I'm assuming.'

'It's important to consider all eventualities.'

'Why?'

'If you know what can go wrong maybe something will go right.'

Follow the river inland beyond the Mountains of Delay.

'Will it?'

'I don't know.'

'Think about it, okay.'

'Okay.'

And so we return to Our Heroine on her Island of Spinsters where she sits, legs dangling over the edge, skipping stones into the sea. Will I take him into my heart/bed/etc.? Shall I? This Island, it turns out, is famous for its Coastal Boomerang Effect, which means that anything you throw (words, stones, goats, etc.) returns to you.

Watch out, Magda! Duck!

By now they're sitting face-to-face in front of the fire. The fire is burning jollily. He reaches across to take her hand which is resting with its mate, palm up, in her lap. His voice has an old-film quality.

Cary Grant: 'Surely you don't mind if I hold your hand.'

Mae West: 'It ain't heavy, I can hold it myself.'

She stops his mouth with a roto-rooter type kiss. She is trying to convince him he's deluded about love.

'It's only sex,' she corrects.

'No,' he insists, plunging further in, 'it's more than that.'

'What could be more?' More, echo the flames in the fireplace.

'I mean, it isn't *only* sex.'

Only a rose. *Rosa spinosissima* spreads by suckering. The word 'only' could be significant, of course. She tilts her glass and sips up some liquid. His earnestness is frightening inside the pink fleece. 'You could take it off, it's quite warm in here.' 'Not yet,' he says.

This is the hard part. This is what creates the updraught that floats her up to the ceiling where she hangs upside down from a beam, rather like a pine marten. She is small and wary and not so gentle, and this is what she observes.

His hand is raised above hers. She registers it as an oncoming attack and tenses, except there is of course no attack, no follow through, no squeezing the life out of. The fingers drop, not in a predatory way nor all at once but like a seabird landing not with both feet at once, but staggered, featherdusting the sand.

She would like to squeeze each finger end until the pink stuff comes. Strawberry syrup, grenadine, suck on the ends, live on his sweetness forever.

In the morning, I sit on the lower step between Housego's knees, my hair wet. He takes the comb, 'Here, let me do it.' It's the kind of fine mouse hair that tangles easily. Through lack of personal kindness towards myself, I tend to yank. Housego lifts up the top hair and deknots the stuff underneath. He does it in layers, in individual strands if necessary like a first-year hairdressing student with a paying customer. Adding dollops of dulcification, deep leave-in conditioner as he goes. Welcome to the Land of Sexual Intimacy and Regular Bodily Kindnesses – missed out on the Victorian Map of Matrimony.

Follow the River of Kisses to its source – beyond the Mountains of Delay into True Love Town – and there, in the very heart of the Region of Rejoicing, you will come to the Lake of Little Darlings.

In the real as opposed to the map world you can follow any of a dozen Lakeland rivers up to their mountain source: Goat Water, for instance, which is in a bowl between The Old Man and Dow Crag. There you can sit, as I do, halfway up the Old Man's screed east face looking down into the tarn, except that a blast of 'unseasonal' snow and wind which hit during the night has turned it into a pool of frozen pale blue buttermilk. An ice of many layers from thin to thick; from dusky purple to a bruised-looking grey. On the surface an exhibition of ice-blown sculptures: geodesic dome, hexagon, tetrahedron. Around the edges a school of shark-snouts in utter white against the blue milk.

Gust-inspired spindrifts, shape-shifting spirals, rolling-pins, hay bales. Sheeted see-through world. Wind to blow the top-snow into ectoplasmic smoke.

I am here to think, to come to some kind of conclusion vis-à-vis Housego. What do you think, Magda? Cold. Nobody knows, tiddly pom. Numb. Dumb. Dumdedumdum.

Enough. Move before you freeze to death, a not very satisfactory solution. Beat yourself on the arms like an Arctic explorer. Walk fast, slipping and sliding on half-frozen scree and half-running causing mini-avalanches. Not to worry. The blood in your feet is now beginning to unthaw, followed by other parts of your body including your face getting red and your heart and lungs doing what hearts and lungs are supposed to do under the circumstances, which causes a slow but sure unthickening of the brain-syrup in your head, excellent for decision-making. Down now at Goat Water, poke a hole in blue ice with your stick and watch as the water begins to flow, slowly at first, then all a-gush. The thoughts are coming, here come the thoughts. The thoughts say ...

It would be nice, it would be so nice.

It would be good, it would be nourishing.

Replenishing redemptive rejuvenating healing

Judicious companion planting, highly recommended by Mother.

The thoughts focus themselves into a list of Arguments For: (1) Regular sex; (2) Regular meals (Housego likes to cook: he makes a carrot soup with coriander that's sweeter than caramelized roses); (3) Regular DIY, garden and treework; (4) Shared use of Land-Rover; (5) Shared use of five children; (6) Regular walking and talking.

*

Then the list gives way, along with the ice, and in that mini ice-framed pool I see ... how it would be fair and it would redress the balance, dress the balance up to such a degree I would not recognize it in its party frock, all bangled and brassed; in fact, the balance would tip so far the other way I would be left with an embarrassment of balance. Good. It would be so good it makes my mouth and other parts of my body salivate just to imagine it. It would cause comfort and crying and noise. It would cause food to be cooked and ears to be washed and wounds to be dressed and walks and cycle rides to be taken. Tantrums. Stories to be read including Flat Stanley for the younger ones and Flatlanders for the older ones. It woud cause the Aga to be stuffed top and bottom ovens both. It would fill the house with a whole Afro-drum orchestra of footsteps. Shadows a-plenty. Mud: five bootpairs' worth, all lined up on racks in the drying room. Larder stuffed with peanut butter and Coco-pops. It would cause the woodland to not be neglected, because Housego would look after it. A live-in woodman who would chop wood and carry wood and all the wood would rejoice because, at the moment, everything is overgrown and therefore struggling for light and he could decide what to do about that, not to mention the falling-down garage which he would cause to be rebuilt to house not only the Land-Rover but all the bikes and trikes etc. of my now jointly-owned tribe. And that would be good and other things too and so it would cause goodness all around, so good, so so-so-good, it would be like the fireworks at the end of Bonfire Night, like a whole spaghetti explosion of goodness, a Hale-Bopp of goodness, a skyful of streaking pulsing tail-wagging millennial goodness. A hoot, a side-split of unlikeliness, a head-wag of 'you don't say!' Which reminds me of the time we were having tea at the Wolf House Gallery and Molly ordered a cherry chocolate crunch square and it weighed about three pounds and Molly said you could make lots of them and use them to pave the garden path and then when people came to tea they could crawl around eating bits off, and the thought of people crawling around eating the paving stones was so hilarious once we started we couldn't stop laughing.

Fom an absence of progeny to a whole teeming Lake Districtful. Hold out your empty arms and here they come, brace yourself ... oof ... a brace of progeny and a man too! A man of spirit and DIY capability, a veritable Paul Bunyan of a man, a man of ecological principles who comes off-the-peg with just about everything, not to mention five children.

And now all that's needed to complete the picture (taken by Bea Merriman) is the black labrador. I could send it to the Aga people for their catalogue, all of us lined up, size-placed from Housego at 6' 5" to baby Housego at around 2'. The stepped step-family. Oh, it could be so good and so funny it makes me drool. Better not drool too much or the drool will freeze on your face.

By now I'm so tempted my knees ache with temptation (and going steeply downhill) not to mention that other over-named part of my body which is now like a frozen chocolate cake yearning to be defrosted and why ever shouldn't it for it would be so good, so yummy-in-the-tummy, so ring-around-the-mouth, so disgustingly good, melted all over, spread all over, head to foot smeared in chocolate with fingerprints and tongue-prints as evidence ... yes yes it would be so good so too-too-good, to the point of too funny and too good and too Death by Chocolate and too Aga-family perfect, and there would come the time when I would look around at my inherited quintet, sextet, thinking,

What are all these people doing here?

Look again at the Map of Matrimony: Land of Spinsters, Country of Single Men. The man goes through high water and a certain amount of hell and eventually takes the hand of the lonely spinster languishing in Languish Town and jumps her onto his dinghy and bobs her over the Sea of Doubt to Acceptation Point over on the mainland. Following a quick visit to Lawyerland they settle at Settlement Bay. They cultivate their children and rotovate their land and activate their organic veggies and off he goes to work in his Land-Rover and she stays at home making maps on her computer and shoving pies into the Aga for when the kids come home from school, college, university, etc.

Happy families

Happy couples
Two by two
Him and her
He and she
A deux à deux
The Map of Matrimony assumes a dyad, a him and a her. It's all genetically arranged, not to mention culturally reinforced. A closed system, a foreclosed system.
Is this really what you want?

33

Maze With Happiness at its Centre

The brain, Jay once confided, is a tree-like structure containing a hundred billion neurons, with the branches of each connected in turn to billions of other neurons, and so on almost *ad infinitum*. Between each of the neurons is a gap. Why does that word stop me in my tracks? *Gap* – that small space – how do you know you can bridge it?

In order for a thought process to take place, however simple or complex, it has to jump the gap/s, which it does on the back of a chemical that trickles between the neurons. Thus, we say our thoughts can 'flow'.

The Maze of Happiness in my map cabinet (Drawer 13) reminds me of that tangle of neurons, or what I imagine they might look like. To a brain researcher – nonsense; but this is not about accuracy but about how we make connections. Keep the leaps small and you'll be safe, you won't fall in.

To be in a maze is to be in a state of bewilderment.

A maze – that confusing and baffling network of paths – is there to lose you; a map, on the other hand, is there to help you out of your bewilderment. This particular maze is a Victorian morality game. It shows a labyrinth of yellow pathways, yellow brick roads. The background or gaps in between are black. How effectively (directly + quickly), it poses the problem, can your brain get you from your starting point on the edge of the maze to the Circle of Happiness in the centre?

First find your starting point.

You Are Here, says the red arrow, committing me to a promising-looking route beginning at the bottom left-hand corner.

Which way now?

As the player, I can take various routes most of which will lead me astray through Passion, Deceit, Falsehood, Dishonour, Oppression, Avarice, Craftiness, Ill-Will, Perjury, Treachery, etc. Given a fair amount of visual, perceptual and spatial ability, however, not to mention patience, I soon find myself on the correct route – Virtue to Honour, Honour to Benevolence, Benevolence to Religion, and so on – landing finally on Happiness, a circular scene just barely decipherable as a village church on a green with some trees and a small but obviously happy family. English rural idyll. Church/countryside/family.

The 'You Are Here' arrow, having cleverly rotated itself, now points to the centre. And I, having used my brain with its clever gap-jumping chemicals to find the way and also managing to avoid most of the routes through misery and treachery – I am also here on the Circle of Happiness.

Congratulations!

A person, having made her way against so many odds to the Circle of Happiness, should be happy. It stands to reason. Unless, of course, the whole thing is a trick. If we assume all those twists and turns symbolize Life and its unpredictabilities, then logically the centre becomes the end-point. Not where people go to live happily ever after but where the dead go. The maze keeps them safe from intrusion except from those clever enough to find their way, those who want badly enough to visit.

Another postcard from the professor. Escher, again; this one is called 'Reptiles'. It features many little alligators or the life cycle of one, depending on how you look at it. The little alligator begins as part of a flat design, but gradually stretches out one 2-D leg, gives it a shake and launches out into real life.

Scuttle scuttle scuttle. Welcome to 3-D land!

Here the little alligator does all kinds of exciting dimensionful things including breathing fire; but soon he gets tired and heads back to take his place in the surface design.

Back to Flatland.

When he's sufficiently rested he will go once again from flat to round, 2-D to 3-D. Round and round, in and out, in theory, forever.

The message on the other side of the postcard reads (in writing so reptilian I have to use a magnifying glass):

Dear Magda,
So sorry ... had hoped to spend time over hol period but alas mother ill not to mention academic pressures, the book ... then there's the daughter in trouble plus a messy business with my ex-wife ... However, I DO intend to get down there for the spring sculpture opening – extraordinary turn of events! and very much look forward to seeing you there. Well, are you?
> Yours,
> Stephen

Monday night.

'Just walk. Weave in and out, change your pace and direction; when you meet someone, greet them.'

We walk and swing about and smile and greet. Backs straight, spines aligned. Perambulating Alexandroids.

Now close your eyes, she says. This changes everything. We walk but we cannot see. There are many things to collide with: walls, piano keyboard, groping hands. I shuffle along, with my bum ruddering. 'Notice what's happening in your body. Keep breathing. If you let go you're less likely to get hurt. Try trusting. Be a cloud.'

How does a cloud move? Were there clouds in Flatland; particles of dust with the moisture squeezed out? Can a pretend-cloud sense the approach of another body? My own instinct is to become compressed – wham! flat as Stanley – a walking cork board, an heraldic shield. Or flatter still, the ultimate Vogue of Flatland, Ms Line. My instinct is to brake, take aim, defend myself – but the whole point of the exercise is to *invite* collision. As a line, especially with my non-luminous and therefore invisible tip, I can be quite deadly. Useful at times, but not now. A line among clouds is simply stupid.

A cloud moves through space. Space is curved, space can be bent. Light travels in straight lines but curves around massive bodies. Shadows can curve and gravity, after all, is curved space.

As a cloud, or indeed any three-dimensional thing, I have many degrees of freedom. I live, after all, in a universe of ten, maybe fourteen, dimensions.

What am I, then? The choice is a terrible one. Like that famous Escher print of the little reptile (courtesy of the professor), I could go round and round, 2-D to 3-D and back again, forever. Alternatively, I could think of Escher's birds. At first they're just a design of triangles but gradually he adds wings, beaks, belly curves. You can feel the loosening of feathers, the grateful circulation of air. Takeoff at last, the defining moment. Black birds and white birds loosed from the strip of paper on which they were drawn.

I float along as instructed. This makes me dangerously soft and open to the other bodies which pass by, bounce off, move through. (Some feel more cloud-like than others.) As clouds we aren't bothered about losing bits of ourselves or being occupied or even dispersing altogether – so much fluff; and anyway, we know that when it's over we will simply gather ourselves together and reform.

We leave the centre together, Housego and I. Low Fellside is steep, its cobbles slick. Feet, gravity, the hinge and swing of his skeleton beside mine. The body's tendency on a steep hill is to pull back but that only makes your feet slip more. There are so many things we cannot say. This condition we also share with the clouds. Our bodies, however, are eloquent to the point of poetry; hands, lips, nerve endings yearning to touch and cling. It seems important however to resist such purely physical impulses, to brush past and keeping on going. For that reason we do not go for a drink together. 'See you at the Opening,' we say. See you.

34

Map of the Rusland Sculptures

Bea persuaded me to meet the sculptors. We met in a pub in Carlisle. They were all young and distressed about the trees and the obvious lunacy of replacing them with so-called Art. It was very awkward at first but they were so sweet, so well-meaning and idealistic it was hard not to like them. They wanted so much to 'do things differently': do their own thing at the same time as developing a 'relationship' with one another as well as with the remaining trees.

Bea kept nodding her head. I didn't really understand what they meant, what it would mean on the day. One of them said, 'Look, we realize we're in a Catch-22 situation. There's no way our work can replace those felled trees. But they're down, there's nothing we can do about that now. Except maybe, you know, when people look at our work it will remind them, so maybe it won't happen again.' They looked at one another, at Bea, at me, wanted so badly for it to be right you could hardly not develop a nod.

'A good rationalization,' I said. It sounded hard. I amended it to, 'A good enough rationalization.'

The amendments will no doubt go on.

As spring approached, the sculptors said they needed more time.

As summer approached, the sculptors appealed for more time.

Just another month, one more.

And so we take a seasonal giant step, straight over Christmas, the New Year, those three precious newborn months. Another postcard from the professor, saying he's sorry not to have been in touch. ('Life intrudes'.) Hopes to see me at the sculpture 'unveiling' in September. A final baby step over summer and into September, almost a year to the day the beeches were felled.

The brochure, with its map (courtesy Dr Magda Beard) and photographs (courtesy Bea Merriman), has been printed and distributed: Dove Cottage, Beatrix Potter Museum, Tourist Information Offices, etc. Once the sculptures have been installed and the unveiling ceremony takes place, they have permission to put them out on display.

No loos, no picnic tables, no caff.

It could have been worse.

Here's a funny-curious thing: of all the people who ought to know about maps, cartographers know the least. Tell us about the map, what is its nature, describe its 'character'. No problem, says the psychologist or philosopher. The linguist will talk about structure, the psychologist psychocartography, the philosopher spatial equivalence. Map of culture, map of language. Their pages will be sprinkled liberally with the word map, the proposition 'map' being taken for granted. Non-cartographers love it, embrace it, make free with it.

Pity the poor cartographer.

My map of the Rusland sculptures is finished. How do I describe it? Having mapped the sculptures' positions among the trees by a kind of supposed spatial simplification, how do I then explain the map itself? You can't explain mapping by mapping, that's the problem. All you can do is use language and language – pathetic, over-complex – almost always fails us.

The sculpture map itself is very simple. It shows the Rusland Valley road with access from the north (Hawkshead) or south (A590, Rusland/Grizedale turnoff). Map reference numbers for Landranger, Pathfinder and Outdoor Leisure maps included. Four red dots mark the location(s) of the sculptures. Reading from north to south, the sculptures can be found, entitled: (1) 'Witness'; (2) 'Memorial'; (3) 'Leaf'; (4) 'Creation's Still'.

It looks quite nice, it does its job, and everyone seems pleased with it. I have been paid a reasonable amount. It gives a small blurb about the beeches; but what about the site itself, its history, geology, ecology and so forth, its visitors both alive and dead? Crack the code, find your way, admire the sculptures – and throw it away. It's only a map after all, a piece of shiny folded paper.

The unveiling of the sculptures. A publicity stunt, low to be sure, but also, as they say, an opportunity. Almost everyone is here: Park Authority reps, committee members, English Nature, the bat lobby, Friends of the Earth, Rusland Valley residents, a few Save the Beeches campaigners and, of course, the sculptors. Not here are those who think the whole idea of the sculptures was a mistake.

My mother is down from Edinburgh, the professor ditto (he by train, she by car); Housego and all his kids, Bea and hers, me and mine. Add one heartbroken Maid – poor thing, she could use a good bash. All present.

August Bank Holiday, almost a year to the day the four beeches, including Molly's, were felled.

The day is hot and hazy, quite sultry, the road full of loose chippings and 20 mph signs. They've been re-surfacing the road. My mother has gone ahead in her car; I'm on my bike. I stop to chat with the farmer, a chance to wag our heads over the increased traffic. 'It's Grizedale,' he says. 'People have started using this as a through road. And now these things, they'll be coming to see them too.' He gestures up towards the beeches. While he talks, I pluck blackberries. Talking and plucking. He doesn't agree with it. 'If you want exhibitions,' he says, 'you can go to Manchester or London. Why spoil a quiet place like this?' I hold out my hand with its little mound of guilt fruit. *Map courtesy Dr Magda Beard*: he's bound to see the small print on the back of the brochure.

He allows himself a single berry. Says when he came here in 1973 his two little girls used to walk along the road. Shows me a picture of them swinging buckets. Now they have another toddler but they don't let her walk on the road nohow. And I say I don't blame him, I wouldn't either. 'That's all right,' he says. 'Enjoy your do.'

*

Artists like to talk about space, about how their work 'sits in space'; how their creations relate to the trees, the road, the sky, the fells, the people. To them this isn't a fragile beech woodland but the Ultimate Gallery.

That's not entirely fair. Even now the sculptors are huddled together worrying over how their pieces may be disturbing 'the natural balance of nature'. They're perched with their wineglasses on the convenient stump of Molly's beech (31). As I approach they get up rather hurriedly. The stump, a year on, is dry; the central honeycomb of rotten heartwood a playground for beetles and ants. Still visible are the sawmarks, tidemarks of dark to light, and of course the rings which if you had the patience you could count.

It makes a kind of sense. After Molly disappeared, the beeches – this one especially – grew great grabby bracts, claw-branched tentacles with which to scoop her up, feed her into its bole hole, its jigged jaws. Out-Maurice Sendaked Maurice Sendak. Made the Wild Things look like the Spice Girls. The Ultimate Mad Vegetable.

Let your monsters out, says the theory. Give them a long lead, let them do their bone-crunching, munching worst and eventually, like played-out children, they'll rub their eyes and go to sleep. Only a beech tree.

I move over to the group now standing beside the felled trunk. Some children, Housego's I think, are climbing on the bottom section, another group are sitting on one of the smaller mid-sections. Beech 31 now makes a convenient bleacher, picnic bench and bar-stool. A man dressed entirely in green hitches a leg up and turns to me. 'And you are ...?' I suppose he means what am I doing here? I tell him I did the map for the brochure. 'Ah, a cartographer,' he says, 'I've always been interested in maps.'

'Have you?'

'Spatial stuff.'

'Uhn-hn.'

'I mean, how d'you measure it?'

'A complicated question. The simple answer is, we measure space by angles. Then we have the problem, assuming you're working with old-fashioned paper maps, of reducing those three-dimensional calculations to two.'

'But what about all that *space* in between the things you're measuring? Is space a load of nothing? Does it go on forever? What happens when you get to the edge of the physical universe?' Watch out, this guy will soon be quoting Stephen Hawking.

I'm rescued by my mother who seems to have taken charge of the professor. 'Darling, I've met someone else from Edinburgh, isn't that a coincidence. He tells me his father's ashes were scattered' – she glances down at her feet – 'well, I suppose somewhere around here, isn't that so?' The professor nods.

'Glad you could make it.'

A camera clicks. My mother whispers to the professor, 'I think it's time.' Slips her arm through his. Made a conquest, she has.

The sculptors are taking up positions beside their pieces. Housego is posed beside a woman in a long skirt with green toenails and hair.

'Where are we?'

'Right there.'

'How do we find the sculptures?'

'Follow the red dots on your map.'

My mother and the professor walk ahead. The path is unclear, the ground uneven. A lot of struggling straggling people. Housego and his green friend fall in beside me. Bea joins us, holding Simon. 'Seen Mick anywhere?' she asks. Housego says he saw him getting out of his jeep with a big bag of food. 'That'll be our lunch,' she says. 'See y'around.'

We stop, along with everyone else, at Sculpture no.1, the furthest north. It's swaddled, as they all are, in burlap sacking. What will be underneath? Anticipation, surprise, the drum-roll of suspense. Holding your breath is exciting too. At a signal from the organizer the sculptor unties the rope and lifts off the bag. It gets stuck halfway. Cameras click, hands help. The sculptor turns his back. I think he's got the giggles.

'Witness' is a geodesic dome mounted on a wooden stump, each of its facets a mirror. The sculptor, straight-faced now, demonstrates how the mirrors reflect the remaining trees. We can see that. 'You look into the dome and the trees are reflected back. It's meant as a reminder. Also it brings light into the wood.' This is a big honour for him; he has many people to thank.

There are blackberry seeds in my teeth, which I worry at with my tongue but do not manage to dislodge. More cameras go off. Granada TV zooms in for a closeup. The sculptor thanks the Park Authority for supporting this imaginative venture.

One down, three to go.

We move on. The ground surface is dry but it's rained a lot recently, so you sense, under the crust, a deep dampness. Patches of new green among the old grass. Dry twigs, bark, leaves; star moss and clover; a surprising number of oak seedlings. The path, hardly a path, winds through thick bracken. Hard on the women in what my mother calls 'unsuitable footwear', mostly teenage girls in monster platforms and Housego's Green Girl in flip-flops. My mother wears arty German sandals, moulded to her feet. She holds her arms above the bracken. 'Try not to touch. I heard its spores are cancer-producing.'

Growing beside the next stump (Beech 38, as was) is a mushroom measuring two feet across, ruffled brown with tawny tidemarks. When I reach down to touch it my mother says, 'Don't, it could be poisonous.' The professor bends to examine its underside. His knees crack. He pronounces it a something-something in Latin. Mother is impressed.

'Memorial' is next, a sequence of four stone slabs meeting at the top and splaying out at the bottom. The slabs themselves are rather like eighteenth century tombstones, very simple with classical chiselled inscriptions but with the addition, at the top of each one, of a photographic inset: 'The Four Felled', taken by Bea Merriman, along with their dates. Here lie the remains of.

Mick meanwhile is leaning against Beech 32 holding a greasy bag and flinging chips into his mouth at a terrifying rate. Beech 32, which once paired Molly's, is much smaller in circumference. It resembles a thin man doing a handstand with his legs pressed tightly together; at the crux, a prominent bulge.

The professor, unhooked from my mother, whispers do I remember the curse of the Thessalian tree cutter? 'Eternal hunger,' he reminds me. No one else knows what's so funny. Housego and Green Girl move three paces away. Bea steps on my foot then moves closer to Mick, reaches into his bag but it's too late. He crushes the empty bag and stuffs it into his pocket. 'How much longer is this thing going on? I'm still hungry. Starved.' The professor and I hide behind another beech.

Ooh, stop, it hurts!

We manage to compose ourselves, follow along to the next unveiling. Two down, two to go. My mother hisses have I lost my senses and stop leading the professor astray. Bea rejoins us. 'Mick's gone off for more food – I think he has a tapeworm.' This is too much, I'm going to pee in my pants. Bea looks as if she might bite me. 'What the hell's so funny?' And then she tells me to shut it and calls me Maphead. *Maphead*? 'It's a kid's book,' she says, 'I'll lend it to you.'

Maphead, hey I like that!

'Leaf' is a huge stone seat in the shape of a slightly incurling beech leaf. The sculptor sits in it to speak, to be filmed and photographed. Behind her Beeches nos.33-36, which have been severely lopped, still look disturbingly like amputees but are starting to heal over and darken with scar tissue, their stumps getting a bit more rounded and weathered. Several of their branches swoop low down, their leaves end-of-summer limp. Dark, thickened and stringy, at the end of their greening. You wouldn't want to eat them.

'Creation's Still' is the last piece. It's been 'planted', as it were, beside Beech 31, along with the other plastic-collared seedlings. It looks remarkably real. The difference is, it will stay a seedling forever. The sculptor is asked to explain the significance of the title. 'Yes,' she says. Her delivery is halting. 'It refers to an ancient connection between planting a tree for the birth of a child, but really you don't need to know that to appreciate it. The piece will convey different things to different people about the nature of creation.'

And now we're back where we started. Someone cracks another magnum over the stump of Molly's beech. I put my hand over my mouth. 'Extraordinary,' says my mother plucking at my sleeve. 'You don't seem to be taking this at all seriously. I must say you've changed a great deal, Magda, and I'm not so sure it's for the better!'

I raise my champagne glass: 'Cheers. That's because I'm all blown up.'

She looks puzzled, as well she might, but never mind. Here come Flat Stanley and his family who *will* understand.

'GEORGE!' said Mrs Lambchop. 'Stanley's ROUND AGAIN!'

Mr and Mrs Lambchop and Stanley's brother Arthur, who'd blown him up, were all thrilled to have Stanley back again in his normal three-dimensional form. To celebrate, Mrs Lambchop made hot chocolate and they drank several toasts to Stanley and also to Arthur for his cleverness. When the little party was over, they all went to bed.

'It had been a long and tiring day. Very soon all the Lambchops were asleep.'

That's the end.

35

Afterword

*A visit to Rusland will appeal to those visitors looking for a
quiet place to roam among ancient preserved beech woodland
where you will find (map overleaf) four sculptures specially
commissioned to commemorate the four beech trees which,
regrettably, in the interest of safety, have had to be felled.
We hope you enjoy your visit to the Rusland Beeches.*

All over, everyone gone home: Bea and Mick, Housego, the kids, the
professor, the mother, the sculptors, the journalists, the camera crew, the
Save the Beeches campaigners, the Rusland Valley residents. What
remains? Deer, birds, bats, owls, mice, moles, voles, ants, ticks.

The sculptures.

The trees.

Me.

This is where the beech avenue begins. It isn't a 'natural' woodland
because the beeches were planted around two hundred years ago, probably by the then occupants of Rusland Hall. Originally there were one
hundred and four. Half were cut down in 1951. Four more were cut
down last year. That leaves forty-eight.

Molly once wrote in an essay for school that she wasn't worried about
them falling down, she thought they'd stand forever, which may have
been a bit optimistic since all trees have a more or less limited lifespan. 'I
like the beeches very much,' she wrote. 'I play there almost every day'.

Since the sculptures were installed traffic, as the farmer predicted, has
increased. It will continue to do so: cars, coaches, road widening, further
tree felling. It hardly bears thinking about. The history of mapping is all

about this sort of thing: expansion, clearances, gobblings up, devastation.

Mapping is also about exploration. Jay thought about this in terms of the human body. No surface or sub-surface of the earth, he maintained, was so plastered with the labels of its explorers as that of our bodies. They mapped us and left their names for us to remember them by: the Fallopian tubes and Eustachian tubes; Bartholin's duct and the duct of Wirsung, the Graafian follicle, Tulp's valve, the circle of Willis, the Islets of Langerhans, Broca's gyrus, Buck's fascia, the loop of Henle, the bundle of His which conducts electrical impulses in the heart, the angle of Louis which tells medical students where on the chest to pop their telescopes.

What do these names tell us? Only that at the end of some experiment – which may have taken an entire lifetime – the explorer-anatomist got somewhere, though not always where he was meaning to go. You mean this isn't the womb, it's the heart? Not the Spice Islands but America? Well, well!

An ending, an arrival, a finding of sorts: You Are Here.

It doesn't tell us the cost: the foundered ships, the broken mad sailors and the fishes' friends. All that boring and not so boring time at sea, the patient observation, explorers and their bloody feet and cracked lips, scientists with fever and wasted frames due to self-experimentation. Painfully, organ by organ, rock by rock, they got to where they were going. Or didn't. Huntington, Parkinson and his tremor, Bell's palsy, Tourette and his tics, Alois's Alzheimer's, Creutzfeld-Jacob and his mad cow, just to bring us up to the present. No woman, so far as Jay knew, had any body part or condition named after her; no place on earth either, so far as I know.

Here's a more upbeat scenario for us here in the Valley. Whereas Grizedale is a vast site with room for hundreds of sculptures, Rusland, with its mile-long stretch of forty-eight beeches, has only four. After the initial flurry of interest no one will bother. More-for-your-money at Grizedale. With luck.

I climb a stile from the Finsthwaite road and cross a field. There isn't really a path but there are more or less obvious ways to make your way along. So I go, quite buoyantly, my new sense of blown-upness giving me extra lift-off. Stepping and peeling and rising until I get to the rocky escarpment high above the beechwood. Here I sit looking out over the world, one of those wide-angle postcard panoramas: The Old Man, Dow Crag, White Pike, Brown Pike, Caw, the Dunnerdale Fells Ridge – all in size-place rather like the perfect Aga family – leading down to Millom with Black Combe lowering in the background and out to the Duddon Sands. The estuary. That place. The whole world in one shot.

I sit and my feet dangle. Children are used to this. A Square back in Flatland could no more sit, in our sense of the word, than a sole or a flounder. Poor old A Square. He came to a much stickier end, by the way, than Flat Stanley.

It was the millennium in Flatland. A Square had, in a manner of speaking, fallen in love. He'd beheld a vision of perfect Circular beauty ('O divine ideal of consummate loveliness'). The Sphere, for that's who it was, was a visitor from Spaceland, the land of Three Dimensions.

A Square could now distinguish between a Circle and a Sphere, a Plane Figure and a Solid.

He told his people how he'd risen through space from where he'd seen into the interior of houses and the creatures therein … into the secrets of the earth, the depths of mines, the inmost caverns of the hills …

Silence!

No one would believe him.

Liar, apostate, criminal.

On the first day of each millenary the Flatland police would search for any misguided persons who pretended to have received revelations from another World. A Square was such a person.

Poor one-planed, one-eyed fool.

They threw him into prison, where he still languished seven years into the new century. His only hope for the new millennium, he wrote, was that his little book might one day be read by 'a race of rebels' who'd refuse to be confined to two dimensions.

From the ridge I can see down through the trees into the Valley, into 'deep space'. No one – I think I can safely say – would lock me up for that. I can also see a small family coming along the road on their bicycles:

Molly, Jay, Magda. Then I can move out of my own body and watch the three of them from a distance, not just from the escarpment but a point in space or entirely outside space. Molly the daughter and Jay the father are a fastish blur while Magda the mother comes in more clearly because she's going slower. They stop and dismount, put their bikes in the falling-down garage and go into the house for their tea. After a few minutes the child re-emerges, gets on her bike and zooms back to the beeches – as it happens, for the last time.

Unlike A Square, no one comes to arrest me or even, these days, ship me off to a loony bin. Imagination, memory, time travel; all are now admissible, even ordinary. If time is the fourth dimension, then I'm merely a visitor going backwards. I could be in hyperspace, or, more likely, they could be visitors from hyperspace. On the other hand I could be in 4-D space, whereas this scene I've just painted, which is in something we call memory, is somewhere back in the third dimension. My fantasy, my fiction.

We can now imagine almost any possibility. In our 'higher' conception of space, we are tending towards some ideal 'superspace' in which every-thing – near and far, past and future, big and small, real and imagined – all come together.

Somewhere in hyperspace, with luck, poor old A Square will be getting my message. Are you receiving?

'Listen,' I tell him. 'You were right. We're no longer confined by limited dimensionality. Three dimensions, peanuts! Mickey Mouse stuff! We're up to eleven –fourteen if you're into time warps, parallel universes, GUTs, supergravity and superstrings. Then there's the Theory of Everything ...'

'Stop! You mean ...' he falters, 'it wasn't the baseless fabric of a dream after all?'

'Nope, it wasn't.'

A tear slides southwards along his square cheek but his banana-mouth goes a-grinning.

Almost nothing, it seems, is impossible. But there is one thing I still find unimaginable, a very simple personal thing: she has not come back and never will. In the space where the child was, a gap; filled with pictures and thoughts and sounds but not her living changing body.

The professor left a note. It said he was returning to Edinburgh – so much work to do! – but he hoped to see me again soon. It was signed, curiously, 'With Compassion'.

Traverse the escarpment where it's bare rock then, lower down, where it gets steeper and more overgrown, scramble. Hang onto roots and slide; eventually drop down onto the forest floor, ankle deep in twigs, old fern mulch, last year's beech casts. Not being gobbled or consumed in any gross digestive way but merely taken in, absorbed. Woman Walking Among the Beeches.

At the same time – this works both ways – the process is reversed. Crunch a fallen nutcase, breathe CO_2, pluck leaves from their branches and feed them into your mouth so it's lined like a nest. Now choose two of the biggest and toughest and place one over each eye. What ho, no snub-nosed hairy sexually omnivorous wildmen or women to be seen doing unpleasant things with animals or children. One heartbroken Maid, tough luck. Now remove the leaves and what do you see? That famous grey that holds light even in darkness. Comparisons have been made with elephants, rocks, ghosts.

'Can I go to the beeches?'

'Now?'

'Now. I want to see the last leaves fall.'

'You can't, it's impossible.'

'Why?'

'Because it's not observable, it happens gradually over time, it's ...'

'But I want to see.'

'All right, then.'

I gave in. We zipped up and went along to the beeches and sat on the wide stone midway between two beeches which would later be identified and stencilled no.17 and no.18. Most of their leaves had already gone. Molly counted: 30 – no, 34 – no, 54 – no ... Each time she came up with a different number. 'It is difficult,' she acknowledged, sporting and generous. I didn't say I told you so or rub it in, so I suppose that made me sporting too. I was having the same trouble. By now the light was poor, the leaf hands hard to distinguish. Last of a tired lot. Scrunched up, windblown, tenacious specimens, they looked as if they might hang on forever. Molly said something to that effect, though I can't remember her exact words. Quoting children, in any case, makes them sound so senti-mental; or rather, it's not the children themselves who come off as sentimental but the person quoting their words. I said I doubted they would hang on forever. 'They might just hang on until they disintegrate, then fall as leaf dust.'

She yawned, 'Think I'll come back in the morning.'

Which she did.

'Well?' I was genuinely interested in the results of my daughter's first foray into observational fieldwork.

Shrug: 'All gone.'

I sit and wait. Another month or more before leaf-fall. I thought going with Molly to watch the last leaves fall was something I was doing for the child, but now it seems as if she was doing it for me.

Breathe in. Let yourself be breathed in, absorbed. Your boundaries, it seems, are becoming porous, a kind of dissolution which is not wholly unpleasant. Biodirectional, mutual. The division between inside and outside blurred.

I looked up the word 'compassion' in the dictionary.

cum + *patior* = 'to suffer within'; or, more broadly, to suffer some-thing to happen; that is, to undergo an experience.

We enter into the experience of others through compassion.

Apparently, it means different things in different languages. In Hebrew, for instance, it's *rachamim*, derived from the word for womb or bowels. (Imagine God suffering constipation when he thinks of the trou-bles of others!)

In Greek *splangchnizomai* means 'to be moved with compassion.' The *splangchna* are the viscera (heart and entrails).

We feel compassion, so it appears, in the body. Does that mean the live, living, body can feel compassion for the dead one?

A cadaver known as 'Adam' can now be inspected on your website, cut into more than fifteen hundred Flatlander slices, providing a microscopically detailed surgical map of his insides.

She is the corpse on the pathologist's slab. She lies there, plus or minus certain body parts, strangely unmoving. She is she and I am I (looking down at her, nodding my head, positive identification, yes), and yet the reverse is also true. She identifies me, observes me, is me.

There is no end to this.